ANDRE GONZALEZ

Time Fugitive

First published by M4L Publishing 2024

This novel is entirely a work of fiction. The names, characters and incidents portrayed in it are the work of the author's imagination. Any resemblance to actual persons, living or dead, events or localities is entirely coincidental.

Andre Gonzalez asserts the moral right to be identified as the author of this work.

First edition

ISBN: 978-1-951762-67-4

Editing by Melissa Prideaux
Cover art by 100 Covers

This book was professionally typeset on Reedsy.
Find out more at reedsy.com

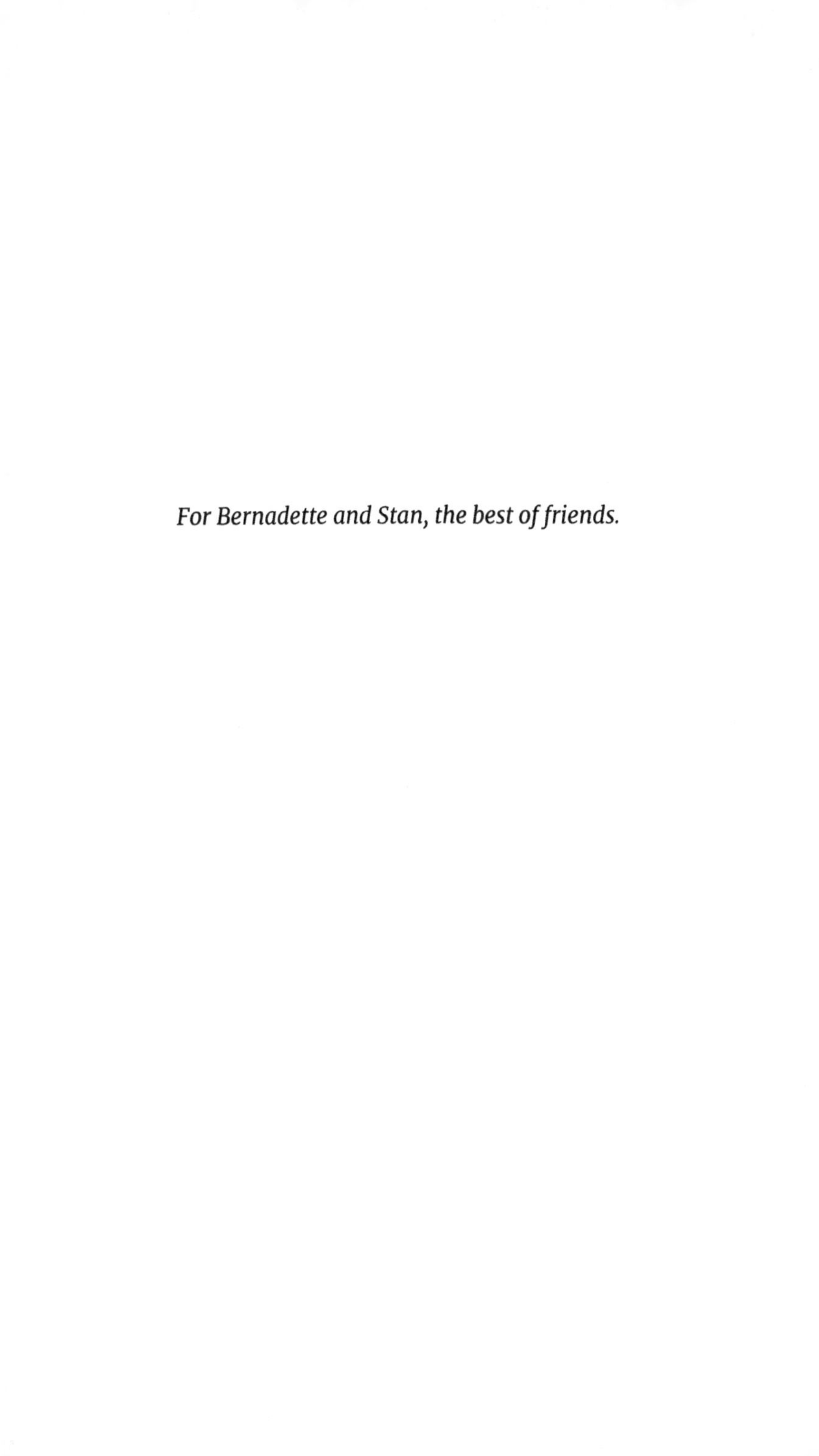

For Bernadette and Stan, the best of friends.

"Life is one long struggle in the dark."

—Lucretius

Chapter 1

September 8, 1898

The girl's screams finally stopped at nine o'clock in the morning.

"Why is the last one always the most difficult?" Doyle Grady asked the ceiling as he lay awake in bed. A thick ray of sunlight seeped through the gap between the two drapes that had remained closed ever since he arrived in 1898.

Only 40,000 people lived in Dallas before the turn of the century, the city still a decade away from its first population boom. Upon his arrival, Doyle immediately bought the bi-level Victorian house a quarter mile east of the Lone Star Saloon. The home stood slightly elevated above the town square, overlooking the dozens of businesses on Main Street.

He could keep his eye on the town, and technically, they could keep their eye on him. That's why the drapes remained closed. No one down there needed to know what happened in this house of horrors.

Doyle yawned, stretching his tired limbs. Carrying the dead weight of the young woman a quarter mile through an underground tunnel had proven as physically demanding as the first two times he had done it.

But she wasn't dead, only heavily sedated. Five milligrams of midazolam slipped into her drink had done the trick. And when you operated the only speakeasy in town—a concept still unknown to the world in 1898—it was rather simple to drug the women he wanted to bring back to his house.

"Did you drink the water?" Doyle shouted, finally sitting up in his bed.

No response was the correct response.

The girl had been screaming and shouting since she woke up sometime around three o'clock. The prior two had only lasted an hour before drinking the glass of water he left for them. This one, however, lasted three hours. Good thing his house was at the top of a hill with no neighbors within a half mile.

"Did you drink the water?!" he shouted once more.

Silence.

A grin touched his lips as he swung his legs over the bed's edge, his feet hitting the wooden floor with renewed enthusiasm. His heart raced. The moment they drank the water was when it all felt real, making him feel *alive*.

He slipped on a pair of fresh socks, hurried out of his bedroom, and headed down the stairs, where he had left the girl handcuffed to the immovable brick stove in the kitchen.

Within arm's reach, the girl could have enjoyed her choice of apples or bananas, along with the glass of water that had been spiked with just enough pancuronium bromide for the paralysis to start within minutes of ingestion.

Doyle ran into the kitchen and found the girl lying motionless on the floor. The glass of water stood empty on the edge of the counter. He shuffled over to stand above her, arms crossed. "You poor, beautiful soul," he said, shaking his head. "Wrong place at the wrong time. Shit happens, right? I know that all too well."

Tears welled in Doyle's eyes. He turned sappy before he killed his victims. It always brought back memories of his wife. Oh, how he missed her. He had quickly learned nothing numbed the pain. Nothing filled the void. He might as well walk around with a hole in his chest, because that's exactly how he felt every miserable day since the love of his life had succumbed to her battle with ovarian cancer.

"Fuck cancer," he muttered as a tear fell to the floor.

A booming knock came from the front door, followed by a familiar squeaky voice.

"Mr. Grady, are you home?" the voice called.

"God dammit," Doyle spat, jerked out of his trip down memory lane. The front door was around the corner from the kitchen, so he didn't need to worry about hiding the girl's body.

Doyle hurried to the door, wiping his eyes free of tears, and pulled it open just enough to stick his head through the crack.

A short man in a stiff three-piece suit stood on the front step, a top hat perfectly straight on his head.

Warren Dinsmore, the biggest prick in Dallas, Doyle thought. He knew Warren wore the top hat to make him appear taller. But Warren wasn't fooling anyone. Even with the hat, the little weasel barely touched five-nine.

"Mr. Dinsmore," Doyle said with plenty of sarcasm.

"Ah, a most pleasant morning, Mr. Grady," Warren replied as he clutched the lapels of his suit jacket with both hands. "I never collected from you last night. It seemed like a busy night for you, from what I could tell."

"Yes, it was. Sorry about that, Mr. Dinsmore. It got late,

and I was tied up with some things. I have your money here." Doyle reached into his pocket and pulled out a one-dollar coin, planting it into Warren's open, pudgy hand.

"Really? You're telling me you sold one hundred drinks last night?" Warren's eyes widened. "On a Wednesday?"

Doyle shrugged. "I tried a new promotion. Called it Ladies' Night. Let all the women drink for free until nine o'clock."

"Free?!" Warren gasped, taking a step back. "That's preposterous."

"Maybe, but it worked. It got all the women in town inside the building, which meant the men followed. And guess who got charged double for their drinks?"

Warren chuckled and shook his head. "Oh, Mr. Grady, sometimes I think you're from the future with these wild ideas. I'll see you tonight."

I'll be gone from this place forever long before tonight, Doyle thought, watching Warren turn around and stroll away, still giggling and saying "Ladies' Night" like it was the most absurd thing he had ever heard.

Warren owned and operated the Lone Star Saloon. Upon Doyle's first visit to the saloon, he noticed only half of the building in use and questioned the vacant space in the back. Warren had used the space as a makeshift office and storage. Doyle, who *was* from the future, proposed a concept called a "speakeasy" to Warren. Women and minorities weren't allowed in the regular saloons, and Doyle framed this as a business opportunity to tap into an entirely new segment of customers.

Warren wasn't caught up in the drama of racism and sexism like most of the other men who patronized his saloon. The man only cared about money and wanted to make as much as he could every damned day of the week. He agreed to Doyle's absurd idea and only asked for one cent from each drink sold, so long as Doyle operated the secret bar entirely on his own.

But Doyle didn't care about any of that right now. He returned to the kitchen and rolled the girl onto her back, her wavy brown hair splayed out in a tangled mess. A guttural noise came from her throat, but her body remained motionless. The spiked water caused complete paralysis of all muscles, including the lungs. He could leave her to suffer for the next eight hours until her lungs eventually ceased to function.

But Doyle wasn't a monster. He never had a desire to put his victims through physical torture. He didn't use them as sex objects. Mental suffering was the only thing he wanted them to go through. The same suffering he and his wife had to endure as they counted down the final year of her life.

Watching the cancer progress over twelve months was no different from being handcuffed to a stove. Seeing the world keep spinning outside while his wife vomited blood inside their once happy home was a trap of its own. Having to go to work as a surgeon every day and perform what the patients described as "miracles" as he saved others' lives had only given him hope for so long. He couldn't give his own wife that same miracle, so why did anyone else deserve it?

He had lost much more than his wife when she passed, a moment that seemed like another lifetime. The months that followed that dreadful day were filled with desires to end his own life. As a surgeon in 2021, he had easy access to the drugs he now used on his victims. He could have just as easily administered the proper dosages to himself and drifted off into the void.

But then he had an opportunity, which momentarily gave

him hope. A purpose. Just as his wife had once been his hope and purpose. But, once again, he lost all that, too.

People didn't appreciate the joy in their lives. How could they, if they never had to suffer to earn it? His only hope for his victims was for them to experience that genuine appreciation in their last moments. The mental strangulation he put them through probably made that difficult, but was that not the point?

"What are you thinking about right now?" he asked the girl on the floor, lowering himself to whisper mere inches from her face. "At this exact moment, your brain and heart are the only two things working in your body. I know you can hear me. Are you thinking about the life you had? All the memories from your childhood? Or are you thinking about everything you're going to miss in the future? A future husband? Kids? You probably would have made a wonderful housewife, as much as I hate to say it. But that's the circumstance of your times. My wife was a pediatric surgeon. Can you even grasp the idea of a woman getting to do such a job? Wherever you go, I hope the world gives you more opportunities than this one did."

He paused and stood on his knees to reach into his pocket for the syringe loaded with potassium chloride, pulling off the cap.

"It's time, you beautiful angel," he said, sticking the syringe into the girl's arm. "This is only going to slow your heart down until it stops beating. It will feel no different from falling asleep."

He pressed down the syringe's plunger until the clear liquid vanished into the girl's body, then replaced the cap over the needle. Without a word, he jumped to his feet and rummaged through the nearby cupboards, where he had stashed a can of red spray paint he had brought from the future.

Across the cabinets, Doyle sprayed two vertical lines six inches apart, then a U-shape beneath them to form a smiley face. "Always keep a smile on your face. It's the only way to get through this life."

He stuffed the can into his pocket along with the syringe and scanned the kitchen. There shouldn't have been anything to leave behind as evidence. He kept a simple life so he could vanish at will.

Doyle hustled back up the stairs to his bedroom and slipped into his shoes, making one last check of the room he had spent most of his six months in 1898. Only clothes and a stack of books looked back at him.

"It's been real, Dallas," he said before exiting the room and descending the stairs. The house was perfectly still and silent, a definite perk of living in this era before automobiles.

Doyle crossed through the kitchen and swung open the back door, where a curvy trail cut across the lawn to a tool shed. The shed had existed as long as the house had, but he built a second wall inside of it to conceal the powerful secret it contained.

A table stood against the back wall, and he crouched down to crawl beneath it, where he had built a swinging door with a latch too small to be seen by a casual observer. Earlier that morning, he had moved aside the piles of junk used to block the door from wandering eyes.

He unhooked the latch and let the door creak open. Heat radiated from the space as he crawled through, sure to replace the boxes and bins of clutter before closing the door behind him. The portal stood beneath a six-foot-tall brick archway, its force longing to pull him through. With his back against the wall, it was only two steps forward before his body would pass through into the next dimension.

Doyle drew a deep breath, heart racing. "On to the next one," he said, taking two steps toward the heat.

Chapter 2

Present Day

Arielle Lucila knew it was urgent when she saw the group email immediately followed by a group text message. Commander Martin Briar requested Arielle and her team report to the downtown Denver headquarters as soon as possible.

She had never received a message of this nature, and her stomach immediately twisted into knots at the unknown lurking around the corner.

Her phone buzzed with a new text message, this one a new group thread with only her two teammates, Felix Francisco and Selena Nicole.

What the hell is going on?!?!?! Selena asked.

Must be important, Felix replied.

No shit, Sherlock, Selena said.

Arielle laughed and shook her head, brushing aside her honey-brown hair. Those two were always bantering, even over a group chat. Arielle typed out her reply. *Let's just head down and see. Half an hour work?*

Everyone agreed to meet downtown at the main headquarters of Road Runners, their secret time travel organization.

Arielle and her team were the top-ranked team of Angel

Runners—Angels for short—who had the unique task of traveling through time to prevent or uncover the truth of past tragedies.

These missions were typically planned out in advance, and they'd have a brief meeting with Commander Martin Briar before starting. Over the hundreds of missions Arielle had completed, she had never received one as impromptu as this one.

Arielle drove downtown in her BMW, enjoying the crisp autumn afternoon. Leaves danced across the ground as gusts of wind brought the early hints of a looming winter. It was a Sunday afternoon in September, and downtown was bustling on one of the rare days where both the Rockies and Broncos had home games. The Rockies were playing meaningless games, leaving the bars and sidewalks crowded with the orange and blue wave of Broncos fans.

Good luck finding anywhere to park, Arielle thought, not bothering with any of the metered street parking. Instead, she headed for a garage a block away from the Road Runners' office.

She parked and strolled out of the garage, finding Selena and Felix already halfway down the block in front of her. Their drastic difference in height made them look like a mastiff standing next to a poodle.

"Hey!" she shouted.

Selena and Felix paused and spun around.

Felix waved an arm for Arielle to hurry and join them. He was always the most stressed out of the three, likely eager to rush into the commander's office to learn the new assignment.

Arielle jogged to meet them, promptly hugging each as they stood in the middle of the sidewalk.

"How are you two?" Arielle asked, forcing her grin of pearly whites. She sensed the tension in the air.

"Oh, just wonderful," Selena responded, placing her hands on her hips. "I was at a beer garden having a nice, relaxing Sunday. And now I'm here."

Cheers and hollering erupted from the bar behind them. The Broncos had just completed a big play to move within the ten-yard line. Felix, the tallest of their trio, craned his neck for a view of the TVs, his brown eyes narrowed on the plethora of screens.

"I'm sure you'll get to finish watching the game," Selena said, smacking Felix on his beefy arm. "Or you can just travel to tomorrow and know what happens."

This earned a round of nervous laughter. Selena was trying to keep the mood light, but they all shared the same dread heading into this meeting. They continued to the office, a marketing firm serving as the front for anyone passing by.

"I was already downtown," Felix said. "Catching the game with some friends at a bar."

"I guess we can't complain too much," Selena said. "We've had an entire month off since the last mission."

"Yeah," Felix said. "Paris looked like a lot of fun."

"As always," Selena replied. "Spent a week there visiting my dad. Then a week in London, another in Madrid. Just got back into town last Sunday to catch up on things around the house."

"Well, you should be nice and refreshed," Felix said.

They walked up the steps and entered the marketing office. Since it was Sunday, the firm was closed. But the actual business they came for lay beneath. They shuffled to the manager's office in the rear and slipped through a secret door that led to the basement.

Selena burned a stare into Arielle as they descended the steps, finally asking, "Why aren't you saying anything, Arielle?"

They stopped on the bottom landing, where another door awaited. On the other side was the Road Runners headquarters, a world of its own.

Arielle shrugged. "I just have a weird feeling about this. For starters, it's Sunday. We've never had a meeting on a Sunday. Then the group email and text message. Everything feels *off* about this."

"How bad could it be?" Felix asked. "Maybe Commander Briar is just trying to get a head start on the week."

"Maybe," Arielle said, not believing a word of it.

She pulled open the door and found the office's main bullpen bustling as always. Teams monitored the activity of fellow Angels out on other missions from this makeshift command center. At least a dozen seventy-inch monitors ran along the walls, all being watched by various people working in the bullpen.

Elijah Ward, Commander Briar's assistant, rose from his seat at the end of the row and rushed over to throw his arms around Arielle in a tight hug. Elijah had always been so flamboyant and positive in past encounters. This time, Arielle sensed tension in his embrace.

"What is it, Elijah?" she asked.

He pulled back, keeping a grip on both of her shoulders as he offered a polite smile to Selena and Felix. "You know I'm not allowed to say," he whispered. "Just be careful, okay? We can't lose any of you three. You're the heartbeat of this organization."

Roughly one percent of the world's population were time travelers. And while not every single one of them was a Road Runner, most of the eighty million time travelers were. Each continent operated under their own sets of bylaws, led by an elected commander, and checked by a Council.

"Elijah," Selena said. "Seriously, what's going on?"

Elijah only offered a tight-lipped grin before backing up and returning to his desk. He picked up his phone and spoke. "Commander, they're here." He nodded and hung up, turning his attention back to the three Angels. "He's ready for you. Head inside."

The closed door next to Elijah's desk was Commander Briar's office. They had sat inside before every mission, but today the door looked intimidating. Arielle had no interest in opening it.

Felix led the way, giving a quick knock before cracking open the door and poking his head through.

"Come in!" Commander Briar said in a convincing tone.

Felix pushed it open all the way, and they all straggled in to sit on the three chairs in front of the commander's desk.

Arielle had only worked with Commander Briar for the past two years, but he had appeared to age at least ten years in that short time. His hair was more salt than pepper, and the bags under his eyes seemed to grow heavier with each visit. His two-year term was coming to its end, and she suspected he looked forward to an extended vacation when the time came.

"Thank you all for getting down here on such short notice," Commander Briar said, leaning forward and folding his hands on his desk. "I hate to call you here when downtown is already so busy, but I had no choice."

He paused and took a swig from the bottle of water next to

his phone.

"Commander, what's this all about?" Arielle asked, shifting in her seat as her body refused to get comfortable.

He cleared his throat. "I've talked to you before about the growth of our organization becoming too much. It happened too fast without proper parameters set in place. We may have won the war against the Revolters, but with almost six million time travelers in North America, it was only a matter of time before someone turned on us."

Arielle's stomach sunk even more. "Do we have another Chris Speidel situation?"

Chris Speidel, intent on using time travel to infiltrate governments and rule the world, had once led an organization, the New Age Revolution, that had gone to war with the Road Runners.

Commander Briar shook his head. "Nothing like that, thankfully. The Road Runners have long operated under the guise that we're all good people. Pure intentioned, if you will. But with the explosive growth, people slipped through the cracks of our recruitment efforts. It's become increasingly impossible to keep tabs on all six million time travelers in North America. Don't get me wrong—we've still done good work. Our prisons are filled with people who have tried to travel through time and cause havoc. But there is now one person who has climbed to the top of our Most Wanted List. Do you recognize this man?"

Commander Briar pulled open his desk drawer and fished out a file, spreading it open and flipping over a picture of a handsome man around forty. He had jet black hair, bright blue eyes, and dimples that highlighted each end of his wide grin—full of perfect teeth, of course.

Arielle's heart skipped a beat as she looked at the photo. "Is that...Doyle Grady?"

The commander nodded. "So you *do* remember."

"Who is this?" Selena asked, directing her question at Arielle.

"Doyle was in my training class when I joined the Road Runners. The Common Training before we all branched out to our different departments. He was some sort of doctor. He struggled through the Common Training and was always griping about why he needed to go through all the levels of training. Everything else was irrelevant to him—he just wanted to be a doctor and not worry about anything else."

"He was one of the top up-and-coming surgeons in the country," Commander Briar added. "We were lucky to have him, but it never panned out. He couldn't seem to wrap his mind around being a time traveler."

"So, what happened to him?" Selena asked. "And what does this have to do with us?"

"Well," said Commander Briar, scrunching his face as he looked down at the file in front of him. "He was ex-communicated by Commander Strike before me. When that happens, we take away a person's Juice and keep close tabs on them for two years to make sure they're not going around spilling our secrets to the public. According to the notes, we actually ended on positive terms with Doyle Grady. He agreed he wasn't in the best mindset—he had lost his wife to cancer before joining us. And both parties agreed he could have a second chance whenever he felt more able to focus on life as a Road Runner. We never had an issue with him after that moment. Until now."

If it was physically possible, Arielle's stomach might have

fallen to her knees. She remembered Doyle vividly. They had bonded over their losses and had long conversations about the pros and cons of going back in time to save their loved ones. But that was only in private. During training, Doyle often kept to himself and stared into the distance.

"There are some concerns," Commander Briar continued. "The problem with taking Juice from someone is that we never know if we got it all. We found the main bottle we first distributed, but if he kept smaller amounts stored in other places, we had no way of knowing that."

"Did he not have a tracking chip?" Felix asked. All Road Runners who worked in the field were required to have tracking chips, just in case they fell into danger. That's what the men and women in the bullpen were watching on all the monitors.

"Yes," the commander said. "But he removed it at some point."

"So this guy is traveling through time illegally?" Selena asked. "Doing some bad things, I presume?"

Commander Briar shook his head. "I wish that's all it was." He rummaged through the file and pulled out a stack of papers, spreading them across the table. Nine different sheets of paper had small portraits in the top right corner with blocks of text on the rest of the pages. "Nine victims. Three in 1898. Three in 1998. And three in 2098. We're confident Doyle Grady killed all of them."

"And we need to catch him," Arielle said, more to herself. "But why is this so urgent if the murders are already done and he's probably vanished to 2198?"

"Well," Commander Briar said, pulling in all the papers and closing the file. He reached back into his desk drawer and pulled out a folded piece of yellow paper, pushing it across his desk. "He left behind a note. And it's addressed to you."

Chapter 3

The three Angels moved down the hall to a smaller meeting room. Commander Briar informed them someone would be along to discuss their plans.

Arielle browsed the note as they strode down the hallway. Both Felix and Selena were pining to know what the letter said, so she read it to them once they were seated at a round table in the conference room.

"Dearest Arielle, I'm so incredibly proud of you. The amount of success you've achieved in such a brief period is nothing short of admirable. I'm sure you remember me from Road Runner training. I think some of the cool kids called me Deranged Doyle, but I only ever heard that in whispers. Maybe I'm wrong?

"Anywho, here we are. Two people who started with the Road Runners on the same day and took polar opposite paths. All I wanted was to help people in need, but the Road Runners felt I wasn't mentally ready for such a task. Ha! Their loss. My mind has always been my greatest weapon, no matter what else has been going on in my life.

"I've followed your work. There is no doubt you're the best in the business. And with still so many years ahead of you, perhaps you can become the best to ever do it. The Babe Ruth of time travel! Our paths may have been different, but I like to think we are still the same. I'm the best serial killer in three different centuries, and you're the best at hunting down the bad guys. Ha!

"Catch me if you can. If you're as good as the world believes, we'll be seeing each other real soon!"

The room remained silent after Arielle folded up the letter.

"This is fucked up," Selena said after a while. "What are we supposed to do?"

"I think you know exactly what we're going to do," Arielle said.

The door swung open, and a man dressed in a suit stepped through, briefcase in hand. He sat down next to Arielle without a word, dropping the briefcase on the table and unlatching it. He pulled out a laptop, flipped it open, and started typing away.

The three Angels gawked at each other in confusion.

"Can we help you?" Selena asked. "Are we invisible to you or something?"

The man held up a firm finger while he finished typing with his other hand, finally clearing his throat and speaking. "Good afternoon. My name is Mark Starnes. I oversee all missions for the Road Runners and am the highest-ranked consultant for the strategy behind all mission work. I've been in this role six years, have worked under three commanders, and have overseen the success of over ten thousand missions."

"We get it," Selena said. "You're hot shit."

He frowned at her. "You must be Selena Nicole. Commander Briar said you don't know when to keep your mouth shut."

Selena gasped. "He would never say that."

"Correct," Mark replied, snapping his fingers. "He didn't

use those exact words, but that's how I translated it. That means you two must be Arielle and Felix."

"Yes, sir," Felix said, sitting stiff as a board. He never did well with confrontation, and Arielle had to hold in a laugh as she saw the fear swimming behind his eyes.

"I'm here to advise you on this mission involving Doyle Grady. Normally, I read the reports from our Research team, then devise my own report, breaking down the strategy for each mission. This one is complicated, however, and will be best to talk out. You three are the best team we have, so I'm open to your input and thought process on how we can approach this."

"Am I in any danger?" Arielle asked.

Mark pointed a commanding finger at Arielle. "Not under my watch. As we speak, a team of guards is being deployed to your home. We'd like for you to start this mission tomorrow, so they'll only be a bother for tonight. They're presence is so you can sleep at night without a worry. We don't know what Doyle's plan is, but we suspect this whole thing is to lure you into some sort of trap. I highly doubt he would even try to attack you at home. He seems to enjoy the challenge of the lure. In a nutshell, he is a sick, twisted bastard."

Selena snickered.

"If he wants to hurt me," Arielle said. "Why are *we* the ones hunting him down? Wouldn't it be safer for another team to take this mission?"

"That's a fair point, but not one we're concerned about. If we assigned another team, there's no knowing how long it would take them to complete the job. You'd have to sit at home. We couldn't risk having you out on other missions, since we don't know what Doyle is capable of. We're not even sure how he's traveling through time—although we suspect he's found old time portals."

"Time portals?" Selena said. "I thought those were a thing of the past."

"They still exist. Never went away. The problem is we don't know how many there actually are. The locations of three hundred time portals are outlined in the Book of Time, but we've discovered two hundred more since."

"Why do you think he's using portals?" Felix asked.

"For starters, we took his Juice. Secondly, the cadence of his murders being every hundred years is more telling. Most portals were set up to jump from century to century. We believe there is a portal for every year of a century, which creates a sort of network of portals for people to access. Think of it like the New York City subway map. It's messy and confusing at first glance, but if you know where you want to go, it just takes some figuring out and you can make it happen."

"So then we haven't discovered all the time portals," Felix said. "Based on what you said, there could be thousands."

Mark snapped his fingers again and pointed at Felix. "Exactly."

"How are we supposed to find him if he's traveling in this network?" Arielle asked.

"Oh, you're going to find him," Mark said. "I'm not concerned about that. What we have in front of us are three different series of murders in three different centuries. I've spent the last three days thinking of the best approach for this, and here's what I've come up with. You use two of the series of murders strictly for research. Learn what you can about Doyle and his patterns. Then, the third one, you'll understand what to expect and can make a concrete plan to catch him before he strikes."

"So you want us to catch him in the year 2098?" Felix asked, frowning.

"I never said that. You decide which two years will be your research, and which one you'll try to catch him in."

"What would *you* do?" Arielle asked, knowing Mark had already considered this.

Without hesitation, he replied, "I'd want to play this game as close to my home turf as possible. It's 2023. The world is drastically different in 1898 and 2098. But in 1998, sure it was different, but it's going to better resemble what you already know best."

"And how do you know it's the same person behind all the murders?" Arielle asked.

"Same methods were used in all three instances," Mark said. "He used a combination of midazolam, pancuronium bromide, and potassium chloride on all nine of his victims. If you're not well versed in your drugs, those are the three commonly used for capital punishment in our current time. As a surgeon, Doyle had access to these drugs. We have no way of knowing how much he could have stocked up on."

"Damn," Selena said, rubbing her temples.

"Damn is right. That's another reason we want to catch him as quickly as possible. Plus, if word gets out about the portals, there will be a fresh batch of criminals taking advantage of them to commit their crimes and vanish without a trace."

"And are we sure it's only these three sets of murders?" Arielle asked.

"No. We've checked 2198 and found nothing. 1798 has been trickier. News spread incredibly slowly back then and is making our research impossible to complete. We haven't ruled it out, but we've yet to find any solid proof he's committed other murders."

Arielle drew in a deep breath and let out a long sigh. "This isn't going to be easy."

"Not at all," said Mark, nonchalant. "That's why we've already compiled hundreds of pages of research to help answer questions you might have about the eras and cities."

"What are the cities?" Arielle asked.

"The 1898 murders are in Dallas, Texas. 1998 was Miami, Florida. And the 2098 ones happened in Oklahoma City."

"If we find the time portals," Arielle said, "can we use them? I assume they'll be nearby his attacks."

Mark tossed up his hands. "If you have your Juice on you, there's not really any harm. However, you won't know where you'll end up. So if you *don't* have Juice, I strongly advise against going through any portals, just so you don't get stranded. Oh, another note, traveling through portals leaves behind a residue. It looks like sawdust, just more powdery. Be aware of that if you decide to step through a portal. Totally normal."

"Thank you for all of this information, Mr. Starnes," Arielle said. "I think we can take it from here. Do you mind giving us a moment to discuss things in private?"

"Say no more," Mark said, closing his laptop and stuffing it back into his briefcase. He stood up from the table and circled around. "I'll compile my report of everything we discussed, along with some more bits of information you might find helpful. If you have questions, shoot me an email—that's what I respond to the quickest. My best advice, above all, is to always remain aware of your era. Dealing with the past is already difficult enough. You're going to find a lot more restrictions on what you can and can't do in 1898 and 2098, so you really have two sets of rules you need to play within. Besides that, I wish you the best of luck."

Mark nodded before he pivoted and exited the room.

All three Angels sighed, the meeting having been a lot to take in.

"I hope you're both ready," Arielle said. "This is going to be our most difficult mission yet."

Chapter 4

They ended up going to Selena's skyrise condominium in downtown. Longing for the constant bustle of nightlife, she had found a two-bedroom apartment in the Spire building, just blocks away from anything that might be going on in Denver.

It was only a ten-minute walk for them to get to her building, plus another five minutes to wait for an elevator to take them to the thirty-eighth floor.

"Whoa," Felix said, once they stepped into her condo. A short hallway led to the living room overlooking downtown, the Rocky Mountains majestic in the distance. "You *live* here?"

Selena giggled. "Pretty cool, huh? It's not a ton of space, only eleven hundred square feet, but it's plenty for just me."

"You're living like a Bond villain," Arielle added. "Impressive."

The Angels were some of the highest-paid members of the Road Runners. While most had opted for bigger properties in the suburbs—like Arielle and Felix—Selena settled into what she called her "dream home" so long as she didn't have kids.

"There's a heated pool on the rooftop if we want to take a swim after."

"Are you kidding me?" Arielle asked. "Selena, we're

starting this mission tomorrow. I don't think tonight is the best time to go for a swim."

Selena rolled her eyes. "I'll do what I want, *Mother*."

"Don't start that shit," Arielle said, jabbing a finger into Selena's shoulder. "You need to take this more seriously. We're dealing with a vicious serial killer. This mission is a whole new beast for us to figure out."

Selena shrugged. "And I get that, but I'm still going to unwind and mentally prepare myself as I see fit. Now, let's get started. I think I have lemonade in the fridge. I'll serve some glasses if you guys want to get settled on the couch. There's not really anywhere else to hold a meeting in here."

After a couple of minutes, Selena joined Arielle and Felix on the couch, sitting between the two of them. Arielle had spread out the files on the glass coffee table.

"Okay," Arielle said, clasping her hands together. She had gone from dread to slight excitement, having full confidence in her team to pull off this insane assignment. "Let's discuss eras. Which two should we use as research, and which one do we want to make our move on Doyle?"

"I agree with Mark's logic," Felix said. "1998 will be the most familiar to us. 1898 in Dallas is pretty much the Wild West. I don't want to get on anyone's wrong side there. And 2098—we have no clue what that world even looks like. So between cowboys on horses and flying cars, I think 1998 is our best bet."

"I agree," Arielle said. "Selena?"

"Works for me," she replied, studying the papers on the table. "You guys notice anything in particular about these nine victims?"

"What do you mean?" Felix asked, cocking his head to look

at them from a fresh angle.

Selena reached forward and shuffled them all around. "It's the same pattern in each era. Two girls and one guy. Do you think there's a reason for that?"

Arielle stood up and studied the pictures, balling a fist under her chin. "I'm not sure of the reason, but it's a pattern. Good catch. Read through these files, and let's see what else we can find."

They spent the next twenty minutes going over the various files about the victims. They each took an era to focus on.

"Anything of interest?" Arielle asked. "I had the 1898 files, and the information is spotty. I know our researchers don't get too close to the crimes. They more or less read the newspaper clippings and *might* pose as locals to ask high-level questions. Depending on the level of danger, they won't even do that."

"The authorities in Florida believe the murders occurred before the victim was even reported missing," Felix said. "Curious if that same pattern is happening with the others."

"Yep," Selena said. "Same for these murders in 2098. Why would someone trying *not* to get caught give us any part of their playbook?"

"It's not that they're being careless," Arielle said. "The psychological traits across serial killers can vary, but a majority seem to be particular in their methods of killing. They believe what worked the first time is how it should always be done. It almost becomes a superstition for them, so they'll actually leave behind several patterns—we just need to know what we're looking for."

"Yeah," Felix said. "Like this red smiley face he spray paints near the last victim. Please tell me that's something else you two are seeing."

Arielle nodded. "The 1898 newspaper clipping mentions a face in red paint. Then they ramble about how the way it was applied to the wall didn't make sense for a paintbrush. Doyle doesn't seem to care if he leaves behind hints that he's from a different time. That might be his downfall if he keeps leaving clues he's a time traveler."

"I got the smiley face in mine, too," Selena said, taking a long swig from her lemonade. "So we've got quick murders before anyone has time to realize what's going on, and red smiley faces."

"Mine doesn't mention anything about the timeline, so we can't confirm that. But that doesn't mean it's not true. They were probably slower to report missing people back then. But how timed apart were your murders?" Arielle pointed at her documents. "For 1898, all three bodies were found in the house after what they believed was at least a week since the last one had perished. I'm assuming forensics weren't quite what they are today, though, so not sure how much we can trust this."

"For these cases in Miami," Felix said, holding a sheet to read closer. "The victims all went missing within the same week. Three days between each of their disappearances and when the bodies turned up."

"All three found in the house?" Arielle asked.

"Yes. So there's another consistency. Doyle has no interest in dumping the bodies. He leaves them in the house, then vanishes. He definitely knows what he's doing. Do we not think it might be worth a look into 2198, just to see if we can catch him off guard?"

"What makes you think he knows we're focused on only these particular years?" Arielle asked. "If he's expecting us, he'll be on high alert no matter what year he's in."

"Well, he left the letter for you in 1898," Felix said. "Another reason we shouldn't bother tampering with anything while we're there. I just had an idea."

Felix jumped off the couch and circled around to stand in front of Arielle and Selena. When an idea caught hold of Felix, it was like he became possessed by it.

"Well?" Selena asked, arching her eyebrows. "Are you gonna tell us something, or are you auditioning for my job?"

"Good one," Felix said flatly. "This mission is incredibly dangerous—I'm not sure if either of you are grasping that. It's not like our other missions when we hunt down unsuspecting criminals. I assume Doyle knows who all three of us are. He's expecting us. He's probably trying to set a trap."

"What are you getting at?" Arielle asked, leaning back and crossing her arms.

"The risk is too high to tamper with a single thing when we travel to 1898 and 2098. If we're truly using those for observational purposes, then let's travel to those eras *strictly to observe*."

"Just to observe? That defeats the whole purpose."

Felix jerked his head from side to side. "The purpose is to *catch* him. But he wants to catch *us*. We know his method for murder and trust me, we don't want to risk having him slip behind any of us and jab us with a needle. Or maybe he'll send a spiked drink our way. I'd rather use 1898 and 2098 to learn everything we can about him and the murders without having to constantly look over our shoulders. We'll move in the background and observe what we can. Maybe ask around, but not too much. We can't risk word getting out that we're looking for him. When we get to 1998 in Miami, then we can be more aggressive, because that's where we're taking him down. What do you think?"

"Sounds like a waste of time," Selena said.

Arielle kept to herself, processing her thoughts.

Felix and Selena looked at her. "Arielle?" Felix asked.

"It's unorthodox. I can't recall that type of strategy ever being used on a mission by an Angel." Arielle shrugged and tossed up her hands. "But this isn't a typical mission. And you're right. Doyle isn't some clueless fool from the past. He's smart, and he's expecting us. Brilliant thinking, Felix."

Felix's cheeks flushed as he nodded in appreciation.

"Notice Commander Briar didn't provide any guidance like he normally does," Arielle continued. "I've learned to read between the lines with him. It means he wants us to figure things out entirely on our own. Mark was there for high-level discussion, but even he didn't really give us anything aside from the best way to approach the three different years. We can pinpoint the exact window of time between the last victim being murdered and the authorities finding out. There has to be some sort of gap—even if it's only a few hours. Imagine getting the first look at the scenes of the crimes before anyone else. Then we can hang around town and hear all the local chatter."

"Oh great," Selena said. "So we're going to leave it up to rumors?"

"Of course not. Sure, there will be rumors, but we'll have more knowledge on the matter than anyone else. That will make it easier to sift through the bullshit."

Felix crouched down, eyes widening as he stared at the nine victims.

"What's wrong?" Arielle asked, shifting uncomfortably in

her seat.

"Now that I'm looking at these upside down, I see it," Felix said, shaking his head.

"See what?" Selena demanded, hopping to her feet.

"It wasn't obvious at first, but it's been in front of us this whole time," Felix said with a nervous chuckle. "We must have been blinded by our own fear, or were in denial."

"Dammit, Felix! *What?!*" Selena appeared ready to jump over the table to shake the answer out of him.

"Look at each set of victims again," he said calmly, spreading the documents out so they could each be in groups of three. "We noticed two girls and one guy for each group, but look closer. They're not perfect matches, but they all resemble us."

Arielle joined Selena in standing, both of them gawking at the portraits on the table, hands placed on their hips as the disturbing reality settled over them.

"Shit," Arielle muttered under her breath.

"Shit is right," Felix said. "The letter may have been addressed to Arielle, but he's coming for all of us."

Arielle nodded. "He's toying with us. This is all some sort of sick game to him. We're absolutely not going to make any appearances near Doyle until we're ready to make a move."

Arielle gathered the documents into a pile and snapped the file shut over them. "Felix, let's head out. We all need to pack because tomorrow we're headed to 1898."

Chapter 5

They arrived in Dallas shortly after noon the next day. They spent the flight figuring out the best point in time to travel back to for the 1898 murders and compared a modern-day map with an 1898 version provided in the mission files.

"We look ridiculous," Selena said, shaking her head as she looked down at her long, flowy dress. She tugged at the collar. "The upper half is suffocating. How the hell did women breathe?"

They had all changed into their outfits to prepare for jumping to 1898. Arielle and Selena wore similar dresses, while Felix opted for a three-piece suit. He could have worn cowboy attire but thought someone investigating a murder would better look the part of an outsider.

Arielle laughed. "We look like we're headed into one of those photo booths where they make you look like the Wild West. All we need is a shotgun and a bottle of whiskey."

"Well, let's get this over with," Selena said. "Did you get the house worked out, Felix?"

"Sure did," he replied. Felix was in charge of living arrangements for their travels through time, along with providing them with the wardrobe to blend in. "There wasn't a ton of real estate, so the house we'll be in is pretty close to town.

Important we play our roles as siblings, because one man living with two women in 1898 will cause a fuss if we don't clarify our situation. We don't need people snooping around us."

"The car is waiting," Arielle said. "Leave your cellphones and any jewelry in your bags."

The Road Runners had acquired three luggage bags from the 1890s. Made of fine leather, they were roughly the size of a modern day carry-on suitcase, only without wheels or a retractable handle. They'd have to lug them around from the narrow grip handles just wide enough to fit a hand through.

Selena gritted her teeth before dropping her phone into her bag. "This is the worst part of missions. Don't you worry about anyone needing to reach you? Your grandma or Javonte?"

Arielle cocked an eyebrow at Selena. "It's only ten minutes in real time. Don't be such a drama queen. My grandma will be fine for ten minutes, as will Javonte."

"And how is that going?" Selena asked.

"It's going," Arielle replied. "We were only dating a couple of months. With our schedules, we rarely see each other, but are making an effort to at least grab dinner once a week."

"Can we discuss this later?" Felix asked, grabbing his luggage.

"Of course. Let's get going," Arielle said, gesturing toward the open door.

Felix had a tattered briefcase he kept the mission files inside and double checked them before they headed off the jet, where a fellow Road Runner waited to drive them across town.

"Good afternoon," the driver greeted them as they filed into the car. He was a lanky man with a bulging Adam's apple to complement a crooked smile. "My name is Rodrigo, and I'll be driving you today. We're headed to east downtown, correct?"

"Yes, sir," Arielle replied. "Thank you, Rodrigo."

The man started driving, staring at the three of them in the rear-view mirror. "My pleasure. I have to admit, when I saw who I was driving today...well, I couldn't sleep last night. It is such an honor. I've been driving Road Runners for five years now and have never driven someone as important as you three. I appreciate the work you do."

"Thank you," Arielle said politely.

"Mind me asking when you're traveling to?" he asked. "Looks like you're going way back in time, judging by your outfits."

"1898," Felix said.

"I'll be damned," he said. "I'm a Dallas native and have traveled to just about every year in our fine city's history. The 1800s are truly special. We're still a small town back then. Peaceful. One thing I can say is that the people have always been kind and caring, even to strangers passing through. I know I can't ask about your mission, but I wish you the best of luck."

"Thank you," Arielle said. "I've done missions this far into the past before, but never in Dallas. Spent some time in Arizona and New Mexico, and I agree, the people were always polite and welcoming."

The driver nodded his head, still watching them in the mirror as though the president had somehow ended up in his backseat.

Please just watch the road, Arielle thought.

Road Runner drivers were instructed not to speak to Angels during transit, but Rodrigo seemed not to care. Arielle didn't mind and would never report a driver. She once had the distinct privilege of driving Commander Briar to the most important mission in Road Runner history. The memories of that day remained fresh in her mind. They had conversed the entire drive, which had been almost two hours long.

"We're going to be in the past for about three days," Arielle said. "Anything we should make sure to see?"

The man bobbed his head from side to side. "Well, I can't say there is anything in particular. Everything you'll need is on Main Street. I don't remember exactly, but you'll probably have three or four saloons you can visit. That's where people spend most of their free time. You'll need to find which ones have the side rooms for the ladies to go to."

"Wait," Selena said, sitting forward. "Are you saying we're not allowed to go into the saloons?"

"Afraid not," Rodrigo said. "They only allow men into the saloons. The only women you'll see inside of them are workers. And they usually get the pretty ones to flirt with the men to keep them there spending money. Like I said, though, at least one or two of the saloons will have a side room where women can spend their time."

Arielle saw Selena's fist balled up and reached her hand over to calm her down. She already knew they were going to have these types of restrictions as women. At least all three of their skin tones weren't *too* dark, or that would have been even more nonsense to deal with.

"I'm not sure it will be of use," Rodrigo continued. "But there are underground tunnels that run under the city."

"Excuse me?" Arielle perked up. "What do you mean? How far do they go?"

"I don't know exactly how far. Quite far, I'd imagine. The

tunnels were dug by the Underground Railroad during the slavery years, but they remain even to this day. People use them today to cut through downtown away from the heat and traffic. I suppose you could do that in 1898. None of these are marked, though. You almost have to stumble across them. Usually in a back room in one of the buildings."

All three Angels exchanged a glance. This driver was giving them incredibly helpful tips without even realizing it.

They exchanged small talk for the next fifteen minutes, finally arriving at a back alley behind Hamm's Alignment and Brakes Garage.

"Here we are," Rodrigo said, killing the engine and turning around to face the three Angels. "Just to confirm with the details provided to me, jumping back from here will land you in the middle of a dirt field in 1898. You should have only a half-mile walk southwest to get to Main Street. You'll find it's a plenty remote area in the past. None of these buildings surrounding us right now existed back then."

Selena opened her door and stepped out, quick to stretch her limbs and tug at the frilly dress that was obviously giving her headaches.

"Thank you so much, Rodrigo," Arielle said, sliding over. "You've been a tremendous help."

The driver grinned. "Just doing my part. Best of luck to you three."

Arielle and Felix exited the car, slamming the doors shut and prompting Rodrigo to drive away.

"Feels weird having such light luggage," Felix said, gesturing to his briefcase and the three vintage travel bags.

"We couldn't exactly plan to carry around our oversized suitcases half a mile through the middle of 1898," Arielle said.

"You have everything important we need, right? Money, maps, notes?"

Felix nodded. "Got all the silver coins we'll need to get around, plus instructions for our house. Our real estate team found no value in buying the property we'll be staying in—it gets demolished in 1923—so they worked out a rental agreement with the landlord. I've been told the house is empty and the doors are unlocked, so we can let ourselves in. We shouldn't be bothered by the landlord, especially since we're only there for a few days."

"So, we rented a house when we only need it for three days," Selena said, rolling her eyes. "Seems wasteful."

"These days maybe," Felix said. "But in 1898, that one month of rent cost twenty dollars. Hardly something our accounting department will even notice. Cheaper than us staying one night in a hotel here today."

The roar of multiple lug wrenches echoed from the other side of the building. Rodrigo had departed the alley, leaving them alone with a couple of dumpsters.

"It's time," Arielle said, reaching into her pocket and pulling out her flask of Juice used for traveling through time. Each Road Runner had a uniquely crafted Juice that enable them to travel through time. "We can't hang out here all day. Remember, we're going to September 8, 1898, at noon. Be specific with your thoughts when you take your sip—would hate for any of us to arrive at the wrong time."

Felix and Selena had already pulled out their flasks and were unscrewing the lids.

"Cheers," Selena said, raising hers high. "See you on the other side."

Felix shot her a glare. "I really hate when you say that."

Selena stuck her tongue out at him before taking a swig. Arielle and Felix followed suit, and they all sat down on the ground, waiting for the world to turn dark. Two minutes later, they woke up in 1898.

Chapter 6

September 8, 1898

The sun blared over the three Angels as they stood up, dusting off their pants.

"Here we are," Arielle announced, rare excitement slipping into her voice.

"Where?" Felix asked, looking around. "There's nothing as far as we can see."

They had indeed arrived in the open space of a magnificently smaller Dallas, Texas. Moments ago, they had been surrounded by businesses and neighborhoods in this same spot. Now, all they saw were a few trees scattered about in any direction.

"Look!" Selena gasped, pointing.

They followed her finger to the sight of three horses galloping in the distance, cowboys riding on top.

"Okay, good," Felix said. "We're definitely in the correct year."

They each let out a nervous laugh.

"What now?" Selena asked.

"Do you have the compass, Felix?" Arielle asked, nodding

to the briefcase still clutched in his hand. Anything in contact with a person during time travel came along for the ride.

"Of course," he replied, squatting down to place the briefcase flat on the ground. He flipped up the latches and rummaged inside for the compass, proudly holding it up. Selena shielded her eyes as the sun reflected off the glass. "Rodrigo said we need to go southwest from here about a half mile. My notes confirm the same thing. Let's go."

Felix led the way, keeping them on track.

"A half-mile walk isn't normally anything to complain about," Arielle said. "But it sure is hot."

"Temperatures can stay in the nineties throughout September in Texas," Felix said. "It doesn't really start cooling off until October."

They trudged along, passing a group of armadillos that scattered away at the sight of humans so far from town. Only three minutes of walking passed before they caught the first glimpse of the town ahead, a row of at least a dozen buildings, none more than two levels tall.

Five minutes later, they arrived at Main Street, a dirt road that split two rows of similar buildings. People strolled up and down the road. Horses slogged along, some huddled in groups at the designated parking areas peppered up and down Main Street.

"Guys," Selena said under her breath. "I feel like I'm in a movie."

"Right?" Arielle replied. "All we need are a couple of cowboys to come barreling out of the bar with their guns drawn."

She sensed the same thing as Selena. Despite her handful of trips this far into the past, it always felt surreal to walk the world of the Old West. Having seen black-and-white pictures in history books throughout school, and even the occasional Western movie her grandfather used to watch when she visited, none of it ever seemed real. Having that entire world brought to life before her eyes was a stiff reminder of how insignificant their lives were in the grand timeline of history.

"So, where is our house?" Selena asked, nudging Felix with her elbow.

Felix looked down Main Street. "It's two blocks behind the general store."

A neighborhood sprawled from directly behind the businesses on Main Street. "Let's check it out," Arielle said, walking ahead.

Dirt crunched beneath each step, the bottom of her dress already turning brown as it dragged along the ground. They passed the bank, two saloons, and a drugstore before an elderly man with an oversized bag slung over his shoulder approached them.

"Afternoon, folks," he greeted, scratching his bushy white beard. Between the beard and the giant bag, Arielle thought he resembled Santa Claus. He wore a raggedy suit, his pants powdered with dirt. "Can I interest you in any housewares? I have kettles, pots, pans, you name it."

"I think we're okay for now," Arielle said, offering a polite smile. "If you could point us toward the general store, that would be great."

"Great, huh?" The peddler cracked a wide grin, seeming to ignore Arielle's question. "You wouldn't by chance need any clocks for your new house, would you?"

"We don't need any clocks," Selena snapped. "We just need

to get to the general store."

The grin remained on the old man's face as he looked at all three Angels. He leaned forward and spoke in a hushed tone. "How's a time traveler supposed to get around without any clocks?" He winked as the three exchanged curious glances.

Felix cleared his throat. "I'm sorry, sir, are you Albert Atkins? I read in the file you might be able to show us around."

The man nodded slowly and plopped his bag of goodies on the ground. "At your service. It's a pleasure to meet you and to have you here."

Albert stuck out a hand, and they all shook.

"Should we be talking out in the open like this?" Arielle whispered, eyes scanning the dozens of people out for an afternoon stroll through town.

"Probably not," Albert said, crossing his arms. "Especially if you're walking around using phrases like 'that would be great.' You must watch your vocabulary when traveling this far into the past. The last thing you want is one of these folks to call you a Yankee. How about I meet you at your house in ten minutes? The general store is at the far end of Main Street, so keep walking and take a left onto Pioneer Way. Two blocks down, you'll find your house on the corner. It's bright yellow—you won't miss it."

"Thank you," Felix said. "That would be mighty fine."

"That's more like it!" Albert bowed toward Felix before picking up his sack and venturing off, still shouting about kettles and clocks to whoever would listen.

"We can't just let that strange man come into our house," Selena said as they continued down Main Street. "We don't know anything about him."

Arielle laughed. "It's fine, Selena. He's a Road Runner and

already knows where we're staying. He's just fully immersed in this era. Who knows, he might even be from the same time as us but has been living here for a long time."

"And that's something Road Runners do?" Selena asked.

"Absolutely. We're Angels, and people like Albert are Guardians. They travel from city to city, era to era, and will stay in one place for twenty to thirty years before moving to their next assignment."

"Guardians?" Felix asked. "I've never even heard of such a role."

"They are somewhat secretive," Arielle explained. "Their primary job is to be involved with the community they live in. They are the ear on the streets, always listening for rumblings of time travel. If they believe a normal person is on to our secret, the Guardians report them for further investigation. Thirty years in the past is a whole new life. So, they offer the roles to people who have nothing left. I was actually offered a role but declined it to become an Angel."

"Fascinating," Felix said, shaking his head. "So these Guardians are planted all throughout time?"

"Throughout all relevant timelines and in every city with a population above ten thousand. There are multiple Guardians in the bigger cities, too."

"Here we are," Selena said. They stopped in front of Dallas General, a poster in the dusty front window advertising fresh apples for one cent each. "Good to know this is here and not a far walk from our house. In case we need anything."

"Like a new outfit," Felix teased.

Selena shot him a dirty look and middle finger before Arielle took the left turn as instructed to start down Pioneer Way. They passed the general store, finding it much more massive than they had expected from the looks of the storefront.

"General stores sell completely random things," Felix explained. "They sell whatever they can get in stock, and there's really no way of knowing what they'll have."

They left Main Street behind and entered the neighborhood.

"I know these homes get wiped away when downtown starts expanding," Arielle said. "But man, they are beautiful. And simple. The best part—none of them look the same."

Each property varied in lot size. Some had bigger yards, while others had none. A ranch-style home could be next to a bi-level home. It provided a uniqueness missing from neighborhoods in Arielle's Original Time.

"Goodness," Selena said. "He was right—can't miss our house. It looks like they used the same yellow paint they use on our roads. At least we got one of the bi-levels."

Felix chuckled. "It's *so* yellow."

"As long as the walls inside don't match, we'll be okay," Arielle said.

They hurried along, eager to check out their home for the next few days. Their house had no front lawn, just a brown picket fence about two feet beyond the front door. Felix opened the gate before climbing up one short step to the door and twisting the knob.

The door creaked open, and they all shuffled into the house. The wood flooring groaned beneath each step they took. They entered the living room, a lone coat rack standing next to the door. Two rocking chairs faced each other in front of a fireplace. The mantel had glass figurines of horses pulling carriages.

"Okay," Felix said, strutting to the kitchen. "It's just a few days, so it'll do."

Arielle and Selena followed Felix, finding the kitchen much bigger than they expected. It housed the dining table, a corner basin, and a colossal steel stove with a thick exhaust pipe running out of the ceiling.

"No cupboards," Arielle said, standing in front of the oven and examining the wall behind it. "Everything is on shelves."

Several shelves seemed to cover every inch of space on the walls, holding all kitchen and dining necessities.

"It all looks organized, at least," Felix added. "Pans and trays by the stove. Plates and cups by the dining table."

A knock came from their front door, and they all spun around. Arielle laughed. "Jumpy, are we? It should just be Albert."

She hurried to the door and pulled it open, indeed finding Albert with his oversized bag full of goodies.

"Hello again," he said with a quick nod. "Mind if I come in?"

"Of course not," Arielle replied, stepping out of the way.

Albert entered their house and plopped his bag on the floor with a satisfied sigh. "Let me tell you, lugging that thing around all day is a workout. Mind if I take a seat?" He gestured toward the chairs by the fireplace. "I'm on my feet all day and never relax outside of lunchtime."

"Make yourself at home," Arielle said, and they followed Albert into the living room. He sat down and immediately massaged his calves with grimy fingers. "I'd offer you a glass of water, but we just got here and I'm not even sure how to go about that. Doesn't look like this place has running water."

Albert chuckled. "Ah, yes, the luxuries we take for granted, right? You should have a freshwater well in your backyard, along with an outhouse—don't worry, they're at least fifty yards apart. For sanitary purposes, of course."

Arielle glanced at Selena, knowing she'd have the strongest reaction to having to use an outhouse. The young Angel looked like she had just bitten into a rotten apple.

Felix stepped forward. "Why don't you tell us about yourself, Albert? When and where are you from? How did you end up here?"

"Certainly," Albert said, shifting his attention from his sore calves to his thighs. "I was born in 1958 in Toledo, Ohio. Lived a beautiful life with my wife and our four kids. We owned and operated the local bookstore. Family business. Lost my dear Merna in 2007 when the bookstore burned down. Our oldest took her own life after that tragedy, and my other three kids blame me for the whole thing and haven't spoken to me since. That's how I ended up as a Guardian. It's far from the life I once had, but it'll do. I get to see the world—me and Merna always talked about traveling the world when we retired. Doing this work helps keep her alive. At least, I feel her in my heart when I go on these wild travels. This is only my third assignment living here in Dallas. Been here for five years out of a twenty-year stint. I peddle random goods, and that keeps me plugged in to the happenings around town."

"We're thrilled to have you here," Arielle said. The three Angels had formed a small huddle around Albert, entranced by his story. Road Runners often took extended trips into the past, helped by the fact they'd only age ten minutes when they returned to their Real Time.

"Happy to help," Albert replied with a tight-lipped grin. "Based on your arrival, I assume y'all are here to investigate those missing people?"

"We are," Arielle said. "How many people know about

them?"

Albert shrugged. "Well, in a small town like this, word gets around. I'd say if someone doesn't know, they must have fallen into their well!" He laughed at himself, shaking his head. "But that's all anyone knows. Two missing people. Thing is, it's not uncommon for people to just pack up and leave town, especially the younger folk. Opportunity can come knocking any time. Better job, better house, you name it. The kids in their early twenties only need an excuse to leave and they'll take it."

"So, their disappearance hasn't caused too much of a fuss?" Felix asked.

"There's always a fuss." Albert stood up, reached into his rear pocket, and pulled out a flask. Accustomed to seeing flasks for carrying their time travel Juice, Arielle thought Albert was about to vanish. But once he unscrewed the lid, she smelled the whiskey immediately. He took a long swig before settling back into the chair. "Right now, everyone thinks those two ran off together. And that makes the locals mad. They take it personal. Like Dallas wasn't good enough for those two kids. If you wanna really see some heads spin, just start a rumor that they fled to New York. But if you're here, this isn't a matter of some runaways, is it?"

Felix and Selena both turned to Arielle, unsure how much information they could provide someone outside of their team.

"You're correct," Arielle said. "We have reason to believe they didn't run away. And there's a third person missing. I'm assuming the word has not broken about that yet. That's why we arrived today. We have a small window of opportunity to find out what happened. What can you tell us about Doyle Grady?"

Albert's eyes bulged at the name. "Doyle? No way. Impossible."

"He's our primary target," Arielle said. "We need to know where he worked, lived, and who he spent his time with."

"I'll be damned," Albert said, rubbing his forehead in frustration. "Doyle came into town a few months ago. All around good guy. Supported the rights of women and minorities. Runs a speakeasy that allows everyone through its doors. He's sort of the leader for the oppressed here—in the underground, of course. How did I not see it coming?"

"Speakeasies didn't exist until prohibition," Felix said. "But since you're from the future and already knew what speakeasies were, you didn't make that connection."

Albert screwed the cap back onto his flask and studied it for a few seconds. "Huh, that's absolutely right. They give us so many things to study and prepare for, but I don't think speakeasies ever came up. Why would they, if they don't exist in this era? Thing is, even though what he was running was technically a speakeasy, it wasn't the first. There's always been an underground for the minorities to gather and enjoy themselves. It's just that no one ever assigned those places a name. They just exist. When Doyle came around promoting his speakeasy, I didn't think nothin' of it."

"That's a big mistake on Doyle's part," Arielle said. "No different from me bringing a cell phone to this era. I'm slightly encouraged, knowing he was that reckless in his approach to fitting in."

Albert laughed, shaking his head. "Fitting in, you say? Far from it. People who are only trying to fit in wouldn't go around town making a name for themselves. People think he is the perfect business partner for Mr. Dinsmore—that's the owner of the saloon where Doyle runs his speakeasy. Mr. Dinsmore just might be the most powerful man on this side of Dallas—again, not someone I would spend my time with if I was trying to blend in."

Arielle scrunched her face into deep thought. "Do you know where Mr. Dinsmore lives? And also where Doyle lived?"

Albert nodded. "Just keep going south if you want to find Mr. Dinsmore's house. About three more blocks from here—you won't miss it. It's the biggest house in town. And for Doyle, he lives on the east side of Main Street. There are a couple houses up on that hill—his is the white one. Are you going to head that way?"

"Yes," Arielle replied. "We need to look for the bodies."

Chapter 7

They marched out of their house, hungry and thirsty. Selena pleaded for them to stop for a meal before proceeding to Doyle's house, and no one argued.

Albert went his own way, vowing to find out everything he could about the missing people and to report back if he learned anything of significance.

The Angels returned to Main Street and had three different saloons to choose from.

"We're going to Lone Star Saloon," Arielle said. "Might as well check out the place where Doyle worked. And who knows, we might see this Mr. Dinsmore."

Lone Star Saloon was on the east end of Main Street, so they passed all the other shops and buildings they had originally seen on their way to the house. They sauntered by a blacksmith building, where a group of workers sat on a bench out front enjoying sandwiches under the beating sun.

When they arrived at the Lone Star Saloon, the three Angels paused outside the entrance, studying a sign hanging to the side of the doors.

Selena laughed before reading it aloud. "Bullseye Whiskey, ten cents. Lone Star Beer, five cents. Free lunch. No spurs inside. Horse thieves and coloreds not allowed. Absolutely no spittin' or fightin' permitted."

"If only we could take a picture of this sign," Felix said, rolling his eyes. "We're really in this era, and it's still blowing my mind."

"You have to take the lead, Felix," Arielle said. "As much as it pains me to say, Selena and I have to remain in the background. We'll do what we can, but our hands are tied."

Felix nodded. "I know. I've been mentally preparing."

And he had. No, he couldn't walk into a room full of strangers with the same confidence as Arielle, but he had observed her actions enough to understand how she got results. With no technology to rely on, he needed to make himself useful, and stepping up for the team was the only option.

Arielle gestured to the double swinging doors. "After you, sir." She shot him a wink that assured him everything was going to be fine.

Felix drew a deep breath. *Here goes nothing.*

He stepped through the doors to find the saloon packed with a lunch crowd. Only men, of course. The buzz of conversation drowned out the sound of an old man strumming his guitar next to the bar. All the tables were filled with men on their lunch breaks, enjoying mugs of beer, chicken legs, burgers, beans, and cornbread. No one so much as turned their head to look at the three time travelers.

A man with a pencil mustache and round glasses noticed them from behind the bar. His eyes bulged as he dashed toward them. "Good afternoon, folks. Is there something I can help you with?"

Felix cleared his throat, heart rate suddenly picking up. "Yes, sir, we're looking for a bite to eat."

The man's eyelids fluttered rapidly as he took a step and examined Felix from head to toe before doing the same to Arielle and Selena behind him. "Certainly. There is one seat open at the bar. The ladies have their own space in the back, but they'll need to go outside and around to the back entrance."

"Yes, sir," Felix said, bowing his head appreciatively. He turned to look at Arielle and Selena, who had already exited the saloon.

With the women gone, the man's lips tightened into an odd grin. "Follow me."

He spun around with grace and pushed through the crowded dining room, Felix trailing behind and catching curious stares from the other men he passed. Only a handful of men were dressed in suits like Felix. The rest were in complete cowboy attire—minus the spurs on their boots—or in dusty, raggedy overalls. A few had soot stains on their faces, and Felix presumed these were some of the town's blacksmiths.

Felix found the lone open seat at the bar and settled down between two burly men keeping to themselves and their juicy burgers.

"Never seen you around here," the bartender said, pouring a glass of water and pushing it to Felix. "From out of town?"

Shit, Felix thought. This is where Selena came in handy. She could whip up a fictional back story in a matter of seconds and deliver it with ease.

"Yes, sir," Felix said, opting to keep the conversation as brief as possible. The less he said, hopefully this bartender would get the hint and leave him alone.

"Passing through or staying for a bit?" the bartender asked, grabbing a toothpick from a carton on the bar and sticking it into the corner of his mouth.

"Staying a few days," Felix replied, looking at the two men on either side of him through his peripheral vision. One kept chomping on his burger, while the other gulped down a mug of Lone Star Beer.

The bartender took a step back and examined Felix once more. "Are you with the government?"

The floodgates of adrenaline opened, and Felix could barely sit still. They had agreed the best angle to explain their presence in Dallas was to inquire into the missing people as private investigators. But what if the bartender asked to see a badge?

I hate this part of the job.

Felix refused to get tangled in a web of lies, so only shook his head. "Not with the government."

The bartender frowned and knocked on the bar top. "I'll be right back."

He darted away, leaving Felix with his glass of water between the two large men. "Hot day out there," he said to the man on his right, who only nodded in agreement, refusing eye contact with Felix.

Seconds later, the bartender returned with a plate of food, sliding it in front of Felix. "Perhaps you're just hungry, but you seem like a man of few words."

Confidence, Felix told himself. *Don't let this guy dictate who you are.*

"It just takes me a while to open up with new people," Felix said. "It's nothing personal—just how I am."

All feeling left Felix's legs. He hated this interaction. It's why he preferred his role of using technology to find the truth, but he had no such option in 1898 and was being thrown to the wolves. All while Arielle and Selena hung out in a back room munching on their own burgers.

"If I didn't know any better," the bartender continued, "I'd think you're in town to look into those missing kids."

Every blood cell in Felix's body came to a screeching halt. Did this man know something about the Angels' presence in the past?

"Missing kids?" Felix replied, raising an eyebrow to feign his surprise. The bartender couldn't have a way of knowing Felix really was here to investigate the matter.

"You haven't heard?" the bartender asked, grinning as he filled a shot glass with whiskey for the man to Felix's left. "Couple of kids went missing last week. They were both in their early twenties, so it's not exactly a crime if they upped and left. But the rumors have been flying. The parents insist their kids had no connection to each other and believe they wouldn't have moved away without a word. Because they went missing at the same time, most folks think they had a secret relationship going on and ran away together. Fresh start for a new life in a new place somewhere."

Felix took a gulp of water. "So, do you think Dallas isn't safe right now?"

The bartender chuckled. "Dallas is just fine. I think they ran away. It can't be a coincidence the two of them go missing at the same time. I think the parents are hiding something. Like maybe they were forbidding their children to date. Wouldn't be the first time a couple runs off without approval from their family, and golly, it won't be the last."

"So, nothing like a serial killer?" Felix asked. This question caused the two men next to him to look in his direction, a move that made his face flush with heat.

"A serial killer?!" the bartender gasped. "Like Jack the Ripper? No, that stuff is for the big cities. Chicago had one a few years back...Holmes was the guy's name. Killed all those people in a hotel. You remember that?"

Felix nodded, clueless.

"Nothing like that here," the man continued. "Now, if one of their bodies turns up, then maybe you're on to something. But I suspect we'll never see them again, and I wish them the best in their new lives."

The bartender spun around and worked down the bar, scooping up dirty dishes and topping off drinks. Some of the crowd started filing out, workers needing to get back to their jobs. A young woman stomped out of a back room and circled the dining area to wipe the tables clean, receiving unsubtle glances and whistles from the remaining men.

She paid them no attention and disappeared into the back with a tray full of plates and cups.

The bartender returned to Felix and pushed over a mug of beer. "On the house. Welcome to Dallas."

Felix grinned. Perhaps he had misjudged the man all along. "Thank you."

"Sure you're not with the Justice Department?" the man asked.

"Justice Department?" Felix asked.

"It's just that you're dressed like them. We've had a few of them come into town over the last week. *They* think there might be something more at play with those missing kids. They ask around, stay in town for a night or two, then disappear. Back to their little office wherever the hell they came from—prob'ly Chicago."

Felix looked around as more people left the saloon and

leaned forward to speak in a hushed tone. "Can I tell you something?"

The man leaned in, reciprocating the lower voice. "Certainly."

They *were* here to find out what happened, and who better to discuss the matter with than the bartender where Doyle also had worked? He hadn't mentioned the name yet, but knew once he did, the bartender would have plenty to say.

Felix looked back and forth between the two men on either side.

"Don't worry about them," the bartender said. "They're good friends."

Felix gulped before speaking. "I *am* here because of the missing kids. Not with the government, but as a private investigator."

The bartender cocked an eyebrow, holding a stern gaze on Felix. "I knew it. I'm not sure how much I can be of help, but just let me know."

"Actually, I was wondering what you can tell me about Doyle Grady. I understand he works here."

The name sent a shockwave through the bartender's body. Felix saw the brief shudder.

"Why, yes, he does work here," the man replied calmly. "Mr. Dinsmore—he's the owner—just visited Doyle this morning to collect on last night's money. Doyle should be in to work tonight. He operates our forbidden bar—where all the ladies and coloreds hang out. But I don't understand why you'd have any interest in him."

"We believe he may be involved," Felix whispered. The saloon had fallen nearly silent now that only four customers remained in the main dining area, plus the two men at the bar.

"Involved?" The bartender arched an eyebrow. "So, you don't think those kids ran away?"

Felix shook his head.

"I'll be damned," the bartender said, clapping the top of the bar. "Willie, Tommy, why don't you clear out the place and watch the door. I need to have a word in private with our new friend here."

The two men sandwiching Felix rose from their chairs without a word, and he figured they both were pushing seven feet. They lumbered toward the saloon's remaining guests and asked them to leave the building, which they did without argument.

"I'm sorry, sir," Felix said to the bartender. "Is all this necessary?"

"Necessary?" the bartender replied with a cackle. "You want to discuss one of our most popular employees potentially being mixed up in a crime? I can't risk any of the customers catching ear of that. Why don't we head to my office? I have the time logs for when Doyle has worked over the last six months, if that would be useful."

Felix's eye lit up. "Actually, yes, that would be great."

"Let's head back. You can bring the beer."

The bartender started toward the door and gestured for Felix to join him.

Unsure, Felix stood up and grabbed his mug of beer, shuffling over. Behind the door was a short hallway with two doors on either side and one at the far end. The bartender turned right at the first door, which was left open.

The door to the bar swung closed, wafting Felix with a slight breeze. He continued into the office, relieved to find a desk covered in folders and papers. The bartender had taken a seat behind the desk.

"So, you're more than the bartender around here," Felix said, taking a nervous sip from his mug. He wasn't sure why he felt so jumpy.

"Bartender?" the man said, shaking his head. "I'm the general manager. After Mr. Dinsmore, I'm the main decision-maker for all happenings in this saloon. Some days—like today—I have to pick up the slack. But I don't mind. The lunch crowd is a gentle breeze compared to the hurricane of the night-time folks. That's usually when we have all hands on deck."

"I see. Say, what's your name? I don't believe I've gotten it."

"Ted Perkins at your service. And you are?"

"Felix. I'd prefer not to share my last name."

Ted shot a quizzical look across the desk. "As you wish. Would you mind closing the door? Don't want any wandering ears to hear us."

Okay, Felix thought. *This is fine. This guy is normal. Has no hidden agenda. And seems interested in helping.*

"Of course." Felix hadn't sat down yet and turned around, walking four paces to the door. "I really appreciate you taking some time to chat with me."

Felix closed the door and turned back around. Ted stood inches away, a brick in hand.

"What—" Felix began, but Ted whipped him across the head with the brick, turning his world black.

Chapter 8

When Felix next opened his bleary eyes, he had no idea how much time had passed. If he had to guess, it had felt like a full night's sleep, but he couldn't know for sure. There were no clocks on the wall in the office, nor any windows to gauge the world outside.

Felix sat in the seat in front of the desk, Ted relaxing comfortably in the chair on the other side. The side of his head throbbed with pain, a headache seeming to engulf every inch of his brain. The room spun around him, and he didn't dare try to stand up, not feeling steady even as he sat. It wasn't until he looked down that he realized he had been tied to the chair by thick ropes around his torso, knees, and ankles.

"Good morning, sunshine," Ted said, offering an evil grin. "I didn't want to tie your mouth shut—that seemed like too much. But I will if you start shouting, are we clear?"

Felix nodded, and even that subtle movement sent a jolt of pain into the side of his head.

Ted laughed. "Good man. Now maybe we can be a little more honest with each other."

"How long was I out for?" Felix asked, his voice groggy.

"Only about thirty minutes," Ted said, putting his boots up on the desk to recline further in his seat. "Now, why don't you tell me who you really are?"

Ted's voice sounded distant, like Felix was still trapped in a dream and hearing it in his subconscious. But he was awake all right. There was no dismissing the burning sensation of the rope around his ankles. Never mind the feeling that his head might explode at any minute.

"I told you who I am," Felix murmured. "My name is Felix, and I'm a private investigator looking into the missing people."

Ted crossed his arms and shook his head. "Not what I want. Where are you from? Why are you here? You're barely older than the missing kids. How are you qualified to look for them?"

Stay calm, Felix reminded himself. He wanted to cry. How long would it take for Arielle and Selena to realize something was wrong? And once they did, could they get past the two behemoths guarding the front door? "I'm a private investigator from Denver, Colorado. The girl's family hired me to look into their daughter's disappearance. I'm more than qualified—I've been doing this job for several years now."

Ted grinned, an evil look that sent chills up Felix's spine. "I suggest you stop with the lies—they'll only get you hurt."

Felix gripped the sides of the chair, anger bubbling up. This man refused to believe a word. What did he want to hear?

"Sir, I'm not lying," Felix said through gritted teeth. "Everything I've told you is true."

Ted snorted, then leaned back in his seat, pulling out a pack of cigarettes and a matchbook from his shirt pocket. He stuck a cigarette in his mouth and lit it with a quick flick of his wrist. Ted took a long drag and blew the smoke toward the ceiling. He put up his feet on the desk, nearly kicking the heavy-duty typewriter sitting in the center. "Doyle warned me you might be snooping around. Said two girls and a guy might show up claiming to look into the disappearance and wanting to pin it on him."

The rage fled from Felix, leaving him confused and clueless how to proceed. Ted must have seen it on his face, because he snickered before speaking again. "What's the matter? Didn't expect Doyle to know?"

"I—we're just trying to do our job," Felix said. "We're not looking to pin anything on Doyle. Just wanted to look around and ask him some questions. We're not law enforcement—we have no way of even arresting him. The facts are all we're after. What the family does with them is entirely their decision."

Ted let out a fake laugh. "Doyle told me you'd say all this." Ted stood up and circled around the desk with slow, dramatic steps. He stopped in front of Felix and leaned against the front of the desk to face him. "Doyle told me a lot. That he has a past that keeps trying to follow him. Now, he didn't tell me *what* his past was, and it doesn't matter to me. I judge people based on what I see with my own eyes, not whatever they might have done before. And Doyle Grady is one of the finest men I know. He has a big heart, cares about people, and has made our saloon a better place since he arrived."

"He's the one feeding you lies," Felix said. "Can't you see that? He's a murderer, and he probably killed those two kids— three by now!"

Ted chuckled. "He knew you'd say that. I once saw Doyle nurse a horse with a broken leg. One time, he even picked up a spider crawling around the bar and took it outside to be free. And here you are, trying to tell me he has killed his fellow humans. I may look like a fool, Mr. Felix, but I'm much smarter than you're giving me credit for. I've known Doyle for six months now. Why would I take your word over his?"

Felix sighed. This battle was lost. He was tied to a chair with no way out. His head burned with pain. Nothing he said mattered. Doyle beat them to the punch and had convinced Ted anything coming out of Felix's lips was pure blasphemy.

"Got nothing to say?" Ted asked, poking at Felix's shin with the tip of his boot.

Felix shrugged. "Doesn't matter what I say. Your mind is made up. Doyle's out there killing more people right now, and you're defending him. I'll just sit here and let it happen, I suppose."

Felix didn't need to act. He was deflated and had lost any will to argue with Ted.

"Doyle isn't a killer," Ted insisted, his tone sounding slightly unsure.

"If he's not a killer, then what is he hiding?" Felix asked. "If you're as smart as you claim, then I want you to seriously think about it. Why would an innocent man go through all this trouble of bribing you to take me hostage? Wouldn't he want to cooperate with an investigation and clear his name? If he didn't kill anyone, then why was he so worried about someone coming to look for him? Innocent people don't have other people hunting them down."

Ted gazed at Felix while taking another drag from his cigarette. He pursed his lips together, refusing to break eye contact.

He's trying to read me. Part of him thinks I'm telling the truth.

Felix held silent, giving Ted the space needed to come to this conclusion. Ted nodded to himself.

"You're a liar," Ted muttered under his breath. "A god-damned liar!"

Shit, Felix thought, his brief glimpse of hope vanishing as quickly as it had arrived.

"Doyle is the smartest man I know," Ted continued. "He told me all about the people after his money—and I know he has a ton. He's paying me to keep you here, after all. A hell of a lot more than I make running the saloon. He promised to protect me, and so far, he's done nothing but that. Even got me a new gun. Wanna see it?"

Felix thought he was going to vomit. Trapped in this office with a madman about to pull out a gun. He didn't see how any of this could end well.

"Ted, please," Felix said.

Ted smiled as he circled back around the desk and pulled open the top drawer, raising a shiny revolver. "She's a beaut', don't you think?"

As long as he doesn't point it at me, I'll be okay. Should I tip myself over? Would that break the chair? How fast would he shoot me if I did that? Does he have the guts to pull that trigger on a complete stranger?

Ted raised the gun and aimed at Felix's face. "Doyle offered me more money if I kill you. It'd be real easy to get away with it, too. People in this town trust me. If I tell them you tried to rob me and I had to shoot you, no one'll think twice. They'll toss your body in the river and wish you the best."

Felix thought the temperature had climbed another thirty degrees in the room. Sweat formed in beads around his forehead, while his heart hammered away in his chest. *This isn't how I die,* Felix thought, trusting the past would take care of him. But Felix had no place in 1898. His murder and disappearance wouldn't be tied to anyone this far into history. They'd always known the past would go to any means to preserve itself, but no one knew if it did the same for the future.

"Doyle's gone," Felix said. "He's playing you like a pawn in his twisted game of chess. If I were a betting man, I don't think you'll ever see Doyle again."

Ted laughed. "Mr. Dinsmore just saw him this morning. Try again."

"I'm telling you, he's gone. He wants you to do his dirty work. He can't actually protect you if he's not here. You'll take the fall, and he'll be halfway across the world. This is what he does. Do you know for a fact Mr. Dinsmore saw him this morning, or is that only what you heard? Have you seen Doyle with your own eyes today?"

Ted opened his mouth, then promptly closed it again. The revolver remained pointed at Felix. "I have no reason to doubt Mr. Dinsmore saw Doyle this morning. It's part of his morning routine. If he hadn't seen Doyle, then we'd all have heard about it. Because once money is involved, Mr. Dinsmore becomes a very vocal man. No Doyle means no money, and I haven't heard a peep."

"Look," Felix said, his rush of adrenaline helping his mind focus on a way out. "I get you're in control of this situation and there's nothing I can do about it. But please, hear me out. You can tape my mouth shut and leave me in this office. I just need you to confirm that Doyle really is still here. If he is, and he still wants you to kill me, then so be it. Collect your money and throw me in the river. But if he's not here, and no one can tell you where he went, then you need to let me go so I can join my team and catch him. We'll leave this town and never look back, and I'll be forever in your debt for your mercy."

The gun trembled slightly in Ted's grip, and after a few seconds, he lowered it. "Shit," Ted said, biting his bottom lip as he stared at the floor. "Doyle always stops in for lunch, but he wasn't here today."

"See!" Felix gasped, wishing he could force Ted to see things from his perspective.

"Settle down," Ted grumbled, waving the revolver at Felix. He eventually dropped the gun on the desk and rubbed his temples in frustration. "I can't believe I'm going to do this, but I'm gonna check and see if Doyle is at his house."

Felix kept his emotions under control. He just bought some much needed time to stay alive. And while he suspected Doyle had already fled, he couldn't predict how Ted would react once he realized Doyle was gone. Would he blame Felix and still kill him? Would the town hold all three of them hostage until they explained where Doyle could have gone? Doyle clearly had a hold on those at the saloon, but did that expand to all of Main Street and its surrounding residents?

There was a chance Doyle hadn't left, either. And if that was the case, Felix knew he wouldn't see tomorrow morning's sunrise.

"I'll be back in a few minutes," Ted said, digging out a raggedy handkerchief from the same drawer he had kept the gun in. "Good thinking about tying your mouth shut. I was just going to have Willie and Tommy stay in here with you, but I'd rather have them stay at the door while I'm gone."

Ted rolled the handkerchief tightly as he shuffled to stand behind Felix. "Open wide."

Felix had no choice but to oblige and opened his mouth like he was waiting for a giant spoon to feed him. Ted covered Felix's mouth with the handkerchief and fastened a knot tightly behind his head.

The flavor of dust and oil mixed in Felix's mouth, making his eyes water. He tried pressing the handkerchief with his tongue, but it was far too tight. The best he could manage were guttural grunts from the back of his throat.

"Perfect," Ted said, patting Felix on top of his head like a little kid. "You stay put now."

Chapter 9

When Arielle and Selena stepped into the separate ladies-only dining area, much to their surprise, it was just as packed as the main saloon. Only one table remained open in the exact center. A few women studied Arielle and Selena as they pushed their way through the crowd, but the majority remained entranced by their own conversations.

The women in the room gossiped about the missing people, everyone seeming to have their own, unique opinions on the matter. One woman claimed to have known the missing boy's family and cited a heated argument the family had about a girl he had been courting. Another woman said this was a lie, that she had actually had dinner with the family after the boy's disappearance, and they said nothing of the sort.

Selena ordered a second beer after finishing lunch and swirled around its final remains as the saloon started clearing out.

"How do you think it's going for Felix?" Selena asked, gulping down the beer and slamming the empty mug on the table. The beer wasn't the greatest, but after wearing this ridiculous dress for a few hours, she found it rather refreshing. And strong. She couldn't recall the last time she had felt a buzz after drinking one beer.

"It's Felix," Arielle said with a giggle. "We have no way of knowing. He's either befriended every single person in the bar or is sitting in the corner by himself."

"That's so true," Selena replied. "He tries to be a closed book, but once he connects with someone, you really can't shut him up."

"Well, if our side of the building is emptying, then his must be, too. We should probably check on him. I'd like to go to Doyle's house sooner than later."

Arielle stood up and tossed two nickels on the table, unsure if tipping was even a thing in 1898. They hurried out of the building, returning to the blistering heat outside their special side entrance.

"Main Street already seems a lot quieter," Selena said as they strolled around the corner of the building.

Arielle nodded. "Think all the racket was just the lunch hour. Now everyone is back at work or home."

They reached the saloon's front entrance and stopped when they saw two massive men standing guard on either side of the double swinging doors. The men's arms were crossed as they stared ahead into the distance.

Selena nudged Arielle with her elbow and muttered, "Do you think something's going on?"

"It seems like it. Let's find out."

Arielle led the way toward the men and kept at least six feet of distance between them. "Good afternoon, gentlemen," she said.

The man on the left turned his head slowly to meet Arielle's gaze. "We're closed," he said in a hoarse voice.

"Closed?" Arielle replied. "I don't mean to bother, but our brother was inside. Can we have a quick look around to see if he's in there?"

The man held his stare on Arielle as he shrugged. "Hey, Tommy, should we let these nice ladies have a quick look around?"

The man on the right laughed, his beefy shoulders bouncing as he shook his head. "Listen, ladies," Tommy said. "Like my good friend, Willie, told you—we're closed. Now leave."

Arielle took another step backwards. Selena crouched to the ground, craning her neck for a view below the swinging doors.

"What's she doing?" Willie asked, pointing at Selena. "Get up, woman."

"Woman?!" Selena gasped, climbing back to her feet.

"Selena," Arielle said sharply, but was promptly ignored.

"I *am* a woman," Selena said, taking a step closer to the men. "Do you have a problem with that?"

Willie laughed. "Get a load of this one," he said to Tommy. "Should we teach her some manners?"

"Take one fucking step toward me and you'll be the one receiving a lesson," Selena said, balling her fists.

"Selena!" Arielle snarled. "Dammit, that's enough."

"Enough?" Selena asked, spinning around to face Arielle. "These two gorillas know something and aren't telling us. The saloon is completely empty."

"Of course it's empty," Tommy said, remaining unfazed. "We're closed."

"Then why the hell are you both standing out here if you're closed?" Selena asked, turning back around. "If you're closed, then shouldn't you be at home? Or do you not have a home to go to? Because gorillas live in the forest."

Willie laughed. "You got quite the mouth, miss. Maybe you really do need to be taught some manners. A lady isn't supposed to talk so aggressive."

"I'm not your typical *lady*," Selena said, taking another step toward the men. Willie uncrossed his arms, hands falling to his sides.

"Selena!" Arielle shouted. "Step back and let's talk this out."

"Listen to your sister," Tommy said, winking at Selena. "She's giving good advice."

Selena tossed up her hands and turned around. "Fine. We can try it your way. But if it doesn't work, we get to bash these morons' skulls."

"What's a moron?" Willie asked Tommy, who only shrugged in response.

"Exactly," Selena said before returning to Arielle's side.

"Enough," Arielle whispered under her breath. "1898, Selena. Women don't act like this." She took two steps closer to the men. "Excuse my sister. We've had a long day of travel and are a bit on edge. Our brother went in there for lunch. We just want to know where he went after you closed."

Willie and Tommy exchanged a glance. Tommy said, "Listen, lady, there were fifty, maybe sixty, people in here during lunch. We don't know who your brother is or where he went."

"Okay," Arielle replied calmly. "I understand that, but why can't we just look inside to see if he left behind a note? We weren't expecting him to be gone already."

"We can't let you inside," Tommy said, nonchalant. "We're closed. And like your sister said, there's nothing inside."

Arielle reached into her bag and pulled out a handful of coins. "I can pay you. Please, just give us five minutes to look inside."

Willie eyed the money, the dials turning in his mind. Tommy, however, waved them off. "We don't need your money. Now leave before I call the sheriff."

Willie stepped forward, the ground rumbling under his heavy footsteps.

Arielle raised her hands. "Okay. We're leaving."

"Good," Willie replied. "Take your monkey-loving sister with you, too."

Selena glared at Willie, and if Arielle hadn't grabbed her by the arm, she might have pounced on the man.

"This way," Arielle said, pulling Selena away from the saloon. They crossed Main Street and sat on a bench in front of the bank.

"What the hell was that?!" Selena asked. "Those guys did something to Felix. Are you blind?"

"I know that," Arielle said. "But we can't just beat them to a pulp in the middle of Main Street. They're still watching us."

They were at least a hundred feet away, but the two men held their ground next to the door.

"Yeah," Selena said. "No way they're leaving now. You should have let me take the one on the left. He needs an ass whooping."

Arielle laughed. "What do you think we can achieve in these outfits? Seriously?"

"Good point," Selena said. "But we may not have a choice. We need to get in there. If Felix wasn't in there, he'd be out here waiting for us. He might have even stopped by the ladies' section to find us."

"I have an idea," Arielle said, standing up from the bench. "Follow me."

Arielle spun around and walked down the side of the bank, stopping behind the building and out of sight from Main Street entirely. Yellow grass and weeds decorated the lot behind the bank, grasshoppers bouncing in every direction with each step the two took.

"What is this?" Selena asked. "You think playing hide and seek with those clowns will make something happen?"

Arielle shook her head. "They're not leaving that door. Let's spare a couple of minutes now. Let them think we've wandered off. Then we can walk along the back of all these buildings and make our way back to the saloon. No one is guarding the ladies' entrance, and it's completely out of sight from those two. I saw a door while we were eating lunch. No idea what it connected to, but there has to be something that leads to the main saloon. They share the same kitchen, after all."

Selena sighed. "That's a long ass walk in this heat and wearing this damned dress. But a brilliant idea."

"I'd love to avoid those men if we can, but if it comes to it, I'd rather fight them inside the saloon instead of causing a scene for all of Main Street to watch. Did you notice if either of them had a gun?"

Selena pursed her lips in thought. "Not that I saw, but we shouldn't ignore the possibility."

"I really don't want a gunfight," Arielle said, patting her leg where she had a nine-millimeter derringer strapped to a garter. "Let's avoid it at all costs. Those guys might be big, but we can take them on without weapons."

Selena shrugged. "I won't shoot until you do."

"Let's go."

Arielle strolled away from the bank. From there, they'd be spotted crossing the road, and it wouldn't take much for Willie and Tommy—despite their obvious lack of thinking skills—to figure out what they were up to. They needed to go to the far end of Main Street to cross and circle back to the saloon.

"What do you think happened?" Selena asked. "Everyone has been friendly, except for Thing One and Thing Two. I find it hard to believe Felix pissed someone off to the point of holding him hostage in the saloon."

"Impossible to say," Arielle said, waving away a couple of wasps swarming around her head. "This is the past we're dealing with. It could be as simple as someone not liking Felix's presence. They're always suspicious around outsiders in smaller towns. Or maybe he was asking too many questions to the wrong person. I'm not concerned about the reasoning. We just need to get him out of there before anything spirals out of control."

"You don't think he would have gone to Doyle's house on his own? Maybe wanting a head start?"

"Not at all. We're on a mission. Felix is going to do everything by the book, so he wouldn't go to that house until I've cleared it."

Just under five minutes later, they had reached the end of Main Street, back at the general store, and crossed the road where they hurried behind the town's church.

"I hope you don't mind me asking," Selena said as they started their journey back to the saloon, "but how is your grandma doing?"

Arielle shuffled her steps upon hearing the question but didn't slow down as she whipped her gaze to Selena. "How did you know about that?"

"I don't actually know anything," Selena said in a gentle tone. "Felix told me you mentioned something on the last mission about your grandma having health issues. Said it was distracting you during the mission."

"Oh," Arielle said, more to herself.

"I'm sorry if I wasn't supposed to know about it."

"No, that's not it. I guess I never told him to keep it a secret, and it's absolutely fine for you to know. I should have told you both before the last mission even started. But yes, my grandma has been diagnosed with dementia. Early stages, so they can give her some treatments that will slow its progress. But there is no cure."

Selena stopped and grabbed Arielle by the arm, pulling her in for a hug. "I'm sorry, Arielle. I know how much she means to you. If you need anything at all from me or Felix, just let us know. We're here for you."

Tears welled in Arielle's eyes as her pursed lips gave the slightest of trembles. "Thank you. She's my only family left, at least that I'm in regular contact with. I always call her before I leave for a mission, and this last time she kept repeating herself. It wasn't anything extreme, but I noticed. It made the conversation feel a little empty. Dementia is a long, sick road. I'm just grateful we only lose ten minutes while on missions. I've been thinking about moving to New Mexico to stay with her between missions. Especially now that we're getting so much time between."

"You'd move to New Mexico?!" Selena asked, but soon realized it wasn't such an absurd thought. Arielle only had her job in Denver and had little else that required her immediate attention.

Arielle nodded. "Either that or moving my grandma to Denver to live with me. I haven't talked to her about either option, but I want to be close to her at all times. The doctors have no way of projecting how quickly a particular case can progress. She can be with me for another fifteen years, or only fifteen months." Arielle shrugged and wiped the tears out of her eyes. "We can talk about this after the mission. Let's keep going. We're almost there."

Chapter 10

Arielle and Selena stood twenty feet away from the saloon's special entrance meant for women. The saloon hadn't closed, but no one remained inside after the lunch crowd dispersed.

"We can go in, right?" Selena asked. They stood in an open space to the side of Lone Star Saloon, out of sight from the primary entrance and the rest of Main Street.

"I don't see why not," Arielle said.

"Do we need a story for why we're back? Or why we're even here in the middle of the day?"

Arielle shrugged. "Only twenty percent of women have a job in this era. The rest are housewives. We might draw some questions, but if we play the card that we're visiting from out of town, they should cut us some slack."

"Sure," Selena said, rolling her eyes. "Just a couple of ladies out day drinking on vacation. Totally normal for these times. Maybe I'll order a piña colada and get really wild."

"Or maybe you can invent the piña colada, get super rich, and live the rest of your life here," Arielle said with plenty of sass. "Then you can stay in that dress for the rest of your life."

Selena flipped her middle finger to Arielle. "Hilarious. Are we going in, or do you prefer we melt out here? I don't see any signs of our friends Tommy and Willie."

"Let's go," Arielle said, strolling up to the swinging doors and pushing them open with confidence.

The bar was deserted. They had cleared all the tables of dishes and wiped them clean. The bar top appeared freshly polished, vacant of beer mugs and shot glasses. The silence was near deafening.

"What do we do?" Selena whispered.

They remained just inside the door and watched two mice chasing each other before dashing out of sight around the corner.

Arielle nodded her head toward a door next to the bar and started toward it. She took soft footsteps, and Selena followed suit. They didn't *need* to be stealthy, but they wanted to go undetected for as long as they could.

They approached the door, this one tall and solid with an actual knob. Arielle reached out and turned the knob, pushing the door open with a creak loud enough to wake up the neighborhood. They stood frozen, grimacing in anticipation of being caught, Arielle's heart hammering in her ears.

Ten seconds passed and no one appeared, so Arielle pushed the door open all the way, relieved it made no more noise. They heard the distant sound of a singing voice, almost opera-like.

Selena stepped through and Arielle closed the door gently behind them. They stood in a short hallway with a door on each side, plus one at the end. Straight ahead, however, was an open doorway that led into the kitchen, and to the source of the singing.

"I love you as I never loved before,
   Since first I met you on the village green
   Come to me, or my dream of love is over.

I love you as I loved you
When you were sweet, when you were sweet sixteen."

A soft piano tune got lost under the white noise of running water and the clanking of dishes.

"What the hell is that?" Selena whispered, stepping toward the door and craning her neck for a view inside. With her head sticking through, she waved her hand for Arielle to join.

Arielle shuffled forward and looked into the kitchen where a man had his back to them. He stood hunched over the basin, scrubbing dishes, while a phonograph in the far corner blared music from a massive nickel horn. The man swayed his hips slowly from side to side as he sang along to the original iteration of "When You Were Sweet Sixteen."

Arielle stepped back and pulled Selena with her. "We need to find Felix," she muttered under her breath. "And I don't think that guy has anything to do with him."

Selena grinned, trying to hold in a laugh.

"This way," Arielle said as they returned to the hallway. "Which door should we check? I can't hear anything else over the music."

Selena put her hands on her hips and studied the three doors. "I'm betting the one straight ahead connects to the main saloon. Let's just have a look?"

Arielle agreed and wasted no time starting for it, passing the two doors with hesitancy. Felix could be behind any of these three doors, but the saloon seemed the most logical place to look, since they had put two bouncers outside the entrance.

"If it creaks, we stop," Arielle said as she reached out for the doorknob. "They'll hear it from where they're standing."

"And if it creaks, they'll hear it regardless if you stop or not," Selena replied. "Might as well go in and take care of them before they realize what's happening."

"No," Arielle said sternly. "We're here for Felix. If it creaks, we turn around and hide behind one of these other doors. We can even go back through the women's saloon, but I'd prefer not to leave the building."

Selena shook her head. "Whatever you say. Open it already."

Arielle nodded and returned her attention to the door, twisting the knob and pulling it open one careful inch at a time.

To their delight, the door made no sound and opened to the saloon, which was as abandoned as the women's side. Two pairs of legs were visible beneath the front entrance's swinging doors.

"Go in," Selena whispered, shoving Arielle from behind until she was standing all the way inside. The scene matched what they had just left on the women's side.

"No one's in here," Arielle said. "Let's go back and check the other doors."

She turned around, and this time gave Selena a nudge to return to the hallway.

"Left or right?" Selena asked as they faced their final two remaining options.

Arielle looked back and forth between the two doors, knowing it didn't really matter. If Felix wasn't behind one, then they'd just check behind the other. But what if he wasn't behind either?

"Open the right one," Arielle said.

Selena nodded and turned the knob. "It's locked," she said, tossing her hands up.

"Relax. Let's try the other door."

Arielle crossed the hallway and promptly opened the door, revealing a dark storage closet. Dishes, towels, and cleaning supplies stood on scattered shelves with no type of organization.

"Felix?" Arielle called into the closet.

"What now?" Selena asked, hands on her hips.

Arielle closed the closet and turned around to face the locked door. "We have to get in there. We're over a hundred years in the past in a small town. People don't lock doors unless they're hiding something. I have my lockpick on my belt. Although, we could probably break in with a stick—these locks aren't that complex."

Arielle never left the house without her utility belt beneath her clothes. She only kept the essentials in it to avoid too much bulk: a small hand gun, two magazines, a lockpick, three throwing knives, one flashlight, and several zip ties.

She started hiking up her dress to reach her belt and struggled with the several layers.

Selena whipped out her hand to grab Arielle by the arm. "Let's ditch the dresses, okay?"

"We can't," Arielle grunted, kneeling down for an easier angle. "We'll stick out without them."

Selena leaned against the wall and crossed her arms while watching Arielle struggle.

After a few seconds, Arielle finally pulled out the lockpick and held it high. "See. No problem."

Selena chuckled as she stepped aside, clearing the path for Arielle to jam the tool into the lock. It only took a couple of twists of the wrist before they heard the click of success.

"Told you," Arielle said. "Nothing to it."

She turned the knob and pushed open the door—this one

with a slow creak that wasn't nearly as loud as the first.

"Oh my God!" Selena gasped, pushing Arielle aside and banging the door all the way open.

Felix sat in a chair with his back to them, ropes keeping him tied to the seat.

"Felix!" Selena cried, rushing around to face him.

Arielle followed, immediately dropping to a knee to untie the rope fastening his ankles to the chair's legs. Selena pulled down the handkerchief stuffed into Felix's mouth, causing him to pant for breath.

Arielle finished untying the other two ropes before circling around to face Felix. Sweat glistened on his forehead, his eyes full of tears.

"I knew you'd come," he said through deep gasps for air, his chest heaving up and down.

"If you knew we'd come, why do you look so worried?" Selena asked with a crooked smile, playfully kicking Felix's foot.

"Well, I *trusted* that you'd come save me," he replied, gradually catching his breath. "But if you didn't, I'm pretty sure I would have died in this room."

"Tell us everything," Arielle said. "Why are you tied to a chair? Whose office is this?"

Felix rubbed the inside of his elbows where the rope had burned into his flesh. "His name was Ted. He's the manager of the saloon. Something's going on. Doyle told Ted that we'd be here and that we'd spread false rumors about Doyle being responsible for the missing people."

"Shit," Arielle said through gritted teeth. "Okay, we need to get out of here. Now!"

Doyle was pulling the strings in Dallas, and if he had already planted the seeds of doubt into everyone's minds, the three Angels would have no way of avoiding a target on their backs.

"You're not going anywhere," a voice called from the hallway, prompting all three of them to jerk their heads toward the open door.

The slow clopping of boots echoed throughout the hallway until Ted Perkins appeared in the doorway, a pistol held in a tight grip, aimed at Felix.

"Looks like Doyle was right, after all," Ted said, stepping into his office and closing the door. "Two younger women and a man will come into town wanting to pin the missing people on Doyle. That's what he told me would happen, and here we are. And he didn't answer his door when I knocked. What have you done with him?!"

"Sir," Arielle pleaded. "Put the gun down."

Ted flashed a grin of yellowed teeth. "I wouldn't dream of it, darling. Why don't the three of you stand against the wall, shoulder to shoulder, so we can have a little discussion."

Arielle raised her hands, showing she meant no harm. "Okay."

She pivoted and started for the wall, turning around to press her back against it. Selena took slow steps across the office to join her, but Arielle noticed Felix holding a steady gaze on the typewriter.

"Your turn, big guy," Ted said calmly.

Felix was still in the seat and had his back to Ted. He stood up, shifting his stare from the typewriter to Arielle, and gave her the slightest nod that only she noticed.

Arielle cleared her throat before shouting, "YOU CAN'T HOLD US HOSTAGE IN HERE!"

She tossed her arms up, flailing them wildly. Selena recoiled and jumped aside, confusion smeared over her face.

They had mere seconds to execute this impromptu plan, but Arielle knew it would work once Ted swung the gun around to her.

As if he had eyes in the back of his head, Felix snatched the typewriter from the desk and spun around in a swift motion, launching the thirty-pound hunk of steel directly toward Ted's face.

Ted whirled his head around too late, eyes bulging as the missile collided with his forehead in a violent *thunk!*

The typewriter crashed to the floor, letting out a brief ring while a handful of keys popped out and rolled around. Ted stayed on his feet for three seconds, no sign of consciousness behind his eyes, blood seeping from a cut on his forehead. He collapsed to the floor, his face once more meeting the side of the typewriter.

"Holy shit!" Selena cried, both hands clasped over her mouth.

"Everybody stay calm," Arielle said, stepping forward to kick Ted's arm to make sure he really was out cold. "We don't have a lot of time. We need to go to Doyle's house right now."

Chapter 11

They bolted out of the saloon, Arielle leading them back through the women's dining area and outside.

"Where are those two gorillas?" Selena asked when they huddled just outside the door.

"Doesn't matter," Arielle said. "They'll be looking for us soon enough, and it's best if we're out of sight."

"Gorillas?" Felix asked, cocking an eyebrow in confusion.

Selena chuckled. "There were two massive men guarding the main entrance. That's how we knew something was going on inside."

"Oh," Felix said. "I was actually sitting next to those guys at the bar. They didn't say a single word to me the whole time."

"Shit," Arielle said, starting away from the building, waving for the other two to keep up. "How much do they know about you?"

"Not much," Felix replied quickly. "They may have caught my name, and that I'm here to investigate the missing people—although Ted has completely twisted that story."

"You didn't mention where we're staying?" Arielle asked.

"No."

With this confirmation, Arielle broke into a mad dash toward the hill that led up to Doyle's house a quarter mile away.

It took them nearly three minutes to reach the house—Arielle and Selena slowed by their dresses. They stopped in front of Doyle's home and gasped for air. Felix walked in circles with his hands clasped behind his head, while Arielle and Selena put their hands on their knees.

"That was awful," Selena said.

"It was," Felix replied. "But we made it. And I'd say we're just far enough out of sight."

He nodded to Main Street down the gentle hill. They saw the buildings and could see the silhouettes of people walking around, but nothing was clear.

"Okay," Arielle said once they had gathered their breaths and were ready to continue. "Keep your eyes open for the time portal. I believe it's somewhere in this house since Doyle would need to be close to it. We can use it in case of an absolute emergency—wish we would have brought our Juice instead of leaving it in the luggage."

"Hell no," Selena said. "You're going to take out your gun now—remember that little tool you have?—and you can take care of them. You insisted Felix and I leave ours since you can handle any gunfight in 1898, or else I'd take care of myself. Besides, I'm not jumping into a time portal crafted by a psychopath with no idea where it will take me."

"It wasn't *created* by Doyle," Arielle said. "He simply found it and uses it. Do you feel the same, Felix?"

Felix looked at Selena and nodded. "Sorry, Arielle. I have no knowledge or experience with time portals. I'd rather not step through one."

"Okay, fine," Arielle said, throwing up her hands. "Selena, get my gun, please. I'm not gonna bother trying with this dress anymore."

Arielle pulled up her dress and let Selena rummage through the layers of fluff and lace to wrestle the gun out of her utility belt.

Felix turned around to look the other way.

"Anything else you need while I'm in here?" Selena asked, her head buried in the dress like a groom searching for the garter belt on his wedding night.

Arielle chuckled. "Just the gun would be great. Thanks."

Selena returned with the gun and handed it to Arielle, who gave it a quick look before lowering it to her side.

"Okay, what now?" Felix asked, continuing to stare down the hill for any sign of trouble. "Are we trusting Doyle is gone? Ted supposedly came up here earlier—that's *why* he left me tied to the chair."

"Why did he come all the way over here?" Selena asked.

"I convinced him he'd never see Doyle again, and that he was making it all up about us being the ones responsible for the missing people. Told him to come up here and see if Doyle was home. But we don't know the answer because he had just returned when you were there."

"I'm confident he's gone," Arielle said. "Even someone with as much narcissism as Doyle isn't going to take any chances. The thrill of getting away with the crimes is probably more of a rush than the crimes themselves."

"So, we're just going to kick in the door and hope for the best?" Selena asked.

"I'm telling you—he's gone," Arielle repeated. "Now, let's head in and see what's waiting for us."

Arielle started for the door and rapped her gun on the glass to knock. She saw nothing through the window, then pressed her ear against it.

"No one's here," she said.

"Or he's hiding," Felix said. "I think we need to slow down a minute. If Doyle's been telling people that we were going to show up to frame him for these missing people, what if entering the house is the exact trap he wants us to walk into? Besides, there are supposedly dead bodies inside. What if Ted saw them? What could he tell everyone once he wakes up?"

"That's why we're moving fast," Arielle said. "We may not be spending as much time in this year as we thought. If the whole town is after us—we just can't."

Arielle turned the knob and wasn't surprised when the door opened. She stepped through first, shouting, "Is anyone here? Identify yourself or you'll be shot."

Only her voice responded via an echo.

The sound of their hollow footsteps bounced around the empty house. Selena recoiled as soon as she crossed the doorway, pinching her nose shut. "Is that smell what I think it is?"

Arielle nodded as Felix copied Selena's action. "Yes, it is. And it's close. It wouldn't be that strong if the body was hidden upstairs or out back."

"How are you not gagging right now?" Selena asked, her voice squeaky because of her pinched nose.

"I wouldn't say I've become used to the smell," Arielle said. "But I've learned how to not let it bother me. Trust me, that stench still makes me queasy inside. Keep your nose plugged if you must, but know breathing in the smell is not harmful. Now, let's look around."

Arielle wandered off, looking left and right as she passed through the foyer. She took two steps into the kitchen before coming to a halt. "That was quick."

Selena and Felix strolled up behind her, hesitant.

"Only one body?" Felix asked as they stared at the dead girl lying on the kitchen floor.

"We just got here," Arielle said. "The other two can be anywhere. This is a big house with a big yard out back, too. Remember, she was likely killed within the last twenty-four hours. The other two would have been killed at least three days ago, assuming the information in our reports is accurate."

She nodded to the kitchen window overlooking the lawn full of weeds and patches of dirt.

"This girl was killed with those poisons?" Selena asked.

Arielle shuffled closer to the corpse and took a knee beside the girl's splayed-out arm. "It looks like it. I don't see any markings on her body that would suggest a struggle. Doyle's smart—we know that much. Why *wouldn't* he bring poison from the future to use on his victims in 1898? Nothing will come up on toxicology reports because the poisons don't even exist yet."

"She was pretty," Selena said, taking a step closer.

The dead girl had wavy brown hair and smooth porcelain skin.

"So, what are we going to do?" Felix asked, wiping sweat off his forehead. The temperature in the house felt just as warm as outside.

"We need to look around the house," Arielle said. "Find anything we can that helps paint a clearer picture of Doyle and what his plans might be. As for the girl, we're not getting involved."

"Why not?!" Selena asked.

"Because word will soon spread about us and how Doyle fled *because* of our arrival. At that point, no one will care about the facts, and they'll blame us for anything found within this house. I'd guess we have an hour tops to get out of here before the sheriff comes knocking, probably less. Let's split up and look around."

"I'll go upstairs," Selena said, spinning away and muttering to herself, "Get me the hell away from this smell."

Arielle stood up and turned to Felix. "I'll check out the rest of this main level if you want to have a look outside?"

"On it," Felix said, equally eager to escape to fresh air.

Arielle left the kitchen and ventured around the living room with a setup similar to their house on Pioneer Way. She quickly concluded that Doyle had never spent time in the living room. Everything was covered in a thick layer of dust, even the lone sofa pushed up against the wall. The mantel above the fireplace lacked a single object. A rack of wood and a fire poker lay on the floor, buried under the same amount of dust as everything else.

"Arielle!" Selena shouted from upstairs. "You need to come see this."

Shit, Arielle thought, dreading the fear she heard in Selena's voice.

"Coming!" she shouted back, and started up the stairs.

Each step moaned until she reached the top landing. The odor of the decaying body hadn't quite reached the top level yet, and Arielle appreciated that fact by drawing in a deep breath. The landing turned into a hallway that led to three doors. She saw a shadow moving in the nearest and stepped into what was clearly Doyle's bedroom.

Selena stood over a desk positioned under a window with the drapes drawn shut. A bed in the middle of the room looked as if Doyle had taken an hour to tidy up to perfection. Clothes stood in neat piles at the foot of the bed.

"Arielle," Selena said, not looking up from the desk where various papers were assembled in organized piles. "I'm scared."

"What's the matter?" Arielle asked, shuffling toward Selena.

Selena took a step back and pointed to a sheet of paper lying on top of the mess. Arielle picked it up and read.

Ms. Lucila,

If you're reading this letter, then the games have just begun. And I know you will, because there is no one better. Right? But see, this is when the world will finally realize that you are not the best. How can you be if I'm always one step ahead? I've convinced everyone of importance in this town that you are a serial killer traveling around the country to hunt your victims. Apologies if that gets you into any trouble, but I'm sure you'll be able to get out of it. You always do.

Do you remember what you told me all those years ago in training? To block out the noise and trust myself. I've taken those words to heart, and now here we are. I have complete faith and trust in myself that I will remove you from the face of the Earth when this is all said and done. And I'll make sure no one can travel back in time to save you, either. Life's just not fair, is it?

Until I see you. With love and respect.

DG

"Nothing to be afraid of," Arielle said, folding up the paper and stuffing it in the bosom of her dress.

"How the hell do you figure?" Selena asked. "This guy *knew* we'd be here. Why else would he have left this letter? And he wants to kill you!"

Arielle shook her head. "I'm not worried about that. He'll need to get close to me to even try to kill me, and if he does, I'll be ready. I know these types of people. He's not going to snipe me from a distance. No. He'll want to get up close and personal. Probably take me to a hideout so he can talk to me and drag out the whole process. We have a bit of a past. "

"A past?! What the hell do you mean?"

"Nothing romantic," Arielle assured her. "I'll have to explain more later. It's complicated."

"How are you not more worried about this?" Selena demanded, hands on her hips.

"Selena, relax. This isn't the first time my life's been threatened."

"Maybe not, but have you ever dealt with a time-traveling serial killer before?"

Arielle opened her lips, but paused. "Well, no."

"Exactly," Selena said, rubbing her forehead in frustration. "This isn't some regular mission where you have the upper hand. Doyle is on a level playing field with us. He can time travel just like us. You need to throw out the rule book and get serious—he can really hurt you. All of us. Felix was already in danger, and we're only on the first leg of this mission."

Arielle tossed her hands up and started pacing circles. "You're right. I've been so used to missions always going a certain way, but this *is* different. Doyle killed that girl downstairs, plus two others. We don't know where those two bodies are, or where Doyle went from here."

"That's why we can't go through that time portal. He could be waiting on the other side."

"And we won't."

They were interrupted by Felix shouting from downstairs. "You both need to come outside *right now*!"

Chapter 12

Sweat streamed across Felix's face as he stood with one foot still out the back door.

"I found the second body," he panted. "In the tornado shelter. And there's something else. C'mon."

He waved them over in a hurry. Felix had worked hundreds of missions in his career as an Angel Runner, but this was his first time finding a dead body on his own. He'd witnessed Arielle kill suspects on prior missions, but this was an innocent person lying lifeless in the shelter outside. And the victim looked like him.

Once Arielle and Selena reached the back door, Felix pivoted around and dashed toward a slightly angled wooden door protruding from the ground just off the edge of the house. He grabbed the handle and pulled the door upwards, the stench immediately shooting out of the dark space like a bat out of hell.

Selena heaved and turned around, clutching her stomach.

"Leave the door open," Arielle said. "The smell will air out in time. You went in there by yourself?"

Felix nodded. "I didn't want to, but once I smelled the body, I felt obliged. It's the missing man. And it ain't pretty down there."

"Of course not," Arielle said. "He was left outside. Probably has all kinds of bugs feasting on the corpse by now, right?"

Felix nodded. He wished he could scrub his mind free of that imagery, but he feared it would haunt him for the rest of his days.

"You said there was something else down there?" Arielle asked.

Selena returned to their huddle, her face a sheet of white.

"Yeah," Felix replied. "There's another door down there. I opened it but couldn't see anything. Way too dark. I took two steps through it and still didn't feel a wall, so it must be slightly bigger than a closet."

"Is it the time portal?" Selena asked.

Felix shook his head.

"Was it hot when you opened the door?" Arielle asked.

"It was actually much cooler than it is out here," Felix said.

"So it's not the portal, then. From what I've read, time portals emit heat. They say you feel like you're burning alive when you step through one, but the sensation only lasts a couple of seconds."

"Wow, sign me up," Selena said, shaking her head.

"Okay," Arielle said, clapping her hands together. "One thing at a time. Let's go to the shed and see what we find. Maybe the third body is there. We already have enough with this letter from Doyle, and it might be time for us to head back to our house to plan our next move. We'll check out the other door in the tornado shelter after the shed, then we can leave. Sound good?"

Felix and Selena nodded. Arielle never had trouble organizing an impromptu plan amid chaos.

"I'm not going near the time portal," Selena said as all

three of them started toward the shed further back in the yard. "What if it sucks us in?"

Arielle giggled, a sound she didn't expect to make under the circumstances. "Again, not how they work. You can walk right up to a time portal and nothing will happen unless you step *through* it."

They reached the shed and Arielle wasted no time pulling the door open.

"No smell," Felix said, relieved. He wasn't sure he could handle the sight of another decaying corpse baking under the Texas heat.

"He must have spent time out here," Arielle said. "Everything is covered in sawdust."

Two tables lined the side walls, completely covered in minuscule wood chippings. A third table stood against the back wall, taller and wider, with various items stacked beneath it: buckets, boxes full of junk, empty milk bottles, and piles of old blankets.

"Are you sure about that?" Felix asked, running a finger through the powdery residue on the nearest table.

"What do you mean?" Arielle asked.

"Well," Felix replied, clearing his throat. "For starters, there isn't a single tool in here. All this sawdust, but no saw. No wood. Nothing. This is the most bare-bones tool shed I've ever seen. There's not even a hammer in here."

"Is it just regular dust then?" Selena asked.

Felix shook his head, examining the substance on his fingertip. "It's too thick to be dust. It definitely looks and feels like sawdust, but if it was, then this shed would smell like wood. Remember, they told us the time portals shoot out a weird dust when they're used."

Arielle closed her eyes and rubbed her temples, drawing in a deep breath. "You're right. We're definitely close to the time portal. Did you notice how much warmer it is in here?"

Selena shrugged. "I just thought it was a hot shed. It *is* ninety-something degrees outside."

"Well, I noticed it," Arielle said, looking around. "But I wonder where it is."

"Hold on," Felix said, glancing up and then down before doing an awkward spin and leaving the shed. Part of planting hidden bugs in various places required Felix to have basic knowledge of structures. Finding any vulnerabilities or hidden compartments had become second nature over his years in the role.

He stomped away from the shed, putting twenty feet between himself and the small wooden shack. After examining the shed for a few seconds, he circled it from the same distance, pausing on each side for a more in-depth look.

"I got it!" he cried out, racing back into the shed, where Arielle and Selena stared at each other in puzzlement.

"Got what?" Selena asked.

"The portal is behind the back wall," he said confidently.

"How can you be so sure?" Arielle asked with a frown.

"Inside," Felix explained, "it's roughly fifteen feet from the door to the back wall. But on the outside, it's almost twenty feet from front to back. I'm betting someone originally built this shed to hide the time portal, then covered it completely up with another wall. That's why there's so much junk under the workbench, and nothing anywhere else."

Arielle looked from Felix to the mess of random objects lying beneath the workbench.

"If you were hiding a time portal, wouldn't you want to

make it hard for some random person to find?" Felix asked, shuffling past Arielle and Selena to crouch down beneath the bench. "Even if someone came in here and rummaged through this stuff, there's so much of it that no logical person would go through every single object. Too much work."

"You seem confident," Selena said, crossing her arms and taking a step back.

"Well, this shed isn't exactly *big*," Felix replied. "Where else could the portal be but behind all this shit?"

Selena giggled, and Arielle stepped forward to help. It took them nearly five minutes to move everything. After breaking through piles of heavy clothes and blankets, they found two rows of buckets filled to the brim with sand and rocks.

"Are you telling me Doyle moved all this, then put it back before crawling through the portal?" Arielle asked, wiping sweat off her brow.

"It seems so," Felix replied, determination filling his eyes as he bit his tongue in deep concentration. "At least we know he takes the secret of time travel seriously enough not to leave anything to chance."

They slid the buckets out from the workbench, where Selena lugged them further away, creating a semicircle around her. More of the sawdust filled the air, and they each took turns coughing from the irritation.

Once the final bucket was removed, Felix panted for breath as he clawed at the small door built into the bottom of the shed's rear wall. "I feel that heat now. Damn."

"Felix, be careful," Selena cried when he reached out to push open the door.

He stopped, mad at himself for not calculating every deci-sion like he normally did. The time portal waited on the other side of the door, and he was about to push it open without another thought. Just because there were about five feet to spare didn't mean he couldn't accidentally fall through the portal.

"Thank you," he said over his shoulder to Selena, his focus returning immediately. Arielle remained crouched under the workbench with him, skin glistening as she looked at him with the most fear he could recall ever seeing on her face. Even for the great Arielle Lucila, the prospect of encountering an actual time portal proved too daunting. He gulped and returned a trembling hand to the door. "I'm just going to push it open."

Felix shoved the small square panel and shielded his eyes as more sawdust puffed through the open doorway. A wave of heat warmed his face like he was standing above a boiling pot of water. He craned his neck, lowering his head toward the open space but keeping a safe distance.

"What's in there?" Arielle asked in a nearly hushed tone.

"I see nothing," Felix said. "But I feel the heat. I'm getting closer."

"The fuck you are," Selena said, promptly dropping to her knees and grabbing Felix by the ankles. "I'm not letting you fall into a time portal. We don't even know if you'd be able to get back."

Felix whipped his head around to meet Selena's terrified gaze. "I'm not going through anything but this little door. Hold my legs if you want, and if I shout, then pull."

He didn't wait for Selena to agree and returned to the door, lunging forward despite the tug of Selena pulling back on his ankles. For being like a little sister, she was always overly worried about him. Felix scooted forward enough to stick his face right against the opening. "Oh my God," he whispered, not sure if Arielle or Selena could hear him.

The floor on the other side of the wall was completely covered in the powdery substance. Rising from the dust was a brick archway about six feet tall, with nothing but blackness filling the space between the arch.

Felix pulled back and twisted around. "I think we can all fit in there," he said excitedly. "I saw the portal. It's against the back wall under an archway. Probably three feet of space for us to all stand in there."

"I'm not going in until you test it to make sure we won't get sucked away," Selena said, loosening her grip on Felix's legs, but not completely letting go.

"Fine. Toss me a blanket. I'll throw it through the door and see what happens."

Arielle moved first, spinning around and reaching out for the pile of blankets they had moved aside. She grabbed two and nearly threw them at Felix. "Throw one just inside the door, then throw another through the portal, if you can."

Felix nodded and grabbed the first blanket, rolling it into a thick ball that would be easier to throw. He crawled back to the door on his elbows, the light brown powder sticking to his sweaty skin. "Here goes nothing," he said, extending his arms and tossing the blanket through the doorway.

He watched it roll to a stop about two feet away from the portal.

"Well?" Arielle asked, a longing for adventure returning to her voice.

"Nothing happened," Felix said, rolling up the second blanket in the same manner. "I'm gonna go in a little deeper, so this can reach the portal."

He stretched out, hands now through the doorway, and

inched forward so that his entire head could stick through. The closer he got, the tighter Selena squeezed on his ankles. She tried to act tough, but clearly had a soft spot for Arielle and Felix, seeing as she always went into a panic if any of them encountered danger.

With his head through the door, the heat elevated to another level. It reminded Felix of all the times he kept his face too low when opening the oven, a lesson that never quite registered over his years of cooking.

Felix held the balled-up blanket in front of him like a football player reaching desperately for the goal line. He reared back and flung it toward the black hole between the archway, eyes bulging as he watched it sail through the air and disappear into the void.

An explosion of the sawdust puffed out from the time portal, covering the walls and floor with a fresh coat of the powder. It also landed on Felix's face, and he blew in every direction to get it off.

"Are you okay?" Arielle called out from behind, prompting Felix to crawl back out to join his team.

Selena broke into hysterics once she saw Felix's face. "You look like someone dumped a bag of flour on your head."

Arielle couldn't help but join in with a loud cackle. After several seconds of sharing a laugh, she tossed him another of the blankets. "Use this like a towel—you need it."

Felix squeezed the blanket as he wiped his face clean, the stale flavor of the powder stuck in his nostrils. "So, the time portal definitely works," he said.

"Great," Selena said. "So we don't actually need to go in there. We'll just take your word for it."

"That's actually not a bad idea," Arielle said. "As much as

I'd love to explore this time portal and study what it can do, we need to move all this stuff back and get to our house. It's only a matter of time before those men find Ted in his office and start looking for us."

"Arielle," Selena said in a shaky voice. She had turned toward the door and was looking outside at the backyard. "It's too late."

Felix and Arielle rushed over to join her, following her gaze to see Willie and Tommy stomping around inside Doyle's house, guns drawn.

Chapter 13

"What do we do?" Selena gasped, spinning around as her eyes dashed all over the shed.

"Calm down," Arielle said, drawing a deep breath. "They're still inside and are going to be occupied with that dead girl's body. We have options. But first, we need to move everything back to block this secret door."

Selena jerked her head viciously from side to side, joining Arielle and Felix in moving all the random shit back to its place in front of the hidden door. "Nope. I already know what you're going to say. You want us to go through that time portal. Sorry, but that's *not* an option."

"Of course not," Arielle snapped back. "But we can hide in that room."

"It won't be much of hiding," Felix said. "We don't have time to move all this stuff back and cover the door. If they come in here, they'll see everything and know exactly where to look for us. Then they'll find the time portal, and that's probably the worst thing that can happen."

"Why don't you just kill them?" Selena asked. "You've taken down more than two guys before."

Arielle gritted her teeth. Killing the two bouncers would be the swiftest plan of attack. "I can't."

"Why the hell not?!" Selena demanded. "Those two gorillas were going to leave Felix to die."

"That might be true, but they're still innocent regarding our mission." Arielle had placed her gun on the workbench earlier, and now picked it up. "Shooting them will be my absolute last resort. They didn't kill that girl, nor are they after us. Well, not in the sense that Doyle is."

"We're wasting time," Selena said, sliding over to stand directly in front of Arielle. "We need to hide or run."

"Felix," Arielle said, turning her attention past Selena. "How big was that tornado shelter, and what kind of stuff was down there?"

"It was about as big as this shed," he replied, unable to look away from the house. "I saw some blankets, flashlights, a toolbox, canned food."

"If we can get in there, that'll be our safest bet. Tornado shelters lock from the inside. Those two wouldn't be able to get us even if they saw us go down there."

"Now!" Felix howled, breaking into a sprint out of the shed.

"What the fuck?!" Selena cried, chasing after him.

Arielle followed suit, furious. Felix had closed the small door leading to the time portal, but they hadn't replaced any of the stuff to block it from view. And they would need to. The house was about to become a murder scene for the authorities to investigate, so it was possible they would examine every square inch of the property.

The three Angels dashed across the backyard and came to a screeching halt just before reaching the tornado shelter. Neither of the men had been visible through the kitchen window, likely prompting Felix's reason for making this mad dash. But Tommy had stood up, having been crouched low in the area where the dead girl lay. He looked over his shoulder, saw the three running, and instantly shouted for Willie.

Tommy swung his gun around and fired a round through the kitchen window. Shards of glass flew, but the rest of the window had splintered to the point of making it impossible to see through.

Within seconds, Tommy burst out the back door, revolver aimed at Felix, who had just reached the shelter's entrance.

"NOOOO!" Selena let out a piercing shriek, lunging for Felix.

Through nothing but instinct thanks to her years of experience, Arielle had already raised her gun and fixed it on Tommy. She pulled the trigger without hesitation and watched Tommy collapse to the ground with a thunderous *thump!*

The crack of the gunshot echoed around them, birds flapping away frantically from a nearby tree.

Willie barreled his way through the door and tripped on Tommy, rolling in two complete somersaults before somehow landing on his feet. He faced Arielle and whipped his revolver in her direction.

Arielle pulled the trigger again, not giving Willie a moment to actually line up his shot. He had still fired a shot, but the bullet sailed errant to the right, lodging into the shed's exterior wall.

Willie looked down at the blood soaking into his green button-up shirt, dropped his gun, and clenched his chest before tipping over backwards. His head landed less than a foot away from his colleague's splayed-out legs.

Selena stood with her hands clasped over her mouth, whimpering. Felix had fallen to his knees next to the tornado shelter, heaving.

"I really thought you two could stomach a couple of dead

bodies by now," Arielle said, lowering her gun. "Especially these two—they were trying to kill us."

Felix gained control over himself and rose to his feet, brushing off his legs. "That was just the past pushing back, right?"

Arielle shrugged. "We found a time portal and were at high risk of having these two also find it. What would *that* do to this timeline we're in? Let's go check out this secret door in the shelter, and get out of here."

Selena threw her hands up. "You still want to go into the shelter?! We need to leave!"

"Yes, I do," Arielle replied calmly. "Tornado shelters aren't supposed to have doors within them. That alone tells me Doyle was up to something, and we need to know what. Now, let's go."

Arielle didn't wait for either of them to respond and stepped around the dead bodies lying on the ground like they were nothing but lawn furniture. She reached the shelter and squatted low to stare into the dark pit.

A set of wide wooden steps descended into the shelter, and Arielle took them, finally prompting Felix and Selena to file behind and follow her down.

"Where is the body?" she asked in a whisper. "The odor is pretty faint already."

Felix stepped next to her and cleared his throat. "It's along the wall under stairwell. I strongly advise you don't look at it."

Arielle wrinkled her nose, feeling the sensation of death crawling on her skin, and took Felix's word to heart. "You said there were flashlights?" she asked, the shelter dim beyond the sunlight beaming through the open door.

Felix chuckled. "About a dozen flashlights in a box. Not sure why Doyle brought so many."

He shuffled toward the opposite wall and rummaged through a mess of items spread across a table, returning with three flashlights and handing them out.

They all clicked them on. "Another sign Doyle was using this shelter intentionally," Arielle said. "There were no such things as flashlights in 1898. These are definitely from our era, which means *he* brought them down here."

Arielle moved her light across the room. An old, dust-infested first aid kit remained on the table where Felix had grabbed the flashlights. On the ground lay a case of water bottles.

"Dasani," Arielle said, laughing. "Doyle was definitely counting on not being caught down here."

"Or he just didn't care," Felix added. "Why go through the trouble of bringing all this stuff from the future? I guess the flashlights make sense, but he still could have gotten some lanterns to use. And Dasani water? He's only a few feet away from a water well."

"Clearly he likes the finer things in life," Arielle said, swinging her light toward the door next to the bottom landing of the stairs. "He was obviously using that time portal to go back and forth to some other time and bring back the goods he wanted to use. That explains why there was so much of that powder."

"If that's true," Felix added, "that means the portals are easy to go back and forth between."

"That might be," Arielle said, strolling toward the door, "but that doesn't mean we're going back to it. Not today."

The door had a bolt lock, which Arielle turned with an

aggressive flick of the wrist. More darkness welcomed them as the door swung open with a blood-chilling creak, and a draft of cold air escaped. Arielle fixed her flashlight to see through the entryway.

"What in the actual fuck?" Selena said, moving next to Arielle with her flashlight turned on.

It first looked like a long hallway, the walls and ceiling made of the underground dirt and sediment. Arielle stepped through the door and drew a deep breath. The musty stench of earth filled her nose, reminding her of a time she had once gone down deep into a mine for a rescue mission.

"I think it's a tunnel," she said, turning back to Selena and Felix, both of whose eyes were bulging in disbelief.

"A tunnel to where?" Felix asked, stepping forward and shining his light from the ground to the ceiling.

"How do you even build a tunnel like this?" Selena asked. "Doyle couldn't have done it himself."

"Probably not Doyle," Arielle said. "Remember our driver, Rodrigo? He said Dallas has underground tunnels. I'll bet Doyle found this one and used it to his advantage."

"How does time pass when going through portals?" Selena asked. "Does only ten minutes pass in your original time like it does with the Juice?"

Felix shook his head. "Nothing changes when you travel through portals. Your entire being—both physical and spiritual, if you will—travels through the portal, and you continue to age as normal. That's why so many of the ancient time travelers are gone. Portals were their only means. The Juice revolutionized and extended the lives of all time travelers."

"Enough about the portal," Arielle said, waving her light across Felix and Selena. "We need to see where this tunnel goes."

"Should we close the shelter door?" Felix asked.

"Probably," Arielle replied. "Just in case anyone else shows up. We don't know how big of a crew Ted has behind him."

"And you have enough rounds?" Selena asked.

Arielle grinned. "Four should be plenty, right?"

They shared a nervous laugh while Felix climbed the steps to close the door and secured the two locks before joining them in the tunnel.

"Alright," Arielle said once they started walking at a casual pace. "I'm trusting this tunnel is safe to walk through, since Doyle must have been using it regularly. But let's remain diligent. He could have traps set up if he believed we were going to find this place. Always watch the step ahead of you, and if something seems off, mention it."

They started deeper into the tunnel, the darkness behind them too intimidating to look back upon, like it might swallow them whole.

"I don't think a trap was his intention," Felix commented after several steps. "You can see the trail in the dirt where he walked. And the footsteps don't all go in one direction, so it's been a lot of back and forth."

"I don't think so, either," Arielle said. "He's not going to try anything while the three of us are together. He'll only take his chance if we're by ourselves, so it's important to always stay together."

They continued on for a couple of minutes, the faint clop-ping of their shoes against the dirt the only sound in the deafening silence.

"So, where do we think this tunnel leads?" Selena asked in a lighter tone. So far, the tunnel's path had remained straight as an arrow, nothing different to see aside from the constant dirt in every direction.

"There are really only two options," Arielle said. "Into town or into the neighborhood. That's the direction it's heading, and there's nowhere else it could go."

"Town makes more sense," Felix said. "Not sure what reason he'd have to go to someone else's house."

"Unless there's another time portal in someone's backyard," Arielle added, believing that was the purpose of the tunnel.

"Isn't it unlikely there would be two portals in the same town?" Felix asked. "Let alone within a mile of each other."

"I've had lots of conversations with Commander Briar, and Mark confirmed it when we spoke with him," Arielle said. "The commander has the Book of Time, which admits there are likely hundreds—perhaps thousands—of portals that were never registered in the database. Even time travelers in the ancient days went through a phase of rapid expansion. Much like we saw too much Juice administered in recent years, they went on a spree of building time portals once enough people learned the practice."

"Wait," Selena said, stopping and reaching out to grab Arielle by the arm. "So you're saying people could have created their own makeshift time portals at home?"

"Exactly," Arielle replied, removing Selena's hand. "I wouldn't be surprised if the one in that shed was exactly that. Let's just be grateful we don't have to deal with the portals anymore."

They continued walking, the tunnel making the slightest of curves. A trail of spiders climbed up the wall, prompting Felix to shuffle to his left. Arielle continued leading the way, her flashlight sweeping back and forth in a fluid motion to illuminate the path ahead.

"Did your parents end up moving to New York?" Selena asked Felix, hoping to break the tension.

He rubbed the back of his head with his free hand before letting out an anxious laugh. "They sure did," he said, voice full of hurt. "They left a week before we started this mission. I at least got to see them off with my sisters."

"That's good," Selena said. "And how are you feeling about everything?"

Felix strolled along faster. "It's been fine."

"You don't have to lie to us. How are you really feeling?"

Felix looked down at his moving feet and sighed. "Did your parents ever send either of you on a guilt trip?"

Arielle laughed. "We're Latino. I think my brother and I were sent on more guilt trips than actual trips."

Felix chuckled. "When I moved to Denver for the Road Runners, I never heard the end of it from my parents. Home was in San Francisco. The family was all there. Why did I need to move halfway across the country? Was I mad at them? They made me feel like the most awful person in existence because I made a decision for myself. God forbid!"

"I had some of that when I went to the FBI academy," Arielle said. "My parents weren't angry, though, more depressed, I suppose."

"I've been thinking about the hypocrisy of it all," Felix said. "My sisters both stayed in San Fran. They wanted to explore other places to live, even within California, but they vowed to always remain close to home. Now our parents are living in New York City without a care in the world. Where's the guilt for them? The contradiction just seems so selfish."

"It's a generational thing," Arielle said. "Families needed to stick together when they immigrated to the U.S. They were treated like third-class citizens upon their arrival. People thought they were stupid because they couldn't speak English. Family was literally all they had to feel safe and grounded."

"That ignorance still exists today," Selena added.

"Sure," Arielle said. "But the times have definitely changed. It exists, but there's a lot less of it. There are some places in Denver where *I* feel stupid for not knowing Spanish now."

"I thought you were fluent?" Felix asked.

Arielle shook her head. "I can carry basic conversations with my *abuela*, but that's about it. Because of the way my grandparents were treated when they came to this country, they never taught my parents Spanish. They wanted them to fit in so desperately that they forced them to learn English. Colonialism still wins all these years later. But you better believe if I ever have kids, they're going to learn every language under the sun."

"You're half French, Selena," Felix said. "Do you know how to speak it?"

"I actually didn't speak it growing up," Selena replied, pursing her lips. "My dad preferred English in the house. But I always felt compelled to learn it because it was my heritage. So I took French in high school and did more courses afterward. I'd say I'm fluent, and almost as strong in Spanish."

"Trilingual?!" Felix cried. "Impressive. I'm fluent in Spanish, too. That's all my parents spoke when we were growing up. I think we might have taught them English because of all the times we needed help with our homework."

"At the end of the day, Felix," Arielle said, slowing her pace, "you can only worry about what you can control—and that's your life. Maybe your parents are more understanding now that they've had an opportunity arise they couldn't pass up. Not everything has to be a certain cookie-cutter way based on how we grew up."

"Good point," Felix said. "We'll be the ones who make the change. No more generational curses."

"Except for the *chancla*, of course," Arielle said with a giggle. "We can't lose that."

Felix and Selena joined in the laughter while coming to a complete stop. They had reached the opposite end of the tunnel, all three of their flashlights falling on a closed black door.

Chapter 14

Arielle handed her flashlight to Selena so she could have two hands on her gun.

"This is it," Felix said with nervous anticipation. "Do we knock first?"

Arielle had already given this consideration during their walk. Since one end of this tunnel had a door, she presumed the other would, too. And now they stood before it, with plenty of decisions to make.

"I think not," she said, taking another step closer to the door and turning around to face Felix and Selena. The blackness behind them could have been mistaken for outer space, but all that mattered right now was what lay ahead. "If there is someone on the other side of the door, we want to catch them off guard, not give them time to take out their gun and open the door for us."

"I doubt there's anyone there," Selena said, examining the door with the two flashlights. "He clearly meant this to be a secret. Why would Doyle have set up a secret entrance to this tunnel on one end, and not the other? Especially if we're in town or the neighborhood. He couldn't risk having some random person stumble across his secret passageway."

"Good point," Arielle said. "In that case, we should be fine barging in either way. Felix, get the door, and I'll be ready here just in case."

Arielle cocked her gun and raised it toward the door. Felix drew a deep breath as he shuffled over and reached for the knob with a quivering hand. He looked back and Arielle nodded for him to proceed. Selena stepped aside to get out of the way of potential gunfire.

Felix twisted the knob and jerked the door open.

More darkness.

"Flashlight," Arielle said, and Selena returned to her side, beaming the light through the open doorway.

"Are those bottles of alcohol?" Selena asked, eyebrows narrowed as she started forward, leading them into a room of a similar size to the tornado shelter.

They all stepped in and closed the door behind them. Tables lined all four walls in the room, nothing but bottles of whiskey and rum standing next to each other. Felix directed his flashlight toward another door.

"Not a tornado shelter," he commented. "Do you think we're under the saloon? Why else would there be so many bottles of booze?"

"Could be," Arielle said, lowering her gun. "Albert said Doyle was running a speakeasy, remember? Did any of you notice where the speakeasy could have been?"

Felix and Selena shook their heads. "If he did it right, then it wasn't supposed to be obvious," Felix said. "But what are we going to do? We can't just walk into the saloon right now."

"I think we can," Arielle replied. "You saw how slow Main Street became after the lunch rush. It's probably going to stay that way until everyone gets off work in the evening. I'd rather take my chances leaving from here instead of going back to

Doyle's house."

"You two realize what's going on, right?" Selena asked.

Arielle and Felix gave her blank stares before shrugging.

"It's simple, you see," Selena continued, picking up a bottle of whiskey to examine. "It's definitely the speakeasy on the other side of that door. Doyle has been running it. He was slipping drugs into the victims' drinks, waiting for them to pass out, then dragged them through the tunnel back to his house where he could take his time. He had this tunnel for that specific reason. Doyle gets to keep a positive image among the public, all while sneaking these innocent people to his house of horrors."

"You came up with that pretty quick," Arielle said, rubbing her forehead. The explanation made perfect sense.

"I've been to every type of bar in the world," Selena said, putting the bottle back down, "and most of them always have a secret room in the back. For the upscale ones, it's a VIP hangout. For the dive bars, it can be an office or storage. I've also seen my fair share of characters within the nightlife industry. Let's just say some of the bar owners were using their private quarters for other matters. This seems no different. Doyle just expanded and dug a tunnel to his house. Like a totally normal person, right?"

Selena let out a disgusted laugh, and Arielle sensed the rage building up within her.

"Okay then," Arielle said. "Game plan. We go through and hopefully no one is there. If so, we slip out of the saloon as quickly as possible and go back to the house. If someone *is* there, we need to play it off like we're supposed to be here. We know the names of Doyle, Ted, and even Willie and Tommy, so it shouldn't be hard to act like we belong."

Felix shook his head. "I don't know about this. My gut tells me we should go back to Doyle's house. We're too close to where we left Ted bleeding out of his head. What if he died? We still don't know. This place could be swarming with police if he did. And with Tommy and Willie dead at Doyle's house, there's no one else here to identify who we are."

"Which is exactly why we'll be able to play it off," Arielle said. "We're guests of Doyle's speakeasy and had no idea what was going on in the main bar."

"I'm with Arielle on this one," Selena said. "Sorry, Felix. But I'd rather be here and have to deal with the police instead of at Doyle's house where there are now multiple dead bodies. How would *that* look?"

Felix considered this, chewing the inside of his lip, then nodded slowly. "Okay. We'll try our luck here."

"After you," Arielle said, shooting Felix a wink as she raised her gun again.

He dragged himself to the door and pulled it open immediately. Arielle was expecting it to be locked, but they found it led to a small lounge area. Circular tables filled the room, and a bar ran along the wall immediately next to the door. The room was dark, minus a beam of light clawing through the bottom of yet another door that waited at the top of a short stairwell.

"Are we in some sort of sick maze?" Selena asked. "Is *this* the game Doyle is trying to play?"

Arielle chuckled. "This is the actual speakeasy." She closed the door behind her and found a plate hammered onto the other side that read *STORAGE*.

Felix studied the room and noticed the nameplate. "So he marked the door as storage. That probably kept most people from venturing into the booze room."

"Even if they did," Selena said. "They probably wouldn't have noticed the other door. This is a really elaborate set up he's put together."

"I told you," Arielle said. "He's a madman."

"I don't care *how* mad he is," Selena said. "We know what he used the tunnel for. This knowledge may not help us in this era, but it's good to know for the other two we need to visit. He's thought deeply about how to get away with his crimes. We can't overlook that. None of this was done on a whim."

Arielle nodded. "He's patient and picks his spots. He probably gives himself very specific parameters for the right time to slip the drugs into someone's drink, and he has to stick to it religiously. I've studied plenty of serial killers, and they can be drastically OCD. In their mind, it's how they guarantee they won't get caught."

"I hate to interrupt," Felix said, starting up the five steps leading to the next door. "But do we need to have this conversation here? I'd much rather go to the house so we can chat in peace."

Arielle chuckled. "You worry too much, Felix. But yes, we should head out. I'd say finding the existence of this tunnel is going to be our biggest takeaway from 1898."

"Not these ridiculous dresses?" Selena asked, doing a curtsy. She and Arielle broke into uncontrollable laughter as they followed him up the steps.

"Our only issue is not knowing where in the saloon we'll be," Arielle said, reaching to grab Felix by the arm. "We know the main bar and the women's bar. Once we step out, follow my lead."

Selena and Felix nodded in agreement, and Arielle lifted her gun once more, aiming at what they hoped would be the final door to pass through.

"Same as before," she said to Felix, whose face twisted with anxiety as he approached the doorknob.

This time, it was locked.

Felix threw up his hands in frustration. "Don't tell me we came all this way to turn back now."

Arielle laughed. "Do you know how you're not being logical, Felix?"

She flashed the light on his face to find it had flushed a soft shade of pink. His jaw clenched as he shrugged in frustration.

"Dumbass," Selena said, gliding toward Felix and smacking him on the back. "You have a lockpick. Even Arielle has a lockpick. Now stop being so worried and pick this basic lock from 1898 so we can get out of here."

Felix let out an embarrassed giggle, his face turning more red. "I'm sorry, guys. I'm still shaken up from throwing that typewriter at Ted. Then watching those two guys get shot dead right in front of me. Never mind being inches away from a time portal and exploring this sicko's tunnel. The last hour has been a lot more than I'm used to dealing with."

"We're not here to judge," Arielle said. "I'll definitely be on the first appointment I can get with my therapist after this mission. Just slow your mind down. You're trying to process all these things at once instead of focusing on what's in front of you. Now, are you going to help us out of here?"

Felix laughed again, this time sounding relieved. "I have my moments. Wow, I feel like an idiot!"

"Good thing you're not actually one," Arielle said, clapping him on the back.

"Okay," he said, shaking his head to break up the mental

clutter. "Allow me."

Felix stuffed his hand into his pocket as he turned back to the door. With a flashlight in one hand and the lockpick in the other, he only needed ten seconds before cracking the lock and opening the door.

For the first time since they had gone into the tornado shelter, sunlight flooded the room. They stepped in, finding a maze of wooden shelves filled with packages of food, more bottles of alcohol, silverware, napkins, and cleaning supplies.

"Where the hell are we?" Selena said, looking around the room. There was a large window to their left, overlooking an open field, tumbleweeds rolling along in the distance.

"We're in the actual storage closet," Arielle said, taking slow steps down the aisle of shelves, using extra caution not to knock anything over. "Don't you recognize it, Selena? We looked in here earlier when we were searching for Felix."

Selena shook her head. "I only got a glimpse. But as long as someone knows where we are."

Arielle shuffled to the end of the aisle and turned the corner, Selena and Felix following. "There's the door," she said, stopping in front of it. "And it should be the last one. That hallway is on the other side. Ted's office is directly across from us. When we step out, the main bar is to the right, and the women's bar to the left. I'd imagine if there's any activity going on, it will be in the main bar, so let's take our chances going the other way."

"And if Ted is still lying there?" Felix asked.

Arielle turned around and leaned against the door. "Look, I don't care what we see when we open this door. We just need to run. No time to linger. Got it?"

Felix and Selena nodded slowly, exchanging a glance while

Arielle turned back around to the door, placing her hand on the knob.

She held up three fingers on her other hand and counted down silently, pulling open the door and taking the first step into the hallway. Ted's office door remained open, but he wasn't on the floor. A pool of blood had dried on the hardwood, voices carrying from the right. The main bar.

Arielle pointed left and tiptoed down the hallway. They passed the kitchen, now deserted, and turned into the women's bar. They let out a collective sigh once finding the bar abandoned, maneuvering through the tables toward the saloon's exit.

The temperature seemed to have risen during their long journey through Doyle's secret tunnel, the air in the saloon baking them. When Arielle reached the swinging doors, she stopped, waited for three sets of legs to walk by, then pushed them open.

The Angels spilled out, a sense of achievement swooning over them. Just being back out in the fresh air, no matter how scorching it felt, was an accomplishment after what they had just survived in Doyle's backyard.

Arielle looked to her right where Main Street remained mostly vacant.

"Let's go back the way we came," she said, starting left to take them along the rear of all the buildings.

Felix and Selena followed without a word, tensions remaining high. They crunched along the dirt path, taking their time behind the buildings concealing their presence, and dashing across the alleyways in between. Five minutes later, they reached the end of Main Street and rounded the apothecary building to cross the road and head back to their neighborhood.

"Well, that was enough action for one day," Felix said.

They all looked down the opposite end where they had just come from, Doyle's house elevated on the hill and distant in the background. Sitting on the bench outside of the apothecary was Ted Perkins, holding up a pouch to his head, presumably filled with ice. In front of Ted stood the town sheriff, hands on his hips as they conversed.

Arielle wasn't sure the other two had seen this, as Felix and Selena carried on with their own chatter. Her heart raced, the floodgates of adrenaline opening once more. She couldn't point out Ted—that would draw attention. He sat only thirty feet away from them, and Arielle could only hope he remained completely consumed in his conversation with the sheriff. They also couldn't come to a complete stop and turn around— that would draw the same unwanted attention, especially knowing Selena would have plenty of questions to shout about the abrupt change of direction.

Arielle put her head down and walked faster, only hoping the other two would get the hint.

They did. But it didn't matter.

"Hey!" Ted's voice shouted, filled with surprise. "That's them! That's them!"

All three looked back in unison. Ted jumped off the bench and tossed the ice pouch aside, using one arm to point at them, and the other to grab the sheriff by the shoulder to spin him around.

"Run!" Arielle shrieked, breaking into a mad dash, hiking up the sides of her dress to make it easier. She looked back and saw Selena doing the same, and Felix running full steam ahead.

Fortunately for them, the sheriff appeared to spend more time at the saloon stuffing burgers into his mouth instead of chasing people on foot. Ted was still in somewhat of a daze and sprinted ten steps before tripping over himself and sliding face-first into the dirt like a baseball player diving for home plate.

Meanwhile, the three Angels moved like gazelles across Main Street, even with the bulky dresses Arielle and Selena had to endure. They didn't slow down upon seeing the struggles of Ted and the sheriff. Felix took the lead, his massive strides gaining more ground than any of them could have dreamed of.

They arrived at their house ninety seconds later, panting for air as Selena brought up the rear and slammed the door shut behind them.

Felix dragged himself toward the fireplace and planted his hands on his knees, sweat dripping into small puddles on the floor.

"What...are we...going to...do?" Selena asked between gasps for air. She plopped down on the sofa, leaning back with her hands above her head.

Arielle, burning up, started taking off the dress. She had kept on a black tank top and shorts underneath, her usual mission attire when she didn't have to dress like a late-nineteenth-century housewife. Once Selena saw this, she jumped off the couch and started doing the same.

They needed a full minute to catch their collective breath and thoughts. Arielle leaned against the mantel and crossed her arms. "We need to leave."

"Leave?!" Felix asked, throwing his hands up. "What about finding out more about Doyle here?"

Arielle shook her head. "It's way too risky now. We'd have been better off if you had killed Ted. Instead, he's alive, knows who we are, and isn't going to rest until he finds us. And in a small town like this, it won't be long until he finds out where we live. It doesn't happen often, but sometimes the best thing you can do on a mission is leave it before you get yourself killed."

"She's right, Felix," Selena said. "I'm not trying to deal with a mob breaking down our door. And who knows what will happen once they find Ted's two goons dead in Doyle's backyard. Besides, we're not even leaving this mission, just this era. Are we going to stop back in our present time first?"

"The instruction was not to return until the mission is complete," Arielle said, circling behind the couch where she had stashed her travel bag earlier. "I have our directions for where to go when we arrive in 2098. I guess it's a good thing we didn't have much time to get settled in here. Grab your things and Juice, and let's go."

They all bounced around the living room like cats chasing a laser pointer, bumping into each other, grabbing any items they might have removed from their bags and left out under the presumption they'd have more time in 1898 Dallas.

After two minutes, they gathered back in the living room, ready to go, flasks of juice pulled out from their luggage. A gun shot fired in the distance, and Selena glanced out the window, shaking her head.

"You were right," she said. "They've already found us."

Arielle and Felix joined her, gawking outside as Ted and the sheriff took their time strolling down the neighborhood block. Ted had his pistol aimed at the sky and fired again. "Come out, come out, wherever you are!"

The sheriff grabbed his belly, cackling with delight.

"Okay," Arielle said, turning back to the center of the room and twisting the cap off the flask. "No time to look back here. We're going to December 10, 2098. Current time of day. See you there."

They all sipped from their flasks of Juice and waited.

Chapter 15

December 10, 2098

"How much longer until the facial recognition software is ready?" Doyle Grady asked.

He had kidnapped a young man by the name of Rowland Reeves, a recent standout graduate in software engineering from Oklahoma City University. And a coworker of Doyle's in this futuristic hellscape.

Rowland was young, handsome, and too smart for his own good. Just like that douchebag who always hung out with Arielle. He even kind of looked like him. Dirty blond hair, chiseled jaw, and the typical smug expression all these academic types seemed to have. Doyle wasn't sure yet if he would kill Rowland after he was done with him. It wasn't part of the original plan, but it was still something that brought him great joy. Maybe. Maybe not.

Doyle believed if the Angel Runners hadn't opted to use teams—fuck you, Commander Briar—he'd already have captured Arielle Lucila and sent their precious time travel world into a frenzy. Why did she get to have all the fun and glory while he suffered a most excruciating cycle of heartbreak and rejection?

Arielle was nothing but a glorified hitman. Hit*woman*, excuse you. Those types of people grew on trees. Teach a person how to use a gun and throw away their moral compass, and you could produce all the hired assassins you needed. But Doyle was a healer. A surgeon who performed miracles with his hands. He'd seen countless patients lying on his operating table, looking death in the eye, only to tell death to take a goddamn hike.

The Road Runners had recruited Doyle to join the Angels as a doctor. A time traveling healer of wounds. Going into the future to get the best medicines ever produced and bringing them back into the past to make people's lives better.

But everything unraveled after the mandatory psychological evaluation performed by a panel of pompous shrinks who already worked for the Road Runners. They deemed Doyle mentally unstable to perform his duties for the organization.

The funny thing about becoming a part of the time-traveling world, only to then be rejected by it, was that they didn't erase your mind. They only took your Juice away, and made you swear to secrecy. They implanted a chip on Doyle's spine—right in that spot where you can never reach yourself, no matter how bad it itches—that not only tracked his movements, but also listened to his conversations. This assured if he ever spoke a word about the world of time travel he had been partially a part of, the real terrorists within the Road Runners—the Secret Keepers—would hunt him down and either kill him on the spot, or banish him to Khronos Island— the time travelers' version of Alcatraz.

But Doyle had no interest in sharing the details with the general public. Most people were too naïve to even believe such a claim as time travel being real. And the ones who might believe it were not the people you'd want to leave with such a powerful responsibility. Gullible dimwits had no business in this same universe as Doyle.

Since Doyle had made an initial positive first impression, he could appeal his status with the Road Runners every two years, under each new commander. Commander Strike had rejected his first appeal, and he was glad to see the torture that befell her shortly after. Then Commander Briar did the same thing two years later.

"Your work speaks for itself," Commander Briar had told him. "But our team worries—and I agree with them—that you are still battling the demons surrounding your wife's death. Take it from me. I once tried to go back in time to save my daughter. While I learned the truth, I never had a chance of actually saving her. My life spiraled from there, and I lost not only my mom, but my entire sense of being. We suspect you won't be able to resist the temptation of traveling forward to get the needed medicine for your wife and bringing it back to save her life. I did the same thing for my mom, and it resulted in an even more horrific fate. It's best we let go of those loved ones we lost. Keeping their memories alive is the best we can manage."

Doyle left the commander's office that day with a new sense of purpose. If Commander Briar, the supposed man of the people, couldn't see things Doyle's way, then no one ever would.

But what pissed off Doyle beyond anything else was Arielle Lucila. They were in the same training class together. They bonded over their grief. Arielle had lost her entire family in a mass shooting at a mall—good job, America—and Doyle lost his wife, *his family*, to cancer.

They were two lost souls who had found new hope in the Road Runners. Doyle had confided to Arielle that he absolutely intended to travel into the future to find that cure for cancer and bring it back to his wife. And Arielle reciprocated by sharing her intent of one day traveling back in time to stop the shooter in the mall and spare her family. They knew they couldn't share these desires openly. The Road Runners had implemented strict rules about tinkering with one's own past, so it remained their shared secret.

But while Doyle was castrated from the Road Runners for this very reason, Arielle Lucila climbed the ranks to become one of the most popular Angels of all time. And in such a short time.

Doyle had reached out when he had first seen Arielle crack the top-100 rankings. He only wanted to congratulate her and ask if she might put in a good word to anyone who could help his cause. But after multiple phone calls and text messages, Arielle never responded. She ghosted him, as people like to say these days. And he never understood why.

"I asked if the software is ready," Doyle said calmly, rearing back a fist and punching young Rowland square on the cheek.

Tears streamed down Rowland's face as he reached up with a shaky hand to tend to the fresh blood drawn to his skin's surface. Doyle had tied Rowland's legs and one arm to a chair, planting him in front of a computer to work with only one free hand.

"I just have a couple more steps," Rowland said, his voice cracking. "Why are you doing this, Elyod? You're going to let me live, right?"

Doyle grinned. He still hadn't gotten used to being called Elyod in this futuristic life, but he'd needed to change his name to blend in.

"Of course," Doyle said, kneeling down to place a caring hand on Rowland's trembling leg. He laughed. "Who ever said anything about killing you? Not me. I think you've put that in your own head, dear boy. I'm not a monster. You only need to do two things for me. Hack into the city's surveillance system and implant the facial recognition software to alert me when my...friend arrives in town. Once that's all done and you confirm it works, you'll be free to go. You and I will be back in the office tomorrow like nothing ever happened. Because if you mention this to anyone, then we'll certainly have a problem."

As if, Doyle thought. He had encountered people like Rowland before and knew a rat when he saw one. Rowland reeked of the filthy alleyways and dumpsters that rats lived in. The college brat wouldn't waste two seconds before calling the police to tell them what Doyle had made him do. No, Rowland was not going back to whatever his normal life once was.

The world had undergone quite drastic changes by 2098. In the United States, the rich continued to inflate their wealth, rigging elections to ensure they'd keep the lower-class slime away from their lavish lifestyles. The revolution everyone had been waiting for finally happened in 2052, when the lower and middle classes fought back. It started with a nationwide workers' strike. Industry by industry, executives scrambled to meet demands and return to business as usual. But the workers never budged. Unfortunately for them, it was too late. The federal government, bought and paid for by their rich cronies, bailed out the nation's executives. Not only did they keep their businesses afloat, they revealed a decades-long secret project that had been years in the making—Automated

People.

Yes, robots that looked and acted like people—without all the bullshit emotions and personal desires—were produced by the tens of thousands and sent to the major corporations around the country. These robots required a single day of training to master their tasks and could work endlessly around the clock. No meal breaks. No work-life balance. And certainly, no spending thirty minutes on the toilet doom-scrolling social media while on the clock. Most importantly, the robots made no demands for higher pay and health benefits.

Introducing these artificial workers had proven only one thing to society: the corporate suits really had zero regard for human life and the workers that had carried their companies for years, some for centuries. These greedy cucks salivated at the opportunity to buy Automated People. For a low cost of $20,000 per "worker" it was only a matter of months before productivity and profits soared beyond their wildest dreams. The striking workers had become instantly irrelevant. Small businesses were trounced by competitors using Automated People.

And the consolation prize for the working class? Free housing in the suburbs, along with a monthly check of $3,000 to cover basic expenses. The government had to make a swift decision to approve this new socialist nightmare because too many of the Automated People were being attacked and destroyed by the pissed-off workers whose jobs they had replaced.

Give people a house and some free money, and they'd leave you alone. The rich took over bigger cities, turning skyscrapers into both office space for all their robots and also housing for themselves. They built forts around the downtown areas, ensuring no bitter poor person could stroll in and damage their new workforce. Permits had to be obtained for simple visits into downtown by anyone who didn't belong.

Living within the fortress of Oklahoma City had been a wild adventure for Doyle. These rich people were so obnoxiously happy, like nothing bad could ever happen to them again now that the dirty poor people no longer infested their cities. It *was* nice not seeing homeless people during a stroll down the sidewalk for lunch. But was it worth the price of dealing with young twenty-somethings that were always out and about, high on cocaine and any other drugs they could get their hands on? Doyle often debated this, but eventually realized he didn't give a shit.

No.

He was here because a time portal brought him to the year 2098, and he needed to continue setting a trap for Arielle. How dare she ignore him after they poured their souls out to each other? And to think he had been going to offer to aid her on the mission to rescue her family.

Doyle shuddered at the thought. How some people could go through their lives as takers and *never* give back to others was beyond his comprehension. Selfishness led to the downfall of society and the rise of the oligarchy in America. Those who loved to take just kept right on taking until they had *their* version of utopia.

People like Rowland, however, were the smart ones. Software engineering became the most important job in the world. The creators of Automated People gave only one warning. Do not let the robots operate on each other. Yes, they could rewire each other to overthrow the world should they so choose. The adaptive intelligence had the ability to grow into that potential disaster, so everyone left any repair work to the engineers. *Human* engineers vetted with background checks, psychological evaluations, and a laundry list of other requirements to ensure that *they* wouldn't program the robots to kill the rich.

"It's ready," Rowland said, sniffling away the mucus that had built up in his nose. He looked up at Doyle, blue eyes wide with terror. "Want to see how it works?"

Chapter 16

After arriving at an upscale hotel in 2098—thankfully in the middle of an empty hallway—the Angels scrambled to find their footing in this new world. Their original plans for leaving Dallas included going to a specific location before drinking their Juice, but Ted and the sheriff changed that.

Thankfully, Arielle had the address for the Road Runners' Dallas office in the year 2098, and they were only a fifteen-minute walk away, according to the young woman working the hotel's front desk.

They lost two hours between walking to the office, introducing themselves to the appropriate parties, then waiting for a ride to the nearest hangar where a jet waited to fly the Angels to Oklahoma City.

Through it all, Felix couldn't help but stop to gaze at Dallas. Long gone were the small wooden buildings from 1898, replaced two hundred years later by some of the same skyscrapers and structures he had known from his Original Time, along with newer ones. They all noted how clean the city appeared, and gawked at the sight of a car hovering fifty feet above the road.

The team at the Road Runners' office explained how a select few billionaires had won the right to test out flying cars, which looked more like miniature helicopters with wheels. Each city would have a handful of the flying vehicles testing the new technology.

The flight from Dallas to Oklahoma City only took an hour, but they all gazed out the windows at the new world below. Even Arielle couldn't help her curiosity, having traveled into the future only twice before—each experience drastically different.

"Those walls around the city," Felix said when they had first taken off and had a bird's-eye view of Dallas. "Are they to keep people out or in?"

"It's keeping poor people out," Arielle said. "I've been to the future twice before, and both times the big cities had those forts built around them. One time was because the poor had overtaken the cities and the rich fled to the suburbs and rural areas. The other time was the opposite. And this instance seems to be the rich running the cities, judging by the hotel we woke up in."

"No shit," Selena said. "Porcelain flooring? Who even does that? I've seen it in rich people's houses, but that entire hotel was made from it. Even the walls!"

"And did you see the cars when we were driving to the hangar?" Felix asked. "We passed like twelve different Lamborghinis. I don't understand."

Arielle chuckled. "I understand plenty. In a nutshell, the top one percent of earners grew to two percent. And those two percent of the population gradually made their way into the cities, enticed at first with affordable luxury housing and office spaces. Once they settled in, they had to drive out everyone else. Crime was on the rise. Muggings were happening daily. So the best thing they could do was remove the problem from society. They loaded the prisons, beat up the homeless to send a message, and doubled the police presence—they had the funds to do it. And that's what sparked the overhaul of society. The walls went up within five years, and they launched a system to track who was entering and exiting the city."

Selena and Felix gave blank stares to Arielle. They had never traveled into the future. While nearly everyone imagined it to be some sort of foreign paradise concocted through their own imaginations, only those who had traveled there understood the grim reality that plagued the world. Commander Briar had shared his stories about the future when he visited once for a mission, citing similar experiences to what Arielle had witnessed.

"Are we going to be in any sort of danger?" Selena asked.

Arielle wrinkled her nose before answering. "Not as long as we're in the city. Now, that's not to say Doyle won't be able to hurt us—he can and will probably try. But we don't need to worry about any other threats aside from him. If we venture outside of the walls for any reason, definitely stay on high alert. For anyone living outside of the walls, society has tipped into full-blown anarchy. Public resources no longer apply to anyone outside, besides their monthly stipends for living. It's everyone for themselves. The crime rate within the walls is zero percent. Outside the walls, it's just under eighty."

"Christ," Selena said, pressing her lips together and shaking her head. "And Doyle lives within the walls, right?"

"We don't know where he lives." Arielle pulled a water bottle from her bag and twisted off the cap. "Doyle had a tracker, but got rid of it. That's why our intel is limited regarding his whereabouts."

"I thought those were impossible to remove?" Felix asked.

"They're hard to remove on your own," Arielle said, taking a swig of the water. "But if you have someone to do it for you, it's just a matter of cutting into the skin and taking it out. My guess is he has a friend just as sick and twisted as him, or he threatened someone's life to force them into removing the chip. Our Truth Keepers found the chip deep in a sewer tunnel in 2021 Las Vegas. He flushed it down the toilet and has been on the run ever since."

She screwed the lid back onto her water bottle and shrugged.

"Well, we knew it wasn't going to be easy," Felix said. "But I think having an enclosed city works to our advantage. We just need to make strict rules and stick to them. Like if we're in a situation that leads to us chasing Doyle beyond the walls, we do *not* follow him. Who knows what kind of mob he'd have waiting for us out there? Within the walls, there is structure, and if we understand that structure, we then understand the limitations of what Doyle can reasonably do."

"That's a good point," Arielle said. "But we're not to leave the city under any circumstances. Not until we're finished here."

The jet slowed to begin its descent. Felix scrunched his face in confusion. "We're landing *outside* of the city?"

Arielle nodded while Selena hopped out of her seat for a better view from the window. They were landing at an abandoned hangar. Weeds sprouted from the cracked pavement of the runway. A couple of planes stood ditched in the surrounding open fields. The barbed wire fence surrounding the hangar and runway lay in scattered ruins. Graffiti littered the walls of both the hangar and the deserted planes.

"Why does it feel like we're landing in the middle of an

apocalypse?" Selena asked, the slightest of tremors slipping into her voice.

"Because we technically are," Arielle said calmly. Yes, she had her own fears about what lay ahead. The Road Runners assured her this hangar was safe and regularly used by the organization. But what if today was their lucky day, and some crazed gunman jumped out of the hangar and started blasting? These people still loathed the rich and surely saw the lavish jets that frequented this landing strip. "The team in 2098 assured me everything is safe here. They're expecting our arrival and will drive us to their office to prepare for entry into the city."

The jet landed, hitting all the bumps and cracks as the wheels came to a stop fifty yards away from the hangar. The pilot, a woman in her early forties, stepped out of the cockpit with a cigarette pinched between her lips.

"Welcome to OKC," she said, taking a drag and blowing the smoke behind her.

"People still smoke in 2098?" Felix asked, genuinely surprised.

The pilot laughed. "They actually don't. Cigarettes got banned some time in the 2040s. But we're time travelers, right? Not an issue to go back in time and stock up. It's the only thing that helps me keep the edge off. Living in this time is not for the faint of heart."

She spun around and fidgeted with the door before getting it to glide open, a short flight of steps retracting to the ground below.

"Thank you so much," Arielle said as they filed down the steps.

The pilot offered a tight-lipped grin, nodding to each of

them. Arielle thought that might have been her first encounter with a Road Runner who didn't seem to enjoy their job. Sure, she could just be having a bad day, or maybe she hated living in 2098. Arielle wasn't here to judge, yet she couldn't help this observation.

Once they reached the ground, a man wearing a navy-blue suit appeared from the hangar and waved them over. He continued walking to meet them halfway.

"Arielle Lucila, I presume?" he asked, sticking out his hand for a firm handshake. He wore reflective sunglasses and had his black hair slicked back. The sun gleamed off all the product he had used to keep his hair in place.

"Yes, sir," Arielle said. "And these are my teammates, Felix and Selena."

They exchanged handshakes. "A pleasure to meet you all. My name is Andrew Adamonis and I'm the Lead Runner here in Oklahoma City. Myself and our team here wish you the warmest welcome."

Andrew had an intimidating confidence mixed with a natural charm. Combine that with a wide grin that revealed pearly teeth, and Arielle thought he could have been a politician in a previous life.

"We're happy to be here," Arielle said.

Andrew ripped off his sunglasses and threw back his head in laughter. "Don't be so outrageous! Nobody *wants* to be here. But I appreciate your sentiment. We understand our partners traveling from the past would much rather return to their Real Time as soon as possible, and that's what we strive to make happen. Come, follow me!"

Andrew pivoted on his leather Prada shoes and started back to the hangar.

"I was told we'd be getting a ride to your office," Arielle said, all three of them struggling to keep up with Andrew, who walked at a pace just below a brisk jog.

"Ahh yes!" Andrew said, waving a hand and not slowing his stride. "We only say that in case the information in your mission files is ever compromised. See, our offices are actually *here*, underground below the hangar. We can never be too careful, especially since we're outside of the city. All information you'll receive is probably a misdirection from the truth. The last thing we want is someone out here to know about our underground operation, hence the mention of a car waiting to pick you up."

The calmness with which Andrew spoke was both reassuring and frightening to Arielle. He seemed to have everything under control, while simultaneously acknowledging there was no way of predicting what could happen outside of the city walls.

They strolled into the hangar, where a handful of aircraft stood concealed beneath massive tarps. As they passed them by, Andrew explained their purposes. "We have two fighter jets that once belonged to the Air Force. Two private jets similar to the one you just arrived on. And a classic 757 commercial airliner. I understand they were quite the norm where you come from. Always blows our mind how many seats they packed together in those things. No care in the world for one's comfort while traveling. Did you really sit next to complete strangers and have to bump elbows with them over the course of a flight?"

Arielle looked over her shoulder to Felix and Selena, who were exchanging glances. Selena rolled her eyes.

"We sure did," Arielle said, playing along with Andrew's

bewilderment at what someone nowadays probably saw as a poor person's means of air travel.

Andrew clapped his hands excitedly. "Fascinating! Well, the future may not be bright overall, but I can tell you flying is a much more intimate and enjoyable process."

Yeah, Arielle thought. *Because only the rich do it now.*

Andrew looked in his mid-thirties. It was hard to tell through the light layer of makeup, an obvious nose job, lip fillers, and Botox injections that kept his skin from moving in any natural way. Even if he was forty, he would have been born in the late 2050s and grown up in this new dystopian world where only the rich had the means to enjoy their lives.

Arielle suspected a long line of generational wealth passed down to Andrew, yet he was still working as a Lead Runner in the most shanty-looking place she had seen in a while.

"Mr. Adamonis," Arielle said, "I'm curious. Do you come from a family of time travelers?"

They had reached a door where a guard stood with a Tommy gun. The question prompted Andrew to stop suddenly, turning around with a wide grin. "Why yes, I do. My family's history with time travel is complicated. My great-grandfather was a member of the New Age Revolution. He oversaw their operations in St. Louis. My grandparents continued his work until the year 2016, when they stepped away from the Revolution. They had quite a powerful leader back then, is my understanding. But they didn't agree with the direction he wanted to take the organization. So, they moved to Oklahoma and started their family, giving birth to my father and aunt. Shortly after that, they were recruited by the Road Runners after the fall of the Revolution, and we've been here ever since. My dad served as a Lead Runner in this very office. I'm honored to continue his work today."

That explains the money, Arielle thought. Time travelers didn't need to be all that savvy to invest in their future. The most common means of making money was to travel into the past, invest in companies like Google or Apple in their early days, then travel back to their present time to cash out. And they could do this continually until their bank accounts reflected whatever number they were chasing. The Adamonis family clearly had enjoyed the fruits of their time traveling privilege.

"Well, that's definitely a rich history," Arielle said, fully intending the pun, but knowing it would sail right over Andrew's head.

"And how about you three?" Andrew asked, his grin somehow widening even more. "Are you also from a line of time travelers?"

"Actually, none of us are," Arielle said. "We're all first generation, if you will."

"Oh, of course!" Andrew slapped his forehead. "If you're from the 2020s, I suppose it's less likely for you to have come from a family of time travelers. I know the Revolution allowed its members to bring new children into the world, but that wasn't really something the Road Runners allowed until right around your present time."

It surprised Arielle how much history Andrew knew about the Revolution and Road Runners. He wasn't just some trust fund kid riding the coattails of his ancestors' success. He cared about his roots and seemed to genuinely respect the work he needed to do.

"Let's head in," Andrew said, spinning back around and patting the guard on his beefy arm.

The guard, whose arms were as big as Felix's thighs, nodded as each of them passed by, following Andrew through the door that led into a stairwell.

The walls in the stairwell were concrete, the steps made of steel. Andrew's voice echoed as they descended. "We keep a guard out front around the clock, just in case anyone comes wandering in. Never have to worry about someone coming down to our office who shouldn't be."

They reached the bottom landing, where another door waited with a panel that illuminated as they approached. Andrew lowered himself in front of the screen, where it mirrored his face. The panel chimed and flashed green while the lock clicked open. "Welcome, Mr. Adamonis."

"Right this way." Andrew pulled open the door and led them into the office.

The layout was similar to their main headquarters in Denver. This was no surprise, seeing as all the offices the Road Runners had created followed a strict design and layout, just in case any of them needed to transform into the organization's main headquarters.

The main bullpen area bustled with about thirty Road Runners sitting at their desks, glancing from their computers to the oversized monitors hanging on the surrounding walls. Doyle Grady's face was splattered across several of the screens.

"You guys are looking for Grady, too?" Felix asked as Andrew led them down the hallway that ran along the conference rooms.

"Like I mentioned, we're here to help you return to your present time as quickly as possible. No one from the past fully grasps how our world works here in 2098, so we like to assist where we can. Before we get started, however, I want to show you what could be our most useful secret. Many offices these days have something similar—but not all, mind you."

He continued toward the end of the hall, passing the kitchen where a couple of people had holograms boxing each other from their handheld electronic devices. Arielle wasn't sure if those were the new phones, or just some enhanced video games. They passed the final boardroom and turned the corner—something that didn't exist in their Denver office.

Around the corner was another door with another guard standing watch, this one holding an AR-15 rifle.

"Good day, Darion," Andrew said, waving a hand.

"Hello, sir," Darion replied, monotone and with a quick nod.

"I'd like to show our new friends here the tunnel," Andrew said. "Just for a quick moment before we head back to start some business matters."

"Certainly, sir," Darion said, shuffling aside.

"Thank you." Andrew stepped forward. The all-black door had no handle, so he simply pushed it open, waving at the Angels to follow him. "This way."

They stepped through and fluorescent lights flickered to life, revealing light gray walls that stretched as far as they could see.

"Is this what I think it is?" Arielle asked.

Andrew clapped his hands. "It certainly is. It's our own private tunnel into the city. We want to be able to bypass all the security checkpoints that are normally required to enter—in case we need to take any weapons in for missions like this. We have another, much smaller office inside the city where about ten people work. Feel free to use this tunnel as needed. Now, shall we head to my office to discuss your plans for capturing this time-traveling serial killer?"

Chapter 17

They met in Andrew's office ten minutes later, stopping in the kitchen to grab drinks and snacks after a hectic day of both regular travel and time travel. The brain fog that often accompanied a trip through time was finally wearing off for all three Angels.

"Very good," Andrew said as he took his seat behind his desk.

Arielle noticed there wasn't a single piece of paper in sight, instead multiple electronic devices, mainly laptops, cell phones, and tablets.

Andrew grabbed a tablet from the corner of his desk and powered it on.

"How much have you learned about Doyle?" Felix asked.

"Well, we've received the reports about his prior crimes in 1898 and 1998 and have been on high alert for any repeat actions in 2098. So far, nothing has come up."

"He hasn't killed anyone yet," Arielle said, folding her hands on her lap. She studied Andrew's office, the complete opposite of what she had grown accustomed to in Commander Briar's barren office with virtually zero decorations. Andrew had landscape paintings of both the current and former Oklahoma City. Dozens of framed pictures hung on the wall showing Andrew with his signature grin, shaking hands with what Arielle presumed were modern-day celebrities. Another dozen electronic picture frames cycled through a different photo every thirty seconds, offering a glimpse into Andrew's personal life. She noticed one where Andrew had his arm around a woman's shoulders as he leaned over to kiss the top of her head.

"And I take it you know when he is supposed to make his first kill?" Andrew asked, his eyebrow cocked slightly.

"Tomorrow," Arielle replied. "Well, I should say the first body will turn up tomorrow, so it's entirely possible the actual murder is happening today…or already happened."

This news soured the expression on Andrew's face. "Well, why aren't you three out there stopping it? Seems silly to come all this way to let an innocent person lose their life."

Arielle nodded. "I wish we could, but we have to stick to our mission objective. We normally stop crimes from happening, but this mission is more than that. We just need to catch Doyle Grady. If murders are stopped in that process, then great. But that's not what we're here for."

Andrew's eyes swam across the three Angels sitting in front of him, and he brushed a hand along his chin. "You know, I could authorize one of our teams to prevent the murders. Perhaps a tag team with you three? They focus on that, and you worry about finding him. I would just need to know the victims' names."

"I'm afraid it's not that simple," Arielle said. "As disturbing as this might sound, we kind of need to let Doyle kill his victims. It's the only way we learn more about his methods."

Andrew smacked the top of his desk, creating a sound that nearly rivaled a gun shot. "*Let* someone die?! You need to understand how ridiculous this sounds to me. We've dealt with our share of death over the years. More than you can imagine. And we've since removed all crimes from our society within the walls. Now you three come strolling into town from the past, telling us a murder is about to happen, and there's nothing you're going to do about it."

Selena cleared her throat and spoke up. "This isn't about us, or you, or even the victims. We have a serial killer on the loose who is hopping through time portals and killing people wherever he lands. We just had to leave Dallas in 1898, knowing three people had been killed there. Don't take this so personally and understand we're only trying to do our job."

Andrew let his jaw hang open. "Everyone said you three are the best team from your era. Now, I don't understand why we even needed a team from the past to come and deal with this matter, but that's not for me to argue with our commander. I will say, I'm not impressed with this process."

"Have you ever been on the Angels?" Arielle asked, remaining calm. She sensed the tension boiling from both Felix and Selena. Felix hated having his work undermined. And Selena couldn't handle being questioned in any capacity.

"I have not," Andrew replied with a fluttering blink. "But that's not the point."

"I think it is," Arielle said flatly. "You don't understand our work or the frustrations we deal with. Do you really think we don't *want* to save these three lives? Of course we do. Our primary job function is all about saving lives. But just like you admitted, you can't argue with your commander, and neither can we. We have strict orders about what we're here to do, and saving a life is not the top priority. Now, with your help, we just might catch this guy and save countless lives across the spectrum of time. You don't understand our way of life, just like we don't understand yours. But we can put aside our differences and make something positive out of this situation. Even without your help, we'll still be out there doing what we can. I'm sure it will be a hell of a lot easier with your guidance, though, so we appreciate any help you *can* offer."

Andrew stared at his desk, drew a deep breath, then pulled open a drawer. In a swift motion, he retrieved a bottle of pills, twisted off the cap, and popped two into his mouth with a shaky hand. He spun around, pulled open another cabinet that housed a refrigerator, and pulled out a bottle of water that he promptly guzzled from.

"Okay," he said after a sharp swallow. "I'm so sorry. Yes, we're all here doing our jobs. Forgive me. I'm just terrified of what's going to happen once there is a *murder* within the walls." He closed his eyes and shook his head aggressively. "Murder. Dammit all! It couldn't have been a robbery? Even arson? But murder! The people, both time travelers and regulars alike, are going to be in a full-blown panic."

If the way Andrew was acting was any sign of how the rest of the population would react to such a crime, Arielle was definitely worried about the repercussions of Doyle running loose in this era.

"Let's not dwell on what *might* happen," Arielle said. "All we can do is focus on the next steps. We need to go into the city and explore. What would you say is the population within the walls?"

Andrew scratched his head before taking another swig from his water bottle. "About 30,000 people. And probably an equal number of robots."

Felix scooted forward in his seat. "How realistic are the

robots? Can you tell them from regular people?"

"Calm down, nerd," Selena scoffed, unable to hide an equal level of fascination in her voice.

Andrew chuckled. "If you glance, you can't tell a robot from a real person. You need to watch how they walk, though. For all the mechanical engineering that went into those things, they could never quite mimic the natural flow of the human stride. They have a slight hitch in their steps, much like a person would have if they were walking on a recently rolled ankle."

"Okay, good to know," Arielle said. "Is there a database of missing people?"

Andrew grinned. "There's a database for just about anything you could imagine. And we have access to it. Have a couple of our own planted within the city's government. There is surveillance that covers just about every inch of public space. And it all feeds into the robots. If they sense danger, they're trained and equipped to help immediately."

"Will they know if we have guns on us?" Arielle asked.

Andrew shook his head. "No, they're not metal detectors. They'll only know if your gun appears on one of the surveillance feeds. Regardless, that shouldn't be a major problem. We've created special identifications for you three to appear as citizens of Oklahoma City, with a designation to carry firearms. So if you get stopped by a robot or officer, just show them your ID, and you'll be on your way."

"Perfect," Felix said, looking down at his 1898 garb. "And I had submitted a request for wardrobe for the three of us."

"Yes." Andrew seemed more at ease as he folded his hands on his desk. "That should all be arranged in one of our conference rooms. You can change into your new outfits, then take the rest in your luggage. Will you be needing a place to stay, or would you like to stay here at the office?"

"A place inside the walls would be ideal, assuming that's where Doyle is staying as well," Arielle replied.

"Well, let's look into it." Andrew tapped his tablet, and the lights turned off while the TV screen on the wall flickered to life.

Doyle's face filled the screen, sending chills down Arielle's back. His blue eyes gazed at her, insanity swimming in them, derangement tucked behind his deceptive smile.

The screen changed to a map of the city, seven red circles along the outer edge. "No one is registered in the city's database under the name of Doyle Grady. We presume he's using an alias, or is living outside the walls, accessing the city through a network of underground tunnels."

"There are *other* secret ways into the city?" Felix asked. "Seems counteractive to having the walls and security."

"People always find a way," Andrew said with a subtle shake of the head. "The areas you see circled on the map are the known entryways. Sewage lines or man-made tunnels. Since they're known, some have been blocked, while others have a camera monitoring the entryway. Not all could be blocked, mainly the active sewage lines."

"People walk through shit to enter the city?" Selena asked, an appalled expression overtaking her face.

"They sure do. And as you can imagine, they're quite easy to spot. But they're getting better about the timing of their arrivals to slip in and vanish. I'd assume they have somewhere to clean up and change clothes. Some people run safe houses for this very reason. I hear it's a rather lucrative business, since they take whatever money the government sends to these trespassers. That said, there are likely other entryways into the city that we don't know about yet. Some that might lead into the basements of businesses, or even private residences."

Arielle nodded, taking a mental note of that specific information. "And what do *you* believe Doyle is doing?"

Andrew sighed and crossed his arms, gazing at the map. "If I wanted to pull off a string of murders inside these walls, I'd probably want to live inside of them. Once you're outside, you get cut off from all the news feeds. It's two separate worlds. Serial killers love to read and watch about their own hype, and he wouldn't be able to do that from the outside. He'd also want to have a quick exit in case things take a turn for the worse. I'm willing to bet he's using an alias and is living somewhere along the outer edge of the city, within a two-minute walk of an exit. Whether that's a regular exit or another unknown tunnel, I can't say."

"Alright," Arielle said, rubbing her forehead. Fatigue was taking over, and something about Andrew's office was pulling her toward sleep. "That's very helpful. If I give you the first victim's name, would you be able to find anything about him?"

Andrew gulped but nodded. "Certainly."

"Rowland Reeves," Arielle said, leaning back in her seat.

Andrew typed the name into his tablet, and seconds later an entire profile appeared on the screen, showing a headshot of a smiling Rowland wearing a light blue graduation hat.

"Let's see here," Andrew said. "Rowland Reeves. Just graduated from the University of OKC seven months ago. Interned for NexaTech Innovations as a software engineer. Left the internship in September to take on a full-time role at Quantum Works, where he's been ever since."

"And do you know what these companies do?" Selena asked.

"I'm not familiar with NexaTech, but I know Quantum Works. They do a few things, but their main contract is with the city. They built the infrastructure for the surveillance system I've mentioned."

Arielle drew a deep breath. "Interesting. I have a hard time believing his murder was random. I'm sure Doyle wants to evade being seen on these security systems. Could he have threatened Rowland to make that not happen?"

Andrew wrinkled his nose. "One person doesn't have that much sway over the matter. Lots of checks and balances for something as simple as turning off one camera."

Arielle glanced at her watch, then looked around the walls for a clock. "What time is it? I'm sorry, but I've now been in three different centuries today and have no bearings."

Andrew laughed, checking his tablet. "I don't envy you. It's about to hit five o'clock. In the evening."

Arielle sighed. A nap would give her a much-needed boost. A full night's sleep would have her fresh and ready to hunt down Doyle with her bare hands. But neither were in sight. "Do you think we could get into Quantum Works to speak with someone this late?"

"Of course," Andrew replied, powering down the tablet and turning the lights back on. "That's a twenty-four-hour job that requires lots of workers. There might be more robots working late into the night, but there's always a handful of people on site."

Arielle stood up and extended a hand to shake. "Thank you for everything, Andrew. We'll take whatever place you can offer us within the city. If you can send us the details, I'd like to head out now and get started at Quantum Works. If we're lucky, Doyle won't ever know we're here."

Chapter 18

Doyle didn't need to climb through a tunnel of shit to get inside the walls of Oklahoma City. He admittedly lucked out when he stumbled across a time portal in 1898, a year he spent venturing around the South and Midwest.

Portals were two-way streets. And the one in Oklahoma City bounced between 1898 and 2098. It took months of wandering around the past until he found the one in Miami that sent him to 1998 and 1798. He had started mapping and charting the time portals he knew of. Some had been passed around by word of mouth, others had been suggested as truth from the Book of Time. In all, he had found seven time portals and intended to use each one to spread his reign of terror throughout the course of time.

In Oklahoma City, Doyle owned two properties. One apartment in a skyrise, and a small ranch-style home just outside the bustle of the big buildings. The wall surrounding the city was a fifty-foot-tall electric fence, and he lived close enough to hear the constant hum of electricity coursing through the wires. Sometimes he'd sit in his backyard and watch birds fly to their most unfortunate death. Once, he even saw a man trying to scale the wall and maneuver his way through the obstacle course of crisscrossed wires with the precision of an adult playing a game of Twister. But the man bumped his head on a wire halfway through, catching fire within twenty seconds like a mosquito in a bug zapper. The stench of burning flesh made its way to Doyle's house and caused him to drool.

Today, Doyle had Rowland tied up in his basement, bound to the same chair from earlier. He'd kill him shortly. Had little choice, in fact. Rowland couldn't be trusted to keep his mouth shut about the events of the past two days. And when you can't trust someone, you remove them from the equation.

Doyle had stepped outside to get away from the screams. While the sounds of suffering normally made him erect, Rowland had not quit. He'd been screaming for four hours straight. Begging, crying, calling for his fucking mommy.

Poor guy.

It wasn't fair to Rowland to be in such a predicament. The kid had worked hard to get a dream job in this nightmare of a world, and it landed him in Doyle's basement with only minutes remaining in his once ambitious life.

Doyle had poured himself a glass of scotch—they at least still allowed alcohol in this hell hole—and sipped it from the swinging bench on his front porch. He knew all of his neighbors' schedules, having observed from behind the curtain in his living room. Doyle refused to be seen or have interactions with his neighbors. For all they knew, he was never even home. He had slipped up two months ago when the jackass nosy husband from the house next door came stumbling out of the house at nine o'clock in the morning—he normally left for work at 7:45 sharp.

Doyle was only trying to enjoy a glass of orange juice from his porch when the neighbor spotted him and tried to play friendly.

"Hey there, neighbor!" the man, whose name Doyle couldn't quite remember, had said. Dale? Gail? Pal? Who knows—there were so many weird names in 2098. "Long time since we've seen you. How's life treating you?"

Doyle had responded by dumping his orange juice on the lawn of rocks. "I'm leaving for vacation. Europe. Be back in three months."

He retreated back into the house before Dale-Gail-Pal could respond. The fucker. What gave him the right to step onto Doyle's lawn and start talking like they were best friends? If he came knocking on his door, Dale-Gail-Pal just might end up with his limbs scattered across I-35 southbound to bumfuck Texas.

That day had been Doyle's worst since living a peaceful six months in Oklahoma. But it was all about to get better.

He finished his scotch and returned inside, Rowland still crying in the basement below where no one would ever hear him. Doyle kept a tidy house—too many mistakes could be made after murdering someone if you had to sift through piles of clothes and dirty dishes to clean up evidence. He rinsed his glass and placed it on the top shelf of his dishwasher.

"God dammit, you sick bastard!" Rowland cried. "Let me out of here!"

Doyle grinned. He always loved when they added a personal touch.

I am a sick bastard, he thought. *But at least I'm not the one tied to a chair.*

He shuffled from the dishwasher to the fridge, licking his lips as he pulled open the see-through door. He rummaged through soda cans, containers of microwave dinners and Chinese takeout until he grasped the black box he kept in the back.

"Hello, my beauties," he said, heart racing as he pulled out the box, placed it gently on the counter, and unsnapped the latches. Inside lay six syringes full of potassium chloride, their sharp needles shining proudly under the kitchen light.

Throughout all his travels, Doyle always made a stop in 2021 to stock up on the drugs he needed to seamlessly kill his victims. Visiting his own past life, where he was a renowned surgeon with a beautiful, loving wife, always sent him into a mental spiral. Yet, he came out of each trip with a renewed sense of purpose. He'd sneak into his old house on the nights his wife was home alone. She would be upstairs sleeping, so he'd give her a kiss before sitting on his couch for a couple of hours. The normalcy kept him grounded and provided Doyle time to reflect on his life.

He pulled out a syringe, admiring the clear liquid death swimming inside. A grin touched his lips as he tucked the syringe behind his ear like a cigarette and closed the box to return it to the fridge.

"Let me go, you piece of shit!" Rowland screamed from the basement. Doyle heard the slightest of wavers in his voice, an early sign that the young whiz kid was finally tiring.

"Just a moment, dear," Doyle called back, giggling at himself.

Sometimes he needed to unleash his inner beast and carry out a savage murder, but he preferred the simplicity of injecting his victims and letting them fall into their eternal sleep. It allowed a brief period where the reality of death clasped its icy fingers around his victims' throats. It opened them up. Made them vulnerable. It fascinated Doyle how much truth a dying person would share before the lights went out. A final confession or cleansing of the soul.

The screaming from downstairs finally stopped, taken over by deep, heavy sobs.

Doyle referred to this as the "mirror phase." Everyone, at some point, has to face themselves in the mirror and confront a disturbing truth. Reality is often harsh, and people do their best to avoid facing it straight on. A cheating spouse. A troublemaking child destined for a life in prison. The worst— an unexpected death of a loved one.

Doyle had his mirror moment three days after his wife had passed away. He had stared at himself in his wife's vanity mirror and could only cry. The reality that she was never coming back took those entire three days to hit him. No more summer evening walks in the park. No more late-night runs for ice cream. Just a life without his one true love. The mirror showed him the truth—bags under his eyes, frazzled, greasy hair that he had nearly pulled right out of his scalp. Doyle had to see his emotional state to confront his reality, and that's why he always kept a mirror in the same rooms as his victims. They deserved their own moment of revelation.

Rowland whimpered like a suffering dog. Doyle tapped the syringe behind his ear before stomping down the stairs.

He kept the basement even more immaculate than the rest of the house. This was, after all, where any murders would take place. The computer and its small desk stood against the wall just to the right of the bottom landing. The body-sized mirror hung on the opposite wall. And that was all he had downstairs. Vinyl flooring made for easy cleanup, plus a closet on the back wall where he'd stash the body until it was time to dump it.

Doyle found Rowland on the floor, tipped over, but still

tied to the chair. The computer screen was open to the facial recognition software, and Doyle clicked through the computer's history.

"I'm impressed," Doyle said, nodding with delight. "You made no attempts to contact someone from the outside world. Not that it would have worked—I blocked any of those capabilities. But it's the trust that matters to me. Perhaps I've misjudged you."

Rowland lay on his side, head pressed against the floor. Strings of tears and mucus hung from the tip of his nose. "I just want to go home," he moaned. "Please. I've done everything you asked. The software is completely ready to use, and I set up alerts if there are any matches to the photos you provided."

Doyle crossed his arms and leaned against the desk. "You've done excellent work, Rowland. But you and I both know I can't let you walk out of here tonight. You may have proven a level of honesty with your work on this computer, but you'll go straight to the authorities."

Rowland shook his head weakly, a fresh wave of tears streaming down his face. "No. I won't. I'll forget all about it. We can walk around the office and pretend not to know each other. I promise."

Doyle couldn't help but laugh, kneeling down and running his fingers through Rowland's wavy hair. "Surviving a tragedy like this is not something you'd ever forget. In fact, it might haunt you for the rest of your life. Always looking over your shoulder. Scared to go out. Who can you really trust in this world?"

"You," Rowland whined. "I trust you like you trusted me. You gave me your word. I did what you asked. Now it's your turn to hold up your end of the agreement."

Doyle spread his fingers and held up his hands. "I'm not the villain here, Rowland. You see that, right? Guys like us have gone through life always getting the short end of the stick. We've had to work hard to get where we are, and for what? Here we are in 2098. Decency is gone. Civilization has morphed into some sick game with robots running the world. Now, I'm sincerely sorry to have put you through all of this, but I'm doing something much bigger than either of us can comprehend."

"Do what you need," Rowland cried, rocking his head from left to right. "But *please* just let me go. Blindfold me and drop me in the middle of nowhere. I don't care. I won't come looking for you."

"It means nothing to you," Doyle replied, paying no attention to what Rowland had to say. Sometimes he could completely lock in to whatever task lay in front of him. A trait that was good for the patients on his operating table, but bad for the innocent victims he snatched out of society. "But Arielle Lucila has done more to disrupt this universe than anyone else. I wouldn't be surprised if it was all her fault society turned out the way it is today. If you tinker with the past, there will be hell to pay. Always. I've been around enough to know that. Most things are best to leave alone."

"What the fuck are you talking about?" Rowland whined. More tears streamed down his face. Surely he could taste the end coming. Doyle was practically feasting on it.

Doyle sat on the floor, scooting so his back could press against the wall. Rowland writhed around, only three feet away. "Let's talk, Rowland. What would you say your biggest regret in life has been?"

"Fuck you," Rowland grumbled. His face turned red, muscles bulging as he tried to break out of the ropes.

"You're not getting out of there," Doyle said calmly. "Do you think I'd go through all this trouble and not make sure the ropes are bound? You're smarter than that."

Rowland took control of his breathing and wiped his face against the floor, leaving a trace of his emotional fluids.

Need to clean that up, Doyle thought.

"You're really not going to let me go," Rowland said, the steadiness in his voice surprising Doyle. It wasn't a question, either. "I don't know what illegal activity you're tied up in, and I don't care. Shame on you for not sticking to your word."

Doyle grinned. "You think you can reverse psychology *me*? Oh, Mr. Rowland, how wrong you are. I wrote the book on mind games. There isn't a trick I don't know. I expected more out of you."

Rowland nodded. "Me too. I should've listened to my gut. I had a feeling you were never going to let me go. Should have refused to help you. Same result for me. All I can hope for now is that whoever you're running from catches you and sends you to a most painful death."

Blood rushed to Doyle's crotch. A soon-to-be victim wishing death upon him. Nothing aroused him more than thinking of his own death. Knowing his miserable life would one day end was perhaps the only thing that kept him pushing forward. Killing Arielle was his ultimate goal—a final piece of the puzzle to fill his void. But if he failed, and Arielle ended up succeeding against him? Well, he hoped she'd make it a dramatic death for Doyle Grady. Up in flames!

Doyle crawled forward and planted a kiss on Rowland's forehead, the salty taste of sweat remaining on his lips as he pulled away. "Oh, Rowland, I promise it will be painful for me, but never for you."

Doyle grabbed the syringe with a quick flick of the wrist and jabbed it into the side of Rowland's neck.

Rowland's entire body jolted. "What the hell?!"

"Shh, shh, shh." Doyle brushed Rowland's hair back. "It's okay. I just injected you with a diluted amount of potassium chloride. You will drift off to sleep in about ten minutes, and five minutes after that, your heart will stop beating. I can't thank you enough for your contributions. Because of you, I just might catch Arielle Lucila and bring her back down to Earth. A fallen angel, if you will."

Rowland cried. A lone, silent tear creating a new shiny path as it streamed down his cheek. "No," he whispered. "You motherfucker."

His chest heaved as he drew deeper breaths. A panic attack.

"Never sell yourself short," Doyle said, continuing to pet Rowland like a dog. "A life ending too soon does nothing to diminish the quality of that life. You've accomplished so much in such little time. And in this messed up world. You should be proud. Do you have parents? Who can I notify about your death?"

Doyle knew the answers to these questions already, but wanted Rowland to confront the ghosts of his past. Rowland was all alone. Dying alone. Just like he would. Doyle had lost his parents as a teenager. His father was killed by a drunk driver—a rich snob executive of some law firm who got to survive. And his mother fell victim to a brain tumor, a tragedy that prompted his initial interest in becoming a surgeon.

Rowland didn't reply. He only gazed blankly at Doyle. *Beyond* Doyle.

"I'm sure your parents will be waiting for you," Doyle whispered. "If that's what you believe in."

Rowland blinked, his breathing growing heavier by the second.

"Tell me what you're feeling," Doyle said. He was having flashbacks to this same experience he'd had with his dying wife. She had squeezed his hand and assured him everything was going to be all right. Confessed her undying love.

"I'll see you in hell," Rowland finally said, his voice groggy and thick with mucus.

The words caught Doyle off guard. No one had ever spoken so harshly toward him after being injected, and he wasn't sure how to feel.

Instead of replying, he held Rowland's head as the young man gradually drifted off. If Rowland simply wanted a peaceful death, so be it. Doyle was here to provide that comfort.

Those ten minutes passed in a flash. Rowland's eyes closed as he started snoring. Doyle lay his head on Rowland's chest, feeling the last moments of life enter his lungs before being blown back out. Death had a certain type of romance about it. Last words. Final breaths. It was an ultimate closure that bordered on pure beauty.

Like clockwork, four-and-a-half minutes passed until Rowland exhaled for the last time.

"Thank you," Doyle said, patting his lifeless chest. As if a sign from the heavens—or Rowland himself—the computer started blaring the alarm he had requested.

Arielle Lucila had just shown her face in Oklahoma City.

Chapter 19

"At least this is better than those dresses from 1898," Selena said. "But I still feel like an idiot. Like what *is* this?"

They had changed into new outfits before leaving the Road Runners' office through the tunnel that connected to the city. The other side opened in a bank basement that felt a bit too familiar for Arielle and Selena.

"So many frills," Arielle said, laughing. "I guess they just moved from the lower half to the upper half after 200 years. Fine with me—at least I can run in this thing."

Arielle wore pink leggings and a purple dress that looked normal from the waist down. The top half, however, was a metropolis of frills and puffy sleeves. Rings and bracelets decorated her fingers and wrists. Gaudy earrings were clipped to her ears to go along with a six-inch burgundy flower in her hair.

Selena wore a similar outfit, only with a soft orange and yellow color palette.

"It's the fashion of the era," Felix said as they strode along the sidewalks of downtown Oklahoma City, en route for Quantum Works. "We need to dress like the rich if we want to get anything done here. If we dress like our normal selves, people will just think we're part of the working staff that comes from beyond the fence. And they'll treat us as such."

"Got it," Selena said. "So the world is still an *awesome* place after all these years."

Arielle giggled. She had felt loose ever since leaving the office. Part of it was the outfit. She could barely take herself seriously. But she also felt optimistic. It had been a while since they'd entered a mission with a clear-cut plan. "You're just pissed that Felix gets to dress normal."

Felix had to put on black jeans, a blue dress shirt, and a black vest. He also had on boots that looked more like galoshes, along with gaudy bracelets and multiple chains around his neck.

"Yeah, I can't really complain," he said. "But I'm not sure how I'm supposed to run in these things."

"No one here is concerned about running," Arielle said. "Remember, there's no crime. What do they have to run from?"

"And why bother running when you can just buy a liposuction?" Selena added. "Have you noticed we've already passed three different offices promoting it? It's like these people eat whatever they want, don't exercise, and just come in for their annual procedure to pump out all the fat. These are the worst kind of rich people—lazy!"

They strolled past two obese men holding hands who gawked when Selena cried her criticisms.

"Selena!" Arielle muttered under her breath, slapping her on the arm as Selena had done countless times to Felix.

"What?" Selena asked, rubbing her arm. "Is one of these rich people going to attack me?"

They couldn't help but break into laughter.

"I can't lie," Arielle said. "It feels so safe just walking around. Usually when I explore a big city I'm always looking over my shoulder. But here...it *feels* like nothing bad can happen."

"It's true," Felix added. "But don't buy into the hype. We all want the world to be a better place, but it only feels that way right now because everyone who the government deems as not safe is suffering outside. And we know all those people aren't bad. Desperate, sure, but society itself has become pay-to-play, and that type of structure can only collapse on itself at some point."

Selena chuckled. "Yeah, and bring down all the liposuction clinics with it."

After two more blocks, they approached a skyscraper standing at least fifty stories tall; the exterior was made entirely of black, reflective glass.

"This is the spot," Felix said, his hand shielding his eyes as he looked up. "Andrew said the building looks like somewhere an evil genius would live."

A giant Q was centered on the top of the building, the white letter standing in stark contrast to the rest of the facade.

They wandered to the main entrance, a revolving door that led into an immaculate lobby. Automated machines moved constantly to buffer and polish the granite floor. The lighting was aggressively bright, but revealed a welcome desk where a man sat upright facing a computer screen.

"Do we just go in?" Selena asked as they all stared through the front windows.

"Of course," Arielle replied. "Does everyone have the badges they had made for us?"

Selena and Felix nodded. Andrew had equipped them each

with pistols, ID cards that allowed them to carry those guns, and badges that showed they worked for the National Security Bureau, a modernized government agency that had national oversight into all crime matters.

Arielle walked first through the revolving doors, Felix and Selena trailing behind.

A group of businessmen passed through the lobby, briefcases in hand as they chattered about the day's work. They paid no attention to the three time travelers.

Arielle looked over her shoulder and nodded toward the welcome desk before approaching the man behind the computer.

The three stepped up and planted their elbows on the desk's elevated ledge. The man stared forward at his computer, navigating the mouse with one hand, and typing with the other.

"Excuse me?" Selena said with plenty of sass.

The man turned his head, his green eyes scanning Selena for two seconds. "Hello, Selena Nicole. How may I help you?"

Selena jumped back, raising her hands. "What the fuck?! How do you know who I am?"

"My facial recognition software can identify anyone registered within the NSB's database. Greetings to you as well, Arielle Lucila and Felix Francisco."

"Wicked," Felix said, jaw hanging open as he leaned in closer. "You're a robot?"

The man, who looked nothing like a robot, turned his head to Felix and frowned. "Sir, we prefer to be called Automated People, or AP, for short. That machine washing the floors is a robot. Are you suggesting I'm on the same level of intelligence as that machine?"

"Of course not," Felix said, shame immediately crawling

across his face. "My apologies."

"Accepted," the fake man said. "My name is William, and you are welcome to call me that. How may I be of assistance today?"

Arielle had expected these robots—Automated People—to have minor traits that gave away their true identity. But she saw nothing of the sort as she gazed at the man across the desk. Not even the voice was mechanical, which she had mainly expected. He sounded real, with natural inflections and flow. Even his movements seemed genuine, his fingers gliding seamlessly from letter to letter on the keyboard. His head bobbed subtly from left to right as he focused on his computer. The production of these Automated People was flawless, except for the slight hitch in their strides Andrew had mentioned, which they hadn't seen yet.

"We need to speak with anyone who knows Rowland Reeves," Arielle said. "Perhaps someone he reports to?"

"Let me see," William said, typing on the computer and focusing on the screen. "Rowland Reeves is employed by Quantum Works in the software engineering department. His direct manager's name is Samia Durian, and it appears she is still in the building."

Felix leaned over the ledge, craning his neck for a view of William's screen. "Are you able to see where everyone is in the building? How did you know that?"

William looked at Felix, and it was in this moment Arielle realized these Automated People couldn't properly portray emotions. A human would have been annoyed by Felix's childlike curiosity by now, but not William.

"Yes, sir," he replied. "Our building is equipped with facial recognition software and knows the exact time each person arrives and leaves. For example, Ms. Durian arrived this morning at 10:06. And judging from the logs of her timesheet, any day she arrives after nine, she never leaves until after seven o'clock."

"I know we just showed up, but is there any chance we'd be able to meet with her?" Arielle asked. "We have some questions about Rowland Reeves."

William nodded. "I see Mr. Reeves did not arrive for work today and has never missed a day since he started in September. If I were to guess, Ms. Durian is likely interested in any relevant information. Let me send her a message."

William returned to the computer and fired off a message, then noticed Felix still gawking at him. "Is there anything else, Mr. Francisco?"

Felix pushed off the ledge and shook his head. "No, I'm sorry."

"Forgive him," Selena said. "He doesn't get out much."

Felix flushed red just as William's computer pinged.

"Ms. Durian is available to meet," William said. "I've added elevator access to your NSB badges. You can use those to take a ride up to the fifty-third floor. She will be waiting for you when you step out."

"Oh," Arielle said, blown away by the sophisticated yet simple way everything flowed within this building. "Thank you."

"My pleasure, Ms. Lucila. Continue across the lobby and you'll find the elevators."

William gestured to his left, then returned to his computer without another word, even as Felix kept looking over his shoulder as they walked away.

"You have *got* to keep it together, Felix," Arielle said under her breath as they approached the elevator lobby. "We're in the future. There's going to be a ton of technology you've never seen before. But you need to at least act like you've been here before. We got lucky William didn't ask questions, but who knows if the rest of the robots out there are as oblivious as he was."

"Automated People," Felix corrected.

Arielle laughed. "Look, I'm all for calling *people* by their preferred pronouns and all that. But give me a break on this one. They're fucking *robots*!"

Selena giggled as she stepped forward to push the call button. "Preach it, sister."

Felix held up his hands in defense. "I'm just trying to play by their rules. I *know* they're robots, but if they ask to not be called that, then who am I to say otherwise? Do we really want to find out what happens if we get on the bad side of one of those things? They already knew who we were just by looking at us for a few seconds."

"Fair point," Arielle said, crossing her arms. "Hopefully we can keep any interactions with them to a minimum."

"Not like you can tell them apart from regular people," Selena said. "I wonder if they date humans. Imagine a charming man like William with none of the emotional baggage human men bring to the table. Could be the perfect relationship."

Arielle laughed. She couldn't deny the logic. But still...

The elevator door chimed while the doors parted. Three women filed out, and Arielle believed they were all robots. The hitches in their strides were subtle, but she couldn't just come out and ask someone if they were real or not. Christ, what a time to be alive.

Once they passed, the three Angels strolled in. Felix tapped his NSB badge against the scanner, and Selena scrolled through the options on the touch screen until finding the fifty-third floor.

"Looks like the top floor," she said with excitement.

"Would you like an express ride?" a voice from the speaker in the ceiling asked.

At least that one sounds like a pre-recording, Arielle thought.

"Yes, please," Selena said, grinning from ear to ear.

"Selena!" Arielle spat. "We don't even know what that means."

"Everybody must secure both hands to a rail before we can proceed," the elevator voice said.

They all looked at each other, then at the handrails lining the walls. No one moved for five seconds.

"Everybody must secure both hands to a rail before we can proceed," the elevator repeated.

"Just do it," Selena said, turning around and grabbing hold of the rail with both hands.

Arielle and Felix did the same, and the doors closed.

"Thank you," the elevator said. "Failure to hold the railing may result in bodily or mechanical harm during an express ride. Commencing in three, two, one..."

The motors running the elevator hummed to life, then all three of them felt a jolt where they briefly lost their footing. The sensation reminded Arielle of trying to stand on a surfboard in restless waters.

Ten seconds later, the elevator chimed and welcomed them to the fifty-third floor. The doors parted, and they stepped out, Felix unable to look away.

"How the hell did they do that?" he whispered to himself.

Standing twenty feet ahead was a woman with her arms

crossed, chewing on her bottom lip. She wore a multicolored suit, a welcoming sight for Arielle, who may have found her way out of the ridiculous frilly outfits.

"You three are from the NSB?" the woman asked, looking them up and down.

"Yes," Arielle said.

"Good. Please come with me. We've been trying to get in contact with Rowland all day."

Chapter 20

From the moment Doyle had seen Arielle and her friends appear on the computer screen Rowland had so graciously set up, he drooled at the thought of getting to kick his plans into motion. It was time to lay the trap.

But he underestimated Arielle's dedication. The bitch arrived in 2098 and immediately went for the jugular. How did she know to start her search at Quantum Works? And why the *fuck* was she already going there?

If these Angels already knew the first victim was Rowland Reeves, what did that mean for the other two he had planned?

None of that mattered. Once they stepped into Quantum Works, how much time would he have before someone came looking for him? They had his address on file, and he could watch them make their way across town. But it seemed wiser to cover his tracks and hide now.

He hadn't even gotten the chance to dismember Rowland's body like he wanted. It was much easier to pack a dead body into a suitcase if it was in smaller pieces.

"Damn it all!" Doyle screamed, stomping his foot. He wanted to punch a hole through the wall, but if the authorities would soon be here, that would create more questions he didn't want to answer.

Fortunately, it was the middle of December, and darkness had already crept over the city.

Doyle stood above Rowland's body, looking down and devising a plan.

Load the body into the trunk. Drive to a safe zone. Dump it. Easy. Just need to take off my license plates before doing it.

"Does that plan meet your standards, Mr. Reeves?" he asked the corpse. "Of course it does!"

Doyle spun and hurried up the stairs, thankful to have an attached garage. That was one detail he hadn't considered when shopping for places to live during his murdering spree through time. But it was now one he'd never overlook again.

He burst into the garage and flicked on the fluorescent light, buzzing immediately. A toolbox lay opened on a table pushed all the way into the corner—it had scraped his front bumper the first time he pulled in—a screwdriver on top.

He spent a couple of minutes unscrewing the Oklahoma license plates from his car, a black 2096 Mercedes sedan that helped him fit in while driving around town. *Fuck you, rich people.*

Next, he popped open the trunk and lined the inside with three trash bags. Even with no blood coming from Rowland's body, Doyle never took a chance. A lone hair could fall from Rowland's beautiful head and send Doyle's life into shambles. Having the plastic bags splayed out reduced that chance and made for a quick and simple cleanup.

He left the trunk open, grabbed a roll of industrial plastic wrap from the garage table, and returned to the basement. Rowland's eyes were glossy as they stared lifelessly at the ceiling. Doyle wasn't the type of person to close them. If Rowland's soul wanted to look at the blank ceiling, then so be it.

"Alright, big fella," Doyle said, moving Rowland's limbs to make the body straight. He unraveled the plastic and started at the feet, taking his time to move the plastic above and under the body, pulling it tight so there wouldn't be any slack that might get caught on something and rip.

It took Doyle five minutes to reach the head, where he took his time making sure every inch of hair was covered. Then he did a second layer, breaking into a sweat as his heart hammered.

He didn't know how long it would be until someone showed up at his doorstep. If Arielle had taken a photo of Doyle to Quantum Works, it could be a matter of minutes before they exposed his alias. But Quantum Works prided themselves on their commitment to privacy. Not just for their clients, but for anyone who worked for them. Arielle would have to make a compelling case for them to share details on such an abrupt visit.

None of that eased Doyle's thoughts, and he finished wrapping Rowland's body like a plastic mummy.

"Shit!" Doyle spat. "The dolly!"

He ran back up the stairs, knees aching, thighs tightening. It had been a couple of weeks since he'd done a formal workout, and he was paying for it now.

Doyle returned to the garage and grabbed the dolly he kept along the wall, running it back inside and down the stairs. He laid it down next to Rowland, rolled the dead engineer onto it, and promptly tied him to the dolly with the same ropes he had used to fasten him to the chair moments earlier.

"I'd have loved to do this a bit slower," Doyle said to Rowland, "but our friend Arielle is already here. Apologies if I bonk your head or anything. Don't take it personal."

A thought had been gnawing at Doyle ever since he saw Arielle and her little friends stroll into Quantum Works like they owned the place. She wasn't a step ahead of him. There was that much to be grateful for. But she wasn't much more than a step behind him. And that was troubling. The bitch was following him, it seemed. Did she actually go through the time portal in 1898? Or had she been planning this for years? She, or someone else from the elitist Road Runners, could have traveled far into the future and studied Doyle's patterns from afar. It would have required no risk to the person investigating, reading briefs of the old crime scenes and drawing their conclusions.

Doyle shook his head. *No. That's not possible. I don't even know how my next two kills play out, so how could they?*

But they could. And would the Road Runners really put their most prized possession at risk based on a whim? These people were calculated. They thought with their heads instead of emotions. That much he could credit them.

"Let's go," Doyle said, hoisting the dolly up and pulling it toward the stairs. He looked up the thirteen steps; lugging a body made it appear like one hundred instead. "From the legs, one step at a time."

His body already sore, Doyle began his ascent with Rowland. He had put the dead body in a seated position on the dolly, ass on the base so the legs would dangle off the edge. By the halfway point, sweat dripped down Doyle's back, making his shirt stick to his flesh.

"Damn you, Arielle," he said through gritted teeth. Her arrival really had made this entire process more difficult than it needed to be. If she hadn't arrived so soon, he'd have taken his time running each body part up the stairs until they were all compacted into a suitcase. And the suitcases made life simple. They gave him options. He could set them on fire. Toss them onto the electric fence where no one would bother chasing after them. The best option was leaving the city. Sure, the folks at the checkpoint would check his trunk, but they never actually opened his luggage. Not for people leaving the city—they were rich and could be trusted, of course. But that option was off the table now. They'd certainly have questions about a dead body in the trunk.

And he couldn't dump the body in a river—too many cameras watched the river for people trying to sneak into the city via boat.

Doyle knew the safe zones away from the cameras. That was all he had wanted to learn through his employment with Quantum Works, but he had gained so much more.

He stopped for a breather with only two more steps to go, wiping the sweat from his brow and rubbing it on the stairs' carpet. He looked at Rowland's wrapped face, eyes still open.

"We had some good times," Doyle said, rubbing Rowland's head. "I want you to know I really did enjoy our evenings out. Maybe after this is all over, I'll come back and have dinner at Rizzuto's in your honor. The four-cheese penne pasta, extra Italian sausage. Just the way you liked it. And a shot of Frangelico to wash it down. It's the least I can do."

Interrupting his thoughts, Doyle's cell phone started ringing.

"What the fuck?!" he grumbled, panic instantly settling in. His phone was somewhere in the kitchen, but the only reason he had it was for work. No one else in this timeline had his phone number except for the people at Quantum Works.

With a flash of adrenaline, he pulled Rowland up the final two steps and laid the dolly down on the landing, sprinting for the kitchen.

He snatched the phone from the table and, sure enough, the caller ID showed Quantum Works.

Doyle licked his lips and gazed around, heart pounding in his ears. Why were they calling him after hours? Minutes after Arielle had walked into the building. Was it some sort of trap?

What do I do?!

It was better than having someone knocking on the door, so he answered the phone.

"Hello?" he greeted, making every conscious effort to sound like someone lounging around at home after a long day at work. His mind braced for any of a dozen possibilities as to who might speak back.

"Hello, Elyod," the voice on the other end replied. "This is Michael."

Whew, a robot!

The robots were the only ones who got to keep normal names in 2098. Michael, William, Emily. Shit like that. When Doyle arrived and was learning the ropes of the new culture, he quickly realized none of the *people* had regular names. He'd met men named Asahel, Increase, and Abimael. Plus women named Clarity, Hester, and Hephzibah.

So he settled on an alias of Elyod to fit in and not draw questions. *Fuck you, weirdos. Elyod Murray at your fucking service.*

At least the surnames had remained normal.

"Michael!" Doyle feigned surprise. "Is there a reason you're calling me so late?"

"Yes, Elyod, and I apologize. The NSB arrived a few minutes

ago, and they believe Rowland Reeves is missing. Our team has not spoken with them yet, but we wanted to be proactive and reach out to all employees of Quantum Works. Do you recall your last encounter with Mr. Reeves?"

Yeah, I just pulled him up the stairs, and now I don't know if I'll be able to walk for a week!

"Hmmm, let me think." Doyle took a long, deliberate pause, counting to five in his head. "I saw him briefly in the kitchen at work on Monday afternoon. We were both grabbing a snack."

"And did Mr. Reeves seem himself?"

"Yes, he was his usual self. He had mentioned going to Rizzuto's Friday after work. I told him I'd have to check my schedule and let him know, but I haven't seen him since to tell him I'd love to go."

Good old Quantum Works. For all the surveillance they conducted around the city and country, they refused to keep cameras within their offices. Once you got through the entrance, they enforced their trust and privacy for all employees.

"Very good, sir," Michael said, the clattering of a keyboard in the background. "If you think of anything else, please let me know. And if you hear from or see Mr. Reeves, call us immediately. Thank you for your time, and have a delightful rest of your evening."

The call ended, and Doyle stared at his phone in disbelief.

Okay, so Arielle and her crew are posing as the NSB. Not good. They haven't even spoken to her yet but are already suspicious. Definitely not good.

He turned to see Rowland's body lying a few feet away from the garage door. "Rowland, my friend. We need to get the fuck out of here."

Chapter 21

Samia led them through a bullpen of empty desks and down a short hallway to a conference room without speaking a word. Arielle could tell she was tense, judging by her pursed lips and stiff shoulders.

"I love your hair," Selena said as they entered the conference room.

Samia had dark skin and long, flowing braids that reached her knees.

This compliment earned a slight grin. "Thank you," Samia said shyly, pulling out a seat. "It's a pain to maintain, but worth it."

Felix ventured to the window, eyes wide with amazement. "Is this the highest point in the city?"

"It is," Samia said. "The founders of Quantum Works have always been ambitious. They want to be the biggest and best, and they believed having the tallest building in the city reflected their beliefs."

"I love it," Felix said, pressing his forehead against the glass and looking down.

"Thank you for meeting with us on such short notice," Arielle said, settling into a seat across the table from Samia. Selena and Felix made their way over to join them.

"I'm concerned," Samia replied, leaning forward and folding her hands on the table. "So I must thank you for coming out to talk. I take it everything is not okay with Rowland if the NSB is involved?"

Felix and Selena looked to Arielle, who first offered a tight-lipped grin. "We know nothing for certain yet, but we believe Rowland's in danger. A tip came in that a known serial killer may have kidnapped him."

Samia smacked the table. "Serial killer?! Someone from outside took him then? I don't see how. Rowland doesn't seem like the type to wander beyond the fence."

Arielle shifted in her seat, knowing the news she was about to deliver could send a wide ripple of panic across the entire city. "Well, that's the thing. We believe the killer is living *within* the city."

Samia stared at Arielle while processing this information, then leaned back, shaking her head. "No. That's impossible. Things like that don't happen anymore. Only outside the fence."

"Like I said, none of this has been confirmed yet, but we're almost certain."

Samia crossed her arms. "Do you understand what this means? A serial killer on the loose in the city. People are not equipped to handle that type of news. *I'm* not equipped. Who am I kidding? Have the police been notified, or is this just an NSB matter?"

"We have not alerted the local authorities," Arielle said, trying to use a caring voice. The fear spreading across Samia's face was growing palpable in the room. "That's because we don't yet understand what the killer is capable of. We think the kidnapping of Rowland Reeves was not random. For a killer to get away with murder in the city, they would need an understanding of the cameras and security system. And that's all powered by Quantum Works, correct?"

Samia rose out of her seat and paced back and forth, eyes glued to the floor as she fell into deep thought. "Yes, that's correct," she said, followed by inaudible muttering to herself. "This can't be."

The Angels exchanged a look. Arielle nodded at Selena, knowing she could adapt and relate to a person in distress.

"Samia, please take a moment to slow down and breathe," Selena said, standing and circling the table to stand in front of the panicking woman. She grabbed her by the shoulders. "This is why we're here. We need to know what sort of knowledge Rowland has about the Quantum Works systems. For starters, what about the security cameras set up around the city?"

Samia nodded, wriggled out of Selena's grip, and sat back down. She drummed her fingers and reached forward to grab a water bottle from a grouping in the center of the table. "Rowland started only four months ago. As a software engineer, the first three months are learning all the systems. We don't use specialists and expect all engineers to work on matters relating to security systems, Automated People, facial recognition, and emergency procedures. But Rowland has proven to be smarter than most. He has a much deeper knowledge of all aspects compared to anyone else with three months of experience."

"Are there blind spots?" Felix asked.

"Blind spots?"

"It's our understanding the security cameras installed cover every inch of the city," Felix continued, standing up and returning to the window. "From what I know about surveillance, that seems impossible. I'm not doubting the capabilities of Quantum Works, but covering every square inch of a city this size? I have a hard time believing it."

Samia drew a deep breath. "You cannot disclose this information to the public, but yes, there are about a dozen blind spots around the city. Why? I don't know. That's a decision from way above me. I'm told there were logistical complications installing cameras in these areas. Some people think the ultra-powerful in town still need places to meet." Samia rolled her eyes. "I have a hard time believing that one because there are so many places they could just meet inside, away from the cameras."

Arielle rubbed her chin. "What are you thinking, Felix?" She rarely knew where his trains of thought were headed.

"It has to be next to impossible to get away with kidnapping in a city this secure," Felix said, turning around and leaning against the glass as he spoke. Arielle imagined how her late mother would have yelled at Felix for doing such a wild thing. What if the glass broke and he fell fifty-three stories to his death?

Mothers.

"It *is* impossible," Samia said. "These things don't happen. There has never been a reported kidnapping since the fences went up and they kicked all the criminals out."

"But nothing is impossible if there are blind spots," Felix continued. "Rowland could have met with someone in a blind spot, not knowing that was the case, only to be knocked unconscious and taken from there. I assume these blind spots are in more remote areas of the city and not down by all the shops and restaurants?"

Samia nodded. "I can get a map of the blind spots, but it cannot leave this building."

"Understood," Arielle said. "And we appreciate that. Now, we want to investigate all possibilities. If Rowland is as smart as he sounds, I don't think he'd have gone off with some random stranger approaching him on the street. Do you, by chance, know anything about his personal life? Family, friends, places he liked to spend free time? Even coworkers he was close with here?"

Samia furrowed her brow, still drumming her fingers on the table. "I know he loved Italian food. Went to this restaurant three blocks from here every Friday after work. Rizzuto's."

"Okay, so that would have been five days ago," Arielle said. "Today *is* Wednesday, right?"

Samia nodded, shooting an inquisitive look across the table before replying. "But he was here on Monday. Worked his regular hours. Nothing seemed out of the ordinary. Then he didn't show up on Tuesday. I called him a couple times but got no answer. Fine, I thought, maybe he got really sick and was sleeping the day away. Those things happen. But when he didn't show up today, I called him every hour, and that's when I started worrying. Rowland has always been an excellent communicator, and it's unlike him not to call, not to show up two days in a row."

A tear streaked down Samia's face, so Felix fetched the box of tissues from the end of the table and pushed it her way.

"And what about the people he spent time with?" Arielle asked.

Samia wiped her tears, then blew her nose. "That's hard to answer. He got along with everyone so well. Even his trips to Rizzuto's, he'd go with different people each week. Few engineers are extroverted, but Rowland is. He has a natural charm that attracts his peers to follow him."

"Would we be able to get a list of all his colleagues?" Arielle asked.

"Sure," Samia said. "But wouldn't you rather just come back in the morning? Everyone will be here. And for Rowland, anyone will be willing to help."

Arielle gulped. "That's a generous offer, Ms. Durian, but I'm afraid we can't wait that long. Every second is precious in a case like this, and we'll probably be up all night trying to find him."

Samia broke into heavier crying, burying her face in her hands as her shoulders rose and fell with each sob. "Please don't let it be too late. He's such a good kid, and has had a hard life."

The three exchanged looks.

"Could you elaborate?" Selena asked, pulling out her notepad and pen.

It took Samia a minute to gather herself before she could speak with confidence. "Rowland lost both his parents in a boating crash when he was a junior in high school. His parents were well off, but the rest of his extended family was not. They all sort of disowned each other once Rowland's parents moved inside the city. When his parents died, none of his family came to the funerals. It was just him plus his parents' friends."

"Did you know him when this happened?" Selena asked.

Samia shook her head. "Of course not. He shared this story with me. But after the funerals, he fell into a deep depression, as anyone would. He was seventeen when it happened, and the state deemed him capable of living on his own, especially with the fortune he had inherited from his parents. That's the thing about Rowland. He was set for life. Didn't need to work. But he put himself through four years of college and has worked tirelessly for Quantum Works. He wants to make a difference in the world. How people who endure so much pain can remain a positive force in the universe is beyond my understanding. They're the real heroes."

Samia's cell phone rang, and she whipped it out of her pocket. Felix immediately craned for a look at the future technology. The size had changed little, aside from the phone somehow being even slimmer. And Samia's finger never touched the screen, but hovered above it, scrolling with the familiar up-and-down motion. "Excuse me. I need to step out to take this."

Samia didn't wait for a response as she spun around in her chair and left the conference room.

"What do we think?" Arielle asked, clasping her fingers together on her lap as she leaned back in her seat.

"I think Doyle knew exactly who he was looking for when he found Rowland," Felix said. "The question is, how close was Doyle to Rowland before he went missing? It's not like he sat outside this office building and waited for some random person to walk out. And to take Rowland after four months on the job filled with training across all aspects of software engineering? It's too precise. No way he could have known all that as an outsider."

"How much more thorough is a Google search these days?" Selena asked. "Maybe Doyle *could* have found out all these things from his basement."

Felix chuckled. "Google still exists, believe it or not, and it hasn't changed. There are other search engines, and it's hard to tell from the interface how effective they are. But let's try."

Felix pulled out his phone and started tapping on the screen.

"Should we have that out right now?" Arielle asked. "I haven't even looked at mine. Our phones still work here?"

"They do," Felix replied, not looking up. "Phone service doesn't work—I'm assuming the old towers we once relied on no longer exist. But the phone powers on and connects to Wi-Fi. That much hasn't changed."

"What if Samia sees your phone?"

Felix shrugged. "Not worried about it. They look similar enough. Check this out. The search engine is called Soaring Eagle. You ask it questions and it returns an answer immediately. I asked it who the smartest person at Quantum Works is, and it gave me the biography of the company's founder, Liam Beasley. I then asked if it could tell me the names of any employees at Quantum Works, and all it could give me were the executive officers. So, no, I don't think the search engines have improved enough for Doyle to have figured this out from home. This is rated as the top search engine in the world."

The door swung open, and Samia stood there with fresh tears welling in her eyes.

"Rowland's dead!" she cried. "They just found his body in a dumpster."

Chapter 22

"What are we going to say?" Selena asked in a whisper.

The three Angels remained in the conference room while Samia left them once more to meet with local authorities gathering in the building's lobby, who she would return with soon.

"What do you mean?" Felix asked.

"We're not really NSB agents," Selena replied, lowering her voice even more. "What if the actual NSB shows up here and questions our authenticity?"

Felix shook his head. "That's not how any of this works. We don't just get fake badges for the sake of the mission. The badges are real, and our names are officially registered in the NSB database. That's why the Automated Person in the lobby recognized us—we're on the books. Let Arielle do the talking. She used to be in the FBI, and that's pretty much what the NSB is today."

Arielle nodded. It seemed a lifetime ago she had been in the FBI's academy, learning the ropes, which included how to interview potential criminals and witnesses. "I don't want you two sitting in silence, though. If you have something to say, throw it out there. Remember, they think we're all NSB agents. So act like it."

There was a rap on the door before it swung open. Samia strolled in first, followed by two police officers.

"Sorry about the wait," Samia said, circling the table to return to her seat. "These are officers Smith and Jones."

Felix jumped out of his seat. "Are you two Automated People? Automated police officers?!"

"Felix!" Arielle snapped like a pissed-off mother.

The two officers looked at each other, and when their faces showed no emotional response, Arielle knew they were indeed robots.

"Yes, we are," said Officer Smith, who looked like a thirty-year-old man. "Is there a problem with that?"

"None at all," replied Felix giddily as he sat back down.

Officer Smith pulled out the seat next to Samia, and Officer Jones, who merely looked like a female version of Smith, sat next to her automated partner.

Samia, however, looked puzzled. "Don't you work with a lot of AP? I thought the NSB employed thousands of them?"

"We do," Arielle said, leaning forward. "Pardon Felix. He used to do office work and just recently got promoted to the field with us."

Selena shot a disgusted look at Felix.

"I see," Samia said. "Anyway, the local authorities are already investigating the area where Rowland's body was found. They received a call from someone who had witnessed a man dumping the body. There was a red smiley face spray painted on the dumpster, like it was mocking the whole thing." She cleared a lump from her throat. "Sorry, this is hard. They're going to review the footage of the surrounding area to see if they can find any clues but wanted to chat with you three first. We all presume you have knowledge worth sharing, since you suspected this was going to happen."

"Did you say the footage *surrounding* the area?" Arielle asked.

Samia looked down and nodded. "I'm afraid the body was dumped in an area where no cameras patrol."

The room fell silent. Arielle knew they'd no longer be able to keep anything a secret. This murder was deliberate, and the locals now knew that.

Officer Smith batted his eyes and crossed his hands. "We need to know any suspects you may have knowledge of."

He spoke in such a stern voice that even Arielle worried he might cause trouble if he didn't get his way. And for all her training and expertise, she had never learned how to fight and disarm a robot.

"I didn't bring any files," Arielle said. "But I have a photo on my phone. Does the name Doyle Grady by chance ring any bells?"

The two officers looked at Samia, who only offered a shrug in response. "Sorry, never heard the name."

Arielle pulled out her phone, still nervous they might suspect her outdated technology, and scrolled through her photos until she landed on the portrait of Doyle. She held it up, and Samia's eyes immediately widened.

Samia touched her lips with a trembling hand.

"You know who this is," Officer Smith said.

Samia nodded. "That's Elyod Murray. He works here. Oh my God, I think I'm going to be sick."

She sunk into her chair, eyes glued to Arielle's phone.

"I'm sorry," Selena said. "Elyod Murray? What does he do here?"

"Elyod has worked here for about a year now. No, that can't

be him."

"Can we run his face through your recognition software and see what it pulls up?" Arielle asked. "Your company touts a ninety-nine percent accuracy rate."

"A brilliant idea," said Officer Jones. "Where can we do that?"

Samia had to climb out of her seat to gain solid footing. *Poor girl's day has been completely turned upside down,* Arielle thought, rising to join her.

"Can you send that photo to me?" Samia asked. "I can get my computer and we can run it through the software in here."

"That should work," Arielle said. "Does email work?"

Samia had started walking and stopped. "Can you not just tap it to me?"

Arielle looked over at Felix, praying he knew what the hell Samia was talking about.

Without hesitation, he said, "We lost our phones in an unfortunate accident right before coming to OKC. They gave us some replacements that are a bit...old. No tapping feature, but we can send emails." He gave an innocent shrug that said *This is out of my hands.*

Samia frowned. "Okay then. Email it over. Like the old days."

She left the conference room, and Officer Smith immediately spoke. "We were surprised to see the NSB here before a crime actually happened."

The three Angels exchanged glances. "Is there a question?" Arielle asked.

"No question. Just an observation. A most fascinating observation. The NSB typically takes forever to arrive at the scene of a crime. Yet here you are. The body isn't even cold yet."

"Well, we've been following the suspect around the country for some time now," Arielle said, questioning what her life had become now she had to explain herself to a robot. "We had hoped we got here in time, but it appears not."

"Or just in time, depending how you look at it," Officer Jones said, tapping the table with a stiff finger. "The killer can't be too far. You said his name is Doyle Grady. Is that an alias or a real name?"

"It's his real name," Arielle said. "He must be using an alias to work here."

Selena slapped the table, startling everyone else. "Elyod! Why didn't I realize it sooner?! It's *Doyle* spelled backwards."

Felix nodded. "Nice job, Selena. I didn't make that connection, either. I'm sure whatever we find now is only going to confirm what we know."

Samia returned with a laptop clutched in her hand.

Arielle was relieved to see a piece of technology she recognized. Felix shifted in his seat, and she nudged him with her knee to keep him under control. He had become like a starving animal in a room full of treats with each product of enhanced technology they encountered.

"Okay," Samia said, sitting down and flipping the laptop open. "Let me open my *email*. It's been a while."

They watched as her finger glided across the touchscreen. Samia must have cried again while she was getting the computer, her eyes redder and more swollen than when she had left.

"Would you like to come see how this all works?" Samia asked the Angels.

"Absolutely," Felix said, jumping out of his seat and hurrying around the table. Arielle and Selena followed with a normal level of enthusiasm, and the three gathered in a tight huddle behind Samia.

On one half of her screen was a program called Recog2099. The software appeared user-friendly, with a lone button to upload a picture into the database.

"Our program does many things," Samia explained. "But uploading a picture for it to identify is one of the simplest tasks it can perform."

On the second half of the screen she tapped open the attachment from Arielle's email, Doyle's face filling the space. She quickly held a finger on the picture and dragged it over to the software.

Samia closed the picture and expanded Recog2099 to fill the entire screen.

"How long does it usually take?" Felix asked.

"Only about a minute," Samia said. "We're working on making it faster, but this seems to be the best we can get it. I mean, it is scraping the photos for nearly every citizen in the country."

"Every single person?" Selena asked, her jaw hanging open.

Samia nodded confidently. "The federal government contracted with us and enforced laws around the country. Any driver's license, ID, or passport photos get uploaded into the system. People receiving government assistance—which is anyone who lives outside the fence—are required to take an annual photo purely so it can be included in the database. There are even talks of the government trying to get photos from school IDs, grocery store memberships, you name it. If a picture is taken of you, they want it."

Arielle bit her lip. She wanted to call out the obvious issues of invading every ounce of privacy people had, but she didn't know this society's views on such a topic. Maybe everyone was fine with it. The rich had their dream lives free of crime and poor people. Everyone else had just enough money to live an interesting life. Was any of this sustainable? She had no way of knowing after only a few hours in 2098.

The laptop chimed, showing Doyle's photo along with his full profile information.

"Elyod Murray," Samia said, shaking her head. "It's him. One hundred percent match."

"Okay," Arielle said. "For starters, his name is Doyle Grady. This Elyod Murray is a new alias he's using. Did he have any connections with Rowland?"

"Yes," Samia replied, her voice shaking. "They worked in the same department. Elyod is the executive assistant for our VP of engineering. It doesn't mean he'd have a ton of direct interaction with Rowland, but he could have if he wanted."

Samia buried her face in her hands and pulled her hair in frustration.

"Can this software tell us if the two were ever seen together?" Felix asked.

"It can," Samia murmured. "But a query like that can take hours to run. I'm happy to start that, but I may not have any information until tomorrow."

"Do it," Arielle said. "We also need the locations of all the areas in town *not* under surveillance. Along with all known entryways and exits—legal or not."

Samia's eyes fluttered as she processed these requests. "I can help with the surveillance matter, but I'm not sure about illegal entryways." She glanced at the robot officers to see how closely they were paying attention to her.

But the cops had turned to watch the three Angels, ignoring Samia.

"Stop treating us like we're invisible," Officer Smith said, standing up. "We're more than capable of handling this investigation. Better, in fact, because we actually live here."

Arielle tossed up her hands. "I'm not here to step on your toes. Only to help."

Even though the robots showed no physical signs of emotion, Arielle felt the bastard judging her. Were they even capable of judgment? Was this robot calculating Arielle and her team and jumping to its own conclusions? Or was it just scanning her face to load a database full of her information—whatever fictional background the Road Runners had created for her?

"We'll be on our way," said Officer Jones, standing next to her partner. "We know of the illegal pathways into the city and will check them out. If you three want to go to the scene of the crime, you're more than welcome. The body was found off Second Street, between Classen Boulevard and Francis Avenue. It's an old industrial park. Lots of abandoned buildings."

Arielle jotted down the intersection. "Samia, can you provide us with all the information on that file for Doy—Elyod? I assume it has his address, phone number, and anything else that might help."

Samia nodded. "I'll respond to your email with that attached. And I'll follow up tomorrow with anything that query turns up about them being seen together."

"Thank you," Arielle said. "We're going to head out and see what we can track down. It was nice meeting you all."

"Likewise," Officer Smith said as Samia walked the three Angels to the door.

"I wish you three the best of luck," she told them. "Let me know if there's anything else we can do to help. I'll be up all night. No way I'm falling asleep."

Selena reached out and rubbed Samia on the shoulder. "We'll sort this out and bring justice for Rowland."

Samia's eyes welled up immediately at the mention of her employee's name. "Thank you."

They left the conference room. Arielle looked over her shoulder as the door was closing and caught a nasty glare from Officer Jones.

Doyle sped through downtown Oklahoma City, blasting Five Finger Death Punch through the speakers, banging his head to the beat. His heart was hammering in his chest, prompting him to crank up the music to drown it out.

The cameras all around town were on him. He could feel them watching like a stalker hiding around the corner, waiting to pounce. Were Arielle and her goons hunting him down? Had the authorities been dispatched to assist?

Tears streaked down Doyle's face as he bit his bottom lip.

Fucking Arielle, he thought. *She arrived way too early. It wasn't supposed to be this rushed.*

"Damn you, little miss perfect!" he screamed over Ivan Moody's manic howling.

He had at least gotten away with three murders in 1898 but was staring at only one completed job in this futuristic hellhole. The next two victims were already chosen, but he had no way of knowing where to find them at this precise moment. And for Doyle, one thing had become overwhelmingly clear during the past hour. He needed to get out of this year.

But Doyle was a man of structure and intense planning. He'd even had the backup plan of how he was going to dump Rowland's body in case he needed to rush. Which he did.

Fucking Arielle.

Yet, he never planned for Arielle's arrival so soon. Being a time-traveling serial killer had proven more complex than originally expected. 1898 was difficult because of how small the town was. He might have been able to hang around longer if he had chosen a place like New York City where he could easily hide and not every single person knew him by name.

And while these big cities in the future had drastically reduced populations, he couldn't step foot outside a fucking restaurant without being spotted on camera. And from what he had learned about the Quantum Works software, his face was likely already arranged to trigger alarms if it showed up anywhere around the city.

I can't just leave here. Not yet. Not with two more kills to make. It was supposed to be three in each city. Three at each stop.

Doyle squeezed the steering wheel and pulled off the road, not even sure where he was. He had only been pressing on the gas pedal as hard as he could, swerving around corners, blasting through red lights. No. Fucks. Given.

His chest heaved, sweat breaking out on his forehead.

Am I dying? he wondered. Drawing in breath suddenly felt like an extreme task. He let go of the steering wheel to find his hands quivering beyond control and had to make a conscious effort to lower the music's volume. He gasped. The walls in the car were closing in on him. Around his destiny. *I can't be dying. This is not how I leave this fucked up world.*

Doyle fidgeted with the switch to roll down the window, couldn't get a hold of it, then flung open the entire door. The chilly night air splashed across his face, bringing immediate relief. A car drove by, blaring its horn at him for hanging out halfway in the road.

"Up yours, jackass!" Doyle shouted at the fading taillights, flipping the bird and feeling somewhat of a return to his normal self.

He closed his door, not wanting any cameras to catch sight of his face, then looked around. In the rear-view mirror, he saw familiar glowing red neon lights running along the edges of an older brick building. A grin spread slowly across his face.

"Rowland, you sentimental son of a bitch!" He cackled. "What are the odds of me driving in circles only to end up at Rizzuto's? This is what I call destiny. Let's call whatever just happened a panic attack and get back to business."

His stomach fluttered with excitement as he leaned over and pulled open the glove compartment where he kept two loaded pistols. He grabbed both, dropping one on his lap, and cocking the other in his right hand.

Could this have played out any more perfectly?

Doyle licked his lips and turned the car around, parking along the curb of the Italian restaurant. The place was packed with people stopping in for a bite after work. Couples cozied up in the booths. Robot servers carried trays of food through the aisles. The waiting area just inside the entrance had at least a dozen cramped in tightly—they normally spilled out onto the sidewalk during the summer months.

Doyle's heart continued to drum, but it was no longer from worry. No. He was going to leave his mark before departing from 2098. His skyrise apartment building, which was purchased under a name Quantum Works didn't know of, was only six blocks away. He could carry out his business, hop in the car, and speed to the building that housed the time portal.

Miami will be better. Lots of people. No cameras at every corner.

I can carry out an undisturbed plan of attack and finally lure Arielle into a trap. This will be one the bitch won't see coming!

Doyle cocked the second pistol before inching the car forward a few more feet.

"Look at all those sweet, innocent people," he said. "Just sitting there, completely unaware their lives are about to change forever. These rich cocksuckers deserve what they get."

Doyle opened his car door, circled around the front bumper, and started firing both guns simultaneously into the restaurant's waiting area. He imagined the alarms going off inside of Quantum Works. Robots and people running around in a panic, calling the authorities, calling Arielle, calling their fucking mommies.

There were only six rounds loaded into each gun, so after he had emptied them, he dropped them both down the storm drain directly in front of the restaurant, and hopped back into the car.

Half the diners inside stampeded out of the building, while the others cowered under the tables.

Doyle sped off, laughing, shouting, pounding the ceiling of the car in pure delight. No, he didn't get to carry out the precise murders he had wanted, but this shoot and run provided a comparable thrill.

Chaos. That's all he wanted. And he got it.

Realizing his speeding car was responsible for the shooting, a handful of Rizzuto's patrons broke into desperate sprints to chase after him. From the mirror, Doyle could see the man leading the charge take a tumble, which then tripped up two others running behind.

Doyle cackled at the sight. Human bowling pins. If only

he had time to turn around and run them over. The thought made his mouth pool with saliva, but going back now would only guarantee his capture. He needed to drive directly to his apartment building and leave this year behind. Leave Arielle scratching her perfect little head, wondering where she had gone wrong once more.

"Sorry, cupcake, our game isn't over yet. Not until I say it is!"

Doyle couldn't keep a smile off his face as he passed skyscrapers in a blur. He didn't need to run red lights because everything had lined up green for him. Sometimes the universe throws a bone your way after all. He was three blocks from freedom and had never felt so alive. The car might as well have been one of those ridiculous flying ones, because Doyle Grady was floating on a cloud. Nothing could stop him. Not Arielle Lucila. Not Quantum Works. Not even the semitruck that made an illegal turn to cut off Doyle.

"Bless you, kind sir!" Doyle said as he swerved around the truck, flipping off the driver.

The engine roared in the silent night. Sirens wailed in the distance, but Doyle didn't hear them. He didn't give a shit about them, in fact.

The building came into sight straight ahead. A glass exterior that looked black in the night, a glowing sign that welcomed visitors to the Mirage Lofts. *Such a hoity-toity name.*

Doyle slammed on the brakes as he approached the building, took a sharp right turn and sped one more block to enter the underground parking garage. Now there were more sirens, and they were drawing nearer. He had hoped the local police would be slow to react, considering it had been several years since they had to encounter an actual spontaneous crime. But they hadn't spared a second in their pursuit. Someone at the police station, probably another shitbag robot, was following him during his cruise through downtown via the cameras. The Quantum Works software even made split-second predictions of where someone in a high-speed chase might drive to. The robots could then read this information and provide the best routes to take to cut off their pursuit.

"Not today!" Doyle howled with glee as he swerved into the parking garage, stopping in the first open space he found—a reserved spot for future residents. He jumped out of the car, engine still running, sirens growing louder.

They know where I am! he thought, running toward the back of the garage that spanned at least two dozen rows of parked cars. An erection pulsed as he ran. The elevator shaft conjoined with a small security office. Doyle needed the stairwell in the back corner, but the security office door swung open, a young man barreling out with terror on his face.

"Hey!" the guard screamed, his voice echoing across the garage. "Hey, mister! Stop right there!"

Doyle didn't slow down, only looking over his shoulder and waving a flailing hand. That poor guard had no chance of catching him.

BANG!

The gun blast made Doyle trip and roll, but the adrenaline brought him immediately back to his feet to continue forward.

A second gun shot came, and Doyle looked back to see the guard standing with the gun drawn from just outside the security office door.

A third shot, and he felt the bullet whiz by his head, maybe six inches.

He never expected some lonely guard, probably a college

student doing his homework, to have such an excellent shot. Where would he have learned such a skill? The shooting ranges had closed down once they banned firearms for all citizens. Even the police had to venture outside the fence to hit the range.

A fourth shot fired, causing a nearby florescent light to explode into hundreds of shards.

"Shit!" Doyle cried, covering his head. "Stop shooting, dammit!"

This time when he looked back, his heart nearly stopped. Next to the guard were four police officers, all with their guns drawn. Running behind them was Arielle Lucila and her team of crackpots. How he wished he could grab Arielle and pull her through the time portal.

Miami, he promised himself.

"OKC Police!" one officer shouted. "Stop and put your hands up, or we'll shoot!"

Doyle grinned. There were at least forty yards between them, and he only had a few more feet to go. Two more rows of parked cars, and there stood the door to the stairwell.

"So long!" Doyle shouted, and started running in zigzags through the rest of the lot.

A barrage of gunfire immediately rained down. More lights exploded. Holes appeared out of nowhere in the concrete walls, sending plumes of gray powder in every direction. The voices behind him cried out in desperation, a jumble of panic.

But none of it mattered. Doyle hit the crossbar that opened the door to the stairwell, skidded to a stop, then ran around the corner of the landing where a door marked for maintenance stood. He clutched the handle and twisted anxiously, flinging the door open and barreling into the maintenance room. Wires and pipes ran in every direction, and Doyle crouched low to crawl beneath a hanging bundle of cords that was at least four feet by four feet thick. Their warmth brushed along his back as he crawled, inching his way toward destiny.

The maintenance room stretched back thirty feet, and he crawled the entire way, gasping for air as the cords pressed down heavily onto his back. The heat rose, practically burning his face. This hidden time portal was just small enough to crawl through.

Doyle made his way through a thin layer of powder, his limbs leaving subtle trails in the residue. The archway stood only eighteen inches off the ground, concealed by the hanging cords. He dragged himself toward it, reaching out with shaky hands that grasped its edges, and pulled his body through.

Doyle vanished from 2098 without a trace.

Chapter 24

When the Angels had stepped out of the Quantum Works building, they heard sirens whining in the distance. An emergency broadcast system announced a shooting had just occurred at Rizzuto's restaurant, only a few blocks from their location.

"Let's go," Arielle said, not waiting for anyone to protest. They ran to the restaurant and arrived moments after the police. News reporters were already interviewing survivors of the attack, where witnesses described a black Mercedes that sped off after a man fired two guns and tossed them into the storm drain. A team of forensics was already preparing to head into the sewers to search for the weapons.

Arielle pulled out her NSB badge and flashed it to the first officer she found on the sidewalk, jotting notes from a witness.

The officer, this one human, examined the badge with a raised eyebrow. "How can I help you?" he asked in a slightly annoyed tone.

"Do we know where the suspect went?" Arielle asked.

"Headed south," the officer replied, keeping his eyes on his notepad and continuing to write. He had to act too good for the NSB, especially with his colleagues around.

"I need to borrow a car," Arielle said. "We just arrived and haven't had a chance to get one."

This statement made the officer look up, confusion inter-twining with a crooked smile. "A car, huh? Well, I'm not a rental agency. I think there's one a few blocks west from here."

"Look, officer, I'm not here to cause you any trouble. You and I both know I have the right to confiscate a vehicle for the purpose of chasing after any suspect deemed a threat to the public—which this man is. I know how to use the radio system in a patrol car. I will find you when we're done and bring it back to you, wherever you are. You can catch a ride from another officer if you need to leave here."

The officer bit his bottom lip and drew a long breath. "Whatever, lady. I guess I don't have a say in the matter. Not sure why you even asked."

"I need the keys, please," Arielle said, growing impatient with this man's ego.

The officer shook his head while he dug into his pockets, pulling out the keys and handing them over as he rolled his eyes.

"Thank you," Arielle said. "And I asked because I was raised to be polite. Like I said, I'll track you down after and personally bring your car back."

The man snorted a rude laugh before turning away and entering the restaurant. Arielle didn't dare look at the scene inside. Having survived a similar, senseless crime, she already knew what the air inside must feel like. Shock. Fear. Guilt for surviving while dead bodies lay on the floor. But the sudden abandonment of everything always drove home a sick feeling in her stomach. When she had survived at the mall shooting, she saw random objects scattered across the floor. A half-eaten corn dog. Shopping bags. A tipped over stroller. They all told a story. They all remained specific memories of that unfortunate day.

She'd see similar things inside the restaurant if she ventured in. Knocked over glasses. Partially eaten dishes. Toppled chairs.

"Arielle?" Felix asked, tapping Arielle on the arm. "Are we going?"

Arielle snapped out of her trance. "Sorry. Yes, let's go."

They all climbed into the patrol car, Felix taking the backseat. When Arielle turned on the vehicle, the radio immediately cried out with the worried voice of dispatch. "Suspect is headed south toward the Mirage Lofts. All available officers head there immediately!"

The dispatch rattled off the address, which then populated on the car's GPS, along with the three best routes and small square symbols representing other vehicles on the road.

"Hell yeah!" Felix shouted from the back. "That's awesome!"

Arielle put the car into gear and sped off just like Doyle had minutes earlier. Dispatch repeated the instruction two more times before announcing the suspect had entered the parking garage at the Mirage Lofts. Elevator access in the building would be turned off.

"Why would he go into the parking garage?" Felix asked as Arielle drove ninety miles per hour toward their destination. The emergency broadcast had served its purpose. The streets were empty of anything not related to the unfolding crime. Only flashing lights were visible on the roads, and they were all headed to the same place.

It only took another sixty seconds for Arielle to arrive at

the Mirage Lofts, where she parked among the cluster of police vehicles huddled outside the garage entrance. Dozens of officers were either running into the garage or holding their ground with guns fixed at the entrance.

"We're going in," Arielle said as she killed the engine and jumped out of the patrol car.

Felix cried out something in response, but Arielle didn't care. She knew the only reason Doyle would have run himself into a dead end was because it wasn't actually a dead end. The building he chose couldn't have been random. With the discovery of an underground quarter-mile tunnel in 1898, Arielle no longer underestimated the intelligence and planning of Doyle Grady.

She ran down the ramp into the garage, finding a row of more cops with their guns drawn. Arielle filed in behind them, Felix and Selena joining her seconds later.

Doyle was across the garage, shouting something inaudible before he turned and ran toward a door to a stairwell. Arielle recoiled at the cacophony of gunfire that rang out. Felix and Selena had dropped to the ground and were covering their heads. But Arielle never broke her gaze from Doyle.

His black Mercedes stood idling right beside them, the driver's door still wide open.

He parked here and ran all the way across. The car is a decoy. He wanted to go through that door all along.

Nearly all the officers broke into a dash toward Doyle, screaming as the door he had entered shut gently behind him.

Arielle broke into a sprint, a couple of cops shouting after her.

"We're with the NSB!" Felix called over his shoulder as he and Selena chased after their leader.

Some other cops joined in the pursuit, but they didn't know what to look for. Arielle expected one of two things. Either Doyle was leading them into a trap, or he would be "missing" entirely, leaving the police to scratch their heads.

With this many people involved, Arielle doubted a trap had been laid out for her.

They reached the stairwell door, Arielle crashing into the crossbar to fling it open. She spun around, looking for any exit points, listening for footsteps barreling up the stairs.

He's not running up the stairs like some common criminal.

Felix and Selena barged into the stairwell, panting for breath.

"A warning next time," Felix said between gasps for air, "would be nice."

"Where did he go?" Arielle asked, nodding toward the maintenance door. "Let's enter with caution."

"Arielle," Selena said, stepping forward and grabbing her by the arm. "Are you sure about this? There are cops here who can take the risk of going into that room. Robot cops who have no actual life to risk."

"This isn't for them," Arielle replied. "Besides, I doubt Doyle is hiding in this room waiting to shoot me. He tossed his guns in the storm drain. He's unarmed, which is why I think the time portal must be in here. Although how it remains hidden from the public is up for debate."

"Another time portal?" Felix asked. "I know we were expecting one, but in this building? Not likely."

Arielle didn't need to listen to any more doubt and proceeded forward, drawing her gun while pressing her ear against the door.

Silence.

She nodded to Felix and Selena before dropping her shoulder into the door to force it open. It glided with no resistance and revealed an abandoned room full of wires, cables, pipes, and drains.

Some of the other police officers had just entered the stairwell, shouting their commands for Doyle to come out with his hands up.

Two rushed into the maintenance room, looked around, and left. Apparently, they refused to see the endless possibilities in front of them. Even if Doyle had no time travel abilities, he could have easily climbed the drainpipes into the ceiling and now be venturing along the building's plumbing. Same with the air ducts and the HVAC system. But Arielle knew better.

The police may have seen an empty room with no suspect, but she knew Doyle had to have disappeared from this very spot.

"What are you thinking?" Selena asked, looking in every direction.

Arielle drew a deep sigh. "This is a big room. I'm not sure why those cops left so quickly, but that's fine. We can't exactly look for a time portal in front of others. Thoughts on where that could be? Could something like that fit above the drains in the ceiling?"

Felix looked up and nodded. "It's possible, assuming they made time portals smaller than the one we found in 1898. Logistically, a portal just needs to be small enough to fit through."

Arielle shuffled over to what looked like the main drain and started climbing. The climb wasn't as simple as she had thought. The exterior of the drain was slick, and she couldn't get any grip, sliding back down like a firefighter in slow motion.

"Shit," Arielle said, taking a step back to examine the drain. "I thought for sure that's where he had gone. Unless he had some special gloves on, it doesn't appear so."

"Are there any ladders in here?" Selena asked, spinning around to scan the area.

"None," Felix replied, still looking up. "I'm not convinced he had a way up there. He must have remained on the ground."

"Are we even sure he came in here?" Selena asked. "He could have gone up even just one more floor and is hiding in a different maintenance room."

Sweat trickled down Arielle's face and she wiped it away with her sleeve. "I can't tell because I've been running so much, but is it hot in here? Hotter than it should be? Felix, are you familiar with these kinds of rooms?"

Felix shrugged. "I've been in plenty of these rooms before and they all vary. Some are freezing, others are ovens. It just depends on the building and where exactly the room is. It *is* warm in here, but we don't have a baseline to compare it to. What about thinking lower instead of high?"

He dropped to a knee and examined the room from the level of a small child. "Crawl spaces galore," he said, shaking his head. "Technically, someone could fit under all the pipes. They leave enough room for maintenance workers to service any leaks as they come up. Hell, he could even fit below that bundle of cords if he really squeezed under them. Both the cords and pipes run back pretty far."

"And what are the cords for?" Selena asked. "We don't want to cut power to the building by accident."

Felix stood up and strolled to the bundle of cords. "What *isn't* here?" he replied with a chuckle. "Power cords, phone lines, DSL cables. Some of this *has* to be outdated by now. It looks like they've just been combining new wires as they add new systems to the building. It's not a hazard, but it's a definite waste of space."

"And which do you think gets less traffic?" Arielle asked. "The cords or the pipes?"

"Definitely the cords," Felix said. "The pipes should be under a regular maintenance schedule to check for issues. There's no such thing for all these wires. They would only get looked at if there was an issue, which is rarely related to the physical wires."

"Well, are you gonna get down there and check it out?" Arielle asked, nudging Felix with her elbow.

He crossed his arms and laughed. "You want the biggest one of us to climb under all those cords? Try again."

Arielle looked at Selena. "We're the same size."

"Then I guess you're taking this one," Selena said with a wink. "I'll have to owe you. No way in hell I'm going near a time portal, if that's what is hiding back there."

Arielle nodded. "Alright then. Me it is."

She dropped to all fours and army crawled toward the bundle of low-hanging cords, the bottom nearly scraping the floor.

"Take your time," Felix called out just as the door swung back open. Officer Smith stepped in and immediately scanned the room.

He saw the bottom half of Arielle's legs sticking out from underneath the cords. "What are you three doing in here?" he asked, looking from the ceiling to the floor and everything in between.

"Looking for the suspect," Felix replied casually.

The robot cop looked in the direction Arielle was crawling,

narrowing his eyes. "Well, he's not in this room. You're wasting your time."

Officer Smith spun around and left as abruptly as he had arrived.

"I don't think he likes you as much as you like him," Selena said with a giggle as the door slammed shut.

"What's going on back there?" Arielle cried out, the weight of the cords pressing into her back.

"Oh, nothing!" Selena replied.

Arielle could barely hear the response from her position. The cords provided a steady warmth along her back, a welcome sensation amid the cold weather blanketing Oklahoma City at the moment.

The crawling became more burdensome the deeper she went into the cords. The muscles in her arms burned as she pulled her body through what might as well have been a swimming pool of mud. Each movement required focused strength. She grew hotter with each stride forward, believing it resulted from the impromptu workout.

But after a whole two minutes of crawling, it suddenly felt like someone had opened a furnace.

"Can you guys hear me?" Arielle shouted. "I'm burning up back here."

"Yes!" Felix called back. "Go slow."

So she did. After crawling another three feet, the cords suddenly rose off the floor and ran up along the wall, disappearing into the ceiling where they branched out to the rest of the building. Right below the sloped bundle of cords was an archway only two feet tall and wide.

"Holy shit," Arielle whispered to herself. She had seen pictures of time portals in text books, part of the broad training all new Road Runners went through. But to have one directly in front of her, the heat blasting across her face, a universe of unknown possibilities waiting on the other side...

She couldn't deny the temptation to crawl right through it, like the portal had a magnetic pull on her.

Come through! We'll have a grand time! she imagined the portal saying in a most welcoming voice. Even for a time traveler, Arielle had little spontaneity thanks to her line of work. Sure, the locations and eras changed, but every mission was just another day at the office.

With the portal in front of her, she considered what life could be like if she vanished into it. How long would it take for Selena and Felix to realize what she had done? Would they go after her? Would the Road Runners have any way of tracking her down if she used a time portal?

The thoughts made her back breakout in gooseflesh despite the scorching heat. She climbed another foot closer, the portal just out of her arm's reach. The light-colored powder they had seen in the Dallas shed lay scattered across the floor.

She scooped up a handful, examining it, wondering what it meant. For Arielle, solving mysteries had become a way of life, and she was refreshed to be holding something she couldn't quite wrap her mind around.

Come in! the imaginary voice from the portal called out. Or was it imaginary? *Come see what awaits!*

As much as she wanted to, a peek at a new life would have to wait. She rose to her knees and hollered toward where Felix and Selena were standing.

"He's gone!"

Chapter 25

Five minutes later, Arielle emerged, covered in sweat and patches of the sawdust.

"You look like a powdered doughnut," Selena said with a chuckle as she helped Arielle get to her feet.

She brushed off the grime from her clothes and arms.

"So, he's gone?" Felix asked. "Does that mean there really is a portal back there?"

Arielle nodded. "And it was just like you said. Small enough to crawl through—not much else."

Felix scrunched his brow and stared at the bundle of cords. "I don't understand why this portal is here. The owner of this building must be a time traveler. There's no other explanation."

"That's a problem for another day," Arielle said. "Doyle's not in this building. We need to go to his house and see what else we can find there. Hopefully something that might give us some insight."

"Let's go then," Selena said, turning around and opening the door. The police lingered at the ramp that exited the parking garage. Doyle's abandoned vehicle remained in the same place, a team of forensics now scrutinizing it with rubber gloves.

They crossed through the garage, strolled up the ramp to curious glances from the local law enforcement—they likely hated the NSB, judging by some of their expressions—and returned to the patrol car.

Arielle punched in the address to Doyle's house, delighted to see it was only a five-minute drive from the Mirage Lofts. She kept her lips pursed tight while driving across town. Guilt had crept into her conscience. Why had she acted like she wanted to disappear through a time portal to leave her life behind? She couldn't dare tell Felix and Selena about it, either. How would they react if their leader expressed a desire to leave what so many considered a dream life?

"Everything okay?" Felix asked. Arielle hadn't even realized he was in the passenger seat this time.

"I'm fine," she said shortly. She shook her head, knowing she needed to give them more than that. "I'm just pissed he got away again. Disappearing through a time portal. Is that a coward move or genius? I still haven't decided."

"It's the move of a twisted individual," Felix said. "Don't beat yourself up. If you're what he really wants, he has to eventually stop running."

Arielle squeezed the steering wheel, flying down the road. "Are we both making the same move? Everything is pointing to a showdown in Miami of 1998. Does he also feel most comfortable there because it's the closest to our Original Time? My biggest frustration is not knowing how he's thinking. Normally, once we figure that out, the mission becomes clear. But not this time."

"We're fine," Selena said from the backseat in a tone that didn't suggest she believed her own words. "We knew this wasn't going to be easy. Sure, it's probably more challenging than expected, but we're making progress. In Dallas, we never saw him. Here, we caught a quick glimpse. That tells me we caught him off guard. No way he intended for us to see him."

"That was the first time I've seen him since 2019," Arielle said. "And it felt so weird."

"Wait," Felix said, sitting up stiff. "You need to tell us everything. I know you've been hiding the truth, and I don't know why."

Arielle squeezed the wheel even tighter. "This was never supposed to be your battle. Neither of you. What happened between me and Doyle is our own business, and I can't believe he's dragging you two into this."

"We're a team, Arielle," Selena said. "We'd never leave you to fend for yourself, even if we know you can."

"I can't go into all the details right now, but Doyle and I had made a deal during our days in training together. He had become like a big brother to me, and I genuinely wanted to help him. But after he got kicked out of training, I was forbidden from speaking to him. I had to completely cut him out of my life, or risk joining him on the outside of the time travel world. And I couldn't do that. I *needed* the Road Runners, so he was left out."

A tear streamed down Arielle's cheek as she kept her focus on the road, Felix and Selena falling silent for a few seconds.

"If he disappears through another time portal, I'm going after him," Arielle said. "I'm going to keep my flask of Juice on me, just in case."

"You can't just go through one of those things without a full understanding of how they work," Felix pleaded.

"I'll be fine," Arielle said. "If Doyle has been doing it with no issues, then why shouldn't I?"

"Because what if that's his trap?" Selena asked. "Could he know you're not familiar with time portals? If so, he could use that to his advantage. You always try to expose and take advantage of your target's weaknesses. Is that not what he's doing to us?"

Selena was right. That was one of the first things taught in their training. Doyle would have learned that, but did he remember after all this time? And not just remember the concept, but the actual in-depth instruction that explained how to best use this approach?

Arielle shuddered as they turned away from downtown towards Doyle's neighborhood. "How long do you think he's been watching me?" she asked. "If he's had this vendetta against me all this time, who's to say he hasn't been following me during all these missions to understand me better? Following *us*?"

"I see your concern," Felix said. "But there's nothing we can do about any of that right now. Instead, we should focus on how to level the playing field. What are *his* weaknesses and how can we expose them?"

They drove in a tense silence for the next minute, Arielle turning into Doyle's neighborhood and creeping along the streets. She went to the end of the road and turned into the driveway.

His house didn't have a single light on. Tall shrubs served as a privacy fence along the side of the house, but they had seen the next-door neighbor's front porch light turned on. Would they be worth asking some questions? How much did Doyle even show his face outside of this house?

"This definitely looks like the house of a serial killer," Selena said, craning her neck for a clear view.

"Do you think he lived in that building we were just at?" Felix asked. "What are the odds of him knowing exactly where that time portal was? We're not paying enough attention to that, but it was all going so fast. I just started piecing this together during the drive over. Why *wouldn't* he have lived in that building, knowing a time portal was in the basement? You really expect me to believe he lives way out here when his best chance of escape waits an entire five-minute drive away? I call bullshit. Or there is also a time portal in this house—which is unlikely because they never built them to be so close to each other. Only a handful of the bigger cities have multiple portals—places like New York, Los Angeles, Chicago. Definitely not Oklahoma City."

Arielle killed the engine and leaned back in the driver's seat. "This is what I'm talking about. Too many questions, with no clue where to find an answer. He could very well have this house plus a loft in that building. But we're so out of our element here. The technology has changed so drastically that I guess you don't even know where to begin a search for information like that."

"I could try to hack into the Quantum Works system," Felix said, staring mindlessly at the house. "But you're right. I have no knowledge of how any of this technology works. It's naïve to assume even the slightest of it is the same."

"Did they never have you go through classes about future technology?" Selena asked. "We had some about the future of acting when I was in training—it was really fascinating."

Felix shook his head. "Afraid not. They mentioned how the future of technology is constantly changing. There was no point in teaching any of it because it could all change by the next day, depending how the future played out."

"Let's not stress over this," Arielle said. "Doyle's already gone. What do we get out of sticking around here and trying to hack into Quantum Works? What we need is to make a firm plan of attack for when we arrive in 1998. No games, no guesses. What's Doyle's weakness? He doesn't have Juice. He can't jump to any era at will like we can. And that's what we need to use to our advantage."

"But the Road Runners don't share the information about time portal locations," Felix said. "At least not the specifics of the location. Not even Arielle has the level of clearance to receive that."

"Even for this mission?" Selena asked, astounded. "There is a serial killer on the loose using the time portals!"

"It doesn't matter," Arielle said. "They want the secret kept as tightly as possible. They don't trust anyone to have knowledge of these locations besides the commanders."

"What if you just talked to Commander Briar?" Selena asked. "Be real. We're not going to tell anyone about the portals, and letting Doyle continue to get away with using them is only going to increase the chances of the wrong person finding out about them. Are they really trusting a criminal to keep the secret? They should want him eliminated as quickly as possible, no matter what sacrifices need to be made."

"As strong as my relationship is with Commander Briar," Arielle said, "he's adamant about the secrets held within the Book of Time. He's told me high-level things that are in it but refuses to give details. I can ask, but it might be a waste of time."

"We're in 2098," Felix said. "What if the secrets have been shared? We can find out who the current commander is and see if they'll tell us. It might be worth a shot since we're already here."

"You want to travel across the country in this current state of affairs?" Arielle asked.

"How bad can it really be to fly from one city to another?" Felix replied. "It's not like we're hitchhiking down the highway."

"The Book of Time has the locations of the time portals?" Selena asked, ignoring the other two.

"To an extent, yes," Arielle said. "All the *known* time portals up to a certain point. Why?"

"Can we not find a way to get our hands on the book? We would only need it for a couple of minutes."

"That is a *major* violation," Arielle said, turning around to face Selena in the back. "We're talking Khronos Island if we get caught. Not worth it."

"Hold on a sec," Selena shot back, leaning forward. "Don't we know when the book was seized by the Road Runners from Chris Speidel's possession? Was there not a period when no one had the book?"

Arielle's eyes widened as she experienced a sudden jolt of hope. "Holy shit! You're right. I was *there*."

"What do you mean?" Felix asked, unbuckling his seat belt, incapable of moving his eyes away from Arielle.

Arielle let out a nervous laugh. "I can't believe that never occurred to me. Probably because that property brings back terrible memories. There was a massacre at Chris's house one day. I was part of a crew that had to stop by afterwards to help retrieve the dead bodies. We lost our lieutenant commander. He insisted on fighting in the field to bring down Chris. They ambushed us. Dozens of Revolters came barging out from behind the house when our team arrived. We never had a chance. It was a major turning point for the Road Runners. After that tragedy, Commander Briar became a madman trying to bring matters to an end—which he did. But the book was later recovered from this same house in a completely remote area of Idaho. And I know where it is."

"And you know a safe time we might get our hands on the book without causing a stir?" Felix asked, now on the front edge of his seat.

"I do," Arielle said with a smile. "A couple months later, I was on a mission with Commander Briar to monitor Chris. But Chris fled the property moments before we arrived. Me and Lieutenant Commander Herrera searched the grounds with a couple of others. I think there was about a twenty-minute gap between when Chris fled the place and we arrived. That's twenty minutes of undisturbed time all alone in the house with the Book of Time. I know which room it was found in, because a lot of things got boxed up to be examined later. I *saw* the book but thought nothing of it because it looks like any old book."

"We're going, right?" Selena asked like a giddy child wanting to stop for an ice cream on the way home.

Arielle looked at Felix, who had an equal amount of elation on his face.

"I don't know," Arielle said. "It's still pretty risky."

"It's not at all," Felix said immediately. "Twenty-minute window? We'll give ourselves fifteen. And I'll make us stick to it. It's worth a shot, and you know it. If we can block the time portal in Miami, we trap Doyle and end this."

Arielle considered this. She looked at Doyle's empty house, which no longer seemed to have any relevance to the mission. Her memories rushed back to her prior two visits to the former

Keeper of Time's house. She had thought she was done with him for good.

Arielle chewed on her bottom lip, in desperate need of a piece of gum. "Okay. Let's do it."

Chapter 26

They never entered Doyle Grady's house in Oklahoma City, as tempting as it was. He had evaded them once more, dancing through time without a care in the world.

Now was not the time for snooping around a house in 2098, when their target would have to be captured in 1998. Felix had argued there could be a relevant clue waiting inside, while Arielle decided they would not go in, much to Selena's delight. She believed anything they might find would only give them reason to remain in 2098, which was no longer part of the plan.

They had returned to the Road Runner office after another long walk back through the hidden tunnel. From there, they jumped to their present time, where Arielle logged on to a computer to pull details from the prior mission she had gone on with Commander Briar to stakeout Chris Speidel's house in 2021.

With the details in hand, they boarded a jet to Twin Falls, Idaho, where they landed and had to drive an hour south to the remote town of Three Creek. Upon landing they jumped back to 2021. The trip felt all too familiar for Arielle. Nostalgia crept in during the drive. The lieutenant commander they had lost that tragic day was more than a leader to Arielle.

Gerald Holmes had been a close friend since her first day with the Road Runners. He had been a trainer before moving up the ranks and specialized in hand-to-hand combat. The two bonded after several sparring sessions and started spending time together outside of training. Their friendship, while strong, ended abruptly when Gerald was promoted to the headquarters, eventually finding his way to the number two position for the organization, where he served under Commander Briar.

They had kept in touch, but hadn't seen each other in person until a chance meeting in the commander's office where Gerald recommended Arielle to assist on the missions to capture Chris Speidel. Looking back, Gerald had played a key part in getting Arielle the recognition needed to elevate her career to the next level. Nearly everyone who had worked on those missions to hunt Chris now held roles of considerable importance.

A tear streamed down Arielle's cheek as she remembered receiving the message from Commander Briar that Gerald had been killed. He had insisted she recuse herself from the job of cleaning up the scene and bringing the bodies home. But Arielle *wanted* to be there. For Gerald. She'd never forget arriving and looking down at her friend's lifeless body. She had broken down and cried for a minute while others did the same.

Am I cursed? Arielle wondered. *Everyone close to me dies.*

She looked at Selena in the rear-view mirror and at Felix by her side. Losing either of them would be the end of her world as she knew it. Selena liked to tease her for acting too motherly, but Arielle felt obliged to look out for them. Not just for their sake, but for her own. She understood that one day she'd have to say goodbye to her grandmother—that was the natural part of life. But she couldn't handle any more loss beyond the expected.

They arrived at Three Creek two minutes before three o'clock on a sunny afternoon. No sign welcomed them to the town with no official population count. But Arielle didn't need that or the GPS. She knew the way once they passed an abandoned shack on the side of the road.

"Two minutes early," Felix said, breaking a long silence. They had taken advantage of the flight from Oklahoma to Idaho by napping. Selena continued snoozing in the backseat during the drive, while Felix read through files about the mission Arielle had completed just two years earlier. "Nice driving."

Arielle tipped her head to the side. "That's all? I was hoping to cut off at least ten."

Felix laughed. They were right on time. Before falling asleep on the jet, Felix had made a schedule with precise times for where they needed to be. With only a fifteen-minute window of opportunity, they had to be strict.

Chris Speidel would walk out his front door at exactly 3:17. The past version of Arielle and her team would arrive at 3:39, but Felix wanted them out of the house by 3:32 to be safe.

"That's the house up there," Arielle said, her heart dropping into her stomach at the mere sight of it. The exterior was a faded brown, a lone lawn chair sat open on the front porch. A maple tree towered on the right side, blanketing the house with ample shade.

Arielle remembered the two bodies they had found behind that tree. Two Road Runners who had clearly tried hiding with no success once the ambush unfolded.

She floored the accelerator to speed by the house. Just knowing in this timeline Chris Speidel was still alive and strolling about inside made her shiver.

Selena stirred awake, stretching her arms wide with a yawn.

"Good morning," Arielle said. "Felix, remind us what happens next."

"We park a quarter mile south of the house," Felix replied, shifting in his seat with excitement. "We wait for 3:15 before starting our return to the house. Assuming we don't see a helicopter or something else arrive, Chris will leave by vehicle. Once we see that vehicle pull away, we make a beeline to the house. Arielle will lead us inside and to the room where the Book of Time is. From there, we'll have approximately fourteen minutes to flip through it and find what we need. I'll keep the time both on my phone and watch—just in case the past tries to get cute. Once those fourteen minutes are up, we close the book, put it back where we found it, and leave. We'll drive straight to the hangar in Twin Falls to prepare for Miami."

"A perfect plan," Arielle said, parking the car on the side of the road. There was nowhere to hide in Three Creek, aside from the two properties they had driven by. They were south of the house, knowing anyone leaving would need to drive north for the nearest airport in Twin Falls. An escape to the south would be careless, leaving Chris a target in the middle of nowhere for hundreds of miles.

Arielle turned the car around so it could face the direction of the house, a blip in the distance just ahead. They had binoculars to watch all activity.

"3:02," Felix announced, putting his phone down and drumming his fingers anxiously on the car door.

"We don't need a minute-by-minute update," Selena said.

"Time is fragile, especially right now," Felix replied calmly. "We have exactly zero seconds to spare. So forgive me for being on top of it."

"Relax, Felix," Arielle said. "I appreciate the sentiment, but it's okay for us to clear our minds for the next few minutes."

"Of course," Felix said, nodding silently to himself.

Ten minutes passed without a word. The tension had grown palpable in the car. Felix and Selena were likely on edge about the prospect of getting to read through the Book of Time. And while Arielle felt the same, she had even more stress about returning inside this house of horrors.

The house itself wasn't an issue, but everything it represented. So many people had been killed on both sides of this time war between the Road Runners and Revolters. These memories were supposed to remain in the past, but Arielle suspected there was no such concept for a time traveler. The past could always be revisited.

Her stomach twisted into knots as the clock struck 3:14, and Felix pulled out his binoculars.

"Looks like a car has arrived at the house," he said, lips pursed tightly. "I see one driver, and three men standing outside the car."

"His crew," Arielle said. "Chris never stayed by himself, especially when so many people out there were trying to kill him. Do you see *him*?"

"I don't think so," Felix replied. "He's supposed to have really white hair, right?"

"Correct."

"Oh, there he is!" Felix gasped. "He just walked out of the house and is talking with the men."

Arielle considered taking out her own binoculars but decided against it. Just because she was back in this time period didn't mean she needed to *see* Chris. He was there, unknowingly breathing in the last moments of his life. She didn't need to see it to believe it.

"Alright," Felix said, his upper lip now curled. "The men all got in the backseat, and Chris is looking at the house."

"I wonder if he knew he was never coming back," Arielle said.

"If he knew that," Selena replied, "wouldn't he have taken more care to hide these valuable items the Road Runners were about to find?"

Arielle shrugged. "Chris Speidel remains a mystery still to this day. He could time travel simply by thinking about it—a perk of being the Keeper of Time. But none of us understood how he used that ability. Like, why didn't he time travel at this moment instead of getting in a car? It was possible he had traveled into the future and saw his death. If he knew he was going to die, maybe he didn't care about any of his belongings. He was selfish and didn't care much for others. People were his pawns in this war, and he couldn't care less if his fellow Revolters died, so long as he stayed alive."

"Okay, he just got into the passenger seat and the car is pulling out," Felix said. "Heading northbound."

Arielle fired up the engine, hands trembling slightly as she gripped the steering wheel. "I'm going to park behind the house. My team lands their jet about a half-mile from the property, and I'd hate for them to see us while they're descending."

"Good call," Felix replied. "You're safe to go now."

Arielle wasted no time putting the car into gear and pulling back onto the road, speeding to the house, arriving in just thirty seconds. She drove around the maple tree and parked.

"We have an extra minute," Felix cried, looking at his watch. "Let's move!"

They all exited the car and marched around the side of the house like a military operative planning a sneak attack. Arielle grew lightheaded as she climbed up the solo step onto the porch. *What if the past pushes back? What if Chris turns around and finds us here, and we ruin everything Commander Briar did in bringing him to his death?*

Arielle didn't share these thoughts with the others, but the weight of the world seemed to have dumped itself upon her shoulders. That was their biggest risk. Changing the timeline of Chris Speidel's life. If he stayed alive because of their visit to his house, they'd all be on the first plane to Khronos Island without a question.

Felix stepped forward and twisted the knob on the door, pushing it. "You two find the book while I stand guard."

"You go in," Selena said, waving Felix off. "You're clearly much more excited than I am about seeing this book."

Felix furrowed his brow. "I ca—"

"Go," Selena demanded. "You're wasting time."

Felix smiled, then followed Arielle into the house.

They looked around, Arielle fighting for a grip over her emotions. The small kitchen to the left. Living room to the right. Narrow hallway straight ahead that led to the bedroom and a bathroom.

"This way," Arielle said, charging into the living room where a bookcase stood against the wall. It was a few inches shorter than Arielle, four feet wide, with three shelves full of books.

"Never would have guessed this homicidal maniac was a heavy reader," Felix commented, but Arielle paid him no attention. She didn't want to talk about Chris, and only wanted to get the details for the time portal so they could leave this house. Just standing in here made it feel like slugs were crawling on her skin.

She crouched for a better view of the options. The Book of Time had no text on the spine, a solid light red cover that was nearly pink after years of being passed around. She shared this information with Felix as she ran her fingers along each book.

"Don't tell me it's missing," Felix said, his face scrunched with concern as he examined the bookshelf.

"Found it!" Arielle gasped, pulling the book from the bottom shelf. Its tattered edges protected crisp pages hardened over what many believed were centuries. A two-inch hour glass was etched onto the front cover, like someone had done the work with a chisel.

"This is really it!" Felix cried out, his anticipation boiling over.

Arielle placed the book gently on top of the bookshelf and flipped open the cover. The pages were yellowing around the edges but remained in fair shape. The contents were still easy to read.

The first page had only a few words that filled the entire space. *IF YOU ARE NOT THE INTENDED RECEIVER OF THIS BOOK, CLOSE IT NOW. FAILURE TO COMPLY WILL RESULT IN HARSH PUNISHMENT, INCLUDING DEATH.*

Reading these words sent a wave of panic through Arielle. She knew, just as well as any other Road Runner, that the Book of Time was as sacred as the original Articles of Confederation in the United States. It was the book that glued together the fabric of the entire world of time travelers. Their original rules and guidelines, storied to have been passed down by Khronos himself, all lived within these pages. Arielle was skeptical the Greek god of time had any involvement with the book, but she lacked proof to suggest otherwise. She supposed believing in the legend was the closest thing the world of time travelers had to a religion.

Felix checked his watch as Arielle flipped the page. "We have twelve minutes. This book is what, three hundred pages? How are we supposed to find anything?"

"It has a table of contents. Relax."

Arielle was the one who needed relaxing. One part of her mind was focused on the book, another on the world outside the house, and yet another on what her life could end up like if they were to get caught.

"Everything is handwritten," Felix said, studying the table of contents and pointing at the header for *TIME PORTALS* starting on page ninety-two.

Arielle flipped to the page, the musty stench of old books wafting to their noses.

The first page of the time portal section showed a sketch drawing of a time portal that looked fairly similar to the one they had seen in the shed in 1898. Darkness filled the space between the arches.

The first lines written beneath the image were dated from the year 1442.

"This book isn't really *that* old, is it?" Felix asked, wonder clinging to each word that left his lips. "The binding of this book looks like it can't be older than the 1700s."

Arielle shrugged. "We're talking about a book passed

around by *time travelers*. Who knows for sure?"

Felix read aloud the opening statement. "Time portals are the lifeblood of our universe. They serve as an interconnected web of parallel timelines. When one passes through a portal, they will leave their existing timeline behind, but are able to return to the same time they had left. Thousands of time portals exist throughout the world, providing ample opportunities for users to visit different eras. While rare, a user may encounter a past version of themselves. This act is possible, but discouraged. If you are dealing with a past version of yourself that is not aware of time travel, the past version of yourself will have difficulty accepting the reality, thus altering their timeline."

Felix stopped and blinked rapidly. "Wait, so if you go through a time portal, you *can* visit your past self? We've never been able to do that with Juice."

"We need the location," Arielle urged, and Felix returned to reading.

"Tampering with timelines is only allowed with proper approval from the Keeper of Time, who holds sole discretion over all decisions related to time travel. The following pages contain the locations of all known time portals across the world. Blank pages are expected to be filled out upon the discovery of new portals. This book shall serve as the only guide for time portal locations. Any duplication or sharing of this information will result in harsh punishments."

Felix flipped the page and found a ledger of time portals broken into several columns: country, state/province, city, coordinates, accessible year.

Arielle was already looking at the next page. "They're sorted by country for the most part," she said, running a finger down the page. "Lots of U.S. on this page."

Felix checked his watch again. "Ten minutes."

They spent another minute flipping across three more pages before finding the city of Miami, Florida. "That's it," Arielle said, some confidence returning. "Wait."

She lowered her brow, noticing there was a second listing for Miami a couple lines below.

"It's fine," Felix said. "Two time portals. We'll block them both. Is there a piece of paper anywhere?"

He stepped back from the bookshelf and browsed the living room.

"Check the kitchen drawers," Arielle said.

They had seven minutes left.

Felix hurried out of the room, returning a minute later with a sticky note and pen. "I want to write these down. Don't trust keeping them in my phone. This way, the coordinates stay with me no matter where we travel through time."

"Good call," Arielle said, snapping a picture of the coordinates on her cell phone as backup.

Felix wrote the coordinates, triple checking each number as he went.

"We have five minutes," he said when he finished. "What else should we look at while we're here?"

Arielle shook her head and snapped the book shut. "This is not for us. Besides, if we have spare time, let's use it getting the hell out of this place."

Felix watched as Arielle crouched down to return the book to its place on the bottom shelf. He opened his mouth to speak, then quickly closed it.

"I'm sorry," Arielle said, looking around the room to make sure they hadn't accidentally moved anything else out of place.

"Put the pen back where you found it. I know how tempting it is, but we're on a mission right now. That needs to be our only focus."

Felix nodded with disappointment, pivoted around to return the pen to the kitchen, then joined Selena at the front door. They left with four minutes to spare, and Arielle was relieved to never have to look back on this house again.

Chapter 27

"We should have looked through more of the book," Felix said, arms crossed as he stared out the jet's window. They were on a flight to Miami, still in 2021, where they would jump back to 1998 after their arrival.

"There was no point in doing that," Arielle said. "We were already breaking a major rule by opening that book. What did we honestly have to gain by looking at more stuff *not* meant for us?"

Felix tossed up his hands. "I'm not a rule breaker."

"You can say that again," Selena added sarcastically.

"I respect the rules in place," Felix continued, shaking his head playfully at Selena. "But I honestly believe that was a gray area back there. Once Chris left the house, we knew he wasn't ever going to return. At that point, the book was no longer his possession. The Road Runners hadn't yet arrived, so who did the book actually belong to for those few minutes?"

"*Not* us." Arielle knew Felix would bring up this matter but hadn't expected it so soon.

"Exactly," Felix said, grinning somewhat madly. "Not anyone. How many people can say they've even been in the same room as the Book of Time? Probably less than five hundred, if I had to guess. And that's going back *thousands* of years."

Arielle laughed, a sound that enraged Felix. "Don't tell me you believe all that nonsense about Khronos. It's called Greek mythology. Myth. Not real. Come on, Mr. Science, you're better than that."

Felix frowned. "You know what else was a myth? Time travel. Yet here we are, about to visit our third century in three days. You're absolutely right, though. I'm a man of science. But even I have to acknowledge there are some things in this world science can't explain. Don't you think I've spent countless hours trying to figure out how all this time travel works? Someone makes a potion in a secret laboratory. We each drink our own and can end up in an entirely different year simply by *thinking* about it! All three of us arrive together in the same place each time we do it, too. Flawless. Never been a mistake. You have no problem accepting that reality but find stories of Greek gods to be ludicrous?"

Felix had lowered his arms, his fists balled up and shaking.

"Is this why you wanted to look through the book so badly?" Arielle asked. "You're looking for answers?"

Felix gave a sarcastic smile. "Of course I'm looking for answers, Arielle. It's my personality to understand why and how everything works. Nothing is exempt from that curiosity. Not even time travel. I don't have the luxury of sitting back and just enjoying it for what it is—like everyone else seems to do. Aren't you in the slightest curious? How does time travel affect us? Are there long-term side effects we're not aware of? There are millions of questions we don't have answers to, but we just accept it all as normal. Like time travel is a typical part of life."

Selena sat in her seat, digging into a bag of pretzels and

watching the exchange. She finally stood up. "That's enough. Felix, you had no right to look in the book. I have to side with Arielle on this one. Rare, I know. Of course, we wonder how this all works, but what does it matter? We're not going to find out, so there's no point in losing sleep over it. I thought it was all a joke when I was approached—who wouldn't? But I've seen some shit in just a few years as a time traveler, and one thing has become very clear. You don't fuck with the people in charge. And that means leaving that book alone."

"See," Arielle said, gesturing to Selena. "Not even the queen of breaking rules wants to tempt fate by opening that book." She crossed her arms and raised her eyebrows, expecting another rebuttal from Felix.

But none ever came. He only sighed and returned to his seat, brushing his dirty blond hair aside to rub his temples. "Okay. You're both right. I got too caught up in my emotions when I saw that book. It's been bothering me ever since we left it behind. I felt like I missed out on a golden opportunity. I still feel that way, but I'm outnumbered here."

"There's nothing to apologize for," Arielle said, sitting in her seat across from Felix. "Trust me, if we had more time and weren't in the middle of a mission, this might have played out differently. We were in a rush, and when that happens, mistakes can be made too easily. And the Book of Time is not something you make mistakes with."

Felix nodded and drew in a deep breath. "Okay. I'll try to let it go. But damn, it was so close! Like missing a lottery jackpot by one number."

"You're a winner in our book," Selena said, unable to hold in her laugh, immediately lightening the mood.

"We have our work cut out," Arielle said once their collective laughter died down. "We have failed on these last two stops. *Failed.* We were supposed to be spending at least a week in each era to find out what Doyle is doing, but we haven't even spent an entire twenty-four hours in either place."

"Is it poor planning or Doyle being a step ahead?" Felix asked, unscrewing the lid off a bottle of water and taking a long swig.

"A bit of both," Arielle said. "I'm not faulting our advance scouting team. I've done a few missions that involve serial killers, and with those, we always arrived either the day before or the day of the first killing. They applied that same principle to this mission, but it's not working because this time the serial killer can time travel. That's why we're going off-script for our stop in Miami. By now, Doyle must know when to expect us. If we arrive even a couple days earlier, we're going to set ourselves up much better. Plus, we need to block those time portals."

The jet rumbled as they neared Miami. The cross-country flight passed quickly thanks to an extended nap before they all woke and Felix wanted to argue about the Book of Time.

Selena started singing the chorus to Will Smith's "Welcome to Miami." Arielle rushed to the window for a glimpse of the Atlantic Ocean in the distance, something she could never resist, no matter her age. Felix remained in his seat, staring blankly at the floor, still pissed off about the book. But Arielle knew he'd be ready to work once they stepped off the jet.

"We're heading straight to the house," Arielle said. "We can make a plan during the drive over. Did you look up those coordinates yet, Felix?"

Arielle had been the first to doze off once they got on the jet. Felix had wanted to strategize during the flight, but Arielle ordered five hours of silence instead, knowing they'd all be better off in the long run.

"I worked for a bit before sleeping," Felix replied, straightening up and clearing his throat. "The coordinates point to a warehouse in Opa-Locka, a city just west of Miami. The building is registered to a company called Rapido Cabinets and Counters. However, that business has been out of operation since 1990. Yet, they've continued to pay their rent every month on time."

Arielle nodded. "It's definitely a time traveler's property, then. Why not spend the money—especially when you can virtually make as much as you'd like—to hide such a powerful secret?"

Felix shrugged. "The big question is who the property belongs to. I couldn't find a name registered on any public documents. The cabinet business was registered as an LLC to a man named Charles Norman. I checked the Road Runners' records and found no such name."

"Could be an ex-Revolter," Arielle said, the thought making her weary. It was an assumption, but what if Doyle was working with a Revolter? Nearly all Revolters had turned themselves in after losing the war against the Road Runners. Ninenty-nine percent, according to the Road Runners. That left one percent out in the world, presumably hiding.

Or helping time-traveling serial killers, Arielle thought.

Felix frowned. "A Revolter? You really think so?"

"Just a possibility. Keep in mind, not all Revolters were involved in the war. Quite a few wanted no part in it, but Chris had threatened death if they left the organization. He needed to keep his numbers elevated to intimidate us. Some had actually gone into hiding before the war took a turn for the worse. They may be going about their lives, unaware they're supposed to turn themselves in."

"So they may not even be a problem?" Selena asked.

"If I had to bet, whoever is paying for this warehouse is not trying to cause trouble," Arielle said, leaning against the window and crossing her arms. "If there are any of them scheming some sort of comeback, it would all take place underground, and they wouldn't be dumb enough to leave a paper trail like monthly rent on a building housing a time portal."

The jet's intercom crackled to life. "Good evening, fellow Angels, our flight is about to begin its descent into Miami. Please fasten your seatbelts to prepare for landing."

They did as instructed.

"I wouldn't worry about Revolters," Arielle continued. "It's a long shot. Honestly, who knows where the money is coming from to pay that rent? It could be a private property of the Road Runners. You're the one who told me they keep dozens of properties off the records for security purposes, Felix. Housing a time portal seems as good a reason as any to keep that information private."

Felix nodded in agreement. "True."

Selena let out a long yawn and stretched as the wheels touched down.

"I know this city is built for you," Arielle said to her. "But remember, we're here on a mission. If we wrap up all of our work, then you can head out."

Selena smirked. "Built for me? Whatever do you mean, Mother?"

Arielle shook her head, unable to keep a grin off her face. While she didn't like the idea of Selena exploring Miami's nightlife in the middle of a mission, she accepted she had no say in the matter. Regardless, Selena always showed up ready to work.

Once the jet landed and came to a stop in the hangar, Arielle stood and faced her team. "We're here. No looking back on the past failures of this mission. We leave Miami with Doyle Grady. No exceptions."

Chapter 28

March 19, 1998

After a quick drive to a car rental agency owned by the Road Runners (they had to operate their own to ensure vehicles were available from all eras), the three Angels had taken their sips of Juice in the offices before setting out into the world of 1998.

They set their plan before they even arrived at their Miami house, a ranch-style home in North Miami, on a residential block sandwiched between a golf course and Catholic school. Plenty of Lexus and BMW vehicles filled the driveways, making Arielle feel right at home.

A short palm tree shaded their driveway where Arielle parked their borrowed 1998 Mercedes sedan. They dropped off their luggage in the house, did a quick walk through to make sure all three bedrooms were in order, then headed back to the car where they set out for Opa-Locka, a fifteen-minute drive west.

"I think going to the portal is a waste of time," Selena said flatly. "No pun intended."

She sat in the back as they drove through the city, forehead pressed against the window as she watched dozens and dozens of palm trees pass by.

"And why is that?" Arielle asked, glaring at Selena in the rear-view mirror.

"For starters, the plan for blocking the portal is weak." Selena sighed. "You want to get there and move random things in front of it. Isn't that what Doyle did in Dallas? He's *already* blocking it. I don't see how us adding to it will make it any different. And there are *two* portals—I don't care what you say otherwise."

"It was a mistake," Felix said through gritted teeth.

When Felix had looked up the second set of coordinates they had found in the Book of Time, they pointed to the middle of Biscayne Bay, about four miles off the coast.

"It's not a mistake, Felix," Selena replied. "They wouldn't mess up something like the location of a time portal."

"So you want to go swimming and find out?" Felix asked. "Be my guest, but I'm not diving into the ocean to look for a time portal. And if Doyle wants to go through all that trouble, then maybe he deserves to get away."

"Enough," Arielle demanded. "Selena, I agree with you about the portal really being out in the water, likely somewhere far below that can only be reached by scuba diving. But we won't be doing that. That's a whole other level of training none of us have. We don't know how to scuba, nor do we know what type of sea life is roaming in those waters. Forgive me for not wanting to get eaten by a shark—I have to draw the line somewhere. What are the odds Doyle knows about that portal in the water? All reports suggest he has spent his time wandering the world in search of time portals."

Selena chuckled, shaking her head. "You can't possibly believe that. We're talking about a man who is literally using time travel for evil. He's not just walking around the country, hoping to stumble across a time portal. He knows where they are. What if he's doing the same thing we just did to access the Book of Time? He may know of another time when the book lay abandoned somewhere."

A knot twisted in Arielle's stomach. Selena was possibly on to something.

"That's preposterous," Felix said, not taking his eyes off the Garmin StreetPilot GPS device on the dashboard. It was the very first edition of a personal-use navigation system, and its basic black-and-white display proved that.

"It's not," Arielle muttered under her breath.

"Excuse me?" Felix asked, still not looking away. "Turn left at the light."

"Forget what I said before. Selena's right," Arielle continued. "Doyle has proven too smart and efficient to be wasting his time walking in circles, hoping to find a time portal. They're not something you just stumble across by accident, either. And he's found at least three that we know of. It's impossible to find one on your own, but three? He's playing with insider information. How else do you explain him being a step ahead of us without using Juice?"

"The point is," Selena said. "We should dedicate all of our time here to finding him. Plain and simple. Knowing where the time portal is, sure that's important. But blocking it isn't going to do anything. If it comes to it, I'll come guard the portal if we think there's a chance he's going to make a run for it."

"Absolutely not," Felix said. "You can't take that on by yourself." Growing up as the only boy with two sisters, it had become a reflex for Felix to be protective of the women in his life.

"Then you'll come with me," Selena replied calmly. "You rarely have anything to do on the last night of a mission, anyway."

Felix let out a nervous laugh. "Us? Guarding the time portal from a psychopathic murderer? Turn right."

Arielle turned the car off the main road and into an industrial complex. Warehouses stretched as far as they could see.

"Let's see what we're dealing with first," Arielle said. "Then we can decide the best approach. We don't even know what size this portal is. If it's as big as the one in the Dallas shed, that will be difficult to block. But if it's small like that one in OKC, we might as well give it a shot."

"Fourth warehouse on the right," Felix said, powering off the GPS system and stuffing the device into the glove compartment.

Arielle slowed as she turned into the parking lot. The building belonged to five different businesses, several of which had semitrucks with their trailers backed up against loading stations. She found the portion of the building marked with a generic sign that read *Rapido Cabinets & Counters.*

The blue lettering on the white sign had nearly faded away completely, an obvious reason no cars were parked in front of its doors.

"I assume this is another easy lock to pick?" Arielle asked Felix as she parked and turned off the car.

"Hopefully," Felix said, promptly fishing the lockpick out of his pocket. He squinted for a better view of the main door in front of them. "I think we're in luck. Come stand guard for me."

Felix stepped out of the car first, practically skipping toward the door with eagerness. Arielle knew he was excited to see another time portal up close. Apparently, that was all it took to make their rather skittish surveillance expert come out of his shell.

He reached the door and waited for Arielle and Selena to huddle around him. With these older locks, he only needed a few seconds and appeared no different from a man fidgeting with his key in the lock. No one was even around to pay any attention to them, and after fifteen seconds, Felix pushed the door open, its hinges screaming into the silent night sky.

"Now what?" Selena asked as they stepped into a pitch-black warehouse. "Are we trusting they've been paying their electrical bill, too?"

Arielle felt around on the wall next to the door until she found a panel of switches, flicking the first one. The light outside the door turned on, and she quickly flicked it back off. The next one turned on a light directly above them, bringing into view a dim open space that faded back to darkness. A third switch powered on the rest of the warehouse, and they now saw several rows of cabinets and countertops stretching to the back of the building. She eyed a crowbar leaning against the wall just below the light switches.

"Holy fucking cabinets," Selena said.

"Well, now we know they actually once sold cabinets here," Felix added.

"Sure, but how long has it been?" Arielle asked. "These cabinet styles look like they're from the eighties."

"Is that regular dust covering everything?" Selena asked, taking a step forward, eyes bulging at the endless cabinets that seemed to stretch in every direction.

Felix laughed to himself. "I get it. The time portal is hidden in one of these cabinets."

"How do you figure?" Arielle asked.

"It's the most logical hiding spot. Looks like there are bathrooms and one office along the side wall, but besides that, there isn't anywhere else a time portal can be except for on this floor."

"But there are at least two hundred to look through. Maybe more."

"Exactly. It's kind of brilliant if you think about it. You need to keep this portal a secret, so you build a cabinet around it, then another, and another. Meanwhile, you're running a fake operation as a cabinet business—just in case any curious eyes wander into here. Nobody would think twice. And why would anyone spend the time to go through each of these cabinets? What's their reason? The portal is hiding right in front of us. We just need to find which one it is."

Selena had continued to inch closer to the cabinets but stopped and turned around to face Arielle and Felix. "And what if someone pops out of nowhere? Do we just run?"

"Run?" Arielle asked. "I have a loaded gun and throwing knives. *They* should be the ones running."

Selena grinned her acceptance of this. "From here, it looks like *everything* is covered in dust. How are we supposed to know which dust is real and which came blasting out of the portal?"

"We don't know," Arielle said. "Let's split up to each take a row, and we'll walk down them together. Three at a time, until we find it. If everything really is dusty, there should be tracks near the time portal, since that's the only thing in this building getting any use."

"Or *extra* dusty," Felix said, his lips twisted while thinking.

"Those portals shoot out so much of that stuff."

"Let's get to it," Arielle said, marching forward and breaking left toward the first rows of cabinets. Felix and Selena joined her, still looking over the massive warehouse that would surely give some contractors wet dreams.

"We may want to focus on the heat," Felix said. "We don't know the last time this portal was used."

They reached the first row of cabinets and Arielle stopped to glance around. "There might be *over* two hundred cabinets. Maybe close to three."

"So, what are we doing?" Selena asked. "Going down each row and opening each cabinet door until we find something?"

"Precisely," Arielle replied.

Selena and Felix split into the next two rows, and they began their journeys up and down the aisles of cabinets. They zigzagged across the aisles, checking a cabinet on the left side before returning to the right for another.

"What are the odds this is all some sort of ploy?" Selena asked as they approached the end of their first rows. "What if the portal is on the roof and we're just down here wasting our time?"

Felix laughed, then quickly fell silent as he considered this.

"There wouldn't be a portal on the roof," Arielle replied. "They're supposed to be hidden. From my understanding, you can't find them using satellite imagery, so that rules out having one on the roof. They must be hidden out of sight, even if that means burying them in a maze of three hundred cabinets."

"A maze would at least make this more interesting," Selena said, and they each shifted down three rows to work on the next set of aisles.

Arielle noticed Felix's face drawn in deep thought. "Everything okay?" she asked him.

"Yeah," he replied absentmindedly. "Just trying to figure which cabinet would make the most sense for hiding the portal. It couldn't have been random."

Selena rolled her eyes. "Can't you just flip open the doors like a normal person? Do you have to analyze everything like it's a puzzle?"

"But it *is* a puzzle," Felix said, as he mindlessly opened the cabinet doors in his aisle. "It's not going to be hidden along the outer perimeter—those are the most likely to have the highest foot traffic. If they believed some time travelers would one day find this location, they wouldn't hide it in the middle aisle, either. If you didn't notice, the exact middle was perfectly aligned with the door we walked through. I doubt that was accidental. Given the choice between left or right, human nature tends to choose the right side, so if I were to hide it, I'd put it on the left - which means we can eliminate the entire other half."

"Felix, please," Selena begged, but he only ignored her.

Arielle rather enjoyed their bickering at this moment, as it brought some spice to a rather inattentive task.

"I counted eighteen aisles," Felix continued. "If I were to hide a time portal, I'd put it just off center to the left of the middle aisle. So I believe we'll find it between aisles six through eight. By the way, Arielle, your estimate was way off. There are at least seven hundred total cabinets in this warehouse."

"Seven hundred?!" Arielle gasped. Part of her believed Felix had somehow cracked the code and was right about the portal's location. They were already coming up to finishing aisles four through six, according to Felix's numbering system.

"Nothing in aisle six, so it must be seven or eight," Felix said. "Would one of you mind switching with me? Aisle nine is the center and a waste of time."

Selena sighed. "I already said this entire visit is a waste of time."

"Just switch with him," Arielle said. "Would hate for you to get sucked into a portal, Selena."

Selena glared at Arielle from across the rows of cabinets between them. When they reached the end of the aisle, Selena grumbled something under her breath as she started down the center aisle. Felix took a sharp turn into aisle eight and slowed his pace, carefully examining the inside of each cabinet as he opened the doors.

Arielle mirrored her pace to match Felix's, considering she was in aisle seven. "Is there something in particular I should look for?"

"No," Felix replied. "Just take your time."

Selena was blasting down the center aisle, twice the distance ahead of the other two.

Arielle was approaching the middle of the aisle, as was Felix, when she reached out and felt it.

All the door handles they had been pulling open were cold to the touch, except for the next one that had the sensation of residual body heat left behind on its surface.

"I think this might be something," Arielle said, pulling the door open.

Felix and Selena both perked up and bolted out of their aisles to join Arielle.

The inside of the cabinet was covered in the unmistakable dust they had seen at the prior two portals.

"I don't see anything, though," Arielle said, taking a step back. She didn't trust these portals and didn't dare risk getting sucked into a random cabinet. Felix reached her first and promptly dropped to a knee for a better view inside the cabinet. He placed his hands on the edge of the doorframe and stuck his head inside.

"Felix, what the fuck?!" Selena cried out.

He pulled his head out, brows furrowed in confusion. "I don't understand. None of the cabinets have this powder inside except for this one. And I *feel* the heat."

"It's gotta be underneath," Arielle said.

Felix nodded and went back into the cabinet, causing Selena to toss her hands in the air in frustration. He brushed off all the dust from the bottom floor of the cabinet, revealing the wooden surface beneath. "It's a false bottom!" Felix cried out, pulling out of the cabinet with a wide smile on his face, the powdery substance coating the tips of his hair. "The bottom is a door."

"Are you going to open it?" Arielle asked.

"Should I?"

"Well, yes. We need to confirm it really is the portal."

Felix scratched his chin. "Okay. Let's have a look."

"Why are you making him do that?" Selena demanded. "What if he falls in?"

"Felix isn't going to fall in," Arielle replied. "His shoulders don't even fit through the cabinet all the way. He'd have to go in feet first to even fit through there."

Felix grunted as he fidgeted inside the cabinet, finally causing a loud CRACK! as the false bottom popped out of place. Dust puffed out of the cabinet, and Felix pulled himself back out, his face now covered.

Selena grinned, and Arielle couldn't help but laugh. It never got old, apparently.

"It was pretty tight," Felix said. "So I'm sure it hasn't been used in a while. But it's there all right. Once I pulled the door up, immediate blast of heat. Just blackness straight below. I think it's one you have to fall into."

"Oh, hell no," Selena said, as if she'd even climb through one to begin with.

Felix stood up and brushed himself off, sneezing out the dust that had collected in his nose. "What should we do?" he asked, reaching over to shove the cabinet, which remained sturdy in place. "It's bolted to the ground."

Arielle nodded, looking into the darkness at the bottom of the cabinet. Somewhere on the other side of that black hole was a universe Doyle would disappear to if they failed to catch him again.

We can't fail this time.

"Do you think it's worth it to move these other cabinets to block it?" she asked. "Or would that make it obvious that something is up?"

Felix rubbed his forehead and looked around the warehouse. "How heavy are those slabs of countertops?" He nodded to a stack of ceramic-tiled countertops along the wall to the left of the entrance.

"It's not granite or marble," Arielle said. "They can't weigh too much, I'd imagine. Plus, they've already been cut, so they should be easy to carry."

Felix grinned. "There's our answer. We place a stack of those in front of this cabinet. I doubt a person could move one by themselves, leaving the portal blocked. As long as Doyle doesn't have anyone working with him, he'll have no way of

getting into that cabinet.”
"Alright, let's get to work."

The Angels returned home after moving ten countertops to block the cabinet housing the time portal. Arielle had kept looking over her shoulder, expecting the past to intervene with their plans. But they had remained alone, and the mood was lighter during the drive home.

Felix had insisted they stop at a Puerto Rican restaurant to pick up three plates of mofongo for dinner. They sat at the dining room table, devouring their mounds of fried plantains and chicharrónes like they hadn't eaten in weeks.

"How are we going to find the first victim in time?" Selena asked once they were nearly finished and everyone leaned back in their seats. "Vanessa something?"

"Vanessa Bauer," Arielle said. "Hopefully, this is easy for once. We have her information in the mission report. We know where she lives and works. She graduated from the University of Miami two years ago and stayed living here. I know it's been a brutally long day, but we might want to head out tonight just to see where she lives. Tomorrow we can start actually following her. We'll need some rest before taking on these next few days."

"And we just follow her until she has an encounter with Doyle?" Felix asked. "Then what? Doyle has an exit strategy planned. He's proven that already. We're not going to walk up to him on the sidewalk and tap him on the shoulder."

"Well, we blocked off his exit," Arielle said with a smirk. "And I guarantee *that's* not in his plan. With no Juice, where will he go?"

"Into hiding," Selena said. "We can't let him get away."

"And he won't." Arielle said. "Let's take this conversation to the car."

Selena rolled her eyes and threw her head back. Felix drew in a long breath and let it out with a steady sigh.

"Just one more hour," Arielle said, gathering the car keys and her wallet. They had already swapped out their IDs from 2098 and replaced them with ones for 1998 that made them appear as valid citizens of the Sunshine State. "I promise. Then we can come back and go to sleep. I'm just as tired as you both."

Felix and Selena begrudgingly followed Arielle out of the house. It was nine o'clock and the crickets had come to life.

Selena stopped on the front porch and looked around the neighborhood. "I don't see any horny housewives waiting to pounce on Felix, so that's a good start."

They all cackled. Felix hadn't been so fortunate on their last mission that sent them to Hilburn, Nebraska in 1978. They piled into the car and Arielle wasted no time pulling out to the road.

"Don't you need me to enter the address on the GPS?" Felix asked.

Arielle raised a hand. "It's fine. I've studied the maps and know where I'm going."

Vanessa lived with three of her friends in an apartment building just south of downtown.

"We have binoculars, right?" Arielle asked, tongue pinched between her teeth as she focused on driving.

"I got mine back here," Selena said, poking through a duffel bag.

"Good. Vanessa lives in a two-story apartment on the bottom floor. We should be able to get a glimpse inside her unit."

With a twenty-minute drive ahead, Felix tinkered with the radio for two minutes, found nothing to listen to, and turned it off with an aggressive tap of the power button.

"You good?" Arielle asked, glancing at the passenger seat. Felix was rubbing his temples, hair a frazzled mess as he kept running his fingers through it.

"Always," Felix replied sarcastically.

"You don't need to lie to us," Selena said, offering her demanding sass. "Just say it already."

Felix sighed. "Fine. I have a lot on my mind with these time portals. I want to go through one."

He let his words hang in the air while Arielle and Selena considered them. Finally, Arielle said, "We can arrange that, but it won't be on this mission. We shouldn't go through without the proper authorization."

"Really?" Felix perked up. "How?"

"I can convince Commander Briar to let us try a portal. Especially if we catch Doyle."

"You two have fun," Selena said. "You couldn't pay me to go through one of those things."

"Suit yourself," Arielle said. "But I'm sure we'll have a good time. They're safe to use. People once used them often, is my understanding. We just need to be trained on how to properly use them so we can get back to where we came from."

"That would be a dream come true," Felix said, sounding like a child getting granted his wish for an ice cream cone at the county fair. "Time portals have always been that mythical thing in our world, like a unicorn. I just want to see what all the fuss is about."

"Is that really all that was bothering you?"

Felix shifted in his seat. "No. I've been reading a lot on the Road Runner news. This next election is ramping up and it's getting ugly. I'm just worried about the future."

Selena laughed. "A time traveler worried about the future. Is that the punchline or the joke?"

"I'm serious. We just got out of this war, and now people are already trying to split the organization again. What happened to how united we were?"

"We were united against a common enemy," Arielle said. "I've heard the rumblings going around about the election, and I think there's nothing to worry about. Remember, the Road Runners were formed solely to oppose the Revolution. This is the first time we've been at peace, and everyone has different opinions on how to approach this new reality. No matter who wins, we'll still be in a time of peace."

"You sound like a politician already," Selena said sarcastically. "When do you announce your nomination?"

Arielle raised her middle finger to the backseat. "Never."

"Oh, please!" Selena laughed. "Not all top-ranked Angels run for the commandership, but when they do, they always win. You people are just so damn beloved."

"You people?" Arielle replied, also giggling. "I'm just good at my job and have no interest in running for office."

"You say that now but wait until you're done doing missions. You're a lifer. When you're not in the field, you'll still be involved. Someone will come along and convince you to run for commander. It's only two years of your life, so why not?"

Arielle wondered if Selena knew something she didn't. It wasn't a stretch for a time traveler to jump into the future and see what might be going on in the world. Had Selena done that, perhaps for another reason, and saw Arielle as the commander? She couldn't ask. Whatever time-traveling people did in their free time was their own business, and much like religion and politics, they frowned upon others asking them to explain themselves.

"We're almost there," Arielle said, needing to change the subject before her mind fell down a rabbit hole.

The late hour in the evening meant little traffic, and they made great time getting across town. Once Arielle exited the highway, they went two blocks before turning into a complex with a sign welcoming them to the Sunrise Suites.

"This is it," Arielle announced as they crawled through the parking lot. "We're looking for building C."

"Over there." Felix pointed across the way to where a large letter "C" stood out from the building's facade.

"From what I studied of the layout," Arielle said. "They're unit is in the back right corner in relation to the main entrance."

She drove along the side of the building, turned off the headlights, and parked two rows back from the unit belonging to Vanessa.

The window was massive and looked into a living room where the glow from a TV splashed across a dark room. Three girls sat on a couch, each holding a small bucket of popcorn.

"How cute," Selena said, looking through the binoculars. "It must be movie night. Should we join them?"

"Is she in there?" Arielle asked, squinting for a better view, but from their distance she could only make out the silhouettes of three girls.

"She's the one that supposedly looks like you, right?" Selena asked. "She's in there all right."

"Let me have a look," Arielle said, reaching back for the binoculars. Selena passed them over and Arielle had her clear view into the living room.

Vanessa sat in the middle of the two other girls, hand moving mindlessly from the popcorn to her mouth, eyes glued to the TV.

"They're watching *I Know What You Did Last Summer*," Arielle said. "My kinda girls to hang out with."

"You like horror movies?" Felix asked, surprised.

"I grew up watching them with my dad," Arielle replied, a grin touching her lips as she thought back to the countless autumn nights bundled up on the couch with her dad while they watched every horror movie they could find. "I've expanded what I watch these days, but a good horror movie always takes me back to those memories."

"Didn't you say she lives with three other girls?" Felix asked, returning his attention to the apartment.

"Yes. I'm not sure what her roommates all do, however. So the missing one could be at work or school. Who knows?"

"Do we have any trackers we can put on her car?" Selena asked. "Might save us some time trying to follow her every move."

Felix shook his head. "I'm afraid not in 1998. The GPS technology isn't advanced enough yet. I could probably get a makeshift one to plant on her car, but we'd need access to the government's satellites to find her. The early 2000s are when most restrictions surrounding GPS technology were lifted, and it became more mainstream."

"We'll have to do this the old-fashioned way," Arielle said, starting up the engine.

"We're really going back?" Selena asked, lunging forward in her seat.

Arielle laughed. "Of course. I said we would. Did you not believe me?"

"Well...no."

They all burst into laughter.

"Usually when we come out for something like this," Selena continued. "You'll find something that needs to be investigated, then the next four hours are gone. It's never point A to point B. No offense."

"None taken," Arielle said. "There are plenty of things I'd like to do right now, but I promised a full night's sleep—which is more important. We can rest easy tonight knowing Vanessa is safe in her apartment with friends. Until tomorrow, let's get out of here."

Arielle drove off, wondering where in the fine city of Miami Doyle Grady was hiding.

Chapter 30

March 20, 1998

The following morning felt more like one Arielle had become accustomed to after four missions with Felix and Selena.

Felix woke at seven and prepared them all a breakfast of eggs, bacon, toast, fresh fruit, and orange juice. Arielle had been up first but spent her time preparing for the day ahead. And Selena was the last awake, dragging her groggy self into the kitchen and plopping down at the table, hair a frazzled mess.

They enjoyed the meal before getting dressed for the day, everyone ready to head out by 8:30.

"Are we clear on the plan for today?" Arielle asked as they congregated by the door.

"You're following Vanessa all day," Selena said with a sigh, flipping her hair to the side. "While me and Felix get to have all the fun of randomly wandering around downtown Miami like we'll actually find Doyle."

"No need for the attitude," Arielle said. "Yes, it's a big city, and I acknowledge the odds of finding him are slim. But that's what we have to work with. I don't think he'll be using an alias like he did in 2098. He only did that because their technology was too advanced for him to get away with living there under his real name. We'd have been able to find him in a heartbeat. He kept his name in 1898, and I don't see any reason he won't do the same here. He has a big ego, and getting away with these murders across the centuries under his real name has to be part of the thrill for him."

"Not that the locals have ever named him," Felix added.

"True, but not the point," Arielle replied, tightening her utility belt beneath a baggy shirt. "The locals don't have a chance of identifying him as the killer, because he didn't exist at the time of the murders. Well, except for these in Miami. But he was a six-year-old boy in 1998, living in Milwaukee. Impossible for anyone to know that he was actually the killer."

"Shouldn't we just kidnap that little boy from Milwaukee?" Selena asked. "Would make a lot of people's lives much better."

"That's a nice thought, isn't it? Unfortunately, that's not allowed within our bylaws. It's illegal to take someone before they committed a crime because you can never say for certain how future events will change the trajectory of a person's life."

"It has some fascinating precedence," Felix said. "A team once went on a secret mission to kidnap Hitler when he was a baby. Didn't tell anyone in the Road Runners what they were up to. They ultimately failed—too big of an effect on history, they honestly never had a chance—and were sentenced to life on Khronos Island."

"Yep," Arielle added. "That actually sparked the law that came into place. We're not allowed to interfere with the trajectory of a person's life before their crimes. They're allowed to maintain their innocence right until the crime.

That's why so many of our missions are based on the crime itself. There are some instances of interference that can be approved by the commander, which has become the routine, but they would never allow something as drastic as taking a future murderer off the streets during their childhood."

"Well, I think that's stupid," Selena said, hands on her hips. "If you *know* someone is going to grow up to be an awful person, you should be able to eliminate them at any opportunity. Especially someone like Doyle, who is using time travel for evil. He's one of our own. The rules shouldn't apply the same way."

"And I agree," Arielle said, knowing how to settle down Selena by pleasing her ego. "But I'm afraid that option is off the table for this mission. Felix, were you able to get everything sorted out for a second car?"

"Sure did," Felix replied. "It should arrive in the next half hour and we'll be on our way."

Arielle turned to Selena, and before she could speak, Selena had already read her mind. "Yes, *Mother*, I made plans last night for places we can explore. Colleges, nightclubs, the hottest restaurants where young twenty-year-olds hang out."

Arielle grinned. Selena always put in the effort and didn't really hate the missions, as she liked to have them believe. She simply hated being micromanaged and preferred to work smarter, not harder.

"Perfect," Arielle said, grabbing her keys off the table next to the front door. "It's a Friday night in Miami, and I plan on following Vanessa wherever she goes, no matter how late."

Selena scoffed. "You're going out for a night on the town, aren't you?"

Arielle batted her eyes playfully. "Maybe. Not like that's

what I *want* to do, but I suspect there's a good chance, considering who I'm following."

"Well then, I'll see you there," Selena responded with a hint of frustration. She was the one who always went out, even on missions. And Arielle always had something to say about it.

"That's fine. I'll call you on our fancy Nokia cell phones. Hopefully, we have signal." Arielle giggled and pulled out the cell phone Felix had arranged for them to each have. It was the brick-style phone with a stub antenna protruding from the top.

Selena shook her head. "This is brutal. We have phones, but no internet on them. Not even any games besides Snake. What shit is that, anyway? Did people really sit there and play Snake for hours when they were bored?"

"They sure did," Felix said, pulling out his phone and waving it in front of Selena's face. "This might be the trip that makes Selena snap. So close to having the technology you want, yet so far."

Selena balled a fist and socked Felix in the arm. "It's not funny."

"Oh, relax," Felix said, eyes watering as he fought the urge to rub where she had punched. "You'll be in a Miami nightclub tonight, and all will be right in the world."

"Well, I'll leave you two to bicker," Arielle said, opening the front door. "I need to head out. I'll see you tonight."

They saw Arielle off as she trotted to the car and hopped behind the wheel. She looked at herself in the rear-view mirror and drew a deep breath. *We'll catch him. Vanessa Bauer will not die.*

She drove to Vanessa's apartment complex, unsure if she would catch her there or if she would already be at Hot Cuts, where she worked as a hair stylist. The Advance team had found out where she worked with no problem but struggled to pin down a consistent schedule. Vanessa sometimes worked mornings, other times evenings. Days of the week were even more sporadic, her schedule impossible to predict.

When she arrived at the apartment complex fifteen minutes later, Arielle was relieved to see Vanessa's car, a gold '95 Ford Taurus, still parked in front of their unit.

Arielle parked in the same spot as last night and killed the engine. With the sunlight already blasting over the city, Arielle didn't need binoculars to see through the window into the living room. Vanessa stood at the kitchen counter, eating a bowl of cereal and flipping through a newspaper.

She stays informed, Arielle thought, beating herself up for not staying up to date on current world events. The task wasn't so simple as she could easily forget *when* she was living.

Vanessa was presumably dressed for work. Black pants and a black shirt, with her hair done up in a high ponytail. She finished her cereal and placed her bowl in the sink when a gray cat jumped onto the counter. Vanessa petted it for another minute, making Arielle gag. Who the hell would let a cat jump on the counter where people clearly ate? She imagined the kitty litter residue that seeped into slices of bread while making a sandwich and had to battle her stomach's will to eject her breakfast.

Once that horrific scene was over, Vanessa disappeared from sight and didn't return for another fifteen minutes. During the wait, Arielle flipped through the mission report to read more about Vanessa's death that awaited in two days. Her friends had reported her first missing on the evening of March twenty-second, after she hadn't called or returned messages for the entire day.

The friends admitted to having a fight at the Night Owl Club before they had all gone their separate ways. None of them had seen when Vanessa had left, aside from stepping outside of the club to cool off after the argument.

If Arielle couldn't get to Doyle before he made his move on Vanessa, she'd be at the Night Owl when the time came.

An image flashed in Arielle's mind of her grabbing Doyle from behind as he tried running off with Vanessa. She yanked his shirt, pulling him off his feet, and threw him to the ground. Kicking and punching every part of his body until she could no longer feel her hands or feet. Until every ounce of life slipped out of Doyle.

This mission was personal. Doyle had called her out from the beginning, daring her to catch him. Leaving his psychotic notes behind, all to taunt her. Tempt her. No mission in her past had ever been this personal. Envisioning her success was one of the first exercises she had gone through with the Road Runners' psychologist. She pictured herself capturing Doyle, bringing him to immediate justice, and the celebration in Commander Briar's office after it was all done.

She couldn't recall ever wanting a mission to be successful this badly. While it was far from true, she believed her entire career teetered on the outcome.

Arielle broke out of her trance, finding her nails buried into her palms to the point a couple of spots were bleeding.

"Shit," she whispered to herself. "Don't try so hard. Nothing easy comes to those in times of desperation. One day at a time."

But Doyle felt so out of reach. He kept evading her, and she had yet to come close. Could he know she was here already?

She didn't believe so, but if he did, what could that mean for the next two days?

Vanessa grabbed her purse and rushed outside, shuffling in a hurry to her car, checking her wristwatch every two seconds.

"Running late?" Arielle said. She never understood how people could have such difficulty getting places on time. All you need is to know the time you need to be somewhere and work backwards to plan a schedule.

Vanessa wasted no time peeling out of the parking lot, so Arielle started her car and followed, oblivious to the pair of eyes watching her from a distance.

Chapter 31

Doyle hid in the bushes thirty feet behind the parking lot behind the Sunrise Suites. His heart raced, pounding in his ears like a not-so-distant drum.

Why the fuck *is she here?* he wondered, bullets of sweat dripping down his face.

Doyle had come to this apartment complex with the simple goal of slipping some of the free drink vouchers into Vanessa's car. If she saw them, she'd return, likely thinking they had fallen out of her purse, or one of her friends had left them in the car from their drunken night out last weekend.

He didn't know if it would even work, but he had to try. He needed Vanessa back as soon as possible, but now the circumstances had changed with the arrival of that fucking Angel, Arielle Lucila.

Why is she here, *of all places? What does she know? What the fuck am I supposed to do?!*

Doyle had nearly started hyperventilating but focused on deep breathing to get himself under control.

He had expected her to arrive, sure. That was her job and naturally part of the cat-and-mouse game.

"Am I supposed to kill this girl today?" Doyle asked himself, grabbing a twig and snapping it in half. It hadn't been part of the plan. No, sir. He wanted at least one more visit from Vanessa before making his move. Maybe she'd visit the club twice this weekend—not uncommon for the locals who fell in love with the place. Fucking kids with plenty of time to waste.

Did Arielle know something he didn't? She wasn't supposed to show up until the day of the murder, which he had no intention of doing today. But were things going to play out differently? Maybe he was going to lure Vanessa back to his house tonight. If matters escalated quickly enough, he couldn't dismiss the possibility. But the thought had never entered his mind. Or heart.

As Doyle's initial fear of having Arielle around faded, he realized the grand opportunity that had fallen into his lap.

A grin touched his lips, his cheeks tightening to hold it in place for the next minute. His heart rate picked up again, but this time because of uncontrollable excitement. Doyle giggled, then laughed. The bushes were shaking. If someone from the apartment complex spotted him, they'd surely think he was a homeless crack addict losing the last marbles rolling around in his head.

But Doyle wasn't going mad. Quite the opposite, in fact. Vanessa could wait. Vanessa was now bait.

If Arielle was in Miami following Vanessa, then she had no clue where Doyle was. She obviously knew Vanessa was going to die at the hands of Doyle—*good Doyle!*—so naturally her logic was to follow Vanessa until she found him.

Doyle licked his lips, his chaotic grin unwavering.

"Oh, my precious Arielle," he said. "Are you really falling into my trap? How could the top-ranked Angel make such a careless decision?!"

If Arielle was too busy pursuing Vanessa, then she'd never

know Doyle was following *her.*

He broke into more laughter. Destiny was finally working in Doyle's favor. He might not get the chance to claim the three victims he wanted in Miami, but getting Arielle was the ultimate prize. So did it really matter?

Doyle bolted to his car and zoomed out of the apartment complex, burning rubber and turning the heads of an elderly couple enjoying a peaceful morning walk.

He knew where Vanessa and Arielle were going, but he needed to make sure. If Arielle actually followed Vanessa to work and stayed there, then he'd happily throw out his plans of luring Vanessa and shift his focus to Arielle.

Drool ran down Doyle's mouth. He could practically taste the feast of removing Arielle from the world. His legs quivered with anticipation, and suddenly, Doyle felt like he could run through ten brick walls. Finally, after all the hardships he had endured with losing his wife, the universe was throwing him a bone. The ultimate bone.

And Doyle Grady was no punk. He would not waste this opportunity, not if he had to dive into South Beach and wrestle a shark—fucking sharks.

He screamed. Howled. Swayed his head to music that wasn't even playing. The music of fate that had swooned over his body and taken a chokehold. A chokehold he rather enjoyed.

Doyle finally drove the speed limit as he turned into the hair salon's lot, where only a handful of cars were parked. It was part of a strip mall, sandwiched between a doughnut shop and a chiropractor's office. The doughnut shop had plenty more traffic, so he parked on that side of the lot and remained back to keep his view on Arielle.

He watched Arielle for the next hour, completely oblivious

to how much time was passing by while they both sat there doing nothing. Seeing her, and knowing she had no clue he was mere yards away, tickled his insides like he hadn't felt in years. Like falling in love for the first time all over again.

Arielle pressed her head against the window, her honey-brown hair flattening against the glass. He imagined grabbing that hair and twisting her head around, having complete control over her. The thought of her screams echoing in his house, where no one could ever hear, made him harder than a boulder.

His fantasies vanished as soon as Arielle opened her car door and stepped out. His racing heart skipped a couple of beats as she started strolling in his direction, prompting him to slouch in the driver's seat.

No fucking way she saw me. Why don't I ever carry a gun when I leave the house? And in Florida! For fuck's sake.

But his panic faded as Arielle turned right and disappeared into the doughnut shop.

Go! he yelled at himself, grabbing the drink vouchers from the passenger seat and throwing his door open.

Stay calm. Walk at a normal speed.

The doughnut shop's exterior was all glass, but the place was so crowded he couldn't even see Arielle in the mob of cranky patrons waiting for their sugar-filled breakfast. His limbs pulsed with adrenaline as he took gradual steps toward Vanessa's car—parked in the back row since she was an employee.

Doyle had wandered off path since he was keeping his eyes glued to the salon and doughnut shop, and a truck screeched to a halt, blaring its horn as it stopped less than twelve inches from his terrified, bulging eyes.

"Get the fuck out of the road!" the driver shouted, leaning out the window of his Ford pickup. The man was red from too much time in the sun, tribal tattoos running all over his arms, and sunglasses that seemed plastered to his face.

Fuck you, Florida.

Naturally, the man drove off while flipping Doyle the bird, and he caught sight of a bumper sticker that said *CLINTON AND GORE OUT IN FOUR!*

How did that work out for you, dickwad?

Doyle had to shake off the urge to chase this troll down and slit his throat. He had more pressing issues and couldn't let the douchebag throw him off his plan. One glance to the doughnut shop confirmed he had plenty of time. Arielle wouldn't be out of there in less than ten minutes, and Vanessa had no line of sight to her car from the salon.

He shuffled to the car, and nearly jumped for joy when he found the windows cracked about two inches on both sides.

Bless you, Vanessa. Everything is falling beautifully into place.

Doyle circled around to the passenger-side window and dropped in the stack of cards, landing them perfectly on the seat next to a pile of nail polish bottles and hairbrushes.

"Jackpot!" he cried, patting the roof of the car and scurrying back to his own. He took one last glance at the line of people now filing out of the doughnut shop. No sign of Arielle. The first part of the trap had been laid, and all he could do now was hope Vanessa would show up at the Night Owl later in the evening. If she did, Arielle would follow, and Doyle was more than ready to meet the moment. First, he'd need to go to his house and prepare for a night of delicious suffering. Arielle wouldn't get the easy way out, either. No silently slipping into the void for the queen of the time travelers. Absolutely fucking not.

No. Arielle would get the full wrath Doyle had saved in his mental reserve just for her. She would beg him to end her life, and he'd do it with pleasure.

He fired up his car and drew a deep breath, a lump forming in his throat as emotions continued to skyrocket.

Tears streaked down his face as he had the most powerful epiphany since the day he accepted his wife was never coming back.

Arielle Lucila would be dead within the next forty-eight hours.

Chapter 32

When Doyle arrived home, he parked in the garage and closed the door before stepping out of his car. Sometimes the annoying neighbor from down the street would trot over and want to chat.

Gloria. The retired woman with nothing better to do than pounce on young men while her rich husband went to the office every day to add to their millions. The husband was the CEO of some local chain of sporting goods stores, and Gloria liked to lounge around on the bed, literally lying on piles of money.

Doyle knew because he watched her from a distance after first moving in. He watched all his neighbors, needing to understand who might pose threats to his work. Sure, Gloria was sixty-five, but she still had the sexual drive of a younger cougar in heat. Doyle might have let her have her way, as she so desperately wanted. But not under the current circumstances. He played cordial and always hurried her off like a stray dog begging for some lunch.

His neighborhood was filled with these types of lonely housewives. Of all ages, too. He'd observed enough activity to know who was having affairs with their pool boys or gardeners. Surely the husbands were out doing the same thing with their assistants "working late."

Fucking rich people.

None of that noise mattered right now. Doyle entered his obnoxiously large house and tossed the keys on the kitchen counter. Too many bedrooms. Too many bathrooms. But dammit, he loved the kitchen. For 1998, it seemed futuristic with its stainless-steel appliances and granite countertops. Not even the warehouse protecting the time portal had many granite options.

Okay, how am I going to bring Arielle back here?

Naturally, she'd be in his trunk, and he'd pull into the garage just as he had done. He'd drug her enough to knock her out and bring her home without a struggle. Carrying her would be easy since she couldn't possibly weigh more than one hundred and thirty pounds.

"Through the kitchen and directly up the stairs to the safe room."

With more bedrooms than he knew what to do with, Doyle had one converted into a soundproof room, fully equipped as a recording studio. He never touched the gear but couldn't afford questions when the contractors showed up to build it. He wasn't the first resident in this upscale neighborhood to drop a hundred thousand dollars on a passion project.

Since there were no basements in Florida, he had no choice but to get creative for a space where he could hold his victims. They loved to scream and shout and pound the floor as they pleaded for their lives. While the houses on the block were spaced apart plenty, he couldn't run any risk of the screams carrying. Or maybe even Gloria would stalk him and get too close for comfort. And if *she* went missing, well, the entire neighborhood would get turned upside down until they found her.

"Need the plastic wrap."

Doyle shuffled into the kitchen and opened the cabinet beneath the sink. He tried to keep things in the same general places, no matter what year he was in. The plastic wrap went under the sink in 1998 and 2098. There wasn't even such a thing in 1898, but he had an underground tunnel, so life was groovy.

He pulled out the roll of plastic—industrial-sized—and brought it to the base of the stairs. Carrying Arielle from the car and through the kitchen wouldn't pose any problems, but Doyle could often struggle to get a dead-weight body up the stairs.

"Skipping leg day always pays a price," he said as he examined the stairs and unrolled the plastic. It had a stickiness on one side that helped it cling to the carpeted steps.

The plastic made it easier to drag the body up and down, and protected any bodily fluids from seeping into the carpet fibers if it came to it. He always performed clean work before moving a dead body out of the house, but a man could never be too safe. There were lots of sick time-traveling superheroes out there, after all.

One narrow staircase with twelve steps leading to the second-floor landing took him fifteen minutes to complete. He walked up and down on the plastic to make sure there were no issues, and clapped his hands when he discovered none.

Doyle climbed back up the stairs and entered the first door on the right, the safe room. He had long ago covered the walls and floor with the plastic wrap, knowing what would eventually take place in this room. He never showed it to the women he brought back to the house, citing it was his private recording studio and he couldn't allow anyone else's energy to interfere with his creative process. For whatever reason, saying this usually made their panties fly off even faster. *Fucking wannabe groupies.*

He'd had the window overlooking the backyard boarded up, the walls insulated and covered in panels of acoustic foam. After it had been installed, Doyle cranked up heavy metal music to the point he couldn't hear himself think. He then stepped outside the house, where he couldn't hear a damn thing coming from within. Not from the front door. Not the sidewalk, and certainly not from across the street.

The soundproofing worked like magic, and Doyle imagined having a longer string of murders in 1998 because of it. A perfect setup like this had made it too tempting. But Arielle showed up, and that plan was out the window.

Now taking his first good look at the safe room since having it installed, Doyle moved aside the guitars and keyboard he had purchased for appearances, shoving them into the corner and clearing space in the middle of the floor.

The lone chair would suffice to tie up Arielle. He'd already swapped out the doorknob to lock from the outside—something he didn't let the contractors do.

"Just need some tools for the evening's events!"

If he was in a pinch, plucking a string off the guitar would make a fabulous tool for choking, but he wanted to be more practical, so ran back down the stairs and into the kitchen. He grabbed some knives, the smoothie blender, even the heavy-duty coffee pot. Moving into the garage, Doyle opened up the toolbox he had yet to touch and nearly slobbered at the sight of a hammer, pliers, and a power drill. An extra roll of thin rope lay on the floor, used for hanging the planters decorating the backyard.

"All of this will work," he said, picking up the pliers and licking them from the base to the pointed end.

Doyle brought the tools into the house and made multiple trips up and down the stairs until they were all neatly organized along the wall in the safe room. Once he finished, he puffed out his chest and stood tall as he looked over the room.

"To the common eye, a simple music studio for some rich playboy with nothing better to do. But to me, I see the most beautiful room of death!"

Doyle closed the safe room's door and returned downstairs, rummaging through the fridge for a beer and cracking it open with a delighted smile on his face.

"Cheers to a fun weekend ahead!"

He raised the beer can to the mirror hanging on the wall in the living room. It had been weeks since he truly looked at himself and was shocked to see the toll his recent adventures had taken on him. Bags under his eyes. Lines at the corners of his mouth. Why were any of these women falling for him at the club? Did money really have that much influence, or had he simply perfected his skills of acting as the charming promoter who could get his way no matter what?

His house phone rang, snapping him out of his thoughts. He'd refused to buy a cellphone in 1998. It hadn't become too mainstream for people to question why he didn't own one. But he had a landline at the house, needing a phone number for his job to reach him. Why the hell was Fernando calling him in the middle of the day? He didn't need to start his shift until seven o'clock. He gazed at the answering machine on the kitchen counter, longing to let the machine take a message. But he knew better. This was not the time to piss off Fernando.

The phone was mounted on the wall next to the fridge, so Doyle shuffled and picked up the receiver. "Hello?"

"Hi there, Doyle," said a woman's voice, forcing a seductive tone.

"Who is this?" he demanded.

"I just saw you got home not too long ago. It's the middle of the day and I'm bored. Aren't you?"

"Gloria?" Doyle replied, tightening his grip on the phone. "How the hell did you get this number? It's supposed to be unlisted."

Gloria giggled. "Silly boy. I can get anything I want. It's always just a phone call away."

"God dammit, Gloria, I've told you to leave me alone!" Doyle said through gritted teeth. He was hardly picking up on anything the woman said, too disturbed that she had somehow found his phone number. What else did she find out about him during her search?

"Oh, Doy," she said, unbothered by his obvious rage. "Can I call you Doy? I know you don't really want me to leave you alone. I recall you once saying, and I quote, 'Maybe some other time.' Don't you remember? Well, mister stud muffin, that time has come."

Doyle took a deep breath. He felt his face turning red, wishing he could rip the phone cords right out of the wall.

"Have you been watching me?" Doyle asked, regaining some control over his emotions. "How did you know I just got home?"

Gloria giggled again. Doyle imagined her lying on her bed, twirling her hair while flirting over the phone like some teenage girl. "I have these things called windows. I was just looking out of mine when I saw your car pull into the garage.

What do you do in that big house of yours? I'd love to come visit sometime."

"Dammit, Gloria. I have a lot to do today. I promise you can come over some other time. How about next week?"

Doyle would be long gone by Sunday night when the time travel world learned of their precious Angel's unfortunate death. They'd unleash every resource they had to find him, and he certainly couldn't hang around Miami to see how it unfolded. A long future awaited of hiding in the wilderness, completely off the grid. At least until he could find a way out of the continent—leaving the United States wasn't enough when the Road Runners' jurisdiction covered all of North America.

"Next week? Really?" Gloria's voice shifted from playful flirting to one of sincerity. She obviously hadn't expected to receive an invitation to Doyle's house.

"Yes. Really." Doyle leaned into this opportunity. "I'll admit, I've tried resisting you. I'm not the type to get caught up in affairs, especially with a neighbor. But knowing that you've been watching me is kind of a turn on. So here's what we'll do. Next Thursday you walk to my house—it has to be here. We can't risk having your husband catch us. You'll knock on my front door. I'll open it, and what happens within these walls remains a secret between you and me. Are we clear?"

Gloria's breathing grew heavy through the phone. "Oh, Doyle. Keep talking like that."

Doyle grinned. "Ah! Not today. You'll have to wait until Thursday. Until then, please let me have some space. Don't ever call me Doy, and have a good weekend."

"How will it not be with you on my mind the whole time?" Gloria asked. Her breathing became faster, and Doyle was fairly sure this titillated woman was touching herself. On that note, he hung up the phone, confident Gloria would remain out of his way for the rest of the weekend, leaving him to focus exclusively on Arielle.

Chapter 33

Vanessa didn't leave work until five o'clock that evening and went straight home. Arielle struggled to stay engaged during the stakeout, reading the entire mission report twice and not finding anything additional of value.

They were alone to figure out the best way to capture Doyle, and following Vanessa around seemed the best option since she would be his first victim in Miami.

Arielle called Selena while driving across town.

"Hey," Selena answered, sounding exhausted. "Any progress today?"

"I'm afraid nothing yet," Arielle replied. "Vanessa worked all day. Took a lunch break at one, where she just walked a block down the road to a deli. Then came back and worked the rest of the day. I'm following her home now. Did you two have any luck?"

"Luck? No. Incredible food. Yes."

Felix laughed in the background.

"Where are you?" Arielle asked.

"University of Miami. We spent most of the day downtown. Checked out some clubs. Not too many were open, but even the ones that were closed had someone in there we could ask about Doyle. No one gave any sort of indication they know him. Stopped at about fifteen different clubs. Then headed to South Beach, poked around some spots there. Came to Coconut Grove, where they say a lot of college students spend their free time. Asked around the restaurants and more clubs, with no luck. That put us about a mile from the university, where we've been for the last hour, chatting with random staff. Felix thinks if Doyle was working at a college, it would be in a role like a custodian so he wouldn't draw much attention and have access to all the buildings."

Arielle nodded. Felix was thinking like an Angel in the field. He was certainly smart enough and just needed the experience to pull it out of him.

"So a total waste of a day," Selena said, sighing.

"It's never a waste," Arielle said. "You explored the city, and you never know when that can be helpful. You've eliminated dozens of locations, which means we can narrow our focus. If Vanessa doesn't go out tonight, I'll grab a map of Miami on my way home. There has to be some pocket of nightlife we're missing."

"So, we get to do this again tomorrow?" Selena asked, her voice filled with dread. "I can't wait."

"I'll probably help you tomorrow if Vanessa goes back to work. I can't do another eight hours sitting in the parking lot. It's too damn hot. And I'm a Colorado girl. This humidity is sticky and gross."

Selena chuckled. "Wow, look at you being a drama queen for once. Just need to bring you to the ocean, I guess."

"Hilarious. Are you going to stay downtown for a bit?"

"Yes. Felix wants to ask around at a few more places. Then we'll probably find somewhere for dinner. We can keep exploring. It's Friday night, so there will be plenty of nightlife."

"You just want to go clubbing in Miami."

"Hey!" Selena said defensively. "I'm just doing my job. Why don't you simmer down?"

Arielle laughed, growing slap-happy after being trapped in the car all day. "Do your thing. I'll call you back when I have an idea what Vanessa is going to do."

They arrived at Vanessa's apartment complex, and Arielle assumed her same position in the back of the lot facing her target's unit. Vanessa took her time going inside, greeted by a roommate, who appeared to be the one missing from their movie night. She had about ten inches over Vanessa and looked even bigger when Vanessa leaned against the counter while they chatted.

The tall girl grabbed a bottle of wine from the fridge and poured two glasses. They clinked and took long swigs before Vanessa retreated to her bedroom, glass in hand, and the tall friend took a seat on the couch to turn on the TV.

Only a couple of minutes passed before Vanessa returned from her room now wearing a pair of jeans and a button-up blouse.

Not exactly an outfit that means she's staying in. Maybe they're just going out for dinner later.

Wherever Vanessa ended up, Arielle was eager to follow. The day *had* been a waste, and she needed to rectify that. If Vanessa went to a restaurant, Arielle would be in a corner booth looking for Doyle. He had to have some sort of encounter with her. He never plucked his victims off the street at random, or even killed them in the heat of the moment. Doyle was calculated. He needed to be to get away with as many murders as he had. Plus, the victims looked like the Angels, and Vanessa was a slightly younger version of Arielle.

She knew Doyle had already met her or at the very least had spotted her and was narrowing his plans to take her life. But where?

The Advance team traveled to six months before a tragedy would occur and notated every movement of their targets. Unfortunately for them, Vanessa had no routine. In those six months, she had never gone to the same restaurant more than twice. Her work schedule was already in shambles. She did frequent night clubs with her friends nearly every weekend, which is why Arielle believed in her gut that's where Doyle had found her. But even narrowing down the list of clubs was tiresome. There were at least a dozen clubs she had visited three different times during those six months. Just because Vanessa went missing from Night Owl didn't mean that's where Doyle had found her. He could have been following her for weeks, leading up to that point.

Arielle pulled out her cell phone again and dialed Selena.

She answered after one ring. "What's up?"

"Did you two check out Night Owl today? It's the club where Vanessa went missing from—er, *will* go missing from."

"Of course we checked there." Selena replied with sass. "That was our first stop. The owner was a pretty rude guy, but he said he never heard the name."

"Damn, okay. Just wanted to check." Arielle shifted in her seat. If the Night Owl was out of the picture for Doyle, they really were wandering blindly.

"No worries. What's going on over there? I assume you made it back to Vanessa's place by now?"

"Yes. She's having a glass of wine with her other roommate—the one who wasn't here last night."

"Ah. Anything interesting about her?"

"She's a tree. Looks athletic, from what I can tell. Maybe a basketball player."

"College player?" Selena asked. "That would connect Doyle to a college campus—if Vanessa ever came out to watch her friend play. But we're having no luck here. Asked ten different custodians by now—some of them are some sketchy dudes."

"And you'd think Doyle would work at a bigger college like the one you're at," Arielle added. "A bigger pool of students to observe and pick from."

"Who knows? There's so many people in this city. Maybe choosing this era to focus on was a mistake. He had fewer places to hide in the other two."

"Oh, shit!" Arielle cried. "The other roommates just parked and are heading in. I'll call you back."

Arielle hung up and watched the two girls laughing as they entered their apartment. They wasted no time pouring their own glasses of wine from the kitchen counter, and the group of them raised their drinks up, toasting to a fun night ahead.

Arielle watched them finish their drinks over the next fifteen minutes. The TV was on, but no one was watching. While the two friends who had just arrived went off to their rooms, the tall girl remained with Vanessa in the kitchen and pulled out a bottle of vodka. She poured four shots and licked her lips with giddy anticipation.

Oh yeah, these girls are definitely going out tonight, Arielle thought, feeling the first signs of hope all day. The potential of just *seeing* Doyle tonight made the whole day relevant.

All four women reconvened in the living room, where the tall one handed out the shot glasses. Arielle couldn't hear them, but knew the sounds of hollering and wooing surely going around the room. They took their shots and filed out of the apartment, purses slung over shoulders, high heels on, hair and makeup ready for a night out.

They piled into Vanessa's car, the tall friend taking the passenger seat while the other two settled into the back.

Driving straight to dinner after a glass of wine and a shot? Arielle thought. *Maybe Vanessa isn't as straight as I thought.*

It didn't matter. Vanessa's fate was linked to Doyle Grady, not a drunk driving accident.

They drove into downtown Miami, Vanessa following the speed limits and committing zero traffic violations. The booze either made her more focused or she could handle a lot more before feeling its effects.

Fifteen minutes later, they pulled into a parking lot for Teleios, a Greek restaurant on a block full of more dining options and night clubs. Thanks to her excessive studying of the map, Arielle knew they were only three blocks from Night Owl. Her thoughts and heart raced in sync. Everything was lining up with her suspicions, and she no longer planned to sit in the restaurant while Vanessa and her friends munched on flatbreads and moussaka.

Arielle parked her car and waited for the women to enter the restaurant. The place was fairly busy, but they only had a ten-minute wait for a table. She had to stick around to ensure they didn't make a last-second change of plans, especially with so many options in the surrounding area.

Through her binoculars, she saw them get seated at a round table in the middle of the dining room and knew they would be there for at least an hour. Arielle tossed the binoculars aside, grabbed a wallet-sized portrait of Doyle out of the mission file, and hurried out of her car, legs now flowing with a nervous adrenaline that made it hard to walk in a straight line.

Fortunately, she had those three blocks until reaching the Night Owl and walked off the nerves. The doors to the club were open, and the music was already booming.

There was no bouncer at the door yet, so she strolled inside to find the club empty, except for the bartenders taking stock, and the DJ testing the lights. Three bars lined the perimeter, and the bartender closest to Arielle looked up with a raised eyebrow.

The woman looked in her early forties and nodded at Arielle. "You're a bit early, sweetie. We won't be set up for another hour."

"Oh, I'm not here to party," Arielle said, immediately regretting her words. *Not here to party? I sound like an idiot.* "I was hoping to speak with a manager, or maybe even the owner."

The bartender put down a glass she had been wiping with a rag and looked Arielle up and down. "Do you have an appointment?"

"I don't," Arielle said, taking confident steps toward the bar. "I'm a private investigator looking into a matter involving a night club employee from somewhere on this block. This might not even be the right place, but I'm making my rounds."

The bartender chewed on her bottom lip, examining Arielle. The owner was somewhere close by, or else she would have dismissed Arielle immediately.

"What's the name of the employee you're looking for?" the bartender asked, picking up the glass and continuing to wipe it.

"Doyle Grady."

Arielle reached the bar and planted her elbows on the top.

The bartender looked blankly at Arielle. "I'm sorry. Never heard that name around here."

"And that's fine, but I'd still like to speak with the owner. I understand club owners talk to each other and share warnings about past or present employees. I hope maybe the owner has heard the name and can point me in the right direction."

The bartender nodded and put the glass down, along with the rag. "Okay. Let me go get him. One second."

She spun around and disappeared down the back hallway. It only took a minute before she returned with a tall man dressed in a flashy suit and jewelry.

"Hello," the owner said, sticking out a hand. "I'm Fernando. Francie told me you have some questions about an investigation. I can assure you we run a clean operation here."

Arielle chuckled. Who knew what Francie had relayed to him, but it was enough to get his interest. Arielle shook his hand. "Thank you for your time, Fernando. But I'm not investigating you or your club. I'm just looking for a man who may have worked at a club on this block in the past year. Does the name Doyle Grady mean anything to you?"

"Doyle Grady?" Fernando asked, taking a deep breath as he looked to the ceiling for his imaginary registry of past employees. "You're the second person to come in here today asking for him. I honestly don't recall ever working with someone by that name. We go through so many employees in this industry."

Arielle heard hints of a Cuban accent in Fernando's speech. "Maybe you'll recognize the face." She reached into her pocket and pulled out the small photo of Doyle, holding it up toward Fernando's eyes.

She saw the immediate flicker of recognition in his gaze.

Only professional liars, which Fernando was not, could get away with concealing this subtle movement.

"Blanco?" Fernando said, his brows furrowed as he studied the picture.

Francie had returned to her post behind the bar but craned her neck for a view of the picture.

The DJ stopped the music, satisfied with all the equipment's performance for the night ahead.

"I'm sorry, did you say Blanco?" Arielle asked.

"That's right!" Francie cried out. "Blanco's real name is Doyle Grady! Jeez, I don't think I've heard his real name since his first day working here."

"This man works *here*?" Arielle asked, heart hammering in her chest. Could Doyle walk through the doors at any moment? What would she do if he did? Hell, what would *he* do? "He *currently* works here?"

"Yes, he does," Fernando said, looking more confused than ever. "Is there a problem?"

Arielle's jaw hung open, and she forced herself to close it. "No problem. I've just been looking for him. What does he do for you?"

"He's a promoter," Fernando said. "He goes up and down the block offering free drink tickets to get people in the club."

"How long has he worked here?" Arielle asked.

"About a year," Fernando said, lips pursed and pointing to the ceiling with his eyes.

"A year?! And you didn't know his real name? How is that possible?" Arielle's voice elevated. She wasn't angry, but it felt like every other emotion was clamoring for her attention at the same time.

Fernando didn't know better, and waved his hands. "Relax,

miss. We've all been calling him Blanco since he started."

"How original, calling a white man Blanco," Arielle said, shaking her head. "I can't believe this. We've been spending all day looking for this man."

Fernando pulled his suit jacket taut. "Look, I'm sorry about the confusion. You're Latina, yes? You know how it is. He's the only gringo that works here, so we started calling him Blanco. He even introduces himself as that to new employees. There are people here who only know him by that name. Even I forgot his real name. He's just Blanco to me. He shows up on time, works hard, never causes issues. Blanco is a part of our community. Even the club regulars know him. Is he in trouble?"

Arielle didn't know what to say. This entire situation had caught her by surprise. "He's not in trouble, but I need to talk to him. Do you know what time he works?"

"He should start at seven," Fernando said, checking his diamond-encrusted watch. "So in a few minutes. He'll stop here first to check in and will hit the street right after."

Arielle nodded and stuffed the photo into her pocket. It was 6:40, and she needed to get the hell out of the Night Owl before Doyle—or Blanco—showed up.

"Okay, thank you," Arielle said. "I'd appreciate it if you didn't mention this conversation to Blanco when you see him. I'll be in touch if I have other questions."

The words practically flew out of her mouth, but she couldn't waste another second. Arielle turned and ran out of the club, looking in every direction in case Doyle arrived a few minutes early to start his shift.

She sprinted back to the Greek restaurant, fumbling in her pocket for her cell phone, which she eventually grabbed, then dialed Selena.

"What's the word?" Selena greeted.

Arielle panted for breath in response. "I found him."

"Arielle? What's wrong?" Concern slipped into Selena's voice.

The restaurant had come into sight, only a block ahead now. The sky had turned to a mixture of purple and orange thanks to the setting sun. Probably a beautiful sight to see if Arielle had any mental capacity to notice. But she didn't.

"He works at Night Owl," Arielle said, slowing her pace to catch her breath. "I just spoke with the owner and showed him a picture. No one knew him as Doyle Grady because they all call him Blanco. He's worked there for a year as a club promoter. Walks the streets outside to bring people in."

"Night Owl?" Selena asked. "The connection's choppy."

"Shit!" Arielle cried, crossing the street to the restaurant. "I said Doyle works at Night Owl. Everyone calls him Blanco."

"Doyle works at Night Owl," Selena repeated. "Got it. And something about Blanco? Maybe you should hang up and call me back."

"Dammit!" Arielle shouted, hanging up the phone and seeing it only had one bar of signal.

She stomped through the restaurant parking lot, glanced inside to see Vanessa and her friends still sitting at their table, and held her phone high above her head, hoping to capture cell service.

By the time she reached her car, she still had no luck. Her hands trembled as she fidgeted with her keys, trying to get the door unlocked.

Then, without warning, her world went dark.

Chapter 34

Selena dialed Arielle for the tenth time in the last five minutes.

"Felix, something isn't right. Stop sitting there and acting like everything is fine."

They finished dinner shortly after Arielle had last called, their conversation broken up by the bad cell service. After twenty minutes had passed without a follow-up from Arielle, they returned to their car, a '97 Toyota Camry, where Selena started dialing.

"Relax," Felix said. "She just found where Doyle works, right? She's probably hiding in a bush watching him or something. No time to talk."

"We need to go there," Selena demanded. "She said he works at the Night Owl, so that must be where she is."

Felix nodded and turned on the car. "Night Owl was our first stop this morning, right?"

"Yes, let's go," Selena urged, slapping the dashboard.

"Okay, settle down. We're close. Maybe ten minutes."

Felix drove off from the pizza joint they had found near the university's campus.

"I'm telling you, she was running," Selena said. "She could hardly breathe and was speaking a hundred words a second. Something was definitely wrong. What the hell would Arielle have been running from?"

"This is Arielle we're talking about. I'd bet my life she's completely fine. She for sure said Doyle works at the Night Owl?"

"Yes," Selena replied, feeling like her own breath was struggling to fill her lungs. "And something about Blanco."

"Blanco?" Felix asked, raising an eyebrow. "Like the Spanish word for white?"

"That's what it sounded like."

Selena couldn't stop running her fingers through her hair. It didn't matter how calm Felix was; she knew something had gone wrong. She'd never heard Arielle speak in such a worried tone before, even if she could only make out every other word.

Selena dialed Arielle again, only to hear it ring and ring. She slammed the phone down. "Fuck!"

"Selena," Felix said in a voice that sounded like he was fighting to keep anger from seeping out. "I need you to relax. I'm sure we'll hear from her soon. End of the night at the latest. It's Arielle. Just breathe. Didn't she once take down an entire cartel by herself? Just to prove she could?"

Selena laughed. That story was as true as they came. Arielle had perched in a tree in Mexico and gradually sniped all the cartel members on a drug lord's property before eventually killing the leader with her bare hands.

"Okay, you're right," Selena said. "I'm sure I'm overreacting."

And now I can't share how Arielle sounded, because Felix only thinks I'm being dramatic.

"Five minutes out," Felix said in a voice that was too relaxed for Selena's liking.

Her legs bounced anxiously, fingers twirling her hair robotically as she tried to clear her mind of negative thoughts.

Arielle had found where Doyle worked with certainty, but what doors did that open? They didn't know how long Doyle had been living in 1998, or what kind of network he had grown during that time. He could have easily turned people to his side, as they had seen in 1898 when everyone in town defended him. If he had done that same thing here, and Arielle was asking around the Night Owl, word could have gotten back to Doyle about Arielle's presence. Unlike 1898, this era has cell phones. And pagers. Actual methods of getting a message to someone without needing to use a horse.

"Please drive faster," Selena begged. But Felix was already going fifteen above the speed limit as they went through downtown.

He looked over his shoulder at her and shook his head. "Relax. We're here."

Selena hadn't recognized their surroundings now that it was night. The scene had completely changed from earlier in the morning when no one roamed the block. Now, people were everywhere. Mostly lined up at restaurants waiting for a table. Others strolled into bars, while a few entered the night clubs.

Felix parked on the curb directly in front of the Night Owl. The club had neon lights around the trim, with a blue and white neon owl perched above the entrance, its wings flapping in a mechanical motion that was painful to watch. But they couldn't deny how it caught the eye's attention.

He turned the key to the off position and drummed his fingers on the steering wheel.

"I don't see her anywhere," Selena said, face pressed against the window as she looked in every direction.

Felix opened his door and stepped out of the car, watching a Lamborghini speed by in the opposite lane. He trudged around the car and started for the club.

Selena jumped out and grabbed him by the arm. "What do you think you're doing?!"

Felix shook his arm free of her grip. "What? I'm going in there to see what's going on."

"We can't just march in there and start looking for Arielle," Selena replied, shuffling around to position herself between Felix and the entrance.

"And why not? You said she was here."

"What if Doyle has people working for him? Or at least someone keeping eyes out on his behalf?"

Felix frowned, took a step back, and crossed his arms. "That seems like a stretch. Besides, that doesn't mean they would know who *we* are. It's not like I'm going in there to ask for Doyle, or even Arielle. I just want to see for myself."

Selena looked around like the world was listening to their conversation. "Okay, fine. We go in. We speak to no one."

Felix nodded and rubbed a comforting hand on Selena's back. "She's fine, okay? Let's have some faith."

Selena sighed as they turned around and strode toward the club's entrance. A mammoth with sunglasses stood guard at the door, checking IDs while keeping a rigid expression.

"Good evening," the man said in a deep baritone, studying the driver's licenses they handed over. He scanned them for a few seconds before handing them back and stepped aside to let them pass.

"Thank you," Selena said, unable to be rude to the bouncer doing his job.

They entered the club and Selena bobbed her head to "No

Diggity" booming through the speakers. It was still early—much too early, in her opinion—for a large crowd in a nightclub. But locals claimed it was impossible to get inside after nine o'clock because of capacity restrictions. Visiting the Night Owl apparently required dedication. There were already a solid sixty people packed onto the dance floor, dozens more lined up at the bars and tables.

"So, what's our move?" Felix asked as they found an open table. They had to lean in to each other to hear over the music.

"Maybe a quick lap around the place," Selena said. "I don't see Doyle, but we don't know what his job is. He could be upstairs or somewhere in the back. He's clearly not a server or bartender."

Felix, being the tall one, looked around the bar like a periscope. "If we see him, what should we do? We're at an advantage because of how many people are in here and how dark it is. We could watch him from a distance."

"Well, if he's in here," Selena said, "then Arielle will be, too. If she learned he works here, she's got to be following him. Did you see her car parked anywhere outside?"

Felix shook his head. "I was paying attention to the cars parked on the street as we pulled up. Saw nothing."

"We don't even know *when* he's supposed to work," Selena said. "What if he doesn't work Fridays? They say this club is busy every night of the week, so it's possible."

Selena kept looking around, praying to catch even the slightest glimpse of Arielle. But she was nowhere to be seen. Felix kept drumming the table as he had the steering wheel earlier. Selena knew he was getting worried, but why did he keep refusing to share that fact?

"Let's take a step back," Felix said, eyes glued to a trio

of girls dancing in the middle of the floor with skirts short enough to leave little to the imagination. "We know Arielle and how she works. If she was running when she called, do you think she was running *to* the club or away from the club?"

Selena grinned. Felix was a master puzzle solver. "Well, if she had just found out Doyle worked here, that would mean she was already here. So running away from the club."

"Okay." Felix nodded in agreement. "And what would make Arielle run? Let's assume she wasn't in danger, because if she was, she probably would've led with that instead of the information about Doyle."

"True," Selena said, now staring at the table in deep concentration. She imagined she was Arielle, going through the same motions she had witnessed countless times. "Arielle has never run from danger. But she runs when she's at risk of getting caught."

Felix slapped the tabletop, the sound lost in the music, but still snapping Selena to attention. "Exactly! Okay. So Arielle was in this building. She found out Doyle worked here. Unfortunately, we don't know *how*, and that matters. If she saw Doyle directly, would she have run?"

Selena jerked her head from side to side. "Nope. After all we've been through on this mission, no way in hell she would let Doyle out of her sight. Even if she had to get out of the club, she wouldn't have run far enough that she couldn't observe the doors. She'd want to follow Doyle."

"Agreed. So, if Doyle *was* here and left, it's safe to say Arielle followed him. That also explains why her car isn't anywhere nearby."

Selena shuddered.

"What's wrong?" Felix asked with a concerned frown.

"I just don't like thinking of Arielle following Doyle on her own. He's dangerous. And sick. We've already seen what he's capable of, and how he's been just one step ahead this whole time. What if that's still the case? What if he was expecting her to show up here, and was ready? We weren't with her. It would be his best opportunity."

Felix shook his head. "Arielle is too aware of her surroundings. She's always ready for the worst to happen."

"What if he created some sort of trap? What if she was running, trying to chase him, and he led her somewhere on purpose?"

The more Selena considered the multiple possibilities, the sicker she felt to her stomach. Here she was in one of the most talked about nightclubs in Miami, and the sound of the music was making her nauseous.

Felix perked up, eyes locked on something in the opposite direction from the dance floor. Selena spun around to look, but only saw huddles of people standing in line for the bar.

"What is it?" she asked, glancing from Felix to the area he couldn't look away from.

Felix made an expression that looked almost like an evil smile. "Doyle works here," he said, though the words seemed intended for himself. "There's a door back there that opens to a hallway. Offices. If Doyle really works here, there's got to be some sort of file or documentation with his information. Phone number. Address. Something."

Selena looked again, now noticing the door that had just swung open and closed. "It's unguarded. I think the bathrooms are also back there, which means we just need to locate which room is the office and find the right time to slip inside."

Felix's lips tightened into a wider grin. "Let's go see what we're dealing with."

Chapter 35

Doyle stuffed Arielle into her own backseat with the calmness and precision of the surgeon he once was.

"Dr. Grady back in action," he said as he climbed behind the wheel and left the Teleios parking lot. The radio turned on with the car, playing "Your Woman" by White Town. Doyle couldn't help but sing along. He looked over his shoulder at a red light and said to the unconscious Arielle, "You're *my* woman now."

After he had prepared his house for Vanessa's arrival earlier, Doyle returned to her apartment complex and waited for her to get home. The sequence of events that followed twisted fate in the most unexpected way.

Of course, Arielle had followed Vanessa home from work. He'd considered attacking her in the parking lot, but there was too much traffic with everyone else returning home. So he had remained hidden and waited for all of them to leave. The closer they had kept driving toward the Night Owl, the more anxious Doyle became. Vanessa was no longer his priority. He couldn't keep his eyes off Arielle, remembering the promises they had made to each other, and how she ignored him after all they had both been through.

Just seeing her opened the floodgates. Doyle was suddenly

back at his wife's deathbed, remembering that feeling of wanting to end his own life. The weeks that followed saw him operating like a zombie. Saving lives no longer brought him joy, but he did it. That was his paycheck, after all. Even a nationally renowned surgeon could go through the motions of their dreaded day job from time to time. But the joy had never returned. Without his beloved wife, nothing mattered.

Looking back, his work took the biggest toll on his mental health. Saving life after life when he couldn't save his own wife may have been what finally pushed him over the edge. All the gratitude his patients showered him with for pulling off such unlikely miracles did nothing to make him feel better. He'd become numb to it all, questioning why anyone bothered going through such extreme measures like a triple bypass surgery, just to keep living in this awful fucking world.

But then he was approached by the Road Runners. At the time, it was exciting. Time travel? He didn't believe it at first, but what did he have to lose? Worst-case scenario, he'd get lost somewhere in the void and could drift away into eternity. But he found a renewed purpose and created his own plans to go back and save his wife. He also made new friends. Several, in fact, but none as good as Arielle Lucila. They bonded over their traumatic losses. They formed a deep spiritual connection. No romance. No fluff. Just two lost souls looking for a better life after excruciating suffering.

"I'll help you if you help me," Doyle said to Arielle's body in the backseat. The same words she had said to him during a private conversation after a long day of training at the Road Runners academy. "DON'T YOU FUCKING REMEMBER?!" he screamed. "Or do you always make promises you can't keep?"

Tears rolled down Doyle's face. Arielle had given him so

much hope when their friendship began. Like everyone else in the organization, he knew early on what she was capable of. Hell, he knew *better* than the Road Runners because he had a front row view every single day at training. It was impossible to ignore greatness when it was right in front of you. If Arielle went back in time to save his wife, he had one hundred percent faith she would get the job done.

And because of that, he was willing to die for her family, if that's what it took to save them. Arielle would live forever in happiness with her parents and brother, while his wife would get to lead a full life. If Doyle had to be the sacrifice to make that happen, so be it. He'd always saved everyone else, so why wouldn't he do it one last time?

He pulled into his driveway and had to park, get out, and open the garage from the keypad since his remote was in his car, which was still parked at the restaurant. When he pulled Arielle's car in, he kept checking his mirrors to see if his nearest neighbors were watching. None were from what he could tell, and he let out a sigh of relief before hopping out to close the garage, leaving the keys in the ignition.

The garage door creaked shut, snapping into place after finishing its descent. It smelled of car exhaust and destiny. Saliva pooled in Doyle's mouth. He was officially out of the public eye, alone in his own property with a knocked-out Arielle Lucila.

"Let's have some fun, darling," he said, shuffling to the car's back door, rubbing his hands together like he was about to dive into a massive feast.

He had lain her across the backseat, and she looked like she was having the most beautiful dreams. If only she deserved pleasant dreams.

Doyle still wasn't sure exactly how heavy Arielle was, nor was he about to find out. Adrenaline had helped him move quickly and efficiently in the parking lot and would now assist him in carrying her body up the stairs. He couldn't recall the last time he'd ever felt this *alive*. Competing in a triathlon with Arielle slung over his shoulders didn't seem too tall of a task, considering how much energy he had.

He opened the car door and pulled Arielle out with ease, cradling her in his arms like a small child. Something bulged against his arms from beneath her shirt, something he'd need to check before tying her up. Arielle's hair fell over her face, and he brushed it aside with the caring grace of a lover. Doyle stomped to the house door and turned the knob. As soon as he pushed the door open, his phone rang in the kitchen, causing an instant ball of horror to drop into his gut.

Gloria, he thought in a panic. *Did she see me pull in? Did she see the body in the backseat? Fuck.*

It rang three more times before he dragged himself to the couch in the living room and dropped Arielle on it. If he didn't answer, Gloria might come pounding on his door next. *I shouldn't have led her on. Stupid Doyle!*

Answering the call was his best bet for keeping her away, so he scampered to the kitchen and snatched the phone off the wall. "Hello?"

"Blanco, where the fuck are you?" Fernando asked, music distorted in the background, which meant he was in his club office.

Doyle's head spun around faster than Linda Blair in *The Exorcist,* searching for the clock on the opposite wall.

Fuck.

He was fifteen minutes late for his shift, and now his asshole boss was hunting him down.

"Fernando!" Doyle cried out, faking enthusiasm. "I'm sorry I'm running a little late. I got tied up in some things around the house. Be there in about ten minutes."

Tied up...good one.

Doyle braced himself for the worst. Not that it mattered anymore. Fernando had proven to be a ruthless man to work for, never tolerating excuses, and quick to fire employees who couldn't adhere to his lofty standards. Being this late to a shift without notification seemed like a guarantee to lose the job he no longer needed.

Instead, Fernando's voice lowered. "Is everything okay?"

Is that actual concern? From Fernando? This day can't get any stranger.

"Uh, yes, I'm fine," Doyle said, twirling the phone cord between his fingers. He had an unconscious time traveler on his couch and so many more important matters on his mind. "Why do you ask?"

"Someone was here looking for you earlier," Fernando said in an even lower tone. "I think she was part of the FBI or something."

Doyle grinned as he looked at Arielle on the couch. "A woman in her twenties, right? Brown hair, athletic build. Kind of intimidating?"

"Yes, that was her. What's going on? Are you in some sort of trouble?"

Doyle laughed, a mixture of relief and boiling nerves. "No trouble at all. She's an old friend of mine from college. She *is* in the FBI, but she always does this. Randomly shows up and messes with me. It's her idea of a joke."

"A joke?" Fernando asked, every ounce of concern fleeing in

an instant. "A fucking joke?! I thought the club was in trouble. Then you. Are you shitting me?"

"I'm sorry," Doyle said.

"Sorry?" Fernando gasped. "Get your *sorry* ass down here right now! If I don't see you in the next fifteen minutes, don't bother showing up!"

Doyle heard the slamming of the phone before the call cut off.

There's the Fernando I know. But he still gave me fifteen minutes after I said I'd be there in ten. What a softy.

Doyle hung up and returned to the couch where Arielle hadn't moved. She had one arm splayed over the edge, knuckles dragging on the floor. Her shirt had rolled up just enough for him to see something black running across her stomach. "What are you hiding?" he asked, squatting down next to her and pulling up her shirt to reveal a utility belt strapped around her waist.

Throwing knives, pepper spray, a nine-millimeter and ammo, and a pouch full of zip ties.

"All this for me, darling?" Doyle asked, flipping Arielle on her side so he could unsnap the belt. "You really wanted to have a good time with me, after all."

He chuckled as he took the belt into the kitchen and tossed it in the cabinet beneath the sink. Maybe he'd come back and use her own weapons against her, but the ones he had in the safe room would suffice for now.

Doyle returned to Arielle, licking his lips and having a sudden urge to dance. He was that overcome with joy. "Alright, up we go."

He squatted down, sure to lift from his legs instead of his back, and hoisted Arielle up and over his shoulder like an oversized sack of potatoes. He swayed gently with her body, hugging her knees as he hummed a soft tune, dancing toward the stairs.

Doyle felt the burn, as expected, during the ascent up. He lost his footing, slipping on the plastic covering, but saved them both from tumbling back down with a quick grab of the handrail.

"Damn, girlfriend," he said, giggling. "How romantic would that have been if we died together? Time-traveling Romeo and Juliet!"

He reached the top landing moments later and turned into the safe room, sitting Arielle on the wooden chair, and tipping her head back to keep her balanced while he hurried over to the wall for the rope.

Arielle had an elevated amount of midazolam coursing through her body, enough to keep her knocked out until the morning. Doyle had brought it for Vanessa, but gladly adjusted his plans when the window opened on Arielle.

Before fastening the rope around her body, Doyle patted down Arielle's legs to search for any more hidden weapons. He only found a cell phone, which he slammed to the floor and stomped into dozens of pieces, then proceeded tying her to the chair. "I'm sorry we had to reunite this way, but I didn't know how else to get your attention. We have to do the right thing, no matter how hard it is. You taught me that. You're going to have a very deep sleep tonight. Do enjoy! I need to go to work—gotta cover my bases and alibis. But I'll be back. Don't you worry. And when you wake, we're going to discuss how you're going to save my wife."

Doyle dropped to both knees after he finished with the rope. He leaned in to Arielle's face and pressed his lips against her ear to whisper. "And after you do that, I'm going to kill you."

Chapter 36

Felix and Selena went into the back hallway, where two lines had formed for the restrooms. The men were on the left, women on the right. The lines were so long they blocked a door with a hanging placard that read *OFFICE.*

"What are we going to do?" Felix muttered as they stopped just short of the lines of clubbers waiting to relieve their bladders.

"Should we just try later?" Selena asked. "I'm trying to think what I can do to draw everyone's attention but can't come up with anything legal."

Felix laughed. "I don't even want to know. But do you really think this line will die down enough for us to make a move?"

"No, I don't," Selena said flatly. "I just need more time."

The last thing Selena wanted was to waste any more time while they didn't know if Arielle was safe or not. But they couldn't make any knee-jerk reactions, either. The most important thing Arielle had stressed over and over was to always consider how the past might push back against an action. They had too many unknown factors at the moment to make such a prediction.

The original timeline of events had Vanessa being killed by Doyle tomorrow night. The past would do everything in its power to conserve that event. If Doyle worked in that small office, what might happen if they barged in? Surely he knew who she and Felix were, even though his obsession was with Arielle.

Clear your mind so the past doesn't know what you're thinking.

Arielle had often told them this, like it was a simple matter. Selena found it impossible to clear her thoughts under the current circumstances. Pounding music, drunk people in a hallway, and no Arielle to be seen. It was all too much for her to process at once. How the hell was anyone supposed to focus on the task at hand?

"Okay, let's go back into the club," Felix said. "Standing in this hallway is just weird."

People were now making out and feeling each other up to pass the waiting time. A woman with smeared makeup had her tongue down another man's throat while keeping an eye open and locked onto Felix.

Felix didn't wait for Selena and started back toward the club, pushing the door open and immediately pivoting back around. He raced to Selena.

"What is it?" she asked, glancing at the door that had gently swung closed.

"Doyle," Felix said under his breath. "I just saw him across the way. He just walked in."

"Shit!" Selena gasped. "What do we do? Is he coming back here?"

"I don't know. I'd guess there's a chance he might."

"C'mon." Selena grabbed Felix by the wrist and pulled him toward the lines. "Face forward and don't look back."

And so they waited in the women's restroom line, which ran along the wall with the office door. The volume in the hallway elevated each time the door swung open thanks to the music pouring in, and when it did, Selena felt the blood in her veins freeze in place. Felix's arm trembled against hers as they both looked down at the floor and waited.

Five seconds later, Doyle passed them by, dressed in a fine suit with his hair slicked back. Selena's heart hammered. The thought of being so close to a crazed serial killer brought a distinct shift in the surrounding energy.

The office door was five people ahead of them in line, so they kept their heads down while trying to steal glances out of the corners of their eyes.

Doyle smiled at the woman blocking the door as he politely asked to pass by. He knocked on the door before pushing it open and disappearing inside.

The line shifted forward, and they were only three spots away from the door.

"What do we do?" Felix asked, no longer hiding the worry in his voice.

"Just listen," Selena whispered. Muffled shouting came from the other side of the door. They exchanged a glance as the line moved up, and they were now only five feet away.

Selena leaned against the wall and wiggled her way a couple feet closer, neck craned to hear the commotion better. The shouting continued. Two men.

"I've done nothing but give my all to this club since my first day!" Doyle shouted. "And you jump down my throat because I was late for the first time tonight? Get real!"

Silence followed for the next few seconds. They moved up further in line, Selena now with her back against the door. Her fingertips pulsed. The door could swing open any moment, and she could stand face to face with the murderous psychopath they'd been chasing throughout time. They had no weapons. When they left the house this morning, their plans were to scout the area, not actually find themselves in a situation to bring down Doyle.

"You're right, Blanco," the other man's voice said. "You're absolutely right. But rules are rules, and I'm going to deduct your tardiness from your next paycheck."

Blanco? Selena thought. *Arielle mentioned Blanco on the phone.*

"I don't even care," Doyle replied. "Keep your money. I expect nothing less."

"Stop!" the man shouted. "Where do you think you're going?"

"I'm going to work. I have cards to pass out, remember?"

Selena heard the footsteps from inside approach the door and hurried forward, bumping into the woman in front of them and making her spill a drink onto the floor.

"Hey, what the fuck?!" the girl cried, streaks of margarita running down her legs.

"I'm so sorry," Selena said, pulling Felix by the wrist away from the door. "I'll buy you another drink."

"Damn right you will," the girl said, her face scrunched up in pure disgust.

The office door swung open and Selena froze, praying the girl wouldn't make a scene that might draw Doyle's attention. But Doyle scurried out of the office and back down the hallway, acknowledging none of the people standing in line. He kicked the door to the club open and vanished from sight.

Felix rummaged through his pockets and pulled out a ten-dollar bill, forcing it into the girl's hand. "Couple of drinks on us," he said. "Sorry again, but we have to go."

They spun around and chased after Doyle down the hall. By the time they reached the door, they saw Doyle making his way through the club's exit.

"Shit!" Selena cried, pushing her way through the crowd. Felix followed with much more ease thanks to the path she had cleared.

They stumbled outside, the bouncer watching them curiously as he held up a line of a dozen people waiting anxiously to enter the club.

The night air was humid and still as they glanced around for Doyle.

"That way!" Selena said, nudging Felix to look up the sidewalk running northbound.

"We can't just follow him," Felix said. "He'll know something is up."

"Fool, we *have* to follow him!" Selena replied through gritted teeth. Her frustration was mounting, not with Felix, but by the panic of somehow ending up in charge of this mission. "Do you see Arielle anywhere around?"

Felix did a double take to make sure. "No."

"Exactly. The last thing she said was that she knew where Doyle works. Oh, and the man Doyle was shouting with in that office called him Blanco. Doyle is Blanco, you see? Arielle got too close. We follow Doyle, we find Arielle."

"What about getting his address from inside?"

"That's not happening. Let's go." Selena started down the sidewalk. Across the street from the Night Owl was an Italian restaurant called Basani's. Doyle strolled into its small parking lot and started sticking business cards under the windshield wipers of each vehicle. Once he finished, he returned to the sidewalk and continued doing the same for each car parked on the street.

Selena and Felix hadn't crossed the intersection, content with how close they already were.

"Is that really the job he's been doing this whole time?" Felix asked, his eyes still scouting the area for any sign of Arielle.

"It's actually the perfect type of job when you think about it," Selena said. "He tries to find victims in their twenties. What better place to work than a nightclub in downtown Miami?"

"How long are we going to follow him?" Felix asked.

"As long as it takes," Selena said. "Until we see Arielle, we have to assume he has some sort of involvement."

"Involvement? So you don't think he actually has her?"

"Of course not." Selena took a few steps back from the sidewalk, still watching Doyle make his rounds up and down the sidewalk. "His goal this whole time has been to capture Arielle. Do you really think if he had her, that he'd just be out here tonight trying to get people into this club? *We* know he doesn't need this job, so why else would he still be out here? I think he probably has some people in his circle, just like he did in 1898. They look out for him, probably warn him if anyone comes asking around. You know Arielle asked too many questions. I'd bet whoever she was asking caught on and is holding her hostage. But now Doyle needs to play nice to get Arielle."

"So then it's someone who also works at the club," Felix said, stuffing his hands into his pockets as a light breeze brushed against his flesh. "Otherwise he'd have left this job."

"The logic makes sense. But who has Arielle? And where are they holding her?"

Selena had been pacing circles, and Felix reached out and grabbed her by the elbow. "You're acting rather calm about this, considering how off the walls you were earlier. Do you not think Arielle is in danger?"

Selena stopped and drew a deep breath. "I'm trying my best to not think of the possibilities—plus, I trust Arielle to stay alive—but I don't think she's in any danger. *Yet.* Not until Doyle is directly involved. So long as we have eyes on him, I'm not going to worry. We're in charge now. Emotions are out the window. It's entirely on us to find Arielle."

"Shit, he's coming back this way," Felix said, twirling around to turn his back to Doyle. Selena followed suit and joined Felix as he started in the opposite direction. "Just play it cool."

"We both have sunglasses in the car," Selena said. "Let's grab them real quick."

They were only a few steps from where Felix had parked, so he hurried to the car and returned with the sunglasses well before Doyle had even crossed the street. They put the glasses on and leaned against the side wall of the club.

Doyle crossed the intersection, clutching a thick stack of business cards in one hand. He strolled in their direction but stopped a group of men and women walking by, handing each of them a card, which they took and then promptly joined the growing line outside the club.

"Must be handing out free drinks," Selena said, craning her neck every few seconds to see around Felix, who stood tall with his arms crossed over his chest.

Further down the sidewalk, where Doyle had just been moments earlier, a group of women came clopping along in their high heels. One waved at Doyle, but he didn't notice. He had ventured off down the street, heading west from the club and disappeared from sight.

"Who are they?" Felix asked, pressing his back deeper into the wall to give Selena a better view around him.

Selena leaned forward and squinted. It was dark, but the group of women passed under the splash of street lights every few steps. "Holy shit. It's Vanessa and her friends."

Chapter 37

Doyle hated wearing suits, especially in a place as humid as Miami.

These flashy fucks and their style, he thought.

Latin music boomed from a nearby speaker as Doyle stood outside the Night Owl Club. It always did, and his head throbbed to the point of numbness. But this was his life in 1998, and aside from the constant pounding bongos, maracas, and cowbell—the fucking cowbell!—Doyle didn't mind his temporary life as a club promoter for the Night Owl, which locals simply referred to as The Owl.

He didn't mind it one bit. His killings were methodical. He wanted victims who resembled Arielle Lucila and her cocksucking teammates. It brought him the most pleasure to see the life slip away from their miserable faces, imagining it was the real Arielle Lucila. He always wanted his first victim in a new city to be one who resembled Arielle, but that wasn't always up to him.

And now, he had the unique opportunity to remove both the real Arielle and the fill-in he'd had his eyes on for weeks. The universe really did work in mysterious ways, and it was a thing of beauty.

Being a club promoter, Doyle observed a constant flow of

men and women in their twenties every night on the job. He'd been doing this for nearly a year now, getting a feel for the crowd and what he could get away with. Despite his earlier argument with Fernando, the club's owner trusted Doyle more than most. This trust led to Doyle getting to spend time inside the club, where he sometimes worked as a personal assistant to Fernando.

It was the typical busy work—fetching drinks, drugs, condoms. Whatever Fernando needed. Doyle was his little bitch boy. How he hated when Fernando would speak Spanish to the women hanging on his arms, only for them to look at him and break out in laughter.

Maybe when I slash his throat, I'll make it in the shape of a smile, since he's always laughing at me.

But Doyle kept his anger in check. Fernando wasn't worth the cocaine residue he left on the tip of his nose. Doyle always arrived with his research completed. In 2002, Fernando would be off to prison for a money laundering scheme where he funneled drug money through the nightclub. And The Owl would be closed forever.

Serves him right, Doyle always thought after brushing aside his fantasies of running a blade across Fernando's throat.

It had taken Doyle time to find who he wanted to target from the constantly revolving door of club guests. Miami was loaded with tourists and thousands of night clubs. He had rarely seen the same face stroll through the doors twice, but when he did, Doyle took note.

Vanessa Bauer had come with a group of friends every weekend for three straight weeks. Mid-twenties, olive skin, long brown hair.

There's my Arielle, he thought when he had first seen her, praying that she would return for a second visit. When she had the following week, he knew it was time to make plans.

Doyle had tested out his methods on other club goers, just to refine his elevator pitch. Apparently, dressing up made him more appealing than he believed. A fancy suit suggested money. And when Doyle asked women to join him at his place a couple blocks over, they knew exactly what neighborhood he was talking about.

He hadn't purchased an unnecessarily expensive home two blocks away from the club for no reason. Fernando didn't know it, but they actually lived on the same block. It was the typical rich Miami playboy type of neighborhood. Flashy cars, boats, light strings climbing up the palm trees.

And that's why Doyle tolerated the constant, booming music during this phase of his life. He could have sex any night of the week and take his pick of women like it was a fucking buffet. See, in Miami, every night is Friday night if you're in the right spot. And The Night Owl was it.

Until Miami, Doyle hadn't enjoyed a woman's warmth since losing his beloved wife, but something about this place made him feel invincible. He'd already lost count of how many women he had slept with just from testing out his scheme. And they all left before the sun came up. God bless Miami!

Aside from his soaring confidence and much needed release of sexual tension, Doyle had a feeling Miami was the place he'd get the real Arielle. He'd set up plans in other centuries only to see them fail. But Miami came through when it mattered.

There were people *everywhere,* unlike the Dallas or Oklahoma he had lived in. He stood on the corner of a busy street every single night, yet never feared being spotted by Arielle or her goons. There was simply too much bustle for anyone to stick out in this city.

But there she was.

Vanessa.

She stuck out only because Doyle had his eye on her. He'd been waiting for her to arrive at 9:15, just as she had done for the past three weeks. People couldn't help but be creatures of habit—a trait that made Doyle drool with glee.

"Hello, darling," he said under his breath, watching Vanessa and her three girlfriends stroll down the sidewalk. *Same friends, same club.*

And Doyle knew that meant she would have the same drink—Sex on the Beach. *Yuck.*

He clenched a stack of cards offering a free drink to anyone entering the club before nine o'clock. Vanessa and her crew approached nearer, the clacking of high heels making it sound like a herd of horses galloping the streets of Miami.

"Good evening, ladies," Doyle called out once they were only twenty feet away. "Back for more?"

Vanessa grinned, flashing the perfect smile between those plump red lips. "Oh, Blanco, you know we're only here to see you."

Yes. Yes, you are.

Doyle theatrically checked his watch. "And you made it just in time. Now, don't you ladies go getting in too much trouble tonight." He shot them a wink, earning a round of giggles.

God, I feel like a fucking douchebag.

"Never," Vanessa replied playfully. "We'll see you in there later?"

"You know it." Doyle cracked a smile before handing out the drink cards to the women and never looked back as they entered the club.

He had his role as a sleazy club promoter down to a science. Charm the women with slick talk and free drinks. Flirt a little. Find them in the bar after eleven to get them more free drinks on his tab, and party the night away. Keep giving them drinks and eventually their trust in him grew while they threw caution to the wind one sip at a time.

In just a few hours, you'll be all mine, Doyle thought, unable to keep a grin off his face. *You'll be* ours.

He remembered Arielle tied up in the safe room already.

Success was only hours away. He could taste it in the air. His first kill in Miami. Arielle's sidekicks would arrive soon—he knew the procedures the Angels had in place, especially with their best asset missing. The Road Runners were quick to dismiss him, but Doyle was a sponge soaking up every ounce of knowledge during his time training with them. Losing his wife had brought an unusual level of focus to his mind. No details slipped by him. He could read a book once and break down every detail, chapter by chapter. Doyle had always been highly intelligent, but his capacity for absorbing information had increased to a level beyond his understanding.

That's why he could remember the drink orders for any woman he targeted in the club. Even weeks later. He had a photographic memory on steroids.

Doyle checked his watch to see that nine o'clock was only five minutes away. It was too late for any newcomers to take advantage of the free drink—they'd never make it to the bartender in time, and Lorenzo ran a tight ship with honoring the time deadline.

The music called on him to enter the club, so Doyle flicked a couple of drink cards onto the sidewalk, more out of spite toward Fernando and the ass chewing he had just endured before starting this shift. *Fuck this job.*

The club's bouncer, a former linebacker at Florida State University, was a behemoth named Jason Henderson. Everyone called him Big J, a name that fit as he stood with his arms crossed, blackout sunglasses, and a scruffy beard that made him look like a bear.

"Big J," Doyle said, clapping him on the back. "I'm all done out here for the night. Let's have a drink later."

"Absolutely," Big J replied, keeping a stern face, allowing a sliver of excitement to slip into his voice.

"I'll see you in there."

Big J nodded as Doyle passed by and entered the club.

The Night Owl had become one of the more popular clubs in Miami over the past couple of years. Celebrities and athletes had found their way to the club and spread the word. And this was with no social media. During his first week, Doyle had the pleasure of briefly meeting Dan Marino, a highlight he hadn't expected to enjoy as much as he did.

Friday night was Ladies' Night at the Owl, which meant there were more men packed into the club than usual. The space had a dance floor big enough to fit one hundred and fifty people comfortably and was touted as the biggest dance floor in Miami. Three bars were stationed along the perimeter, and there was a second level where they kept the VIP booths and tables.

On the main level, there were only ten standing tables that were often fought over by three hundred people nightly. This evening was no different, but Doyle spotted Vanessa at the table nearest the bar. He tapped his breast pocket to make sure the midazolam pill was there, just in case—he still had access to hundreds of the pills whenever he wanted to pop back to his present time.

He doubted he would *need* to use it to get Vanessa to his house. His main issue was how to get her separated from her friends, a more advanced technique he had worked on in weeks past, with varying difficulty depending on the woman's loyalty to her friends.

Fortunately, Vanessa had come out with the same girl-friends as she had the prior two weeks, so Doyle already understood the moves he'd need to make. He'd seen enough friend groups in the club to understand they mostly followed the same dynamics. There was always a loose cannon, who didn't necessarily need alcohol to make out with different men throughout the night until finding the one she wanted to leave with. Some were courteous enough to tell their friends they were heading out, but most did not.

In Vanessa's group, this was the tall brunette who played collegiate volleyball at some nearby state university. Both of the prior weekends, she had ventured off with different men.

Then there was one who just wanted to dance the night away. This was Vanessa's friend who somewhat resembled Selena. However, Doyle wouldn't dare kill two women from the same circle of friends—that would only make his life hell once the investigations started. He preferred to stick around when possible, to at least see how matters unfolded.

Each group also had the responsible member. The one who worried what everyone else in the group was up to. This one was a tiny, yet fierce woman called Debbie Richards. She and Vanessa were the only two Doyle had formally met. And that was because Debbie inserted herself into the conversation as soon as Doyle had approached Vanessa on the first night they met. Debbie often chased down her tall volleyball friend but had never stopped her from leaving with strange men.

And that left Vanessa, the friend in the group who looked like she'd rather be anywhere else, but came out because that's what her friends wanted to do. She never had more than three drinks during her stay, just enough to get a pleasant buzz and dance a few songs before retreating to Debbie, who had to bitch about every pair of eyeballs staring at her ass.

Why do you hang out with these people? Doyle thought as he saw Debbie throw her head back and laugh. Eliminating Debbie from the picture was the first step. He'd never be able to get Vanessa out of here as long as Debbie was circling them like a hawk.

Doyle went to the main bar in the center, where he had struck up a friendship with Lorenzo, a bartender working his way through medical school. It pained Doyle that he couldn't share his true past as a surgeon, instead pretending to be someone who dreamed of going to medical school. They bonded over this, and Lorenzo never asked questions when Doyle ordered the most random groupings of drinks. For all he knew, Doyle was still working as the promoter, even from inside the club.

As an employee, Doyle bypassed the line and stood at the side of the bar where servers picked up drink orders for the VIPs upstairs.

Lorenzo was finishing off a margarita when he noticed Doyle. "Blanco, good sir," he hollered over the shouting crowd surrounding the bar. "Another good night?"

Doyle nodded. "As always."

Lorenzo wore a jean vest to show off his biceps. He had obviously put plenty of work into getting as shredded as possible. Doyle wondered if he did this for fitness reasons, or to earn more tips. Even when the ladies were getting free drinks, they'd still throw massive tips at Lorenzo, just so he would acknowledge them with his endearing smile.

Doyle had learned most of his moves by observing Lorenzo. While the bartender didn't use his charm to lure women to his house—at least, not to Doyle's knowledge—he had a natural way of communicating with both the men and women spending their time at the Owl.

Lorenzo was always smiling. Doing so hurt Doyle's cheeks after ten minutes, but he had no choice. No one would respond to the creepy man standing in the corner with a serious countenance.

"Need any drinks?" Lorenzo asked, wiping his hands on his apron and shuffling over to Doyle.

Doyle looked at the table with Vanessa and her friends.

"Yes. I need a dirty martini, Sex on the Beach, and two shots of tequila."

Lorenzo nodded. "On it, boss."

I fucking hate when men call me that.

Doyle waited, but not long. Lorenzo had some of the quickest hands he'd ever seen work behind a bar. While the other bartenders around the club had to check recipes and take their sweet ass time pouring drinks, Lorenzo could fill three different orders at once. He never had to check a list of ingredients, somehow knowing every drink. He had that medical brain that needed to retain more information than most people.

"Drinks up!" Lorenzo called out as he poured the two tequila shots, holding the bottle well above his head, yet still landing the stream of liquid precisely into the shot glasses.

"You're a magician," Doyle said, offering one of his forced smiles as he slid the drinks onto a small round tray.

"Anytime, boss."

Gag me.

Lorenzo spun around to take the next order, and Doyle reached into his pocket for the pill, which he quickly dropped into the tequila shot intended for Debbie. He waited twenty seconds for it to dissolve, then started for Vanessa and her friends. He had to dodge a couple of drunks to avoid spilling the tray. The servers didn't get paid enough.

Finally, he reached the table and turned on the charm. "I wasn't sure if you ladies had gotten your drinks in time, so I got you some."

He lowered the tray onto the table, earning giddy applause from Ms. Volleyball. "Dirty martini for you," he said, placing it in her hand.

"Thank you, kind gentleman," she replied, cracking a wide grin and eyeing Doyle.

I'm not here for you, skank.

"Sex on the Beach," Doyle said with confidence, handing the drink to Vanessa.

"How did you know?" she asked. "I've been hooked on these drinks for the past six months."

Doyle tilted his head. "Just a hunch. And two shots of tequila."

He pushed the shot glasses across the table toward Debbie and the dancer, sure to give Debbie the one that he had slipped the tablet into.

Debbie studied the shot glass, grabbed it, and held it high. "To free drinks!" she cried out.

The other girls followed suit by raising their beverages, cheering and hollering.

This is going to be way easier than I—

Debbie tipped her shot glass over and poured its contents onto the tray, glowering at Doyle.

"Debbie, what the fuck?!" Ms. Volleyball shouted across the table.

Debbie slammed down the shot glass and tossed her hands aggressively in the air. "Do you really expect me to trust a drink from some random stranger? I don't know who this guy is, and neither do any of you. I'd think twice about drinking anything from a random man. We know better, ladies."

Clearly out of spite, Ms. Volleyball chugged her martini like it was a glass of water.

Vanessa put her drink down, crossed her arms, and shook her head. "That wasn't cool, Debbie. This is Blanco. He's a promoter for this club. Why would he slip something in your drink when he *works* here? His job is to *literally* make sure you keep coming back."

Debbie jutted out her chin, not giving a shit what anyone had to say. "I don't take drinks from men I don't know. We've met this guy, what, twice? He might have an agenda. There's a lot of sick people in the world, and most of them are *men*."

"You're so fucked up," Ms. Volleyball shouted, now stretching her majestic arm across the table to point a finger in Debbie's face. "You need to get laid already. Maybe you'd be more fun to hang out with."

Debbie's jaw dropped, her face turning red, even noticeable in the dim club.

"Fuck you, slut!" Debbie shouted back, smacking Ms. Volleyball's hand out of the way.

Ms. Volleyball put her hands on her hips, grinning like a lunatic. "At least people don't bitch about going out with me. Unlike *someone* else."

"Ladies!" Vanessa screamed, smacking the top of the table. "That's enough! Blanco was just doing a kind gesture for us. Something I'm sure he'll never do again now." She turned to him. "I'm sorry about my friends but am truly thankful for the drinks."

Doyle brought back his smile. "It's totally fine. For what it's worth, your friend isn't wrong. There are a lot of sick people out there. I've seen plenty of them in action right in this club. Maybe not the best approach, but she isn't completely wrong in rejecting a drink."

Panic was settling in for Doyle now. He had only brought the one pill, and it was now a dissolved mess on his tray. How would he get Debbie out of the picture now?

"Look," Doyle said, raising his hands up to show his innocence. These women didn't know about the murderer standing in front of them. The man who had killed people across the depths of time. They just saw a club promoter in an itchy fucking suit. "I'm happy to get you another tequila shot," he said to Debbie. "You can even join me at the bar to watch it get poured."

All the friends swung their heads around to look at Debbie, who kept a stiff expression.

"Fine," she said, letting out a sigh. "Let's go."

She didn't wait for Doyle before starting toward the bar. Vanessa grabbed Doyle by the arm as he picked up his tray.

"Thank you," she mouthed.

Doyle grinned and followed Debbie to the bar. He needed to figure something out. And fast. Arielle would wake up in nine hours.

Chapter 38

"So, what's going on back there?" Doyle asked Debbie while they waited at the side of the bar. "The mood was very tense."

Debbie's face had been stuck in an eternal scowl since they left her friends, but it softened at the corners once Doyle forced some sympathy into his voice.

"I don't know," Debbie replied, fidgeting with her fingernails. "I try to make sure no one goes home with a serial killer whenever we go out. And those *bitches* can't ever appreciate that I'm just looking out for them."

Serial killer? Debbie, your dark thoughts are practically my language.

"I know what you mean," Doyle said. "I, too, have friends who don't appreciate what I do."

Debbie's eyes widened. The last thing she expected was to have anything in common with the man whose free drink she had swiftly dumped out to prove a point. "Do tell. And explain how you deal with it."

Doyle gave a gentle grin like he had a secret he didn't want to share. "Well, like I mentioned, I see the good, the bad, and the ugly working in a club. I know every play in the book. And you're absolutely right about men slipping stuff into drinks. It happens at least once a weekend—that we know of. There are also sneaky women out there, granted, not as bad as spiking a drink. But there are the freeloaders, who bounce from man to man for free drinks, leading them on all night before leaving with their friends. Now, I don't even have an issue with that. If I had beauty to lure men into buying me drinks, why wouldn't I?"

Debbie laughed at this, and Doyle wasn't sure why. She was plenty attractive, perhaps the second-best looking out of their group, right after Vanessa. Maybe she had never considered such a ploy and was now contemplating a fresh approach to these horrid nights out.

Lorenzo slid over two new shot glasses full of tequila while Doyle continued. "There are also women who order their own drinks all night, strike up a conversation with a man, and maybe even get cozy and cuddly in a corner of the club. All to tell the bartender to move their tab to the man's. And of course it's without their knowledge. Shady people out there."

"I wish I could say I'm surprised," Debbie said. "That sounds like something Lauren would do. She's the tall one."

Doyle needed no explanation and knew exactly who she was talking about. "All this to say that I'm much like you. I warn my friends about these types of women. You could say I've gotten pretty good at spotting the patterns and can pinpoint who exactly would try to pull these stunts—a perk of working here for a year. But do you think they listen to me?"

Debbie grinned. "Of course not. Ugh, it's so frustrating." She balled her little fists and pounded one on the bar top. "How do you deal with it? You're only trying to look out for their best interests."

Doyle leaned in toward Debbie, catching whiffs of a fruity perfume. Up close, she had gentle eyes, almost hypnotizing.

Too bad her face was always stuck in a death stare. "You gotta let go. It's so hard to accept, but we are not their parents. They're going to make the decisions they make with no regard for the advice we give them. It's a hard pill to swallow, but I've found I can enjoy myself more when I go into it with those expectations. I don't even waste my breath anymore. Just let them make their mistakes. They always find their way back, and when they do..."

"You get to tell them *I told you so!*" Debbie said with a hearty laugh.

Not at all the direction I was going, but sure.

"Exactly," Doyle said, nodding along, much like you would to be polite to the old man rambling on the bus. "Your name is Debbie, right?"

"Yes." Debbie's eyes fluttered as she pursed her lips together to keep in another grin. All the smiling had to have been making her face sore. Doyle understood. Maybe in another lifetime they could have made a good couple. But not this one. No, sir. In this one, Debbie was just another roadblock to yet another successful kill.

"Well, Debbie," Doyle continued. "My friend Lorenzo here was kind enough to pour us some new shots. I'm sorry we got off on the wrong foot. Let's toast to new beginnings."

Doyle grabbed his shot glass, still unsure if his impromptu plan would work, and handed Debbie hers. He raised his high in the air.

"To new beginnings," Debbie said, elevating her glass.

They touched glasses and downed the tequila. Debbie made the typical face of most tequila shot victims, like she had swallowed a whole cockroach.

"Whoo!" she cried out after, eyes watering. "Stings so

good."

There we go.

Doyle glanced over his shoulder and saw Vanessa standing alone at their table. "Tell you what. Order whatever drinks you want tonight and put them on my tab."

Debbie's eyes bulged as she stuck her face out in disbelief. "I couldn't possibly—"

"I insist. You ladies have been here three weeks in a row now? Consider it a thank you for making my job easier. Lorenzo will take care of you."

Doyle said this loud enough for Lorenzo to point at him and give a thumbs up.

"Wow, thank you," Debbie said. "I know everyone calls you Blanco, but what's your real name?"

Doyle gulped. It was an innocent question, but considering the circumstances that would hopefully unfold in the coming hours, one he couldn't afford to answer. "I'm sorry, Debbie, but I prefer to keep my real name private when I'm at the club. Like I said...lots of crazies out there."

Debbie's smile disappeared for the first time since making its debut. She couldn't hide her disappointment. Maybe they made a bet to see who could find out his real name.

Do you talk about me, Vanessa?

Doyle couldn't help but wonder, considering she had looked their way at least seven times since they came to the bar. Was that jealousy swimming in her eyes?

Don't worry, Vanessa. I'm only here for you tonight.

"Where are all my friends?" Debbie asked, letting out an exaggerated sigh. She had finally caught sight of what Doyle hoped would not send her back into a tailspin of panic.

"I'm sure they just stepped outside," Doyle said with complete composure. "Things were pretty heated."

Debbie wasted no time hurrying off and pushing through the crowd to return to Vanessa. Doyle followed behind.

"Hey," Debbie said, rubbing a hand on Vanessa's back. "I'm so sorry about what I did. I just had a fantastic conversation with Blanco and feel much better."

"She even takes drinks from me now," Doyle said playfully, but Vanessa kept a stern expression.

"They left," Vanessa said flatly, pursing her lips and staring blankly at Debbie. "They left because of *you*."

Debbie took a step back and placed a hand on her chest. "Me? No."

"Yes. *You*. What are you not understanding? You do this shit every time we go out? Telling us who not to talk to. Or telling us to stop drinking. You're the opposite of fun. And tonight, we get a round of *free drinks* from Blanco, and you fucking dump it out? What's happened to you?"

Debbie's typically hardened face trembled on the verge of tears. She wasn't used to being called out for her actions, and Doyle figured these past ten minutes would be good for her growth as a person.

"I..." Debbie began, but had no words to complete. Her lips quivered as tears welled in her eyes.

Poor Debbie.

Doyle wished he could comfort his new friend. They'd just shared a bonding moment about this very issue, and now it was all unraveling. But comforting Debbie could cost him Vanessa. And he needed her in his house tonight.

"You need to make this right," Vanessa said, brows furrowed in rage. "I think you can still catch them—they headed outside to call a cab."

"What?!" Debbie cried. "They were just going to leave you here?"

"Yeah. With you. Lucky me?" Vanessa rolled her eyes and turned around to face the dance floor, where everyone else was having the time of their lives.

"Nessa, I'm sorry," Debbie pleaded. "I'll make this up to you. Blanco just gave me a lot to think about, and I promise I'll change. I can fix this. Stay here."

Debbie hugged Vanessa, who allowed it, but offered nothing in return. She smiled at Doyle before running out of the club.

Doyle's stomach fluttered with anticipation. What the fuck just happened? He now stood alone with Vanessa, all three of her friends nowhere to be seen.

Holy shit. What do I do?

He never expected this to fall into his lap. Arielle was tied up in the safe room, and now Vanessa just needed a nudge in this vulnerable moment.

"Hey," Doyle said softly. "I'm sorry about your friends."

Vanessa turned back around, tears streaming down her face that she promptly wiped away. "You have nothing to apologize for. What were you two talking about over there, anyway?"

She couldn't conceal the curiosity in her voice. She *needed* to know what her friend had discussed with him.

"It was actually about this," Doyle said. "The way she acts with you all. I told her I was once the friend who was just like her. I cared too much. Couldn't mind my own business. I told her she needs to trust her friends. It's the only way forward before she pushes too far."

Vanessa snorted. "Well, it might be too late for that. She pushed, and they left."

"What is this really about?" Doyle asked. "Do you want to

step outside and discuss it?"

Good Doyle. Get her relaxed outside of the club. Be the sounding board she needs to vent to. The trust already has a foundation, now hammer it home.

"Aren't you working?" Vanessa asked, looking around like she was about to do something illegal. "I'd hate to get you into trouble."

Doyle shook his head. "It's totally fine. I have free rein. And right now, one of our best guests is crying in the middle of Night Owl. I need to make it better."

Vanessa smiled and nodded. "Okay. I'd love to talk."

Doyle led the way outside, clapping Big J on the back. "We're coming right back in. Just need some air."

Big J nodded, keeping his hands crossed over his belly.

All the smokers huddled to the right of the entrance, a hazy cloud hovering above them and their raspy laughter. Doyle took Vanessa further away, nearly to the intersection where a line of cars waited for a green light.

"So what's going on?" Doyle asked, tugging on his necktie. "Debbie seems like a good-hearted person."

Vanessa laughed, looking at the ground as she doodled on the sidewalk with the tip of her heel. "Maybe *too* good-hearted. This blowup tonight wasn't just about what she did to you—sorry about that, by the way."

"Water under the bridge," Doyle said, flashing a quick grin.

"This has been months in the making. I've actually been friends with Debbie since my freshman year of college. We'd go to parties, and she'd always be worried about people drinking too much. Or the police showing up. Like, Debbie, these are *college* parties. People are going to cut loose. But she's always been a worrier."

Doyle nodded along, setting a mental timer for when Debbie might crawl back down the sidewalk with their friends. He couldn't rush Vanessa, but he'd move the conversation along where he could.

"I know the type," he said. "And she's kept worrying even more as you get older."

"Exactly!" Vanessa shouted, stomping a heel. "It seems like she gets worse every week."

"I can't speak on her behalf, but after the conversation I just had with her at the bar, I believe she's going to do better. No more panicking Debbie."

Vanessa giggled at this. The tears were long gone. She seemed to enjoy Doyle's company, almost as if there was a connection between them. Or at least a fate.

"I hope you're right," Vanessa said. "Because we all live together, so it's not exactly like we can brush this under the rug. If my other two friends found a way home, Debbie's going to be there later. And you know Debbie now. She's not one to shy away from confrontation."

Doyle shrugged. "Friends fight. It happens. Sometimes those fights can end friendships. But if it was really that fragile to begin with, is it even worth the struggle? True friends stick together like family, and I think that's what you have."

Vanessa grinned from ear to ear. "I like that. Who would have thought you had so much wisdom?"

"Like I said, I'm an observer. I see everything here. Happy newlyweds. Cheating spouses—sometimes in the club at the same time. People on first dates. And so many groups of friends. Maybe I should open a counseling service on the side with all the messes I've seen."

"Not your worst idea."

"Oh? And what is? The tequila shot I gave to Debbie?"

Vanessa cackled with delight, clutching her stomach. "No you didn't! Too soon!" She slapped him playfully on the arm, letting her fingers linger a second longer than necessary.

Now.

Doyle forced a fake chuckle. "Say, I could use a break. I just live a couple of blocks away from here. Care for a drink at my place? Then we can head back and hopefully your friends will be here."

Vanessa's head whipped toward the affluent neighborhood, eyes widening. "Wait. You live in *Sunset Harbor*?"

Doyle nodded. "Easy commute."

Vanessa's jaw hung. "Hold on. I'm not trying to jump to conclusions or make accusations, but don't you have to be, like, really rich to live there? Aren't you just a club promoter?"

Doyle smiled, showing his teeth in an expression that was far out of his comfort zone. "Well, yes, I *do* help promote the club. I'm good friends with the owner. We're business partners."

Vanessa's eyes fluttered in amazement. "Okay. Wow. Yes, let's go. Sorry, I don't mean to sound like some gold-digging whore. I was going to say yes, regardless. I'm just caught a bit off guard. Thought you were someone else completely."

Doyle raised his hands. "It happens. That's why I can't get in trouble if I leave here. They can't exactly fire me."

The lies kept pouring out of his mouth, but he didn't care.

"Well then, lead the way, good sir," Vanessa said, sticking out her arm for Doyle to grab.

They intertwined at the elbow, a perfect fit. Doyle started off toward his neighborhood, mouth pooling with saliva at the mere thought of having both Vanessa and Arielle in the safe room at the same time.

He looked over his shoulder at the Night Owl, touched by all it had done for him, including this ultimate parting gift. He would never step foot back inside that club again, and Fernando could go fuck himself for all he cared.

The night was young and full of possibilities. So much so that he didn't notice the man and woman following in a car several yards behind.

Chapter 39

They reached Doyle's house ten minutes later, arm in arm, enjoying a casual conversation about how life had brought them to Miami, while crickets chirped beneath the moonlight.

Under other circumstances, Doyle would have considered the night romantic—in fact, it still was, in his own sick, twisted way. Vanessa radiated a lavender scent, and if Doyle didn't already have Arielle tied up inside, he probably would've succumbed to Vanessa's tantalizing attraction. He fantasized about throwing her on his bed and jackhammering for twenty minutes of pure ecstasy (he had a numbing cream, thanks to his time as a surgeon).

But tonight was not about pleasure. He had to think with his head instead of his dick—a wise lesson for all the young boys out there—if he wanted to accomplish the business at hand.

"Beautiful night," Doyle said when they reached his sidewalk, and he stopped.

"This one's your house?" Vanessa asked, eyes bulging at the mini mansion. Her amazement hadn't waned during the walk over.

"Sure is. My humble abode." Doyle unhooked his arm from Vanessa as he reached into his suit jacket for his house key. He rarely entered through the front door, but with his car sitting abandoned in the Teleios parking lot—as it would be for the next several days—he had no choice tonight.

They strode up the walkway, Vanessa gazing at the amazing portico while her clopping heels echoed around the neighborhood. He prayed to every god floating in space Gloria wasn't having one of her bored moments staring out her window. She at least knew where Doyle worked and shouldn't expect to see him this early on a weekend night.

Doyle wasted no time inserting the key and had to fight every instinct in his body not to look over his shoulder. He was this close and couldn't scare off Vanessa now. He needed her comfortable, to the point of never wanting to leave. Because she wouldn't. And some horny cougar down the street would certainly not be the one to unravel it all.

Fuck it. If Gloria shows up tonight, she's never leaving this house either.

Doyle was completely in the driver's seat for what felt like the first time in years. Arielle was tied up in the safe room. Vanessa now stood in his foyer, the door locked behind them. And a time portal waited for Doyle once it was time to leave town and disappear from 1998.

The universe is finally paying me back after all the heartache it's caused.

"This house in stunning," Vanessa said, her mouth agape while her eyes wandered in circles, admiring the ridiculously overpriced abstract art hanging on the walls.

Fucking scam artists.

"Care for a drink?" Doyle asked, stepping further in and tossing his keys in the bowl standing next to the door.

"Please and thank you," Vanessa replied. "Do you need me

to take my shoes off?"

You can take off anything you please.

"No. Not at all. Make yourself comfortable. *Mi casa es su casa.*"

Vanessa giggled, and Doyle wondered if her chugging that Sex on the Beach at the club had loosened her up.

Loose is good. Loose is relaxed. Why ever leave? You can stay here forever.

Vanessa kicked off her shoes anyway, and shuffled to the couch, plopping down right where Arielle's head had lain hours ago. She swung her feet up, allowing her hiked dress to reveal smooth, athletic legs.

Doyle proceeded through the living room, keeping his eyes ahead on the kitchen, stealing a split-second glance from the corner of his eye. *Jesus Christ, this chick* wants *me.*

His legs wobbled as he entered the kitchen, growing terrified he lacked the strength to resist Vanessa. Leaving behind any traces of DNA *inside* of a murder victim was the most reckless mistake a killer could commit. Doyle had strict guidelines to avoid this pitfall, one he had so far relentlessly upheld.

But tonight, Doyle felt like a god. He could not be stopped. So why not give in to some inner desires? Not even a top-notch forensics team could trace DNA through a time portal. Could they?

Doyle entered the kitchen and spun around to face the counter, having a clear look at Vanessa around the corner with a crane of the neck. His mouth went dry, so he opened the cupboard above to pull out a bottle of wine and two glasses.

Doyle hated wine. He had the bottle from eight months ago when one of his flings had brought it over to enjoy with dinner. They had instead ripped each other's clothes off and spread their juices all over the house for the next hour. The pot roast had burned to a char, so they ordered Chinese, never touching the bottle.

But Doyle felt locked in tonight. He'd yet to see Vanessa have wine, but something in his tumbling gut told him to open the bottle. It had been years since he last used a corkscrew, so he needed a moment to refresh his memory, but when that cork popped out, Doyle licked his lips with great pride.

Don't even need to slip anything in her drink. She's already in the palm of my hand.

He poured the wine and returned to the living room with a strut in his step.

"A nice glass of chianti for the lady," Doyle said, extending the glass to Vanessa. "Could I interest you in a side of fava beans? Maybe a liver?"

Vanessa howled in delight. "Shut up! You're a Hannibal fan, too?! I think we're going to get along just fine."

"Hannibal?" Doyle responded, cocking his left eyebrow. "It's Jodie Foster for me. She really gets me going."

Vanessa had to hold her glass up as she tipped over and laughed into the pillows. "Oh, stop it! You're too much."

"Let's make a toast then," Doyle said, inching closer to the couch. "To new friends."

"To new friends," Vanessa repeated, eyes moving up and down Doyle's body.

Fuck. Nothing good is going to come once that wine glass is empty. Except maybe me. Ha!

They tapped their glasses together, but never took a sip. Their eyes locked so fiercely, Doyle imagined he could hear Vanessa speaking to him through some sort of invisible tunnel only they could see.

Doyle gulped, each limb frozen in place. "So? What would you like to do this evening?"

Stupid Doyle. You know *what she wants to do. What do you expect her to answer?*

Vanessa took a sip of her wine, then undid the top button of her blouse with her free hand. "Oh, not much. You?"

She left a red lipstick mark on the wineglass, and oh, how he wanted those same marks all over his chest.

Calm yourself!

The phone rang, and they both whipped their heads toward the kitchen in surprise.

"Fuck," Doyle muttered under his breath, shuffling for the phone.

Who the fuck is calling right now?

He reached the phone, but didn't pick it up, staring at it while it rang for the third time.

"Are you going to answer that?" Vanessa asked, returning to her relaxation on the couch by taking a longer drink of wine.

If it's the club, Fernando just wants to chew me out. Scream for a couple of minutes to make himself feel better. But I can't tell him I quit, not in front of Vanessa when I just told her I'm a part owner.

"No." Doyle took a step back. "I'll let the machine get it. I have much more important matters to tend to."

Good Doyle.

He started back toward the couch, immediately regretting his decision. If Fernando left a message, Vanessa would now get to hear it, since the answering machine sat on the kitchen counter right around the corner.

The machine clicked into action, and Gloria's voice followed.

"Hey there, lover boy," she said.

Jesus fucking Christ!

"I thought for a minute you were having a party without me, but I may have been wrong. There have been two people standing outside your house for the past ten minutes. One keeps staying on the sidewalk, while the other goes up to your front door. They look suspicious, so I thought I'd let you know. I'll keep an eye out until you get home. I can't wait for next week. Bye."

Gloria hung up, and Doyle hadn't realized he was staring blankly toward the kitchen while she spoke. Vanessa buttoned her blouse back up and slammed the wineglass on the coffee table, splashing a couple of drops on the white carpet stretching beneath the table and couch.

Doyle examined the drops that looked just like blood.

"What the fuck?!" Vanessa cried, jumping up and balling her hands into fists. "Lover boy? I get it, you're rich and single. I'm not the first woman in here or the last, but for fuck's sake, have some decency and don't let your hoochies call while I'm lying on your couch."

"Wait, it's not what you think!" Doyle replied, leaping across the living room to stand in front of Vanessa. "That's my neighbor. She's crazy. She thinks we have something going on, and I've never even touched her."

"Get the hell out of my way," Vanessa said through gritted teeth. "Thank you for a nice evening, but it's over. Besides, there's two people standing outside your house. Are you not going to do something about that?"

Doyle grabbed his hair and started pulling. "Please. Just sit back down on the couch, and I'll deal with all of this. Give me ten minutes."

Who the fuck is outside my house?!

But Doyle knew. The cocksucking Angels were surely snooping around for Arielle. But how did they find him so quickly? They weren't even in the parking lot when he kidnapped her—he'd scouted the area three times before making a move.

"Ten minutes?" Vanessa asked, hands on her hips, eyebrows raised to her hairline. "Some whore calls you and tells you people are standing outside, and you want me to wait ten minutes like you're running to the store to buy another bottle of wine? You must be out of your mind. I'm getting the hell out of here."

"STOP!" Doyle screamed and jumped, stomping both feet when he landed.

Whatever confidence Vanessa had been trying to portray vanished in an instant. She stood there, eyes wide, mouth hanging open.

Doyle saw the fear in her eyes—he never mistook the fluctuating pupils and sudden twitches that accompanied pure horror in a person's eyes.

"I'm sorry," Doyle said in a calmer tone. "But you can't go. The people out there might be dangerous."

"Dangerous? Are you in some sort of trouble?" Vanessa had taken a step back and pointed her feet toward the door. Doyle knew to always check people's feet to understand their desires.

If she made a run for the door, he'd have no issue stopping her. But if she took another step or two away from him, what would that mean? It was impossible to build concrete trust in a matter of minutes, but she had agreed to come to his house, so not all was lost. She must have had even a fraction of faith in Doyle to follow him to an unknown place.

"I'm not in trouble," he said, his gaze moving to her eyes to show he was telling the truth, then down to her feet to make sure she didn't run. "But there are some people after me."

Vanessa snorted and tossed her hands up, then took one more step backwards. "People after you, but that's not trouble?" She pressed her lips tightly together and shook her head. "I was wrong about you. Thought you were a normal guy with his shit together. But you're just like all the other sad sacks in this city. Desperate. Willing to say or do anything just to get laid. You work at a nightclub, so I'm sure you won't have a problem with that. I really need to be going now."

She took another step back, and Doyle caught her eyes glance at the door. Her voice was firm, but her trembling arms suggested otherwise. She was out of his arm's reach.

Doyle took a slow, steady step toward her. "Please don't go. I told you I can fix this."

Vanessa's eyes danced in every direction. She hadn't given up on the door but was looking for anything else. She no longer felt safe.

"I'm going," she said, and it nearly sounded like a question as she took yet another step back.

Her high heels were by the front door, but Doyle doubted she'd stop to grab them. Not if she really felt in danger.

"Vanessa, please."

You sound fucking pathetic. Let the girl go. Cut your losses and deal with Arielle. She was the main prize all along.

But Doyle couldn't risk having that front door open again. Not if the Angels were outside snooping around his property. If a panicked woman went running out of the house, they weren't the type to knock on the door to ask questions. They'd barge in and demand answers. Then what? Doyle couldn't possibly take on two Angels by himself.

I don't even know if that's who's out there. Fernando could have finally figured out where I lived and sent his lackeys to scare me straight.

Vanessa must have seen Doyle tied up in his thoughts, because she broke into a sprint for the door. Doyle realized in time, jumping over the coffee table and lunging toward her, diving and wrapping his arms around her knees like a football player making a textbook tackle.

Her foot kicked him in the jaw while they went down, but he didn't feel it thanks to the adrenaline racing through his body. They both let out heavy grunts as they hit the floor, Vanessa immediately wriggling to get out of his grip. She freed one foot and kicked him in the face.

"Get the fuck off me!" she screamed as loud as she could.

"Shut the hell up!" Doyle muttered, grabbing her free leg and squeezing it in his embrace. He didn't care if Vanessa wanted to fight, but the last thing he needed was her making noise that could be heard from outside.

Doyle climbed on top of Vanessa, flattening her beneath his body as she scratched and clawed at his back. She spit in his face, causing an instant erection.

"Get the fuck off—" she screamed, cut off by Doyle's hand cupped over her mouth.

"Shut up!" he whispered, looking around for anything he could use to keep her silent.

Vanessa's heels were the only thing within reach, so Doyle stretched out for them while keeping a hand over Vanessa's mouth. She rammed her knee into his crotch, sending shock-waves of pain into his abdomen.

He rolled off Vanessa but had the heel clutched tight as she scrambled to her feet. He kicked her in the shin with just enough force to make her fall back down. Doyle rose to his knees, pain still shooting in bursts from his throbbing testicles.

"You bitch!" he growled, rearing back the shoe and swinging it forward. The heel caught Vanessa square in the temple, blood instantly spurting out as she collapsed unconscious.

Doyle lay on his back, panting for breath and wiping the sweat out of his eyes. She had gotten him good. He had the urge to vomit, but knew he just needed to pass the time for the pain to fade.

Breathing exercises got him through the next five minutes, and Doyle rolled his head over to see the pool of blood fanning out from Vanessa's head had doubled in size.

She's dead, he thought, not needing to check for a pulse. He'd seen enough dead bodies in his life to know with a close look.

"Dead," he said. "God dammit, Vanessa."

Once the pain had subsided enough for Doyle to get back on his feet, he stood over her body and calculated the best approach for cleaning up this mess. Then he remembered what had started this debacle.

The two people waiting outside his house.

Chapter 40

Felix returned from the front door, having pressed his ear against the cool wood for the past minute.

"I couldn't hear much," he told Selena. "It's too muffled. Maybe laughter, some light conversation for sure. And I think I heard a phone ring."

Selena glared at the front door like it had a secret. "What do you think we should do?"

"We need to find Arielle. If she didn't follow him here, then we're just wasting our time. And like you said, until Doyle has Arielle, she can't be in too much danger, right?"

Selena sighed and bent over to place her hands on her knees like she had just finished a marathon. "Something feels off about all of this. We can't just turn our back on Vanessa. We *know* he's going to kill her tonight. What good are we if we can't stop it from happening?"

"True," Felix said, chewing on the inside of his lip as he stared at the moon shining fiercely above them. "But that was always part of the past's plans—Vanessa dying. I'm hesitant to get tied up in that situation for what it might inadvertently do to Arielle. Even if we tried to kill Doyle right now, that doesn't get us any closer to Arielle. We *need* to know where she is."

Tears rolled down Selena's cheek as her breathing increased. "We're so *fucked*, Felix. How are we ever going to explain this to the commander? Arielle is missing and we have *no idea* where she is." She broke into a heavier sob, prompting Felix to look around to make sure they weren't drawing any unwanted attention. "This can't be happening right now."

Felix rummaged in his pocket to make sure his lockpick was there. "Come with me."

He grabbed Selena's wrist and pulled her to the side of the garage. They leaned against the siding, Selena still breathing heavily through the tears.

"Listen up," Felix said, sliding in front of Selena and lowering both of her hands away from her face. She looked up at him with every ounce of anguish trying to writhe through the moisture on her eyeballs. "We're being too indecisive. I'm taking control of this mission until we find Arielle. Doyle at least knows where Arielle is. Since we didn't bring any weapons with us, we're going to break into this garage, find some tools we can use, and shake this guy down until he gives us an answer. We can tie him up and let Arielle decide what to do with him. Do you know how Arielle has so much success on her missions?"

Selena shook her head, the tears gone, fear fading by the second.

"She makes a plan before barging into a room," Felix continued. "Then goes full throttle until the job is done. No hesitations. No questions. Just a pure trust that her plan won't fail her."

Felix saw Selena had just about returned to her normal self and released her hands.

"We don't have a plan, though," she said, wiping her tears

with her arm.

"I'm aware," Felix said. "But we're going to make one now. I've studied enough houses to know how to break in. I have a good idea about the layout inside. All we don't know is *where* Doyle and Vanessa are. If we're lucky, they'll be upstairs, and we can sneak up on them. If not, and we see Doyle on the main floor, we need to charge toward him with no hesitation. Don't give him a second to react. Unlikely he's just sitting there with a gun, but if he's supposed to kill Vanessa tonight, we don't know what he has nearby. Do you think you can handle all this?"

"For Arielle," Selena said. "I'll do whatever it takes. We owe her that much."

Felix grinned. "My thoughts exactly. Let's check the back of the garage."

They passed through a narrow path between the garage and a row of bushes. It was too dark to see exactly how big the backyard was, but Felix had no reason to believe it was a standard size, judging by the magnitude of the house.

"Jackpot," he said when they reached the back and found a door leading into the garage. "It's always fifty-fifty if a garage has one of these doors. Must be our lucky night." He reached for the knob and turned it, instantly grinning. "*And* it's unlocked."

Felix pushed the door open with caution. The garage was pitch black, so he fumbled around the walls until he found a light switch and flipped it up to the buzzing sound of a fluorescent light.

Selena gasped and clapped her hands over her mouth.

"Holy shit," Felix said, following Selena's gaze to Arielle's car parked in the middle of the garage.

They locked eyes, struck by disbelief.

"Was this part of the plan?" Selena asked, mouth still open.

Felix was speechless, looking at the car as if it wasn't real. Wishing someone would pinch him so he could wake up from this nightmare. "The plans have changed. Arielle is here, and we need to hurry. Look around for anything that can be used as a weapon."

Felix spun, his legs wobbly as nerves settled into every nook and cranny of his body. He found a toolbox and opened the top, locating a wrench, and stuffing it into his pocket. The weight of this evening had snowballed into chaos. He supposed the responsible thing to do was leave and return better equipped with a plan, but they didn't know how much time they had before Doyle would call checkmate. They didn't know if they were already too late. The thought of Arielle lying dead inside forced Felix to stifle nausea.

Selena had shuffled over to a set of standing shelves, examined the contents and snagged a loose screwdriver. "Bug spray?" she asked. "We can spray it in his eyes."

Felix nodded seriously. "Anything will do at this point. I've got a wrench."

"Look, Felix!" Selena gasped, pointing to the opposite corner of the garage. Tucked into the corner, next to a ladder, stood a sledgehammer. "Too heavy?"

Felix couldn't help but smile. "Not at all. I'm not sure I have the stomach to bash a man's brains in, but I'll give it my best."

"You've never *needed* to bash someone's head," Selena reminded him, which oddly put him at ease.

I can do this. For Arielle. For all of Doyle's victims. And for the Road Runners.

"Okay, we're as ready as we're going to be," Felix said,

hoisting the sledgehammer over his shoulder and shuffling to the door that led into the house. "Eighty percent of people leave this door unlocked. I'm going to turn the knob, and if it's unlocked, we're going in. Stay as quiet as possible. Tiptoe. Stay behind me."

Selena nodded, determination swarming over her face.

Felix drew a deep breath as he faced the door, reaching out a hand that was shaking like a severe case of Parkinson's. Destiny waited on the other side of that door. In this moment, Felix realized fear only came from within. Situations were only scary if you let them be. Yet so many people surrendered to fear, thanks to some inner voice that whispered sweet terrors in their ear. Felix refused to succumb to the pressure of the occasion and grabbed the doorknob.

He twisted it, and it never stopped. He paused before pushing open the door, expecting Doyle to ram into it at any second, or maybe swing it open and start firing. A grisly image flashed in Felix's mind of him and Selena dead on the garage floor. So close to saving Arielle, yet oh so far.

Fuck that, he thought, and pushed the door open.

Straight ahead was a stairwell. Kitchen to the right with only the light above the sink turned on. Phone on the wall. To the left was a living room. Two wine glasses on the coffee table, both half empty. Further left was the front door, and a body lying in a red pool of blood that had soaked into the carpet.

Felix's heart froze. *Please don't be Arielle. Please God.*

He stepped into the house, Selena practically on his back, her fingers wrapped tightly around the screwdriver in one hand, the bug spray in the other.

The house was silent. Too silent. With a better look, he

realized the body was Vanessa and not Arielle.

He knows we're here. Why else would he abandon a dead body?

Felix turned around and pressed a finger to his lips. Selena nodded and followed him deeper into the house. After five steps, they were in the open space between the kitchen and living room. The sledgehammer's handle wore into Felix's shoulder. He wanted to put it down, maybe find a knife in the kitchen, but they had zero seconds to spare. They needed to find Arielle.

Felix stopped and nodded toward the stairs, then pointed up with complete confidence. He knew Doyle was up there. If he had been on the main level with them, he would have already made his move. Doyle wasn't one to run in this situation. He'd come too far in his endeavor to capture Arielle. Now that he had her, he wouldn't dare cower away from *his* moment of destiny.

They reached the bottom of the stairs, and Felix saw they were all covered in a plastic wrap. Bloody footprints were on the first couple of steps. The landing at the top was wide. Even if Doyle was waiting around the corner, Felix would still have enough time to react. He clutched the sledgehammer's handle, becoming one with the tool.

He tiptoed around the bloodied footprints, prompting Selena to follow suit. The plastic scrunched beneath each step, the sound amplified by the surrounding silence. Even a light rainfall or outdoor breeze would drown out the noise of their ascent, but they had no such luck tonight.

Selena remained one step behind Felix as they continued up, one crinkle at a time. She had matched his steps to reduce the amount of noise, but if Doyle was even half listening, it was still enough to hear.

With two more steps to reach the landing, Felix grabbed the railing with his free hand and pulled himself to the top to skip the remaining steps.

He looked right down a long hallway, relieved to find no one waiting for him. A wall was to the left, providing relief that they wouldn't have to cover two directions while moving down the hallway.

Selena joined Felix, and they peered down the hallway, looking left and right for any sign of which door they should open. The first door on the right was cracked open a couple of inches, the glow of a light splashing into the hall.

Felix tightened his grip on the sledgehammer and started toward it, hands positioned ready to swing, his face inches from the door. He peeked through the crack, but only saw open flooring, all of which was covered in the same plastic.

Selena breathed down his neck, craning for a look, and retreating once she realized there was nothing to see. Felix glanced over his shoulder and nodded for Selena to stand aside.

Once she slid over, Felix leaned into the door with his shoulder to push it. A long, whiny creak sounded from the hinges as it swung open, revealing Arielle tied to a chair, eyes half open and dazed.

Behind her was Doyle, grinning, with a knife held to Arielle's throat.

Chapter 41

"It's about damn time," Doyle said. He gripped the chef's knife steady against Arielle's throat. "Where's the other one of you? The pretty one?"

Felix gulped. "She's not here."

"Don't fucking lie to me!" Doyle snarled. "I know there were two of you outside."

"She's still outside," Felix replied calmly, making every mental effort to keep his nerves in check. "I didn't let her come in. Didn't know how dangerous it would be."

Felix scanned the room. Every inch of wall space had been covered in soundproof foam. No windows, no closets, just an empty room where no screams could escape.

Doyle laughed, a maniac sound that sent chills down Felix's back. "And you were right about that, blondie. Very dangerous indeed. Why don't you put that sledgehammer down before your friend here gets hurt."

"Okay."

Felix was in no position to argue, especially with Selena hidden just outside the door. His life was in her hands now. He lowered the sledgehammer off his shoulder and squatted to place it gently on the floor.

"Good boy," Doyle said.

"Arielle, are you okay?" Felix asked.

Her eyes were blinking rapidly, head bobbing side to side as she made guttural noises from her throat.

"Don't mind your queen," Doyle said. "Your arrival made me wake her up early. She was supposed to be knocked out until the morning, but I had to wake her to see her friend get killed."

"You drugged her?" Felix asked, eyes locked on Arielle. "Midazolam again?"

"Ah! You've been doing your homework," Doyle said with a widening grin. "I feel honored. When did you find out about the drugs I use?"

"We've known since the beginning," Felix said, trying desperately to communicate with Arielle through her eyes, but hers were heavy and puffy and didn't appear to really *see* Felix in front of her.

"How impressive. Midazolam is quick and easy to use. Based on the dosage, you can know exactly when it will wear off and the patient will wake up. Quite reliable, if I say so myself. Unlike your friend here." Doyle patted the top of Arielle's head like she was an obedient dog, his other hand still pressing the knife against her throat. "But that's nothing a little flumazenil can't get rid of. I had to slip her some once I realized you were here. She should be fully awake in another five minutes—it's fast acting."

"What do you want, Doyle?" Felix asked cautiously. He noticed the variety of weapons leaning against the walls, but he had no move to make. Not as long as the knife was on Arielle's throat.

"Don't be so rushy," Doyle said, cackling at himself. "I *wanted* Arielle to keep her word and save my wife. But now, I'm not sure you're going to allow that to happen. If you take one more step toward me, I'm going to slit her throat. I suppose I'll never make it past you—such a big, burly man. I guess that means my life will also end here tonight, but isn't that the beauty of death? The closure of it all? I send Arielle to her destiny while falling to mine. It's romantic. We're kind of like soul mates."

Felix remained frozen in place, terrified to make a sudden movement, but his mind raced with possibilities for getting out of this mess. "You and your wife were soulmates. Not Arielle. You know killing her won't bring your wife back. Why does she have to suffer? Why did anyone else have to? I'm sorry about your wife. I really am. But why go on this rampage? What did Arielle do?"

Doyle's grin softened, but the lunacy remained in his eyes. "Me and Arielle had a *deal*, and she refused to hold up her end of the bargain. Not just refused, but completely cut me out of her life like I never existed. Like we never bonded over our grief. The world is full of people who only look out for themselves. They say anything to get what they want and don't give two shits about the trail of destruction they leave behind for everyone else to deal with. And I was going to help Arielle in return! That's the worst part. I was going to bring back your family, you *bitch*!"

Doyle looked down at Arielle, his teeth gritted in rage.

In that split second, Arielle threw her weight sideways to tip the chair over. The knife grazed her throat, creating a thin cut. Doyle looked down in disbelief, and that's when Felix reached into his pocket for the wrench, his heart pumping adrenaline that made his vision pulse as he focused on Doyle's face.

He reared back the wrench and followed through with a

perfect throw.

Doyle jumped aside, dropping his knife as he landed on the floor. The wrench hit the foam wall and didn't make a sound until it crunched the plastic on the floor. Doyle scrambled to his feet, grabbed a hammer lying next to the wall, and charged at Felix like a rabid running back.

Felix lowered himself to absorb the blow, but dove out of the doorway once Doyle pulled the hammer back and swung with all his body weight behind it.

Doyle lost his balance and tumbled into the hallway. Selena lunged out of nowhere and blasted the bug spray. But Doyle had his back to her, screaming as he half-crawled, half-ran into the bedroom across the hallway.

"Get him, Selena!" Felix shouted, rising from the floor and pulling Arielle's chair back up to a seated position.

"He's going to the time portal," Arielle said, just loud enough for Felix to hear. "Beat him there. Go!"

The words hit Felix's ears, and he wasted no time darting out of the room. In the bedroom across the hallway, Doyle opened the window facing the front yard and hopped out where the portico above the front door caught his landing.

"Shit!" Selena cried, chasing after him.

"Get Arielle and meet me at the time portal!" Felix commanded as he turned the corner to blast down the stairs. He heard the garage door motors humming and wished they had thought far enough ahead to eliminate the possibility of Doyle escaping in the car. But they were too consumed with Arielle to cover all their bases on such a last-minute plan.

Felix broke right for the front door, flung it open, and sprinted across the front lawn just as Doyle had pulled out of the driveway. He didn't bother trying to slow Doyle down, not in a car. The madman would surely run him over without remorse.

Smoke spewed from Arielle's tires as Doyle sped off down the street, just when Felix reached his own car and jumped in.

An older woman in a white silk gown chased after the car, shouting, "Doy! Come back!"

Felix shook his head, having no idea what that was about. With a quick turn of the ignition, he drove in the opposite direction, having studied maps of the area just as extensively as Arielle. They knew the best routes to the time portal from each neighborhood within a ten-mile radius of downtown Miami. And Arielle had made sure they focused on key areas like the Night Owl since that's where Vanessa had last been seen. Even tied to a chair inside a serial killer's house, Arielle had already put in the work to give them an advantage at this exact moment. Felix only needed to beat Doyle to the warehouse to alter his escape plans.

He turned out of the neighborhood and zoomed down the main road. Since it was late, traffic was light, and he only needed to slow down at red lights to check for crossing vehicles before committing a violation and proceeding through. In the name of justice, Felix threw the rulebook out the window.

The engine thundered as he soared away from downtown, street lights blurring by. No nerves were bubbling within, only a sense of fate. Arielle had always talked about being ready for anything, understanding that even though she was the leader of their tight-knit team, anyone could be called upon to meet the moment.

Confidence is when preparation and faith in yourself cross paths. Felix thought of the words Arielle had delivered several months ago when they were all still getting to know each other.

And he was prepared. Felix knew the route Doyle was currently taking to the warehouse but also knew his way would get him there faster, even with a fifteen-second late start.

Faith in himself?

He found it funny how an arduous situation like this had forced him to push all doubt aside. He had no time to let fear hold him back. Over their past four missions working together, they had each grown a deeper appreciation for their work and cherished their spot as the top-ranked team of Angels. No one else in the entire world of time travelers had expectations as high as this team, not even Commander Briar. They had become the epitome of what a team of Angels could be. Their individual strengths complemented each other's weaknesses. They worked selflessly as a crew.

Even Arielle, who had been adamantly against working with a team after years of tackling missions alone, had learned to step back to let them shine as a unit. They were on the same page, even when they weren't together. Felix and Selena kept their focus when they realized Arielle was missing. They understood what needed to be done and executed a plan that didn't quite work to perfection.

But it worked.

Arielle was alive, and Doyle was about to encounter a roadblock in his plans to escape.

"You're toast, Doyle," Felix said, turning into the warehouse parking lot. No other cars were in sight outside of Rapido Cabinets and Counters. He parked ten spaces away from the entrance and turned off the car, dashing through the darkness to enter the building.

Just as he stepped in and closed the door, he saw headlights appearing down the street, racing toward the warehouse.

Chapter 42

Felix turned on the warehouse lights. He doubted Doyle would question why the lights were on, nor did it matter.

The serial killer only needed to get to the time portal to escape this botched attempt at killing Arielle. If he vanished, he'd buy himself more time.

Felix knew this and grabbed a crowbar lying on the ground below the light switch panel. A car door slammed outside, so Felix sprinted to the nearest row of cabinets and crouched low to hide.

He didn't know what Doyle was carrying with him and couldn't risk exposing himself. A crowbar had no chance in a gunfight, and until Felix could confirm there was no gun, he had to play it safe.

According to their original numbering, Felix was hiding in the tenth row, sitting on the floor and keeping his breathing under control. When the door swung open with a bang, he held his breath to ensure silence.

"What the fuck happened in here?!" Doyle shouted. He slammed the door shut and stomped toward the mess of cabinets the three of them had rearranged before leaving the building during their first visit.

Arielle had insisted they rumple the layout, both to buy them time and to throw Doyle off his plans if it came down to this. She had been right on both fronts.

Doyle's stomping came to a halt when he reached what was once the middle row of cabinets, now a clusterfuck of wood in no particular order.

"You've got to be fucking kidding me!" Doyle screamed at the top of his lungs, kicking a cabinet hard enough to splinter wood. "God dammit!"

Felix kept his cool while Doyle grabbed cabinets and threw them aside. He'd have to move at least fifteen cabinets to reach the time portal, and that was assuming he chose each one correctly along the way. Even one step in the wrong direction could cost him an extra dozen cabinets before reaching his target.

"Did you do this, Arielle?!" Doyle shouted, his voice echoing around the warehouse, his heavy gasps for breath making Felix wonder if he was having a panic attack. "You bitch! How did you know?"

The rummaging continued for Doyle, and Felix figured it was safe enough to peek over the cabinet for a better look. Doyle's hair was a sweaty, tangled mess dangling over his forehead. He no longer looked like a psychopath hellbent on killing everything in sight, but a man of magnified desperation.

Felix calculated the distance between him and Doyle to be fifty feet apart and wanted to approach him from the front-door side of the warehouse to obstruct the obvious path out.

He has to have a gun. No way he'd come here without one.

How Arielle made decisions on the fly, Felix would never know. Did she just flip a coin to decide if it was a good idea to charge at someone or not?

"I'll hunt you down if it's the last thing I do!" Doyle shouted as he continued grabbing cabinets and hoisting them aside. "Arielle *fucking* Lucila!"

Felix had to stifle a laugh. It was beyond satisfying to watch Doyle have a mental breakdown. He had come here assuming it would take five seconds to slip into the time portal and prepare for his next encounter with the Angels in some other century. But like Mike Tyson once said, everyone has a plan until they get punched in the face.

Doyle was actually making steady progress toward the center of the cabinets. Felix didn't remember which one exactly housed the time portal, but he knew it was time for action once Doyle reached the stack of countertops and was actually succeeding in moving them one-by-one. Perhaps Doyle was much stronger than they had presumed.

He stood up, the crowbar much lighter in his hands compared to the sledgehammer. A former baseball player, he'd have no issue swinging and making contact.

Doyle had gone in too deep and was so focused on finding the portal that he never noticed Felix shuffling around to position himself between Doyle and the exit. There was another exit in the back corner of the warehouse, but it had to be at least two hundred feet away. Doyle would never beat Felix in a foot race covering that much distance.

Felix cleared his throat to get Doyle's attention, but he was too busy talking to himself, cursing Arielle's name after every other word as he punched and kicked any cabinet in his way. He looked like a child throwing a tantrum in a messy room with toys all over the floor.

"Looking for something?" Felix called out much louder.

Doyle froze in place like he had been caught doing something illegal. He made no movement for a gun, or any weapon as he turned around wide-eyed.

"You!" Doyle grumbled, pressing his lips tight together. "You assholes did this, didn't you?!"

Knowing he would not get shot, Felix's confidence soared even further. If only he had a gun himself, this whole mess would already be over. "Of course. You didn't think we'd let you get away too easy, did you?"

"Tell me which one has the portal," Doyle demanded, balling a fist and slamming it down on the nearest cabinet. Blood oozed from his wrist, but Doyle didn't appear to notice.

"Why would I do that?" Felix replied, taking a step closer.

"Put down the crowbar and fight me like a man," Doyle said, grabbing a chunk of splintered wood from a busted cabinet and pulling the piece all the way off. It had a sharp point but wouldn't do nearly as much damage as Felix's weapon.

"Fight like a man?" Felix asked, raising an eyebrow. He'd never felt so in control of a situation. And he loved it. "Odd words from a man who wastes his ability to time travel by killing innocent people. Did you fight those kids in Dallas like a man? Or were you a coward? What about Rowland in Oklahoma? Did he have a fair chance?"

Having studied Doyle for so long on this mission, Felix understood this sad murderer's entire pride and existence centered on his ego. Attack the ego and Doyle would unravel even further than he already had.

"Those people were part of the plan," Doyle said, inching backwards. "There were supposed to be more, but you jackasses kept showing up before I could finish the job."

"Ahh, yes," Felix said, taking another step closer. Doyle had cleared a path between the cabinets as he searched for the time portal, and they now stood facing each other roughly ten yards apart. "I forgot we were supposed to *let* you kill all those innocent people. That was part of the plan, too, right? Getting away with murder was supposed to be easy when you can time travel. Looks like you're not as good as you thought. So unprepared. There were supposed to be three bodies in 1898, but we only found two. I suppose you also weren't prepared enough to make the third kill?"

Doyle shook his head. "I threw that third body through the time portal. Just wanted to see what would happen. And fuck you, I'm more prepared than you'll ever be."

"Is that so? Then how come you're having such a hard time finding your way out of here? See, Arielle was *actually* prepared. She knew from the day we arrived here that you'd try to escape through this time portal. So we blocked it off. If you were truly prepared, you'd have an alternate plan. But you don't. I can see the fear all over your cowardly face."

Doyle threw the splinter of wood at Felix, missing wide by an entire arm's length. He hoisted up the final countertop and tossed it aside like the Incredible Hulk, then promptly kicked another cabinet and tore off another piece of wood, wielding it like a sword.

"What's the matter, Doyle?" Felix continued, taking small steps every few seconds. Doyle had nowhere to go. Cabinets were piled together behind him. He could always try running on top, but Felix doubted he'd get too far that way. Something shifted within Felix, though. He wasn't entirely sure but suspected Doyle had actually come close to the time portal. If Doyle felt the heat, things could get ugly. "This obviously ends tonight, so I just want to know why you did all of this. Losing your wife can't be easy."

"STOP TALKING ABOUT MY WIFE!" Doyle screamed. Tears streamed from his eyes, leaving shiny trails down his cheeks.

"I see," Felix said. "Do you think your wife would be proud of you after everything you've done? You were both good people at one point, right? No way she'd ever approve of what you've done as some sort of sick revenge for losing her. You realize no one killed your wife. Or do you blame yourself?"

"STOP! SHUT THE FUCK UP!"

"Doyle Grady. A top surgeon in the country. Could save everyone but his own wife. You were only good until it really mattered."

Doyle's face turned red as he clutched his hair with one hand, still holding out the wood in front of him with the other, veins bulging as thick cords on his neck. His crying intensified, bottom lip quivering beyond his control.

"So you got invited to join the Road Runners," Felix continued, now fifteen feet from Doyle. "Naturally, you thought you'd use time travel to go back and save your wife. But you found it nearly impossible to interfere with your own life. Too dangerous and complex. We've all been there. You thought seeking help from a fellow time traveler would solve the problem. Easy, right? Someone else could go back and interfere with your life. Why not offer them the same thing in exchange? But nothing's that easy, Doyle. Just because we can move freely through time doesn't mean everything else is simple. Arielle didn't betray you. She was loyal to the organization while they kicked you out. They forbade her from speaking to you, or else she would suffer the same fate."

Doyle took two steps back and stopped, his eyes darting to the cabinet on his left. He drew a deep breath and shook his head, wiping his tears away. "You're right. I'm completely in the wrong, and I deserve whatever punishment I receive for killing all those innocent people. But I'll never apologize. I followed my heart to make the situation right in my eyes."

Felix watched Doyle's feet shuffle to the left a couple of inches. He stuck out a toe under the cabinet to his left.

Shit.

Doyle pulled the cabinet door open with his toe, letting out a wave of heat that reached Felix in seconds. He grinned as he dropped the wood. "But my time for justice won't be today. You'll never catch me. You're just a poor man's Arielle, you piece of shit! See you in hell!"

Doyle crouched, poised to jump into the time portal, when a gunshot blasted from behind Felix.

The top half of Doyle's head exploded in every direction like a watermelon being dropped off the roof of a ten-story building. What remained of Doyle's body fell forward, blood pouring like a river from where his head had been just seconds earlier.

Felix fell to his knees and vomited. He'd never seen such a grisly scene and wasn't sure how he'd scrub the image from his memories. After relieving his nausea, he looked back to see Arielle and Selena in the doorway, Arielle lowering a shotgun.

Selena stood with her jaw hanging, unable to keep up with Arielle, who had started toward Felix. The gunfire was still echoing throughout the warehouse. The sound clung to Felix's mind and body as he tried to process what had just happened.

Arielle reached him and tossed the shotgun aside. Felix dropped the crowbar and hugged her, breaking into heavy sobs as he buried his face in her shoulder.

"I'm so proud of you, Felix," Arielle whispered into his ear as she consoled him. She ran her hands up and down his trembling back. "You were perfect."

Chapter 43

Present Day

As soon as the Angels returned to their present time in Miami, they took Arielle to the Road Runners' office for medical evaluation. Blood screening showed the midazolam was out of her system, while a minuscule amount of flumazenil remained. The doctors had no concerns and wrapped a bandage around her throat, clearing her for a return trip home.

Before they could board a jet to Denver, Arielle received a call from Commander Briar's assistant, Elijah Ward, informing her the commander would soon land in Miami and wanted to meet the team at Surfside Beach for a post-mission briefing.

They headed to the beach, ordered a round of margaritas from one of several available beachside bars, and found a cozy spot at a table shaded by a towering palm tree.

"Arielle, are you sure you're okay?" Selena asked. "I've never seen you this quiet after a mission."

Arielle sipped her margarita and studied the glass, making streaks across the condensation with a lazy finger. "I'm okay. Still in shock, I guess. That was the closest I've ever come to death on a mission, and I can't stop replaying the events that led to Doyle capturing me. How could I be so reckless?"

Selena grabbed Arielle's hand across the table and massaged her palm. "Stop beating yourself up. You did nothing wrong. This mission was dangerous from the start. Doyle was ready for anything. He had an advantage as a time traveler, unlike our other missions."

Arielle sighed and stared out at the ocean. A cruiseliner sailed far in the distance. A flock of seagulls wandered the sand, and a group of friends were tied up in an intense game of volleyball.

"And how are you doing, Felix?" Arielle asked. "That was quite the scene you had to witness."

Felix shook his head while staring at the table. "I've booked an appointment with a therapist tomorrow. Wish I could erase the image of Doyle's head exploding, but guess I'll have to settle for learning how to cope with it. You want to join me, Selena?"

"I'm okay," Selena responded. "It was tense, sure, but I'm not feeling all that bothered by it. Relieved, in fact, knowing that bastard is dead. You should take all the time you need, though."

"Enough about that. How did you two get to the warehouse so fast?" Felix asked, not hiding his urgency to change the subject from his mental stability. "You were only a few minutes behind me."

"It's Arielle," Selena said. "Once I untied her, we went through Doyle's house, found the shotgun, then went outside and Arielle hot-wired the first car we found. Quite simple, really."

Felix blinked rapidly. "Wait. You killed Doyle with his own shotgun?"

Arielle grinned for the first time since arriving at the beach.

"Romantic for us soulmates, isn't it?"

"We should have never done this mission," a voice said from behind. Arielle spun around to see Commander Briar leaning against the palm tree.

Felix jumped out of his chair and ran over to shake the commander's hand.

"You three stay seated," the commander said, shuffling toward the table and sitting down. "I'll join you."

"Why did you come all the way out here to meet us, Commander?" Selena asked. "We would have been home in about four hours."

"A few reasons," he replied, crossing his hands on the table. "I needed some fresh air. I love the beach. And I want to speak candidly with you three. As you know, all conversations are recorded in my office. And while I'm the only one who can access them now, it doesn't mean someone else won't in the future. First off, I want to apologize for putting you three in such a dangerous position. Your job comes with plenty of risks, sure, but you're never meant to have a knife on your throat or to get drugged. Jesus Christ."

The commander shook his head.

"You have nothing to apologize for," Arielle said. "We understood the danger this mission presented when we accepted it. It was uncharted territory for the Angels, and now we know. We pulled it off, and we're all alive in one piece. That's all that should matter."

Commander Briar nodded and licked his lips. "That's fine and all, but I couldn't stop thinking about how awful things could have turned out. I let the Advance team have it before I got on the plane. This is just as much their fault as anyone else's."

"Commander," Arielle said sternly. "This is no one's fault. Doyle Grady understood *how* we would hunt him. It didn't matter what the Advance team ever found. He was always going to find another way around getting caught. The only mistake, I think, was never allowing him to join the Road Runners."

"What?!" Felix asked, jolting forward in his seat. "You'd want to work with that guy? After everything you just went through."

Arielle smiled. "I know it's disturbing to say, but I met my match in Doyle. He's my photo negative. The yin to my yang. He's the evil genius version of me. And if he had joined the Road Runners, I'm not so sure he would have taken the dark path. He would have broken some rules, sure. Desperation will make a person do that. But haven't we all had to break some rules to get where we are?"

Commander Briar frowned as he stared at the table in deep thought. "Interesting take, Arielle. You never cease to amaze me. That doesn't erase my guilt, however. I signed off on this mission. I put my legacy ahead of your safety. My term is ending, and I was scared it would get erased by whatever wild direction the next commander is going to take the Road Runners."

Arielle threw her head back and laughed, the motion stretching the cut on her throat to cause a slight burning sensation beneath the bandage. "Commander Briar. The man who defeated the Revolution. Your legacy is set in stone. You are the Abe Lincoln of the time travel world. No one will ever forget you or what you accomplished."

Commander Briar chuckled. "I think Abe has a few inches on me."

"Maybe you can travel back to make sure," Selena said, and they all shared a laugh.

"Were you really going to help Doyle?" Felix asked Arielle.

She nodded and closed her eyes, remembering that day as vividly as yesterday. "We were young and grieving. And I absolutely intended to save his wife. I was going to do that first, then he would go back and stop my family from going into the mall that day. Said he would rear end their car and cause a scene to stall just long enough. And back then, we didn't know the rules of time travel. We didn't know what seemed like such a simple plan would probably be impossible to carry out. But that conversation gave us both hope for a life without pain. Sometimes hope is all it takes to push you over the edge."

"Sounds like a future campaign slogan," Commander Briar said, shooting a wink at Arielle.

"Ha! In your wildest dreams. Have you thought about what you're going to do when your term is up?"

Commander Briar nodded. "That's part of why I'm here—just been needing a reason to come out. I'm not entirely sure what I'll do, but I want to be by the ocean. Back when Chris killed my mother, the Road Runners had me hide at a place called Crooked Island. It's part of the Bahamas and was an absolute paradise. With everything that was going on, I strangely felt at peace. I want that feeling again. I can step away and know everything will be fine. The Council I put in place will always protect my interests, even while I'm away. I understand that now, and that's why I want to take advantage of stepping out of the spotlight."

Felix offered a sorrowful frown. "It's only been two years with you in charge, but the Road Runners without Commander

Briar seems so wrong."

"I wouldn't stress too much about it. The job fell into my lap, against my will, and things kept working out in my favor. Besides, I'm old news. The future is in your hands now. Don't blow the opportunity."

"What are these new candidates like?" Felix asked. "What's the inside scoop?"

Commander Briar waved him off. "Like I said. Don't worry. Regardless of who wins, the organization will be moving in a different direction. It shouldn't have any effect on your jobs—not from what I can tell. They're more focused on expanding the Angels, actually. All the candidates agree the Angel Runners are a strong suit and we should invest more into them. Outside of that, it sounds like there are plans for time travel businesses. Secret businesses that would only be available to those who have cleared the strictest of qualifications."

"Wait, like businesses facing the general public?" Felix asked. "How on earth do they plan to get away with that?"

The commander shrugged. "Not my problem. I'd be surprised if they ever get that running, honestly. Not as long as my Council remains in power. But I guess we'll wait and see. My best advice for you three is to stay together as long as you can and just worry about your missions. Everything else is noise, especially around election time."

Commander Briar stood up and pushed in his chair.

"Where are you going?" Arielle asked.

The commander chuckled. "I told you already. I didn't really come out here to hang out with you three. There are some beachside condos I've been wanting to check out in the area. As much as I'd love to return to the Bahamas, I want to stay stateside, at least for the next commandership, just in case they need to call me in for advice or assistance. Maybe I'll get a vacation home on Crooked Island for now."

"Bouncing between different beaches?" Arielle said, standing up. "Not the worst of your choices."

She gave him a hug that he gladly returned.

"You're the best there is," he whispered into her ear. "And the others are following in your footsteps. You're all going to do big things. Stay safe out there."

Commander Briar wished Felix and Selena farewell before trudging away down the beach.

"Well, that was random," Selena said, earning a round of laughter from the table. "But I must say, Commander Briar has it all figured out. Quite the life he's putting together once he can step away from all this."

Arielle sat back down once the commander was out of sight. "What if we stay here a couple more days?"

Felix and Selena both raised their eyebrows in unison.

"For...relaxation?" Selena asked like she was terrified to know the answer.

Arielle smiled. "Yes, for relaxation. We're already here. Beach. Drinks. Nightlife. What else do we need? We can spend a couple days in the sun doing absolutely nothing."

"Wow," Selena said, taking an extra long drink from her margarita. "Maybe some of those drugs are still in your system. I don't think I've ever heard the word *relaxation* come out of your mouth."

Arielle giggled. "No drugs, I promise. I don't know. Nearly dying put some things in perspective. Did you know we only have to do one mission per quarter to hold on to our top ranking? Those were some details I received in an email from

Commander Briar in his subtle way of telling me to take it easy. That's assuming we complete the missions successfully."

"Just promise me one thing," Selena said. "No work talk during these two days. Not a peep until we're back on the jet. Think you can handle that?"

Arielle grabbed her drink. "Oh, I can definitely handle that. I'm not even going to think about the mission recap I need to write until we're back in Denver. I don't want to hear the name Doyle Grady ever again. The three of us know what happened in that house, and let's leave it at that. I killed a man. Yes, I know it's a part of my job, but that doesn't make it any easier. No matter how awful of a person I remove from existence. I'm going to need some time to unwind from this mission. And taking those three months off just might be what I need."

"We're here for you," Felix said. "You name it, and we'll take care of it."

Arielle grinned. "I already told Felix I was proud of him at the warehouse. But I'm proud of you, too, Selena. Everyone pulled their weight on this mission and that's the only reason we won. We'll always look back at this mission as the one that shaped us into who we truly are. The best team of Angels in the world."

"Arielle Lucila!" Selena said, slapping the top of the table. "Are you bragging? Not being humble for once?"

Arielle shrugged. "What can I say? We've earned the right to brag. Just this once."

They ordered a second round of margaritas and chatted the night away, the chaos of the mission fading as gradually as the setting sun.

Arielle Lucila Series

Have you read all the books in the Arielle Lucila series? If you weren't aware, these books can all be enjoyed as standalones.

Check out the entire series, also available in Kindle Unlimited:

Angel Assassin (#1)

Secrets in the Vault (#2)

Dirty Money (#3)

Time Roller (#4)

Time Fugitive (#5)

Author's Note

Thank you for reading Time Fugitive! I enjoy serial killer books, and have been toying around with the idea of a time traveling serial killer on the run for a few years now. As with any time travel story, the mechanics are always the hardest thing to nail down. Factor in a set of rules that already exist in this current universe I've created, and it didn't quite work.

That's why I introduced time portals—although they've been mentioned in prior books—for this story. Once the rules of the portal were figured out and I found the best way to make them work with the existing framework of time travel, the story started coming together.

I had so much fun writing the scenes from Doyle's perspective. I've always been a fan of the fictional bad guys who seem friendly on the outside, while having a monster lurking inside. Think Patrick Bateman from *American Psycho*, or Joe Goldberg from the *You* series.

My intent was for this book to be enjoyed by both time travel and serial killer fans alike. Writing this book has made me want to write more books in the serial killer genre, although I have some other projects already lined up.

Thank you to everyone who helped make this book possible, starting with my editor Melissa Prideaux. Without your touch, this story would still be a jumbled mess.

To the Gonzalez Gang, thank you for the constant outpouring and support. On the days when I just don't feel like going, a few minutes in the group sparks my motivation to get behind the keyboard and make the magic happen.

And thank you to my wife, Natasha. We've taken a big leap of faith, and I can't imagine anyone else by my side in the process. I love you.

Andre Gonzalez
July 20, 2023 - February 9, 2024

Join Newsletter

If you enjoyed this book, be sure to join my newsletter to stay up to date on future releases, promotions, and lots of glimpses into my writing career.

Plus, I'll send you a bundle of four novellas just for joining!

Head to BookHip.com/LNNVQF to sign up!

Enjoy this book?

You can make a difference!

Reviews are the most helpful tools in getting new readers for any books. I don't have the financial backing of a New York publishing house and can't afford to blast my book on billboards or bus stops.

(Not yet!)

That said, your honest review can go a long way in helping me reach new readers. If you've enjoyed this book, I'd be forever grateful if you could spend a couple minutes leaving it a review (it can be as short as you like) on the page of the retailer you purchased this book from.

Thank you so much!

Also by Andre Gonzalez

Arielle Lucila Series:
Time Fugitive (#5)
Time Roller (#4)
Dirty Money (#3)
Secrets in the Vault (#2)
Angel Assassin (#1)

Wealth of Time Series:
Time of Fate (#6)
Zero Hour (#5)
Keeper of Time (#4)
Bad Faith (#3)
Warm Souls (#2)
Wealth of Time (#1)
Road Runners (Short Story)
Revolution (Short Story)

Amelia Doss Series:
Salvation (#3)
Nightfall (#2)
Resurrection (#1)

Insanity Series:
The Insanity Series (Books 1-3)

Replicate (#3)
The Burden (#2)
Insanity (#1)
Erased (Prequel Short Story)

The Exalls Attacks:
Followed Away (#3)
Followed East (#2)
Followed Home (#1)
A Poisoned Mind (Short Story)

Standalone books:
Snowball: A Christmas Horror Story

About the Author

Born in Denver, CO, Andre Gonzalez has always had a fascination with horror and the supernatural starting at a young age. He spent many nights wide-eyed and awake, his mind racing with the many images of terror he witnessed in books and movies. Ideas of his own morphed out of movies like *Halloween* and books such as *Pet Sematary* by Stephen King. These thoughts eventually made their way to paper, as he always wrote dark stories for school assignments or just for fun. Followed Home is his debut novel based off of a terrifying dream he had many years ago at the age of 12. His reading and writing of horror stories evolved into a pursuit of a career as an author, where Andre hopes to keep others awake at night with his frightening tales. The world we live in today is filled with horror stories, and he looks forward to capturing the raw emotion of these events, twisting them into new tales, and preserving a legacy in between the crisp bindings of novels.

Andre graduated from Metropolitan State University of Denver with a degree in business in 2011. During his free time, he enjoys baseball, poker, golf, and traveling the world with his family. He believes that seeing the world is the only true way to stretch the imagination by experiencing new cultures and meeting new people.

Andre still lives in Denver with his wife, Natasha, and their three kids.